DATE DUE			

THE WOMAN WHO WAS GOD

BOOKS BY FRANCIS KING

The Needle
Act of Darkness
Voices in an Empty Room
One Is a Wanderer (Selected Stories)
Frozen Music

THE
WOMAN
WHO WAS
GOD

A Novel

Francis King

Weidenfeld & Nicolson

New York

499 0586

Published by Weidenfeld & Nicolson, New York
A division of Wheatland Corporation
841 Broadway
New York, NY 10003-4793

Published in Canada by General Publishing Company, Ltd.

Library of Congress Cataloging-in-Publication Data

King, Francis Henry.
    The Woman who was God : a novel / Francis King. — 1st ed.
        p.   cm.
    ISBN 1-555-84-248-8
    I. Title.
PR6061.I45W6 1988   87-36875
823'.914—dc19   CIP

Manufactured in the United States of America
Designed by Irving Perkins Associates, Inc.
First Edition
10 9 8 7 6 5 4 3 2 1

TO
MARGOT AND RONALD BOTTRALL,
old friends

HOME

I

She imagines it as a novelist might imagine it.

In the subtropical moonlight, the dilapidated building, half palace and half prison, looks like the skeleton, bleached by the sun, of some vast prehistoric monster which once lumbered out of the ocean to expire from a mortal wound or sickness. The insect life that all through the long day whined and crepitated within its labyrinthine corridors of bone is as inert as the palm trees that all day threshed in the scorching wind. The tender lolls at the rotting jetty, and the mangy, emaciated dog, tethered in its kennel, no longer rattles its chain and howls.

He lies out naked on the high brass bedstead, with the mosquito net wavering, a flurry of snow, about him. That snow fails to cool the burning of either his body or his mind. Runnels of sweat gleam, like the silvery trails of a slug, on his torso and down the cheek that is turned to the open window. Beyond the window, the silence is momentarily broken by the chatter of some creature, bird or beast, in the tree dripping fleshy lianas.

He stirs, he raises his torso, clutching the back of the bedstead with both hands. He swings his legs off the damp, tangled sheet onto the cracked marble of the floor beneath it. He feels the chillness on hot soles. He slips his feet into sandals, stooping to fasten the thong first of one and then the other. He reaches out for his shorts, lowers them, then throws them away from him. He brushes at a mosquito whining in one ear. His sandals slurping on

3

the marble, he makes his slow way out of the room and down the glimmering corridor, past the doors behind which other people, some known to him and some unknown, grunt, snore, sigh, or murmur in their sleep. He is wholly naked, a boy-man of nineteen, with blond hair curling in tendrils round a face burned by the sun to the color of the wood of the banisters along which his hand, the nails carefully tended, now slides.

The wicker lounging chairs are still out on the verandah, and the bottles and glasses are still out on the wicker tables, to be cleared by the black, white-robed servants who will rise silently at dawn over the ridge of forest above the house. He touches the back of one of the chairs, feeling its dry roughness on the moist smoothness of his palm. He walks down the seven steps, each fissured and clogged at the back of its tread with ocher dust, and then, raising his arms from his body so that the wind that has all at once jerked up from the sea can buffet around them, he takes the path of sand, embedded with seashells, which in the moonlight looks to him like a stream glinting with fish. The dog hears him and for a moment, having recognized his scent, rattles its chain and whimpers. He walks on, arms still extended, as though he were walking a tightrope.

The waves lisp on the luminous crescent of the beach, as they sweep in and then fold one over the other. They hiss as they retreat and once again surge forward. He stands and feels the icy spume between his toes and on his ankles and splashing upward onto his thighs. He stoops, makes a cup of his hands, and fills it with the salt, sticky water. He pours it over his chest, cooling its fever. He walks on, with the silent house on his right and the murmurous sea on his left. The sand squelches abrasively under his toes.

Beyond the wide crescent of sand there is another, smaller one, out of view of the house. Fringing it there are palm trees, crowded close together, which look in this light as though they had been cut from tinfoil. Dwarfed among them there is a humped bush that exhales a peppery odor. He tears at it as he passes and holds the raceme, bone-white where he has made the

4

vicious fracture, up to his nostrils. He breathes deeply, then breathes out on a long, tremulous sigh.

Nine jagged rocks look like the ruins of a dolmen, the entablature shattered so that no devils or angels will now ever sup at it. He stares at the rocks, hands on slender hips, while a heel grinds deep into the sand. Then he leaps up the smallest of the rocks, feeling now the soft wetness of the algae and now the rough dryness of the tufa against his prehensile toes. From one rock, birdlike, arms extended like wings, he flies to another, rearing up behind that, and so on and on, until he is perched, a silvery eagle in the moonlight, on the highest and sharpest of all. He raises those arm-wings, as he peers down into the huge, unwinking, lustrous eye of the rock pool beneath him. He raises the arm-wings even higher, joins them, and then, then, then . . .

She has imagined it as a novelist might have imagined it. But she knows, as the reader of a novel would know, that it could not have been like that.

II

It could not have been like that.

Ruth St. Just waited in the restaurant on the top of the Kensington High Street store for the man whom she had once known so well that every action, word, and even look of his had filled her with a sense of dreary predictability, but who had now become so much of a stranger that she could not even guess why he should have chosen to meet her in this of all places.

When she had telephoned from the country to tell him that she must see him, she had at once recognized his weariness and wariness, as though he had decided that she was yet again about to ask for one of those loans of money that so often, to her shame, eventually became gifts.

"Well, yes, yes, of course." In the past she had heard him be similarly evasive with his widowed sister when, from time to time, she telephoned him out of the lonely desperation of her Belfast life. "Is it *very* urgent?"

"Yes, I'm afraid it is."

"Oh, in that case . . ." He told her that the next day he would be valuing a house for an Arab vendor in Upper Phillimore Gardens and that he could see her after that for "a cup of coffee." She smiled at that word "vendor." She had never heard anyone but a real estate agent use it. In fact, she had never heard anyone use it since her divorce from him.

The Times crossword rested on the table to the right of the elbow she had propped there. From time to time, tilting her head sideways and downward, she would gaze at it briefly. Once she even picked up her pen, lying beside the paper, and began to write a word. Then she realized that the word was one letter too long and therefore could not be the right one.

Most of the customers of the restaurant at that hour between elevenses and luncheon were elderly and shabby. They shuffled slowly and jerkily the length of the counter, with the mob-capped, fresh-faced girls crying out peremptorily, "Yes, please! Next, please!" to wait patiently, trays propped on the rail to their left, in the queue to the cashier, and so to move on, singly or in twos or threes, to one of the Formica-topped tables, each with a cut-glass vase of artificial flowers on it. One old woman, in what Ruth could see were "good," if worn, shoes and a "good," if threadbare, tweed coat and skirt, dropped her stick as she impatiently yanked a paper napkin out of the dispenser. Ruth at once jumped to her feet and picked it up for her. The old woman repaid her with an extraordinarily beautiful smile, irradiating a face that had previously looked distracted and woebegone. Momentarily Ruth felt moved. It was as though, as she was peering out of a window into some drab street, a shaft of sunlight had touched her for a second.

Reseating herself, she looked at her watch. Mark was late, as he was always late. In the old days, Mr. Erskine, exasperated, or Miss Wordsworth, plaintive, would ring to ask where he was. This or that client was waiting for him outside this or that empty flat or house. "Oh, but he left ages ago", Ruth would lie, even though he had only just rushed out of the door. "I simply can't imagine what can have happened to him." Often she would even fancifully elaborate—"They're digging up the bottom of the road, so it could be that he couldn't get his car out," or "Perhaps he's again having clutch trouble, he had to call the Automobile Association last weekend. Oh, I do hope he hasn't broken down again."

As she gazed around her, she all at once noticed that among the shabby elderly people there were a number of even more shabby young ones, with pale faces and long hair and long coats or skirts, sidling furtively about the restaurant, always without trays. She felt a pang, like a knife suddenly thrust under her heart, when she saw that one of these, a youth with a straggly golden beard and a gold ring in one delicate ear, might almost have been her Jim at what she had always thought of as the "lost" period of his life. But now, ah now, her Jim was even more lost, lost beyond recall.

She stared at this beautiful, tall, emaciated youth, wondering what he could be doing, as he edged between the close-set tables, glancing down now to left and now to right. Eventually, without asking her permission, he placed himself at the table of the old woman whose fallen stick Ruth had jumped up to retrieve. He sat with his chair turned away from the old woman, one leg crossed high over the other and his hands deep in the pockets of the khaki greatcoat which, falling open, revealed that, instead of shirt or sweater above his ragged blue jeans, he was wearing a red-and-white-striped pajama top. The old woman eyed him with a mingling of fear and distrust from under waxy, wrinkled lids, as she poured out a cup of coffee from a dark brown Denby Ware pot and then, cradling the cup in both tremulous hands, raised it to her bunched lips to sip. When the boy, his back still half turned to her, began a low, tuneless whistle, the old woman frowned and began to gulp the coffee instead of sipping at it. She also had a Danish pastry before her, and with a small shake of her head, as though in silent admonishment to herself as much as to him, she cut it into halves with the knife beside her and then cut one of the halves into halves again. She picked up a quarter, raised it to her mouth, and popped it in. Her blue eyes fixed above the young man's head, she began slowly to chew.

The young man fumbled in the pockets of his greatcoat and eventually brought out a used match. Without ever looking at the old woman, so close to him across the table, he inserted the match under the nail of his left forefinger. Still chewing, the old woman gazed at this action with not so much distaste as horror. She again raised her cup in a hand that now trembled even more than before and, having placed it to her lips, took two or three small sips. Then she got up, nervously brushing crumbs down from her tweed skirt, before she removed her stick from the back of her chair and picked up her black leather gloves. Now at last the young man looked at her, amused and implacable. She was at pains not to look at him as she limped off.

As soon as he was alone at the table, the young man swiveled around in his chair, stretching out his legs, drew the old woman's empty cup toward him, and then raised the Denby Ware pot. As one hand held the pot aloft, so the other went out greedily for the plate with the three quarters, so neatly cut, of the Danish pastry on it. He gulped from the cup and crammed one sugary corner of the Danish pastry into his mouth. Then, suddenly aware that Ruth was staring at him, her hand with the pen in it poised above her crossword puzzle, he stared insolently back at her. Ruth at once looked away. It might have been her own Jim scavenging for food, just as all these other pale, gaunt young people sidling up and down between the tables were scavenging for it.

"Hello, Ruth! Sorry to have kept you waiting." Mark spoke to her as if she were one of those tiresome individuals who asked to be shown properties far beyond their means, not because they had any intention of moving from where they now lived but because they could not think of any other way of passing a morning or afternoon. "Didn't you get yourself some coffee or something?"

"No, I was expecting you to get it for me." She smiled wanly, elbows on table and chin propped on hands.

She had always expected him to do everything for her. He wondered how she managed now, living alone in the country, with a restaurant to run. "Okay." He sighed. "Two coffees it is, then. I presume you still take milk and no sugar?"

She nodded. "Milk and no sugar." She was pathetically grateful to him for remembering that.

"Something to eat?" All at once, against his will, he felt tender, even loving toward her.

"Nothing to eat."

The young man reminded her of some bird of prey as, the outsize greatcoat fluttering around him, he all at once rose from the table at which he had been sitting, circled the two tables beyond it, and then alighted on a chair beside a third, where a couple of ample middle-aged women, shopping bags around them, were talking, the brims of their hats almost touching, in a confidential undertone. One of the women broke off what she was saying, turned her head, and gave him a penetrating stare. "Do you mind!" that stare said. Insolently the young man stared back. Then he fumbled, as before, in the pockets of the greatcoat, brought out a crumpled cigarette butt, plugged his mouth with it, and leaned forward to ask for a light. Ruth could hear, even from the distance at which she was sitting, "I'm afraid I don't smoke," from one of the women, and "This is a nonsmoking area, you know," from the other. The young man smiled, putting the cigarette butt back in his pocket.

"There we are!" Mark set down a Formica tray with two cups, two teaspoons, two dark brown Denby Ware pots, two miniature cartons of milk, and two paper napkins embossed with the name of the store. "Sure you don't want anything to eat?" As soon as he had asked that, he wished he had not done so. It would be just like Ruth to change her mind capriciously and send him back to that bloody queue.

"Nothing."

Mark seated himself opposite her, making the metal chair all at once look flimsy and fragile. His increasing girth caused the buttons to strain at his dark gray pin-striped waistcoat. His face sagged. He had been late for Ruth, he was going to be late for that appointment. He was going to be late for everything that day. Gloomily, as he poured out the coffee, first for her and then for himself, he saw the inexorable chain of cause and effect, each link unbreakable. Unless, of course, he sacrificed his lunch hour. But why the hell should he do that? Well, they'd better get on with it.

"You're looking well," he said, even though, with those bruise-like shadows under strained eyes, she looked nothing of the kind.

"And you," she said perfunctorily. He had put on even more weight in the five weeks since their last meeting. That dentist's nurse must stuff him with the same relentless efficiency with which her employer—to whom Ruth had reluctantly felt obliged no longer to go after the "break"—filled his patients' teeth.

"So what is it, then?" They rarely met, and whenever they did, it was because she wanted something of him. He, who had once been so exigent, now never wanted anything of her.

"It's this Jim business." She should have said "this James business," since Mark had always obstinately refused to use the diminutive, but it was too late now to correct herself.

"You're not still brooding about it?"

"It couldn't have been like that."

"Like what?"

"His death. He couldn't have died in that way."

"I don't see why not." Then all at once he allowed the irritation which simmered away within him whenever she spoke of their son's recent death to surge to the boil as he had never done before. "Why the hell not?"

"He couldn't swim. He was terrified of water. You know that, Mark."

He knew it. In the shallows, first at Brighton, then at Vouliagmeni, and then on the island of Hvar, he had forced their slender, girlish son into the water. "Here, give me your hand. Here, put your arms around me. Here, let me put my hand under your chin. There's nothing to be afraid of." But the boy was always afraid. Suddenly he would be thrashing about in panic, letting out one shrill yelp after another, like a dog pinned under the wheel of a car, and clutching his father so tightly around the neck that he might have been making an ineffectual attempt to strangle him. Mark would feel a profound shame as the people around them on the beach or in the water stared with pitying contempt. Later, when he had grown older, the boy would sulkily decline even to enter the water at all, preferring to sit or lie out in the sun, his mother beside him, while Mark, a strong swimmer, propelled himself out and out and out, as though to get as far away from the two of them as possible.

"He might have learned to swim."

Ruth shook her head decisively.

"Why not? Out there, in that climate, by the sea. Away from you," he added cruelly. He had always thought that Ruth's excessive love, an encumbrance to the boy in so many different ways, had also been an encumbrance in this, both metaphorically and literally sinking him.

"People don't get over that kind of irrational terror."

"Of course they do. Every day." He was about to cite the case of his present wife, the dentist's nurse, who had gotten over her irrational terror of dogs because he had insisted they must have one, a huge Alsatian offered to them by a neighbor, whatever she felt about it.

Again she shook her head. "He wouldn't. I know he wouldn't. Not that terror."

"So?" Surreptitiously he glanced at his watch. He was already overdue in Earls Court Square.

"So . . . He didn't die like that. He couldn't have died like that. It would have been inexplicable enough if he had gone into the sea. But to have climbed up some rocks and then to have dived into a rock pool . . . Don't you see, Mark?"

He raised his cup and drained what was left in it. The coffee was surprisingly good here, good and extremely cheap, that's why he came to the place despite all the weirdos. "They all say that's how he died. Why should everyone lie to us?"

"That's what I keep asking myself." She might have added: That's what obsesses me. "There's something so strange about it all. Sinister." Her eyes tracked the young man, who, now with a radiant black girl in tow, was once again strolling between the tables. Eventually he sat down at one and the girl sat down beside him, huddling close, as though for warmth. He put out a hand to investigate a half-eaten sandwich on a plate before them. "Yes, sinister," she repeated with a little shudder.

"I think you're imagining things." That was what he used to tell her when she first began to suspect him of infidelity with the dentist's nurse. "You know you tend to do that."

"Yes, that's what I tried to believe. Tried, tried. But now that I've thought about it—oh, over and over again, so often . . ." Through the interminable hours she had lain awake, imagining it as a novelist might imagine it. "They've been hiding something from us."

"They? Always 'they'! Who's 'they,' Ruthie?"

"All of them out there. The police. The Embassy. The British Council. The doctor who did the autopsy. The French priest. Above all, that dreadful woman on the island."

"All of them?" He was dryly ironic. "Dear Ruthie—you've too much imagination. Always did have. That's what first made things so difficult between us."

"I'm not showing too much imagination, Mark. I'm merely showing a modicum of intelligence."

"Anyway . . ." Again he glanced surreptitiously at his watch, putting his hands under the table and then using one to jerk up the shirt cuff from the wrist of the other. "Does it really matter how he died? He died." He shrugged. "That's it. Terrible for him, terrible for us. But whether he died as they said he did or whether he died in some other way . . . I can't see that it matters."

"You wouldn't." It was as if, in her sudden fury, she had thrown a bucket of icy water in his face. "I have to know. And if anyone was to blame . . ."

She was implacable. As always when she was in this kind of mood, he felt obscurely frightened. He also felt angry. By now that North Country couple were probably walking away from Earls Court Square to a telephone booth, from which they would ring Mr. Erskine, always exasperated, or Miss Wordsworth, always plaintive, to ask what had happened to him. He pushed his cup away so fiercely that he all but knocked it over. "At all events, what is it that you want me to do?"

"I want you to back me up."

"How?"

"He named you as next of kin on that British Council form. Yes?" She hated to have to say this, since she hated to have to face it: inexplicably he had named his father, not her. "That makes it difficult for me. If I want another autopsy, an autopsy over here . . . Or if I want a fresh investigation."

"Oh, Ruth, Ruth, Ruth!" All at once moved to pity, albeit against his will—leaving her, he had vowed that he would never again allow her to force that emotion on him—he held out his hand to her across the smeared Formica of the table. "I'd do anything to help you. But *this!* Nothing's going to bring him back. Let's face it. He's gone. That's it. You—we—have just got to pick up the shattered pieces and get on with our lives."

She stared piercingly at him. "There are no shattered pieces for you."

"Of course there are!" But he was cruelly aware of the hollowness of his own indignation. "I adored that boy. I absolutely adored him." He almost added: Don't forget that when we split up it was with me that he sided, he wanted to be with me.

She compressed her lips. "I can see it's useless."

"I'd do anything for you," he repeated. "You know that. But to go on nagging away at . . . That way madness lies, Ruthie."

She stared out over his shoulder at the golden-haired boy and his black girl. They were now leaning toward each other, laughing. "Perhaps I am mad. I'm sure they think I'm mad at the Foreign Office and the British Council."

"Of course you're not mad. But grief can do such odd things to one. And living as you do—alone—in that isolation in the country . . ."

She gave a derisive laugh. "Alone, isolated! Do you think that no one else works in my restaurant, and that no one comes to eat there?"

"You know what I mean." He stooped and picked up his battered briefcase, her first Christmas present to him after their marriage. "At night—so far from anywhere—no one for company . . . After all, you're really a town girl, aren't you?"

"You won't help me."

He rose. "I can't, over this." She always had this amazing ability to make him feel guilty, however much he resisted it. "Sorry, Ruthie." Now he looked openly, even ostentatiously, at his watch. "Must fly. Ought to have been in Earls Court Square ages ago. God knows what will have happened to the couple I was supposed to be seeing." He put both hands on the table and then leaned across it. "Forget all this. Put it out of your mind. What's the point? What *is* the point?"

Her lips barely moved in her pale, resolute face as she said: "One has to keep faith with the dead." She stared intently at him, and he forced himself to hold her stare. Then she looked away as she added: "Otherwise everything is just a sham."

At that point he consciously gave up. It was no use arguing with her, no bloody use. She had become so odd since the tragedy—understandably, since, once the break had taken place, James had really been the only person of importance in her life. "Well, I'll be on my way. Coming?"

She pointed to the coffeepot. "I'll stay a little longer. I've nothing particular to do for the moment."

"All right, old girl." He paused, once again moved, against his will, by her bleak, stoical forlornness. "No hard feelings?"

She smiled, lifting up her cigarette packet from where she had put it down beside her *Times*, and rotating it between her strong fingers. "No hard feelings."

He winced almost visibly at the irony.

As he began to walk away, head lowered, in his stained Burberry, the battered briefcase under one arm, she could not resist calling out to him: "Oh, Mark, Mark!"

He turned fearfully. What did she want of him now? "Yes?"

"Tell me—why did you choose *here* for our meeting?"

"Why not? Wasn't it all right?"

"It was fine. But couldn't we have met at your house? No farther, really, much easier for talking."

He took two clumsy steps back toward the table. "Well, the trouble was that Gloria—Gloria had something on." He knew that she knew he was improvising a lie, but by now he did not care. "This is her day off and she has these relatives . . ." He left it like that. Let Ruth herself decide what Gloria and the relatives were doing.

"I see." The tone was derisive and dismissive.

After he had gone, she gazed down at the crossword. But so far from her being able to solve even one of its clues, the words were all a blur. Then, all at once, she was aware that two people were about to seat themselves at her table. She looked up, startled. It was the pale, beautiful young scavenger and the radiant black girl. She stared at them and, ominously impassive, they returned her stare. Then they drew back chairs.

A moment later the boy was stretching a hand across the table. Ruth, head lowered in a pretense of looking at the crossword, gazed sideways at the hand, its nails long and tended with surprising care. *That hand could be Jim's.* She heard the boy say in a deep, husky voice: "D'you think you could spare a fag?"

She put a protective hand over the cigarette packet between them. "No, I could not." Despite her fury, her voice did not tremble. "Why are you sitting here without even asking me? There are plenty of empty tables." She looked around the restaurant as though to confirm this. "What do you want?"

"Okay." The boy rose, making a placating gesture with both his hands. The black girl rose with him. "Okay. That's all right." He began to wander off down the restaurant, between the close-set tables, until he found one, recently left empty, with plates of half-eaten food on it and a carafe with some red wine glinting at its base. He slumped down in a chair, and the girl, who had been following some distance behind him, slumped down in another, opposite him. They both began to laugh, heads leaning toward each other, as she had seen them laugh before.

Ruth looked at the boy's laughing mouth. The teeth were large, regular, and white. *It might be Jim laughing.* Then, uncannily, she seemed to hear Jim speaking, as she often now did in the murky twilight between sleep and waking: *I was a stranger and ye took me in; naked, and ye clothed me; I was sick, and ye visited me; I was in prison and ye came unto me.*

She got up, slipped into her coat, put her bag and her *Times* under an arm, and then picked up the half-smoked packet of cigarettes. Clutching the packet against her breast, she walked slowly past the table at which the boy and girl were lounging. As she did so, she tossed the packet onto it. She might have been chucking a crust of bread to two pigeons.

They both looked down at the packet, amazed. Then they looked up. Without a backward glance, Ruth walked on.

III

"TIRESOME WOMAN!"

As he stood, hands in the pockets of overtight trousers, staring morosely out of the window, Fred Tracer was referring not to the woman being dragged along Horse Guards Parade by her umbrella, as though she had just descended from the stormy skies and the umbrella were a parachute, but to another woman, whose son's file, full of her letters and other people's letters and memoranda and minutes scrawled with Foreign Office initials, he was holding in one hand. To him all women were tiresome unless they were either extremely clever or extremely attractive.

Miss Lumby, who was neither of these things, looked up from her daily chore of winnowing the contents of his pending tray.

Things, she would remark to her female colleagues, would pend there forever if she did not unhook them. His depending tray, that was all she really was, she would often add. "I can't help feeling sorry for her," she now said, since feeling sorry for Ruth had become, in an odd way, a part of feeling sorry for herself.

"You'd do better to feel sorry for all the people whose time she's managed to waste. And that very much includes you and me."

Miss Lumby sighed, partly because the draft of a letter clearly intended for the out tray had strayed into the pending one and partly because, when Fred Tracer had deputed her to parry Ruth's impassioned demands on the telephone or had asked her to type his answers to Ruth's no less impassioned letters, it was with Ruth and not with her own boss that she found herself sympathizing. "So terrible to lose an only son like that. So far away, in such peculiar circumstances."

"He was so far away because he clearly wanted to put as much distance as possible between his mother and himself," Tracer retorted sharply, leaving the embrasure of the window. As the woman in Horse Guards Parade had turned the corner into King Charles Street, her parachute-umbrella had all at once been blown inside out. Somehow, he did not know why, that had cheered him.

"I'm sure he must have loved her." Miss Lumby hoisted an enormous stack of reference books and files and then rested her chin on top of them, so that all at once she was transformed into an upended human bookcase.

"We often want to get as far away as possible from people we love." Tracer was crisp.

Miss Lumby staggered across the room with her burden. Of course the brute wouldn't dream of hurrying over to open the door for her. Somehow, with one hand under the books and files and the other groping blindly, she managed at last to find the handle and turn it. With difficulty she swiveled her head. "I agree with her that there's something fishy about the whole business." She felt both exhilarated and frightened by her own defiance.

"Yes, there very well might be." He surprised her by agreeing.

"But for God's sake don't tell her so. You'll only encourage her in what, let's face it, has become an obsession."

"I suppose if you have nothing else in your life, then an obsession is one way of filling it."

"True enough, my dear. But we don't really want her obsession filling *our* lives. Do we?"

Miss Lumby edged her way out, and then miraculously succeeded in shutting the door behind her without dropping a single book or file.

Alone, Tracer furtively took a small comb out of his bottom desk drawer and eased it through the sparse reddish hairs, which he had taken to coaxing across what would otherwise be the bare dome of his head. He began to wonder what the tiresome woman, until now never seen although so often heard on the telephone, would prove to be like. Miss Lumby, who was one herself, had said on more than one occasion that she was "clearly a lady." But something about the accent had made Tracer doubtful of that.

He was seated at his desk, yet again flicking over the pages of the voluminous file, when, at exactly the appointed time, Miss Lumby brought in his visitor. Holding a dripping umbrella as far away from herself as possible, Ruth used her other hand to pull off what struck Tracer as an extremely unbecoming waterproof hat, more suitable for a postman or a streetsweeper. As he stood up to greet her, she seemed deliberately not to look at him for several seconds on end.

"Shall I take those from you?" Miss Lumby knew that Tracer would hate to have umbrella and hat dampening his carpet or chairs.

"Would you? Oh, thank you." Ruth now began to take off her raincoat.

As raincoat, hat, and umbrella passed from one woman to the other, Tracer was annoyed to detect an immediate warmth, even complicity, between them. More seemed to be passing than just the three objects. But what it was, he was not sure. "Thank you, Barbara," he said, curtly dismissive.

Miss Lumby, ignoring him, turned again to Ruth. "A cup of coffee? It'll warm you up."

Ruth shook her head. "No, thank you. But it's sweet of you to offer."

"Do have one if you'd like one," Tracer said grudgingly. "Why not?"

"It'd be no trouble," Miss Lumby put in, smiling at Ruth, her head on one side, in a manner that made her all at once look girlish, even pretty. "We now have one of those machines. Horrible coffee, I'm afraid. But at least it saves trouble and mess."

Ruth smiled back and again shook her head. "No, really. I arrived here far too soon, so I went into a café, rather a nice one, just by Westminster Station."

Tracer had moved behind his desk. "Well, Barbara, I'm afraid it rather looks as if your offer is not going to be taken up. So I suppose that Mrs., er, St. Just and I had better get down to business."

"What a charming woman," Ruth said, when Miss Lumby had closed the door behind her.

Although Ruth had not so intended it, Tracer took the corollary of this to be that he was not charming. Well, that was something of which he had been humiliatingly conscious all through his life: he lacked charm. "Yes, *un bon oeuf,* thoroughly so. And she's really super at her job. Totally dedicated," he added, all at once feeling loyal and generous in thus effusively praising someone whom he usually nagged at and denigrated. "Please." He pointed to the chair opposite the more comfortable one on his side of the desk.

Ruth sat down, crossing one leg over the other. The legs, Tracer noted, were shapely, giving the impression of belonging to a body younger than the one, ample at the bosom and heavy at the hips, now leaning toward him.

Opponents warily sizing up each other, they were each reluctant to open the interview. Tracer drew the file toward himself, gave a dry little cough, and squinted down at it from under caterpillar-hairy eyebrows, even though he needed no reminding of its contents or of her reason for being there. Ruth, a naturally nervous person, felt nervous now. But she had long since learned how to use a jolly, comradely, no-nonsense manner to conceal her nervousness. Faced with a mastectomy, she was the kind of person who would cheerfully ask the surgeon: "Won't life become rather lopsided for me?" Faced with the guillotine, she was the sort of person who would no less cheerfully tell her executioner: "Now do please try not to leave my hair in a mess!" The jocularity would not make the mastectomy or the guillotining any easier for her; but it would certainly make them easier for the persons about to inflict them. Now, in a pretense of relaxed good humor, she leaned forward and said: "You think me a terrible bore and a nuisance, don't you? Of course you do!"

"Not at all! By no means!" Tracer protested, although he thought her both those things. "What could be more understandable than a mother wishing to discover precisely how her son died?"

"Understandable but tiresome." Ruth's use of that second adjective reminded Tracer uncomfortably of how he had stood at the window and, looking out, had exclaimed partly to Barbara Lumby but chiefly to himself: "Tiresome woman!" People who battered at others with their obsessions, whether they were ambitious, obstinate members of Parliament who occasioned the drafting of answers to supplementary questions to the Foreign Secretary, or sad, troubled nobodies like the one before him now, *were* tiresome.

But "Good heavens!" he protested. "I'm—we're only too happy to assist you in any way we can. That goes without saying. It's just that . . ." His voice trailed away as, small, pudgy hands resting on the file open before him, he again looked across at her from under those caterpillar-hairy eyebrows. In contrast to the vivaciousness of his manner, his eyes, Ruth noted, were tired and dull.

"It seemed better to come and talk to someone here, rather than to continue to write letters and telephone. Even if that did mean leaving my little business and making a journey up from the country."

"Quite so," Tracer agreed, even though, when Miss Lumby had first told him of the suggested visit, he had burst out tetchily: "I'm sure she has nothing to say that she hasn't said ad nauseam in letters and on the blower." He turned over a page of the file, and peered at the minuscule handwriting of a comment by the head of the legal department. It read: "This is a potential source of embarrassment." How right he had been! Tracer looked up: "And what exactly is your, er, little business, Mrs., er, St. Just?" Inquisitive by nature, he really wished to know. She looked the sort of woman who would be running not a business but a docile husband and family.

"A restaurant. In the Cotswolds."

A member of the Wine and Food Society and a frequent contributor of recommendations and criticisms to the *Good Food Guide*, Tracer wondered if her restaurant could possibly be that delightful place, its beamed ceilings so low that one was obliged constantly to stoop for fear of grazing one's head, where he and Anne-Marie—funny girl, why had she never written after her return to Lyons?—had been served those delicious ramekins of gratiné of smoked haddock in a béchamel sauce, followed by pink saddle of lamb with the crispest of snow peas. No, he decided, she did not look the sort of person who would run that sort of restaurant. Hers would be called something like "Ruth's Kitchen" or "The Appleblossom," with set luncheons being served at "very reasonable" prices to genteel women shoppers. "A restaurant? I've often thought I'd like to run a restaurant," he now said, although he had never thought anything of the kind. "Hard work, I should think. And did your son help you with your restaurant before he went to Africa?"

"Jim was totally uninterested in it. Just as he was totally uninterested in what he ate." She leaned forward in her chair, hands clasped. "I opened the restaurant when my marriage broke up. Jim had just started boarding school."

Tracer looked across at the window, the white paint of its frame chipped and grimed, and its panes smeared with the rain that gusts of wind kept spattering across them. He had better bring her to the point, if he was to get to the Reform Club by one. "I wish we could do more about your, er, Jim. But as I've explained to you over the phone—and in my letters too, of course—our room for action in these matters is, of necessity, circumscribed."

Suddenly, like an uncontrollable tick convulsing a previously tranquil face, the nervousness that Ruth had so far been success-ful in concealing seized her and shook her visibly before him. Her voice both hardened and grew shrill, making Tracer think: Oh Christ, I hope she's not going to create a scene! Fiercely she told him: "I'd have thought your people out there could have made rather more effort. Yes, I must say that, since I feel that! I'm sorry. But I do wonder if they really care a damn."

He controlled his annoyance, deliberately bringing down his voice in both pitch and volume. "Of course they care, Mrs., er, St. Just. I'd have thought that was all too obvious from the very full reports I've relayed to you. As far as it's been possible to make inquiries, my colleagues and I have conscientiously made them. But you must appreciate, understand—of course I've already told you all this in my letters and on the phone—in matters of this nature we have little, if indeed any, jurisdiction." He saw that Ruth, leaning forward with one hand on the desk, was about to interpose something, but this merely had the effect of making him hasten. "I do not have to tell you that, although Saloum was originally an arbitrary creation of French colonialism, it is now an independent nation. Like all nations that have only recently achieved independence, it is jealous of it. To suggest—as you appear to be doing—that the Saloumese police have been cor-rupt and inefficient or that a Saloumese pathologist, even though trained in Paris, has been unable to perform an adequate autopsy, is not, I'm afraid, the sort of thing to be well received out there by the Saloumese—or, indeed, by our own people."

Blood had surged up into Ruth's face, making it look blotchy and puffy. "So it's a matter of indifference to *our people*"—suddenly there was a crude, jeering sarcasm in her words and the way she spoke them—"if a British subject has been so foolish as to let himself get murdered?"

22

THE WOMAN WHO WAS GOD

Tracer restrained his anger, as she had been unable to restrain hers. "You must be fair, Mrs. St. Just. And that, if I may say so, is an unfair comment. An unjustified one, wholly unjustified. Of course His Excellency and his staff in Siné and of course our vice-consul, Mr., er, Diamont, in Bissance, are all deeply concerned. But, as I've repeatedly tried to get you to appreciate, there's little more they can do than they've done already."

"I expected you to say that. And what about this woman?"

"What woman?"

"This woman who seems to think she's God."

"Do you mean Madame Vilmorin?"

"The one they call Mother."

"I'm quite sure no one at the Embassy calls her Mother." A laugh erupted from him, as brief and explosive as a sneeze. "I certainly can't imagine Sir Francis Portman doing so."

"It was, as you'll know, at her ashram—or whatever she chooses to call it—that my son met his death."

Met his death? Died? Tracer thought how odd it was that the former sounded so much more accusatory than the latter. "Yes." He nodded. "And I'm sure the Saloumese police must have questioned her thoroughly."

Ruth's face was still unattractively blotchy and puffy from the blood congested in it. "She's said to be a rich woman, extremely rich. Her disciples have made her rich."

He nodded. "Yes, that seems to be the gossip. But what precisely is the relevance of her richness?"

Ruth smiled and shrugged her shoulders. "I'd have thought that only too obvious."

"If you mean that, being rich, she was in a position to buy police protection, then I must object, object most strongly. I know Saloum well. I was *en poste* there a few years ago—before, let me hasten to add, Madame Vilmorin established her, er, center. I think you may have a false idea of the kind of country Saloum is. It's not another Uganda or Zaire—far from it. It's one of the few countries of Africa to have been unshaken by civil war or even tribal dissension since it achieved independence way back in the

23

fifties. President Mamadan is a remarkable man, literally a philosopher-king." He swiveled his chair around in the direction of the window, so that now she was seeing him in profile. "Of course not everyone in his government or his civil service is honest. No one would claim that. After all, here in England we also have our bad apples—don't we? But there seems no reason for supposing that your son's death wasn't fully and fairly investigated—or that there's been any kind of cover-up."

Ruth rested her head against the back of her chair and then closed her eyes, as though in preparation for sleep. When, after a few seconds, she reopened them, they glittered with angry scorn. "I didn't really believe I'd get anywhere on this visit. Well"—she raised one hand to her graying hair—"I can understand your attitude. Better to give a tacit nod to a cover-up than to endanger relations between this country and Saloum."

"Mrs. St. Just—I've already been at pains to tell you—we do *not* believe there's been any kind of cover-up. The Embassy has gone into the whole matter, gone into it thoroughly. That is the conclusion. No cover-up, none at all." He swung his chair back to face her. "You're being unfair, you know, grossly unfair."

"The body," Ruth persisted.

"The body?"

"What has happened to my son's body?"

"Well, I gather that—since no instructions have yet been received as to what you and your former husband wish to have done with it—it is still, er, being kept. But clearly the Saloumese would like those instructions."

"I should like a postmortem to be performed in England. As I wrote to tell you. You ignored that request."

Tracer drew a deep breath and then puffed it out. "There are a number of difficulties there. Firstly, it is, of course, your former husband whom your son named as next of kin. And your former husband informed us that, being himself perfectly satisfied that your son died as a result of an accident—as the Saloumese police and the pathologist maintained from the beginning—he wished the body to be cremated in Siné, just as soon as you had also given your consent. Secondly"—he was now speaking with weary patience, as to some fractious child, offspring of others, whom he would dearly like to slap but did not dare to do so— "there is, of course, the question of expense. I know nothing about your means, Mrs. St. Just. But if the body were to be flown back here, you or your former husband would of course have to pay for that. H.M.G. would certainly not undertake to do so, not in these circumstances."

Suddenly his weariness had also infected her. For the moment, she had no more will to protest or argue. She would have to look elsewhere, do something else. Again she inclined her head back against the resilient upholstery darkened by other heads, and again she closed her eyes. She must have been an extraordinarily pretty woman when young, Tracer decided. In fact, she was an extraordinarily handsome woman now. But tiresome, tiresome, tiresome.

Ruth again placed a hand on the desk. "I mustn't waste any more of your time. Or any more of mine," she added dryly. "I can see I've reached the end of the road here. But I've not yet reached the end of the road altogether. By no means. I think you're all due for some surprises, you and your colleagues. Yes, I rather think so."

As she rose to her feet, Tracer, rising too, gave her a smile of pitying superiority. He had no intention of attempting a riposte.

"That nice woman took my things."

"Yes, you'll see her on your way out through her office. Her name's Miss Lumby."

With ironic courtesy, they shook hands. "I don't imagine you'll see me again," Ruth said. "But you'll hear of me. Yes, I think I can promise you that. You'll hear of me."

He replied stiffly: "I'll be happy to see you at any time."

In the outer office, the connecting door closed, Ruth said, "Oh, thank you, Miss Lumby," as the other woman tenderly helped her on with her raincoat and then handed her her hat and her umbrella.

"I put them by the radiator. I hope they're a wee bit drier."

"Oh yes. Oh, thank you."

Miss Lumby, with her slight stoop and her pigeon-toed walk, followed Ruth to the door and then out into the passage. "I'll have to accompany you downstairs." She gave an apologetic smile. "Security. You know what it's like these days."

Ruth nodded over her shoulder.

"This lift's due for replacement," Miss Lumby said, pressing a button worn from all the other fingers that had pressed it, year after year.

"Looks about time," Ruth said, peering down the shaft.

"Long past time."

At the sound of the elevator clanking down toward them, Miss Lumby gathered all her courage, as she invariably had to gather it for any disagreement with Tracer. "I wanted to tell you. I have a hunch. I don't know much about it—only what I've read in your letters or in office minutes or what you've told me on the phone—but I think, I'm sure, you're really on to something."

"You believe that?" Eagerly, Ruth put out a hand and almost touched the other woman's arm. "You do, really?"

"Yes, I do, I do!" Miss Lumby gave a surprised, delighted laugh, as though only now had the full truth come home to her. "But don't quote me, please never quote me! Promise?"

"Of course I promise. Oh, but that cheers me up a lot! Thank you, thank you!" This time Ruth not merely touched Miss Lumby's arm, but gripped it fiercely.

The elevator rocked to a halt, its door clattered open. The two women emerged, Miss Lumby to be greeted by a woman of about her own age, who was waiting with two other people, both middle-aged men in glasses. "I'll bag a table, Babs," the woman said.

"Oh yes, dear, please!"

At the entrance, Miss Lumby took Ruth's hand in hers and leaned forward, as though afraid of being overheard by the heavily moustached security man at his high desk. "More power to you!" she whispered. "Remember—I'm with you, with you all the way!"

* * *

Ruth decided on an impulse—although she was the least impulsive of people—that, instead of at once returning home as she had planned, she would go over to the Tate Gallery to look at the Turners. After all, it was Jim who had persuaded her, shortly before his ill-fated departure for Saloum, that it was Turner and not, as she had until then always believed, Constable who was the greatest of English painters.

She cowered under her umbrella at the bus stop, while the gray, cold rain sliced downward at her legs out of a gray, cold sky.

"Been waiting long, dear?" A motherly looking woman with two shopping bags had come up behind her.

"An age," Ruth answered in stoical resignation, as a gust of rain rattled against her umbrella like grapeshot.

"What a day! And poor Princess Di's launching that ship on Tyneside, isn't she?"

"Is she?" Ruth did not care about poor Princess Di. But she did care about her own chilled, wet legs.

Behind the bus stop there were three telephone booths. In one of them, Ruth suddenly became aware of an elderly intellectual-looking man, with thick white hair receding in deep waves from his high forehead to cascade on the collar of his dapper army greatcoat. What was he doing? Certainly not phoning. A cleaner perhaps—despite his appearance? Open penknife in one hand, he was scratching in total absorption at the doors and even the windows of the booth. Then, evidently despairing of the efficacy of the penknife, he began to use the long nail of a forefinger crooked with arthritis.

But of course! Suddenly it came to Ruth. Inside each booth there had been stuck innumerable prostitutes' notices. She could imagine them. "Severe French mistress ..." "Chinese bow-fronted chest for sale ..." "Lover of watersports ..." "Strict-tempo dancing lessons ..."

Laboriously, the old man rubbed and scratched, now with penknife and now with fingernail, in an obsessive crusade, surely doomed to failure, to eradicate all this sad, squalid evidence of what he presumably saw as depravity and sin and what Ruth could see only as loneliness and inadequacy. Of course his task was hopeless. He might succeed in removing every one of the notices in those three booths, but all over London there were other booths with other advertisements and, in any case, in no time at all these three booths would also once again be full of them. It rained into the sea and still the sea was salt.

The man suddenly realized that she was staring at him. Then he glared at her through a smeared pane, knife gripped in one hand while the long, inward-curving nail of the crooked forefinger rested on the pointed end of his chin. Terrifyingly, he had been transformed in that moment from a gentle, shabby, elderly intellectual—a librarian, musician, or schoolteacher—into a demon with blazing eyes and mouth pulled aslant in a wild grimace of loathing.

Ruth recoiled. All too clearly he was mad.

Then she heard the woman behind her cry out in joy: "Here it is! Here it is! At long last!"

IV

"I DON'T THINK this meat is quite cooked through, dear."

The Brockhursts, three of Ruth's Saturday "regulars," a retired master butcher, his ailing wife, and his Pekingese-breeding spinster daughter, had arrived early, as usual, in order to be sure of their table by the window. They rarely spoke to each other, preferring to look out moonily at the genteel bustle in the high street. It was Mrs. Brockhurst, usually so self-effacing, who had summoned Ruth to complain.

"Well, it is beef," Ruth replied, in a tone far less conciliatory than she generally employed to her customers.

"It's bleeding," Mr. Brockhurst said. "There's blood on the plate."

Surely a master butcher ought to be used to bleeding meat? And surely he ought to know that beef should be eaten rare?

"If you don't like it like that, I could cook it a little longer for you."

"Would you, dear?" Mrs. Brockhurst, who often said that she hated a fuss, had already repented of having made one now.

"What about yours?" Ruth asked the Brockhurst daughter, Hazel, a middle-aged woman with naturally fuzzy gray hair smoothed down over the top of her crown and then bushing out from the two old-fashioned grips that held it in place over her delicately pointed ears. Hazel, having roused herself from a reverie of taking one of her Pekes, Wang, to stud to a Cruft's champion in Taunton, vigorously shook her head. "Oh, mine's fine. Thank you, Mrs. St. Just."

"And yours, Mr. Brockhurst?"

"Mine'll be all right. Not to put you to any trouble."

"It'll be no trouble, if it's not all right," Ruth said crisply, as she hurried off to the kitchen with Mrs. Brockhurst's plate. Once there, she told the Belgian girl, Toinette: "Give this a few moments in the microwave."

Mrs. Brockhurst leaned across the table and whispered to her husband: "She's not herself, is she? It's not like her to be snappy."

"I must say I didn't care for her tone," Mr. Brockhurst agreed, chewing on meat that was not merely red but tough. Mrs. St. Just needed some advice on buying, he decided. He pulled out a piece of gristle from his mouth between forefinger and thumb, and squinted at it professionally before putting it down on the side of his plate.

"She's rattled, poor dear." Mrs. Brockhurst sighed. "One can see at a glance she's rattled."

"That's hardly surprising." Fond and admiring of Ruth, Hazel always looked forward to Saturday lunch at the restaurant. "She's been through a lot—and is still going through a lot."

Mrs. Brockhurst nodded in sympathetic agreement. "The loss of her only son. One must make allowances."

FRANCIS KING

Mr. Brockhurst clearly did not think that Ruth's loss of an only son obliged him to make allowances for inferior cuts of meat. "There was something about it in *The Star* yesterday. So Jock at the garage told me. Didn't see it myself."

"There's been a lot about it in the papers," Hazel said. "Even *The Times*. She must hate all the publicity."

"Not a bit of it," her father contradicted her robustly. "If there's publicity, who started it?"

Frowning at him, Mrs. Brockhurst extended a warning hand across the table, as though to snatch away his plate. She had noticed that Ruth was making her way toward them with the beef, now cooked to a dark mahogany.

"I hope that'll be all right."

Mrs. Brockhurst was not the sort of person to say: It's far from all right, now you've overcooked it. But she thought this, as the three of them chewed in unison, their eyes fixed on two pubescent girls and a boy, the nearest that the village had so far gotten to punks, who were indulging in a lot of giggling horseplay with the one bicycle, old-fashioned and rusty, that they had among them.

When Ruth was back in the kitchen, thinly slicing more beef with an electric carving knife that always filled her with an irrational dread of an accident, the young waiter, Ned, who had once again either forgotten or deliberately neglected to shave, hurried in to tell her: "There's a guy wants to see you."

"Not another complaint about the beef!"

"No. This guy says he's got an appointment."

"But he's not due till four!" Ruth guessed that it must be the journalist who had tried to interview her over the telephone and who, when she had objected to that—"I must see people face to face if I'm going to tell them things of importance to me"—had then, grudgingly, proposed a visit.

"Said he got here sooner than expected."

"Very much sooner. Far too soon."

From the voice on the telephone she had expected, she did not know why, some middle-aged, gin-sodden old hack, with

30

swollen, purple hands and nose, nicotine-yellowed nostrils, and gray flannels baggy at the knees. She had certainly not expected this personable young man, with a deeply cleft chin, glossy black hair falling in deep waves almost to his shoulders, and an athletic torso draped in an overlarge, fleecy, pale blue sweater with "Missoni" embroidered on it in dark blue silk. Still less had she expected a tall, big-breasted, big-nosed girl, in a precisely similar Missoni sweater and tight-fitting white trousers, leaning against the wall beside him.

"I'm Mrs. St. Just."

"And I'm Larry Granger." He extended a hand, a gold bracelet dangling loosely from his wrist. "And this is Clare." No surname.

Clare smiled, still leaning a bony shoulder against the wall. "Hi."

"I wasn't expecting you so soon. As I told you, I run this restaurant, and we're just in the middle of serving lunch. If I don't keep an eye on things—my chief helper's down with flu—then they tend to get into a mess."

"Yes, I'm sorry. The thing is that we were planning to cadge lunch off Clare's parents, but then, when we got to Woodstock, we found there'd been some muddle and they'd gone up to London. We probably passed each other on the way without realizing it! So we thought we'd sample what you had to offer—if that's all right with you, that is."

Ruth nodded, coaxed out of her previous exasperation by his good looks and charm. "Of course. Have lunch on the house. I've just had a cancellation, so you can take that table for two over there. It's a bit near the kitchen door, I'm afraid."

"Oh, that's terrific. And it needn't be on the house, though it's kind of you to offer. Expenses," he added.

"For your friend too?"

"Oh, we'll somehow work that out."

The Brockhursts had been attempting to eavesdrop on this encounter.

"Not from round here," Mrs. Brockhurst now leaned across the table to whisper.

"London, I'd guess," Mr. Brockhurst whispered back. "Wonder what all the palaver was about?"

"I heard him say something about her parents and a muddle over lunch," Hazel volunteered.

Mrs. Brockhurst shrugged. Then, in her uncharacteristically belligerent mood of that day, deciding they had been waiting far too long for their next course, she turned and called out over her shoulder: "Ned, Ned dear! May we have a little peep at that gorgeous sweet-trolley of yours?"

After having selected some Black Forest *gâteau* for herself, Mrs. Brockhurst asked Ned sotto voce, as he set down the plate before her and then licked daintily at a blob of cream that had come off on his thumb: "Ned, tell me, do you know anything about that couple over there? We were wondering. She's so beautiful, isn't she? Like a model. Her face is so familiar. We saw them arrive in a sports car—a Morgan or something like that."

Ned, who often said that he liked to keep himself to himself, was not going to satisfy this craving for gossip. "I've no idea, Mrs. Brockhurst. I've never set eyes on them before. They must be passing through—on their way to Stratford, I shouldn't wonder."

"Let's make pigs of ourselves," Larry was saying to Clare, oblivious of the interest that the Brockhursts were taking in them. "Not this wretched *table d'hôte*."

"At a place like this the *table d'hôte* is often fresher," she remarked sagely. She had worked in a Brighton restaurant not all that different from this one during a summer vacation from Sussex University. "I'm afraid nothing's going to be all that hot, is it?"

"Sorry. I made a boob there. I don't know why, but when I chatted to her on the phone, I got this crazy idea that hers would be the sort of restaurant about which one reads, 'At last! A first-class nosh-house in a culinary black hole!'—or something like that. Anyway, we'll console ourselves with a bottle of champagne."

"If they have such a thing."

Ruth did have such a thing. "Are you celebrating?" she asked, as she instructed Ned where to set down the ice bucket and how to place the bottle in it.

Larry shook his head. "Just coming here. And meeting you." The insincerity was blatant. But despite it, Ruth warmed yet further to him.

When Ruth had returned to the kitchen, Clare giggled· "Oh, you do lay it on!"

"One has to. Pai l of the profession."

"The long day wanes," Ruth remarked to Ned, as four o'clock approached. The Brockhursts, who had sat on, glumly obstinate in their curiosity, long after people whom they had preceded had paid their bills and left, had just aroused themselves to ask for what Mr. Brockhurst, who had never lived in America, for some obscure reason always called "the check."

Ned glanced up from stacking plates in the dishwasher. "Sorry?"

"Tennyson." Ruth was too tired to explain any further.

Clare looked flushed from too much of the champagne and too much of the Armagnac that had followed it. She and Larry were leaning toward each other conspiratorially, conversing—as, to the Brockhursts' annoyance, they had been conversing throughout their meal—in near whispers.

Ruth came over to their table with a breakfast cup of strong black coffee in one hand. She set it down on their table and then drew up a chair from another table to place between theirs. "So that's that. I've precisely two hours of rest before dinner's upon me."

"You work hard," Larry said, genuinely sympathetic. He had noticed how strands of hair were sticking to her damp forehead, and how her eyes looked curiously unfocused.

"Very hard. And the restaurant makes so little that I often ask myself if it's really worth all the trouble."

"Have you eaten?" Clare asked. She, too, felt genuinely sympathetic toward this handsome, harassed woman.

"Oh, I snatch this and that, when I have a moment. The staff are eating now. They're a good crowd, I love them all, but they're terribly inexperienced, with the exception of the chef."

I'd have guessed he was inexperienced too, Larry felt like saying, remembering the mushy *petits pois* and the treacle pudding that had stuck uncomfortably to the roof of his mouth. Instead: "It's a very attractive house. And well situated."

"From 1724. But mucked about. I couldn't afford to do much to it. But at least I had the hardboard stripped off the doors. Can you imagine? And off the staircase, which had been totally boxed in."

"Vandals," Clare murmured, helping herself to another of the mints that Ned had brought with their coffee.

"Do you mind talking here? Or would you prefer to go upstairs to my flat?"

Ruth was disconcerted when, instead of saying that no, of course they did not mind, Larry answered: "Oh, why don't we go upstairs? We've sat on here such a long time, and the room's become so full of smoke." In fact, he was merely obeying the injunction of his canny first editor, on a small West Country newspaper: "When you're going to write about an animal, always try to surprise it in its natural habitat."

Ruth rose wearily, abandoning her half-drunk cup of coffee. "I do wish Mr. Brockhurst—he was the man sitting over there—wouldn't light up that pipe. It's so inconsiderate."

"You should tell him not to," Clare said, also rising.

"Should I? I suppose I'm not tough enough."

"My guess would be that you're a very tough lady," Larry said.

"Is that a compliment?"

Larry merely smiled.

Later Larry was to describe Ruth's flat to Clare as "chintzy," and Clare was to describe it to him, more charitably, as "cozy." Since it occupied the top of the house, where the servants' quarters would once have been, its rooms were small and low-ceilinged, and the long corridor that gave access to them was narrow and gloomy.

"Thank goodness the stove hasn't given up the ghost," Ruth

said, going over to stoke it. "I love this stove. I couldn't get through the winter without it."

"Don't you have central heating?" Clare asked, with the surprise of someone who has grown up with it.

Ruth shook her head as she removed a black velvet coal-glove from her right hand. "Only in the restaurant. Too expensive to install it up here."

Larry and Clare had seated themselves side by side on a long sofa from which Ruth had hurriedly scooped up newspapers, magazines, books, and some knitting. "I'm afraid I tend to use this sofa as a table as well as somewhere to sit." The sofa, covered in a faded chintz of pink cabbage roses on a lime-green ground, was more comfortable than it looked.

"Can I get you something?" Footsore and with her back aching, Ruth prayed that neither would say yes.

"Just a glass of water, please," Clare said, stretching her long legs out before her and then massaging her thighs.

"And for me too," Larry said.

Because she had become used to being asked for it by American tourists, Clare got some ice out of the refrigerator in the kitchen and put it in the glasses. While she was doing this, Larry nudged Clare and pointed at a watercolor of a sunset over the Giudecca. "Not bad," he said. "Brabazon."

"And who's he when he's at home?"

He ignored the question, as he peered round the room. "Better than anything else in this room. Repro furniture, repro pictures."

Ruth returned, a glass in either hand. "There you are," she said, setting them down.

Larry fiddled impatiently with the combination locks of his small attaché case, swearing under his breath, and eventually got it open. "Do you mind a tape recorder? I have such a wretched memory." In fact, his memory was excellent. But by now he had grown used to people denying they had said things he had reported them as saying, and he liked to have this safeguard.

Ruth was dubious, staring down at the machine with brows

drawn together in a mixture of puzzlement and distaste. "Oh, all right," she at last conceded.

"In the old days, journalists had pads and pencils and shorthand. Now they have tape recorders," Clare commented obviously, sipping from her glass.

Ruth's decision, reached on hearing this remark, that the girl could not really be all that bright, served only to develop an already incipient irritation with her. After all, since she was clearly not a newspaper colleague, it would have been more courteous if either she or Larry had asked at the outset if Ruth minded her presence.

Larry switched on the tape recorder. "I'm hopeless with this thing. In fact, I'm hopeless with anything mechanical. People are not at all pleased when I interview them, and then discover at the end that nothing has been recorded."

"I don't think I'd be all that pleased in those circumstances," Ruth said, surprising him, as she often surprised people, with an unexpected tartness, as though suddenly they had bitten on a lemon pip in an oversweetened apple puree.

"Where shall we begin?" Larry asked, his head on one side as he smiled at Ruth, now seated in an armchair even lower than the sofa. "Oh well, let's begin at the beginning. Why not?"

Ruth began at the beginning, in a clear, strong voice, so unlike the one, tremulous with emotion, with which she had previously spoken to Larry on the telephone. Her son—James, Jim—had decided that, after all, he did not want to go to university, at least not immediately, brilliant though he was, and so—oh, how she wished he had never seen the ad in The Times!—he had applied for this job in Saloum, of all dreadful places. He was, well, rather a romantic sort of boy, and perhaps Saloum struck him as rather a romantic sort of place. He spoke fluent French—he had stayed with a family in the Dordogne for most of the previous summer holidays—and no doubt that had been a help to him at the interview. No, it was not a British Council job, it was a job at a private school, not in the capital, Siné, but in this place called Bissance. Yes, Bissance. No, she herself had never heard of it either, until he had told her about it. The British Council had been asked to recruit someone suitable for the job, that was their only involvement really. The pay was poor, the living conditions were poor. Probably that had also helped him, there were few other applicants.

At this point Ruth paused. Face unnaturally flushed, she turned to Larry. "Is this the sort of thing you want me to tell you?"

"Of course " But already he was wondering how much of all this he could use.

"I didn't want him to take the job. I wanted him to go to university, but that was only a small part of the reason that I didn't want him to take the job. There was this, this"—she broke off and gazed, frowning, at the glowing stove before her—"this hunch. I knew even then that something terrible would happen to him." Silent now, she continued to stare into the heart of the glow.

"And . . . ?" Larry prompted.

Ruth gave herself a visible shake, and then resumed her narrative. At first things seemed to have gone well. He had written enthusiastically about the town, about the school, about his pupils, and about his colleagues, all of whom were either African or French. Then, well, his letters had seemed to cloud over. That was the only way she could put it. They had seemed to cloud over. Nowhere in them did he openly state that he was unhappy or even discontented, but somehow, she could not say how, she had known that he was both these things. So it had come as no surprise to her when he had written to say that he had asked to be released from his contract at the end of the second term, and was planning to join a community—yes, "community" was the word he had used—on an island off the coast. "The island is called, called—Ellampore." For some reason she always experienced difficulty in getting out that name—all too familiar though it was to her.

"And what exactly was this community?" Larry asked.

"There was something about it not long ago—before his death—in *Time*. This woman, this American woman, who's partly

37

Japanese and who was married to a Frenchman—that's how she first went to Saloum, he had some job there—runs it as though . . . as though she were God."

"She's the one they call Mother?" To Ruth's surprise it was Clare who put the question. Ruth had assumed—wrongly, it now transpired—that the girl knew nothing of the story.

"Yes, they call her Mother. There's this house on the island, once a prison, and they all live there together, under her rule." She gave an abrupt, nervous laugh. "Essentially it seems still to be a prison. Yes." She leaned forward in the low armchair, hands clasped together, as though all at once submerged in some terrible but fascinating dream. The blood had drained away from her previously flushed face, leaving it gray and clammy.

"What precisely was your son *doing* in this—this community?"

"I don't know. I honestly don't know. His letters became fewer, shorter, more and more evasive." And her own, she all but added, had become more frequent, longer, increasingly anxious. "That wasn't like him. Before that, he used to tell me everything. No secrets. We were very close, as a husbandless mother and an only son tend to be very close."

"And then?"

Her lower lip trembled, as though she were about to burst into tears. "Then I got this phone call from my former husband. He had had a call from someone at the Foreign Office. The man at the Foreign Office, I learned later, had suggested that my former husband should break the news to me in person. But my husband phoned to tell me." She spoke the last sentence with so intense a resentment that her auditors were startled. "It was said to have been an accident." She got up and with jerky movements began once again to pull on the black velvet glove. She turned to Larry. "I've told you this part."

"But why are you so certain that it couldn't possibly have been an accident, as they all claim?"

"I've told you that already!" As she threw Coalite into the stove, her exasperation was all too apparent. "He couldn't swim. He had this quite irrational terror of water. He wouldn't even go

38

in at the shallow end of a swimming pool. So it's out of the question that he would have dived, yes, *dived* off a high rock into a rock pool below it."

"Then what do you think happened?"

"I don't know. I just don't know. I've been trying to imagine it." Night after night she lay sleepless, trying to imagine it.

"Do you think someone killed him?" To Ruth's annoyance, it was Clare who put the question.

"What else can I think? Someone killed him, now there's a cover-up."

Larry was gazing at the black glove on her hand. "The woman they call Mother?"

Ruth shrugged. "Possibly. Or with her connivance. She seems a strange, sinister sort of woman. She has this power over people. She has all this money."

"And you think the Embassy's somehow involved in the cover-up?"

"Again—possibly. I don't know. All I do know is that they don't seem to want me to get at the truth. That was obvious when I saw someone at the Foreign Office last Friday."

"Probably they don't want to upset the authorities in Saloum?"

"That's how it strikes me. But I don't care a damn about the authorities in Saloum. I want to get at the truth." She threw on the last bit of Coalite and then banged shut the door of the stove, before tearing off the black executioner's glove from her right hand. "There's one odd thing. There's this man called Eugene Diamont—our consul in Bissance. Bissance is the nearest town on the mainland to . . . to Ellampore, and so it was he who was in direct charge of things. I telephoned him, because his letters were so vague, scarcely bothering to answer any of my questions. He was equally vague on the telephone. But there was one interesting thing he told me." As so often during the last days, Ruth could now once again hear the voice, emerging through the static, with that faint accent that made her ask herself: French, Indian, African? "But my dear Mrs. St. Just," that voice told her, "you really mustn't make these reckless insinuations. Madame

39

Vilmorin is known to me personally—and her community is known to me. In fact, I was there only a day before the tragedy. It was a Sunday. I often go to Ellampore on a Sunday—or even for the whole weekend. If you knew Madame Vilmorin as I know her . . ." I don't trust that man, Ruth had said to herself, as she had replaced the receiver. "I don't trust that man," she said now.

"You think he was involved?"

"I don't know if he was involved in Jim's death. But I'm absolutely certain he was involved in the cover-up."

Later, when Ruth had brought in a bruised fiberglass tray with tea things on it and they were sipping the dark, bitter Indian tea and eating *petit-beurre* biscuits, Larry said: "One has to be careful with a story like this."

"Careful? How careful?"

"So much is suspicion and supposition. Isn't it? Libel. The nightmare of every journalist and editor."

"You mean of all this I've told you . . . ?"

"I'll have to be extremely careful." He stirred his tea, smiling down into it. Then he looked up, still smiling. "Of course one can hint at things. I'm rather good at that. One writes between the lines, and people—if they're bright enough—then read between them."

Clare nodded. "Larry's got a real gift for that."

"You see, what I feel, think"—all at once Ruth was neither calm nor coherent—"what I want, if there's enough of a scandal, if public opinion over here is aroused, then, then perhaps the Foreign Office, the government, will do something positive. They must do something positive." She appealed to them. "Mustn't they?"

"One certainly hopes they will." Larry evaded the question. He put out a hand, the gold bracelet dangling, and switched off the tape recorder. Then he said, "Let's make sure we've got all that," and pressed another button.

Ruth was irrationally convinced that, after she had expended so much energy and emotion, the tape would now prove to be blank. But after a click and a whir she heard: "I'm hopeless with this thing. . . ."

"Not all that hopeless," she said in smiling relief.

"Obsessed," Larry said, using a word many had used already and many more were going to use. He was at the wheel of Clare's car.

"Do you think she'll get anywhere?"

"Who knows? Somehow I doubt it."

"It really depends on you."

"On me! You flatter me. My piece will certainly be cut and will probably be spiked. As I told her, I'll have to be terribly careful."

"What are you going to say? Tell me. Come on, tell me." Clare shook his arm, making the car swerve dangerously. "How will you describe her?"

" 'Bereaved mother'?"

" 'Tragically bereaved mother.' "

"Hm. Better."

" 'Tragically Bereaved Mother: The Mysterious Death of My Only Son.' How about that for the headline?"

"Too long. 'Yesterday Mrs. Ruth St. Just, an attractive divorcee, spoke to me in her cozy flat above her popular Cotswolds restaurant about the mysterious death of her son, James, on the Saloumese island of Ellampore. Once a base for pirates, Ellampore has recently achieved fame'—no—'notoriety as the headquarters of a secret and, some would say, sinister sect. . . .' " He broke off, laughing.

"*Was* Ellampore once a base for pirates?"

"I haven't the foggiest. But it makes it sound more interesting."

"Silly!" Clare put up a hand and tweaked his ear, provoking a delighted yelp. "Do you think that boy was really murdered?"

He shrugged. "She certainly thinks so."

"He might well have been."

"Yes, he might well have been. But how's she going to prove it?"

V

THE PEOPLE OF THE VILLAGE, even those who thought of themselves as her friends, had long since felt that, tiny step by tiny step, Ruth had either been precipitated into, or had herself precipitated a seemingly irreversible process of distancing herself from them. She was like someone in love, who can only with an effort focus attention on anyone but the loved one. She was like someone mortally ill, who, awaiting death like a bride her bridegroom, is incapable of sparing more than momentary attention for those gathered for the celebration of that dark, final union.

These were, for the most part, decent, tactful, reticent people; and so, as in the case of a love affair or a death sentence in their small community, they rarely spoke to Ruth about her obsession, despite the increasing publicity in the newspapers. But inevitably they spoke about it to each other. The kinder of them said that Ruth was no longer herself, as though it were some simulacrum that, distantly polite, welcomed them to her restaurant, entered their shops, nodded and said a hurried good morning or good afternoon in the High Street, and parried their invitations to bridge parties or cocktail parties. The less kind of them said that Ruth had become odd—as though she were now one with poor, harmless Miss Foxton, obliged to quit the primary school at which she had taught for so many years because of the mania that sent her marching up and down the village streets, ranting unintelligibly to the inanimate world about her.

In the kitchen, when Toinette told Ned that she'd better get Mrs. St. Just's permission before slipping out for a second to say good-bye to her boyfriend, a soldier returning to Germany after a brief leave, he replied: "Oh, don't bother about getting her permission. Just go, love. In the state she's in, she's not going to notice."

When at a meeting of the Women's Institute, old Mrs. Perrott, always out of touch because of the distance of her dilapidated thatched cottage from the village, suggested that "that nice Mrs. St. Just" should be asked to join the subcommittee for the summer fete, the vicar's wife said in a hushed voice, almost as though Ruth might be outside the door listening: "Oh, I hardly think . . . not at this moment . . . ," and everyone silently nodded.

As she went about her tasks, Ruth often found herself marveling that, with such scant and intermittent attention, she could nonetheless manage to perform them little worse than in the past. She ordered the food, she oversaw the staff, she dealt with bills, bookings, and letters of inquiry or complaint. She had always been efficient, and she continued to be efficient now. But when, at the close of a long evening, she at last retreated upstairs to the flat to lie down on the sofa, her head deep among its cushions and her eyes shut, she would find that she could summon up almost no recollection of anything that had happened. Vaguely she would remember that there had been some sort of altercation between Toinette and Ned over a borrowed corkscrew, that there had been some sort of muddle with a local firm over the table for a birthday party, that there had been some sort of unpleasantness with a pushy North Country couple over a bottle of wine. But she could not have been more precise. Through all these things and over all these things, there was the constant thought of Jim and the mysterious manner of his dying.

Larry's article had appeared. It said, as he had warned her it would, far more by implication than directly. It suggested, as he had not warned her it would, the possibility that, just as a jolt may cause a hair-crack hardly visible to the eye in a piece of delicate porcelain, so her bereavement might have unhinged her in a manner so subtle as hardly to be noticeable. Ruth did not care for that suggestion, but she was not surprised by it. She accepted that many people—even someone who knew her as well as Mark did—took the view that, in her conviction that Jim had been murdered, she was not being wholly rational. What she found much harder to accept was Larry's tone of condescending pity. Sad, lonely, bewildered, bereaved, frustrated: well, yes, no doubt she was all those things, but she did not like him to call her them in print.

The day after the article had appeared, as she once again lay in her now habitual manner on the sofa, doing nothing, observing nothing, almost thinking nothing, the telephone began to shrill. Her first impulse was to let it ring. No doubt it was a wrong number, Toinette's boyfriend from Germany, or someone asking her to do something she had no wish to do. When, however, the telephone shrilled on and on, she at last clambered wearily off the sofa and in stockinged feet limped over to it. "Yes." Earlier that evening that same sharp monosyllable had made Mr. Brockhurst remark to his wife: "She's not going to go on getting customers if she answers the phone like that."

"Mrs. St. Just? Is that you, Mrs. St. Just?" It was a woman's voice, somehow familiar and yet unidentifiable.

"Yes."

"Oh, Mrs. St. Just, perhaps I've phoned too late. Perhaps I've woken you up."

Ruth glanced over to the carriage clock on the chimneypiece. "Not at ten thirty-seven."

"Oh, I'm so glad. I had to work late this evening. I've only just got home. . . . Are you there, Mrs. St. Just?"

"Yes, I'm here."

"It's silly of me. I haven't told you who I am. Please forgive me."

"Yes, who are you?"

"It's Babs—Barbara—Lumby. Remember me? At the F.O.? We talked on the telephone, twice, three times, and then you came to see Mr. Tracer." Miss Lumby sounded as though she had rushed to telephone after racing up a flight of stairs. It was her eager breathlessness that had prevented Ruth from identifying her sooner.

"Yes, of course I remember you." Both Ruth's voice and her stance, previously so rigid, now relaxed. "How are you, Miss Lumby?"

"Fine, fine, thank you. And you?"

Had Miss Lumby called merely so that each of them could inquire about the health of the other? "Yes, I'm fine too."

44

"Good. Oh, good." There was a silence. Then Miss Lumby, sounding even more breathless than before, said: "I expect you're wondering why I called?"

"Well, yes, I suppose I am."

There was a brief, embarrassed giggle at the other end of the line. "I read the article." In the ensuing silence, Ruth waited. Then Miss Lumby went on, in a voice so confidentially low that Ruth could only just hear it. "So did someone else." Another silence. "You know whom I mean?"

"I think I can guess."

"I shouldn't really be telling you all this, and you must never, ever, let on that I have. You won't, will you, Mrs. St. Just?"

"Of course I won't."

"He was furious about the article. And he brought it to the attention of some other people—no need to give names—who were also furious." Again there was that brief, embarrassed giggle, suggestive not of a middle-aged woman in a position of responsibility, such as Miss Lumby was, but of a mischievous schoolgirl. "I really called to warn you, Mrs. St. Just."

It suddenly struck Ruth that Miss Lumby might be repeating her name like this because it gave her some kind of weird pleasure to do so. "Warn me?"

"He—that person of whom we've been talking—said that what you'd told that journalist and what he had written was libelous. He said that if you'd said such things or that journalist had written such things about some private person or organization and not the F.O., you'd have been lucky not to have been sued."

"I really cannot see anything libelous in saying or writing what one believes to be the truth."

"The libel laws are so strict—and so odd. Often they just don't seem to take into account whether a thing is true or false. Do they? Mrs. St. Just, I do think you should be careful."

"It's terribly sweet of you to phone me like this, and I am, I am grateful." Ruth meant it: she was touched by Miss Lumby's solicitude and, yes, she was grateful. But the warning struck her as

45

preposterous. She went on: "But if being careful means dropping the whole thing, then—no."

"What you told that journalist about Mr. Diamont." Miss Lumby pronounced the name as an English one—not as a French one, as Ruth had done when telephoning Diamont and speaking of him to Tracer, in both cases uncorrected. So presumably the name was English. "That made Mr. Tracer particularly cross. He said that Mr. Diamont could sue you and the paper on the basis of that. It implied that at best Mr. Diamont had been negligent and at worst had been involved in some way in the death of your son. Or at least in a cover-up after it."

"Nonsense."

"I'm only passing on to you what Mr. Tracer said."

"Yes, of course, Miss Lumby. And, as I said, I'm very, very grateful to you. But if Mr. Diamont takes it into his head to sue— or anyone at the Foreign Office does—well, so much the better. It may help me to drag the truth out into the open."

"Oh, Mrs. St. Just!" There was another silence, during which Ruth all at once felt an intense exasperation. It was wrong of her, she knew, but she could not help it. "Well, I mustn't waste any more of your precious time. But I did think . . . I did think that I must let you know how certain people had been reacting."

"Thank you, Miss Lumby, thank you very much."

"Thank *you*, Mrs. St. Just."

Ruth could see no reason why Miss Lumby should thank her. "Well, good night, Miss Lumby."

"Good night, Mrs. St. Just."

Ruth once again stretched out on the sofa, her clasped hands behind her head and her eyes closed. She smiled to herself. All at once she looked relaxed, contented, happy, as no one had seen her look for a long, long time. She was glad that the article had annoyed Tracer and all those anonymous people in the Foreign Office. She was even glad of the talk of a libel action. Again she smiled, then she laughed out loud.

She opened her eyes and stared up at the cracked, grimy ceiling—that was the worst of having a stove, she had often told

herself, it made everything so dirty. Then she screwed up her
eyes, as though in an attempt to decipher something inscribed up
there. An idea had come to her, at first no more than an amorphous wisp of vapor curling round her brain, then solidifying,
then growing and growing.

Yes, that was it, that was it. That was what she must do.

"We thought we'd have one of these workers' cooperatives,"
Ned said. "You know the sort of thing. The six of us. Well, five, I
suppose, seeing that Mrs. Potts is only half-time."

Ruth felt saddened by the hopeless ambition of the whole idea.
"But Ned, dear Ned, what about the money? I'm only taking this
step to raise some cash."

"We have some savings," he said, brushing with his hand at the
lapel of the grease-stained white jacket that only yesterday Ruth
had told him to send to the laundry. "Between us, that would be
something."

"Unfortunately, more than something is needed."

Perched on a corner of the table that he had just laid, Ned
swung a foot back and forth, head on one side. "There's the
bank," he said. "A loan."

"Well, you could try," Ruth conceded, although she knew that
the trying would come to nothing.

"Why don't *you* try?" he suddenly leaped to his feet to ask. "Yes,
that would be best."

"Try what?"

"You don't really have to sell. You could borrow the money you
need on the security of the restaurant and the flat. We'd look after
the restaurant for you while you're away. We could manage." His
gray, peaked face was eager. "How about that?"

Ruth nodded. "Yes, that idea did come to me. But what I have in
mind may cost me, oh, far more than I could borrow. And . . ."
Her voice trailed off. She knew now that she wanted to sell not
merely to pay for her journey out to Saloum, but also to divest
herself of all possessions and responsibilities, like some anchorite
setting off into the desert or some Crusader setting off for the

Holy Land. She shook her head. "No good, Ned dear. I have to sell, there's no other way. If you and the others can come up with the sum, well, nothing would please me more. I'm very fond of you all. You know that, I think." She put a hand on his shoulder, feeling its fragility beneath the coarse and greasy cloth of his jacket. The contact filled her with a sense of pathos. "God knows you've often driven me round the bend, Ned, often, often. But— you're a good boy."

Gratefully he smiled up at her, his sand-colored eyelashes blinking rapidly over his pale green eyes.

She knew at once that despite his peevishness, his snappish-ness, and his constant flow of disbelieving or disparaging com-ments, this viewer, the seventeenth to call, would buy the restaurant and flat. He wore a dark blue pin-striped suit, cut in such a way that it flared out, skirtlike, over his ample thighs and bottom; moccasin-style shoes of a leather so pliant and soft they might have been slippers; and a camel's-hair overcoat that kept slipping off one of the shoulders over which he had draped it. Although his name was Italian, he spoke with a Cockney accent.

"That'll have to be seen to." He seemed to have that to say of almost everything she showed him as, hand massaging chin, he stared in a fiction of despairing disbelief at the *batterie de cuisine*, at the vast Esse cooker, at the fuse boxes, light fixtures, linen, crockery, cutlery.

In the flat, his hand once again to his chin, with a bloodstone in a chunkily ornamental setting glinting on his ring finger, he raised his head to sniff repeatedly, like a sanitary inspector about to detect bad drains. "You've some damp in here."

"Oh, no, there's never been any damp."

He shrugged, turning down the corners of his small, pettish mouth, while his hand went out to stop the overcoat from slipping yet again off his shoulder. The implication of the *moue* was obvious: no one would expect a vendor to tell the truth. Vendor! She suddenly thought of Mark. Perhaps she should have asked him to act as agent. He might have let her off paying a commission.

In the bathroom the plump, carefully manicured hand with the bloodstone ring on it pulled at the flush, and then the dull, discontented eyes stared down into the swirl of water. Ruth knew what he would say. He said it: "That'll have to be seen to."

"Seems perfectly okay to me. Always has been."

Again he shrugged, again the corners of his mouth turned down.

Now he stood on tiptoe and stared out of the bathroom window. "Not much of a view." But how many people, using a bathroom, would stand on tiptoe to find a view?

Patiently resigned in the certainty that at last she had found a buyer, Ruth said, "The water meadows are rather beautiful in the summer."

"That's probably why you have all this damp. The water meadows." He spoke as though he equated water meadows with death-watch beetles or dry rot. He extended a hand to the wall above the washbasin. "Yes, damp."

In her bedroom, without asking if he might do so, he began to open the built-in cupboards, even getting on a chair to reach the highest of them. He peered at the contents. Then, closing the last, he commented: "These look pretty antiquated."

"They were here when I came. But they can't be all that old."

"They'll have to be seen to."

The long, tedious inspection over, they sat facing each other, he on the sofa, an arm extended along its back, and she on the straight-backed chair that she always seemed subconsciously to choose when dealing with business. When, stirring herself, she offered him a drink, he asked for some Perrier water—"I'm on the wagon at the moment."

"I'm afraid I haven't got any Perrier water. Sorry."

He looked disbelieving: "I thought in a restaurant . . ."

She explained that the restaurant was closed on Monday and none of the staff was there. (Hadn't he noticed that for himself?

He was quick enough to notice patches of damp on the walls or cracks in the brickwork. She was damned if she was going to trek down to the restaurant again to fetch the Perrier herself.)

Eventually he compromised, with an ill grace, on some ginger ale. "Is it low-calorie?"

"I'm afraid I've no idea." She turned the bottle around and peered at it. "Yes," she lied. The lie gave her pleasure, but she later decided that it would have given her even greater pleasure to have answered no.

He sipped dubiously at the ginger ale. "I wonder if I might ask you a personal question, Mrs. St. Just?"

"Ask anything you like." She smiled. "Whether I'll answer is another matter."

"Why are you selling?"

"Because I have—other plans."

They held each other's gaze challengingly. Then, because she knew he thought she was lying, as he had so clearly thought throughout the interview, she gave a little smile and told him: "No, I'm not selling because the place doesn't pay. In fact, it pays reasonably well and, if run better, would pay even better. What it needs is a skilled restaurateur. I've never been that. Just an amateur, really."

He looked pleased by what he clearly took to be an oblique compliment to his own professionalism. He had already boasted to her of his success with a wine bar in the City and with a pizza parlor—his own phrase—in the West End.

"Well, I'll have to think about it," he said at last. "Before reaching any decision, I must go over the accounts. As I told you."

"Of course."

As they passed through the empty restaurant on their way out—the sight of the unoccupied tables always filled her with an unreasoning depression—she halted to say, "If you do decide to buy, there's just one thing."

"Yes?" He became suddenly wary, as though he suspected that she was about to reveal something appallingly wrong with the house or the business.

"The staff here is an extraordinarily nice and happy crowd." Nice and happy! Would he really care if the staff he employed were either of those things? Efficiency and skill would be what he wanted. Poor Ned, Toinette, and the rest of them had no abundance of either of those qualities. Nonetheless, Ruth pushed on. "I think they'd be willing to stay if you wanted them."

"Well, let's see, let's see. We mustn't rush our fences. You don't even know that I'm going to take the place off your hands now, do you?"

But she knew, she knew.

SINÉ

I

RUTH CRINGED and threw up an arm to shield herself from the sunlight as, the last of the passengers but for a mother with two small, fractiously bleating children, she stepped out of the plane. She scrabbled for her dark glasses in her handbag. It was some time before she realized that the name being chanted rather than spoken at the bottom of the gangway was her own. Given a French pronunciation, it sounded wholly alien.

"Yes, yes!" she cried, picking up the overnight bag she had set down beside her and hurrying toward the black girl with artificially straightened hair parted in the middle and drawn back into a loose bun under a beige and brown *poilu's* cap tipped over one eye.

"I'm Mrs. St. Just. That was the name you were calling, wasn't it?"

The elegant, beautiful girl merely smiled and gestured with her clipboard at a young man standing a few feet away from her. Hand raised to shield his eyes from the glare, even though he was wearing heavy steel-framed dark glasses, he was already staring over at Ruth. Now he stepped forward.

"Mrs. St. Just." He put out a hand. "I'm Denzil Rawson. Welcome. You don't know me, you've never heard of me, but I'm from the Embassy. I thought I'd come to meet you. That way things would be quicker and easier. Things are rarely either in Saloum."

"Oh, thank you. I'd never expected . . ."

But he had already turned away from her to address an elderly man in a threadbare uniform of tattered blue trousers and faded blue shirt, a monogram on its breast pocket, who had been desultorily excavating a hole in the tarmac with the big toe of one foot.

"Don't go with the others," Rawson told Ruth, as he now returned to her, picked up her overnight bag, and handed it to the old man, who had followed with a curiously stiff, jerky walk behind him. "If you come this way with me, we'll get you through in a jiffy. Or at least in what passes for a jiffy in this country. That, of course, is assuming the baggage handlers haven't taken yet another break."

"I could really have carried that little bag myself," Ruth said, as they began to walk under the scorching sun to a long, low, white building with "AEROPORT DE SIN" blazoned across it. "Aeroport de Sin"? As Ruth gazed at the words, Rawson laughed and said: "I like that, don't you? The E with the acute accent fell off and of course no one has bothered to replace it. It was like that when we arrived, it will be like that when we go. But don't let that 'Sin' mislead you. There's crime in Siné, lots of crime. But of sin it's hard to find anything. Except, of course, among the expats."

In a moment they were through the passport control; the large perspiring black official hardly glanced at her passport before he franked it with the gleeful force of someone stamping on a cockroach. He then pointed at two rattan chairs, his jolly smile—Ruth at once warmed to him—revealing teeth that seemed to have been encased in silver paper. To Rawson he said something in French.

"He suggests we sit here until the luggage has been unloaded. It's cooler than in the concourse. The boy will bring the luggage through."

Ruth was to get used to ancient servants being called "the boy."

Rawson crossed his legs carefully, so as not to crease the trousers of his beige raw-silk suit, and then drew out a folded handkerchief from the breast pocket of his jacket, with which he began to dab at his forehead and the back of his neck. Ruth watched him, thinking how handsome he was, in an elongated, aristocratic way. "How one sweats in this country!" he said. But to Ruth, who could feel her underclothes sticking disagreeably to her, he looked remarkably cool. He adjusted the cuffs of his shirt, twitching at them fussily. "You must be careful of dehydration. An English tourist died of it only last week."

"I didn't know that one could *die* of dehydration. Unless, of course, one was lost in a desert." She gazed around, at the passport officer, whose forearm muscles bulged under the rolled-up sleeves of his khaki shirt; at the pock-marked, lethargic sentry with a rifle across his knees, lolling on a chair beside the doorway that led out to the concourse; at the coils of flypaper, black with flies, hanging from the cavernous ceiling; at the shutters from which many slats were missing or tilted askew. Then she looked across at Denzil Rawson, who at once responded with a smile. She leaned forward to say what she had failed to say before. "I never expected anyone to meet me."

"H.E. thought it the least we could do."

"But how did you know which plane to meet?"

He smiled. "Easy. There aren't many planes, and there are only three in a week from London. You said you were arriving at the weekend, so it was an obvious assumption you'd come on the Friday plane—there being no planes on Saturday or Sunday."

She felt suddenly attracted to him, so neat, so clean, so cool, so handsome, so efficient.

"You'll be staying here for a while, I take it?"

"Here? You mean in Siné? Oh, no longer than I can help. I want to go down to Bissance—"

"Up to Bissance," he corrected with the same fussiness with which he had twitched at his shirt cuffs. "North."

"Up to Bissance as soon as I can. And from Bissance I must then go on to—to Ellampore." Once again she stumbled before getting out the place name.

He gazed at her with a disquieting mixture of puzzlement and pity. He sighed. "We want to do anything we can to help you."

"Well, that'll be a change!"

He laughed, not in the least offended by her tartness. "Haven't we been helpful so far?"

"Hardly."

"Everything is always more complex and more difficult in our job than outsiders ever realize."

The old man whom Rawson had called "the boy" had now appeared in the doorway. He seemed to be afraid of walking past the sentry. *"Me voici!"* he called out with the strangely sibilant accent that the Saloumese gave to their French. He was straddling Ruth's two bags with his sticklike legs in their dark blue cotton trousers, as though to protect them from some marauder. Ruth suddenly remembered that she had never given him the baggage tickets. She wondered how he had recognized what belonged to her.

Rawson got up. He did so slowly, as foreigners soon learned to do anything not urgent in the heat of Saloum. "Well, that was quicker than I expected. As a rule everything in Saloum takes longer than one expected. Is that all?" He indicated the two pieces with a foot shod in lizard skin. Ruth nodded. "For the luggage to have come through so fast and for nothing to have got mislaid—that's certainly one for the book. You've brought good luck with you."

"I hope so. Good luck is what I need at the moment."

The old man staggered ahead of them with the two large suitcases and the overnight bag. The muscles at the back of his legs and in his scrawny arms were stretched taut, as were those in his neck. Appalled, Ruth wanted to rush forward to help him.

Under a vast tree, whose trunk, in its yellowish-pink rawness, looked as though the bark had been ripped off it in strips, was a black Rover car with a black chauffeur at the wheel. The chauffeur, his peaked cap tipped over his closed eyes and his mouth wide open as his head lolled back against the upholstery, was in a deep sleep. With the signet ring on his left hand Rawson rapped on the window, closed presumably to retain the coolness of the air-conditioning, and then, having achieved nothing, rapped once again. At the second rap, the chauffeur jerked forward, pushed up his cap, and jumped from the car. "Sorry, sir!" Coming from The Gambia, as Ruth was later to learn, he spoke English.

Yawning, the chauffeur opened up the trunk of the car, revealing that among much else it also contained three coconuts. Then, without making any attempt to assist, he watched as the old man, breathing heavily with a low, whistling sound, as of a kettle coming to the boil, heaved up first one of the suitcases and then the other. Rawson rattled the change in his trouser pocket and eventually produced two coins. He held them out without looking at the old man. Reluctantly the old man took the coins in his palm and stared down at them with the crestfallen look, seemingly close to tears, of a child balked of its expected pocket money; then, holding out his hand, with the coins still resting on its palm, he repeated, "*Quatre, quatre, quatre.*"

Rawson made a gesture as of brushing away a cloud of gnats. "*Assez! Va t'en!*"

The driver joined in. "*Va t'en! Va!*" His gesture was more violent, as though he were pushing someone invisible out of his path.

The old man stared first at Rawson and then at the chauffeur. He muttered something under his breath. Then, forlornly, bony shoulders sagging, he began to wander off.

"My cases are very heavy," Ruth said, as she clambered into the back of the car.

"Not nearly as heavy as those of most travelers." He clambered in beside her. "You see, whatever you give them, they always ask for more—as a matter of principle. You'll learn that."

"I have a feeling I've a lot to learn."

"Where do I go, sir?" the driver, who had an amiable, spherical face, with a large, straggling moustache stuck in the middle of it, turned round to ask.

"La Pinière," Rawson told him. He looked at Ruth. "That's where you've booked?"

Ruth nodded, wondering how he knew.

He must have guessed that she was wondering, since he now said: "It had to be either La Pinière or La Flèche d'Or, so I got my secretary to ring up to inquire. She rang La Pinière first and La Pinière it was. Odd name. There's not a pine tree in sight. Perhaps the French owners were homesick for the pines of their homeland."

"Is the hotel all right?"

"All right? Oh yes, perfectly all right. You could imagine you were in any luxury hotel from Miami to Tokyo. Clean, efficient, comfortable. Mind you, I prefer La Flèche d'Or myself. But then I'm a romantic. It's the old hotel," he explained. "The hotel that existed long before anyone had thought of freedom for any colony in Africa. Although it now has air-conditioning, a swimming pool, and a nightclub, the travel agents still avoid it. It's seedy, rundown."

They had reached the outskirts of the city. Gimcrack housing estates, composed of groups of square white-washed bungalows fenced off from each other by rusty barbed wire sagging from poles set askew in soil the color of rust, reared up all about them. "QUART DE BRIE" Ruth saw picked out in flints, glittering in the sunlight, on a bald hillock above one estate. "Why Quart de Brie?" she asked.

Rawson shrugged. "Why anything here? That next estate is called Amitié and the one after it Liberté. But I'd imagine there's little friendship or freedom in either."

They passed a crescent of beach, with garishly colored cabins and beach umbrellas and innumerable people, white and black, crowded together as though some huge wave had tumbled them all up, higgledy-piggledy, with the matted seaweed, the crushed cartons, and the Coca-Cola cans. Then the car was traversing the port, with leggy gantries, ships with smokestacks that looked as if they were stained with iodine, and near-naked dockers straining like ants under huge loads. Beyond the port, there were low, wrinkled expanses of sand, with basinlike indentations in them, from which there sprouted misty, pale green emanations of scrub. Staring out of their car windows, they were silent. Then Rawson turned to her. "Nearly there now. Place de l'Indépendance."

Here there were high-rise blocks of apartments, with washing fluttering from the upper stories and offices and shops on the ground floors. There was a movie theater, looking like a Turkish bath, with an outsize picture of Brigitte Bardot appearing in some ancient film, mounted just beneath its squat dome. There was a bus station, with hordes of people, some in Western clothes and some cocooned as though in white bandages, squatting patiently under trees while waiting for their transport.

Suddenly Ruth experienced an unfamiliar claustrophobia in the sealed car, with the air conditioner making a persistent noise like the whine of a mosquito hugely amplified. "Would you mind if I opened this window?"

Rawson did mind. But he shook his head politely. "Go ahead."

Ruth wound the window down, then rested her arm along its ledge. The sun was like fire on her bare flesh, but she let it remain there. A breath of air scorched her neck, as the driver accelerated to pass an overladen truck lumbering along in the center of the road. "Very hot," he muttered, furious that the window had been opened.

The truck they had passed now rattled and thudded past them, all but grazing their front left mudguard. The driver laughed and accelerated in pursuit. But traffic lights stopped him before he could again overtake the truck. In front, the truck, piled high with old tires, was spewing a foul-smelling blue-gray smoke. Ruth began to cough.

As she coughed, a handkerchief to her mouth, she all at once experienced a moment of terror. A creature, whether man or woman she could not at first be certain, with white, disheveled hair and white robes fluttering in the wind, was leaping toward her—yes, it was at her that the wild eyes were staring—on a single shriveled leg and a crutch that was no more than two pieces of wood fastened together with rope. The creature—she saw now that it must be a man—was screeching as though in an incoherent fury. Before Rawson or the driver had become aware of him, he had raised the hand not holding the crutch, its fingers bent into the palm to make a tight fist, and had begun to beat on Ruth's arm, still outstretched along the ledge of the window. At once she pulled away her arm and cowered back in her seat. After seeing what happened, Rawson put a hand into his pocket and, as the lights began to change, drew out some coins and flung them in a wide arc out of the car window and into the crowded road.

Having given another grating screech—whether of joy or rage, it would have been impossible to say—the man at once began to hop in all directions, unmindful of the braking, hooting traffic, as he attempted to retrieve now one coin and now another.

The car surged forward. "A beggar"—Rawson sighed—"one of hundreds." He peered into her face and noticed, with concern, that it was drained of all color. "He scared you. But most of these poor wretches are harmless. Harmless but persistent."

Ruth closed her eyes, then opened them. "How strange we must seem to them, passing like gods on our mysterious errands from one building they will never enter to another they will never enter. . . . Do you always give them money?"

"Good heavens, no. I'd be broke if I did."

"So in that too you're like a god. Capricious."

"Oh, there's nothing godlike about me!"

Two soldiers sat on duty in wooden sentry boxes on either side of the open gates to the hotel, legs crossed at the ankles and rifles across bare knees. To the left of the gates, up an incline that looked, in its dun bareness, as though it were some vast ant-heap, there stood a corrugated iron shack, open on the side that faced the road; woodsmoke, raw and pungent, billowed from the chimney sticking out of it at an angle. Rawson followed Ruth's gaze. "That's where the sentries and the touts go for their food."

The hotel was a tall, glass-fronted slab, designed by a famous Belgian architect whose name Rawson, clearly to his annoyance, had forgotten. Its foyer was so chilly that Ruth put her arms around herself, wishing she had a cardigan, as they waited for the smartly uniformed clerk, his crinkly hair glistening with oil, to finish with an American guest who demanded to know where she could buy amber, real amber, not this fake stuff that was always being pushed at one.

Registration at last achieved, Rawson said: "You'll want to unpack, take a bath, perhaps have a zizz. So I'll leave you now, shall I? But if you've nothing planned for this evening, my wife and I would love to take you out to dinner."

"What time is it?" Ruth looked at her watch.

"Only two hours ahead of English time. That means it's"—he consulted the wafer-thin gold watch on his fragile wrist—"twenty past four. People eat late here. Shall we pick you up at about seven-thirty?"

"Yes, that's fine. Thank you."

A grave, tall, handsome busboy, in a spotless white uniform, white socks, and white canvas shoes, was waiting patiently beside her luggage. She leaned forward to whisper: "Should I tip him?"

"It's a good rule in Saloum to tip everyone you can afford to tip." He put a hand in his trouser pocket. "You probably haven't got any small change. Here, let me give you this."

"Count it. Then I'll know what I have to repay you."

He laughed and shook his head, as, watched by the busboy, he emptied the coins into her palm.

In the room, the busboy opened the door to the bathroom and said, "Bath," turned on the television and said, "Television," and drew the curtains together and said, "Drapes," before once again drawing them apart. *Madame désire quelquechose?*

Ruth shook her head. She felt in the pocket of her blouse for the loose coins, brought out three or four, and handed them to him. *"Merci,"* she said, in a French accent as poor as his English one.

He stared down at the coins in his palm. Then he looked up at her and smiled. He said nothing, he did not move.

Again she put a hand into her pocket, to find that there were still more coins in it. She brought these out and gave them to him. Impassively he inspected them, as they lay with the other coins in his cool, cupped palm. Then he made for the door, still carrying the coins on his palm. *"Merci, madame."* The door shut quietly behind him. There was no way of telling whether he was pleased or not.

Ruth went to the window, sealed because of the air-conditioning, and adjusted the Venetian blind so that she could look out of it. From the seventh floor, she was gazing down on a swimming pool, its water a brilliant, seemingly artificial blue, with the sea, a muddy gray-brown, separated from it by a high rampart of barbed wire. By the rampart, under the shade of a tree like the tree at the airport, its trunk strangely raw-looking, there stood a squat soldier with a rifle. There were white bodies in the pool, and white bodies lying around it. A black waiter moved toward them, carrying a tray loaded with glasses and bottles.

She moved away and began to unpack, even though it seemed a waste of time to do so when tomorrow or the day after that or the day after that she would be setting off for Bissance and, eventually, Ellampore. The drawers were lined with crisp, clean paper. At the bottom of the built-in cupboard there was a heavily starched, blue cotton bag with "Blanchisserie" embroidered on it. She went into the tiled bathroom, and although her flesh was now cool from the air-conditioning, she ran cold water from the faucet over her hands and forearms.

She had wanted to treat Denzil Rawson, as she had wanted to treat everyone at the Embassy, as an enemy. But now, after all that courtesy and kindness, how could she do so? She felt bewildered and balked. She lay down on the bed, its linen fresh and smelling of lavender. Then, after a few seconds, she got up and began to run the bath. She knew that she could not sleep and she had no desire to read. But after that seeming assault by the wild, incoherently gibbering beggar, she was afraid to go out on her own. In the end, she turned off the bath and stood at the window, watching the people splashing in the pool or roasting their bodies around it.

They seemed strangely remote from her, almost another species.

II

RUTH KNEW AT ONCE that Denzil Rawson's wife, Peggy, had once been a dancer. She held herself erect, firm chin uptilted and wiry body taut. When she walked, it was with a strut and swagger. When she stood, her feet were turned outward at an angle to each other. Her hair, parted in the middle above a low, wide forehead, was held in a snood that looked as if it had been woven from gold wire.

"We thought we'd take you to a fish restaurant we know—by the sea, a little way outside the city." Peggy spoke over an angular shoulder, as they emerged out of the air-conditioned coolness of the lobby into the slowly expiring warmth of a day that already seemed to Ruth to have been interminable. "We think it the best there is here, but some people don't agree."

"I'm sure I'll agree."

"One's nervous of taking a restaurant owner to a restaurant," Rawson said.

"I'm no longer a restaurant owner," Ruth said, disconcerted that he was so well briefed about her. "And in any case, my restaurant wasn't all that good."

The car to which they strolled, with the nerveless languor that afflicted everyone white in Saloum, was not the chauffeur-driven Rover but a Peugeot 205, with innumerable indentations and scratches on a gray body thick with dust. Rawson noticed that Ruth was appraising all this damage. "Don't imagine that Peggy and I are both appalling drivers. Don't even imagine that Peggy is—though she's not all that hot. Here everyone constantly bangs everyone else's car. I think people regard it as a way of being informal and matey—like Italians and Greeks constantly patting and stroking each other."

"Shall I drive?" Peggy asked.

"No, dear, I'll drive."

Peggy pulled a face at Ruth, as she held open the rear car door for her. Then she slipped in beside her. "Well, in that case, let's pretend that Denzil's our chauffeur. It's *very* smart to have a white chauffeur out here. H.E. doesn't have one, but to H.E.'s constant chagrin the French ambassador does. Mind you, the French ambassador's chauffeur was born here and bred here—and he drives terribly badly. But he *is* white. Denzil and I call him the White Elephant, firstly because he's so huge and secondly because he's so useless—always getting lost and arriving late."

This car, unlike the other, official one, had no air-conditioning.

But as they meandered along a road that followed the serrated edge of the coast, with sheer drops to a sea alternating swaths of green, blue, and red in the dying light of evening, the air through the open window beside her was cool on Ruth's face and bare arms. Peggy chattered away, while Rawson, suddenly thoughtful, even morose, frowned at the road ahead of him. It was probably as well that he concentrated on his driving, since trucks constantly hurtled around bends on the wrong side of the road or attempted to lunge past in the face of oncoming traffic.

Peggy spoke with a childish enthusiasm of their life in this country so unlike any country in which she had ever lived. She spoke of the market and the food that she bought there ("cheap, cheap, incredibly cheap"), of their three servants ("of course one has to watch them like a hawk"), and of the black children, offspring of a Nigerian diplomat, with whom their children played. Of this friendship she remarked, clearly puzzled: "It's odd. None of the children, neither theirs nor ours, seems to realize that there's this difference of color. I suppose that's good," she added, as though not really sure.

The restaurant, called L'Aiglon, was perfectly situated above a small, quiet bay. Little more than a large bamboo hut, with a narrow, stony path zigzagging down from it to a crescent of sand beneath, it was strung with Christmas lights glittering in colors as various as those of the sea in the last glow of sunset. Parked behind the restaurant there were a number of cars, the majority with diplomatic corps plates. Peggy eyed them ruefully. "How shabby Big Bertha looks in company like this!" Ruth wondered why they should have given the name Big Bertha to a car as small as the Peugeot.

A diminutive boy in ragged shorts and an undershirt torn at the shoulder was walking toward them, accompanied by an emaciated mongrel at the end of a length of rope with many knots in it. "M'sieur, m'sieur!" he hissed in the sibilant way of the Saloumese. He would look after the car, he offered.

Rawson nodded wearily. "It's a kind of blackmail," he explained to Ruth. "What he means is not that he'll look after Big Bertha but that he and his mates won't damage her."

"Is the blackmail expensive?"

"Oh, God no! The equivalent of five or ten pee. That's why one goes along with it."

In one fist the boy was clutching a peeled stick, with which he occasionally swished at the dog without actually hitting it. Each time the dog saw or heard the stick descending, it would pull on the rope, cowering away. The sight filled Ruth with anger. "Does he have to do that?" she asked. But Rawson ignored the question, as he pointed downward, telling her: "Look, look! Isn't that incredibly beautiful?"

Yes, it was beautiful, with late swimmers bobbing up and down in water that was now the color of blood, fishermen squatting out on a ruined sandstone jetty, and innumerable boats scattered like confetti as far as the horizon. But what the boy was doing to the wretched dog was far from beautiful.

"Come!" Peggy summoned her.

The owner of the restaurant was a plump, balding Frenchman, in an open-necked, short-sleeved blue Thai silk shirt, which shimmered as though it were a part of the ocean, tight-fitting white cotton trousers, and narrow white espadrilles. Seeing them, he rushed over. "Monsieur Rawson!"

"Pierre!"

The two men embraced each other. Then Pierre took Peggy's hand, bowed over it, and raised it to his lips.

Rawson grasped Ruth's arm above the elbow. "Pierre—this is a visitor from England. Mrs. St. Just." Pierre hesitated for a moment. Then he took the hand that Ruth was holding out to him, bowed over it, and kissed it too. His lips were soft and damp, and at that proximity, he smelled to Ruth of fried fish.

As he led them to their table, Pierre began to explain, in voluble French, what he could offer them that evening. They were lucky, a fishing boat had just come in, everything was fresh, perfectly fresh. He pulled back a chair for Ruth. This table offered a wonderful view, yes? Ruth agreed that it did.

"Would you like to see the menu or shall we leave everything to Pierre?"

Rawson had addressed the question to Ruth, but it was Peggy who answered: "Oh, let's leave everything to Pierre. We always do. Like Mother, Pierre always knows best." She smiled coquettishly up at the Frenchman, as he unfolded a stiff white linen napkin and placed it over her sharp knees.

"*Bon, très bien. Vous avez tous confiance en moi!*" Then in English, as he shook out Ruth's napkin with a ripping sound: "And for wine? Some Muscadet?"

"Some Muscadet. Yes, why not?" Rawson put his elbows on the table, rested his chin on his hands, and gazed down at the bay with obvious satisfaction. Then, as Pierre hurried off, he turned to confide in Ruth: "I'm afraid the Muscadet is not all that good. And it costs about as much as a bottle of vintage champagne back home. But at all events it's better than the local stuff—which I can't recommend."

They began with the smallest of sardines, fried so crisply that they might have been whitebait, sprinkled with lime juice. "Yes, Pierre was right," Peggy said, spearing another on her fork and popping it into her overwide mouth. "These sardines must have come out of the sea only a moment ago." She crunched on the morsel. "When you get to Bissance, you must have the regional dish there. It's called *poulet au Yassa*. It's somehow better there than anywhere else. You cut up the chicken and marinate it in lime juice and peanut oil, with onions, pimiento, salt, pepper, lots of pepper. After that you drain the chicken pieces and grill them over a charcoal fire—it must be charcoal—and then you put the pieces and the marinade and all the other ingredients in a pot and let everything simmer for about, oh, an hour. Of course, you serve it with rice."

"Sounds delicious," Ruth said, wondering how her customers would have appreciated such a dish.

"You're going to Bissance because of the death of your son?"

Peggy queried, reaching across Ruth for some salt. Ruth had already noticed with what speed she was eating, as though she were late for an appointment.

Rawson shot a warning, even angry, look at his wife, but either oblivious of it or determined to ignore it, she went on: "I wonder if you'll discover anything."

"I wonder too."

Rawson laid his knife and fork down on his plate. He leaned forward and spoke patiently: "I'm afraid there's nothing to discover. Honestly. You must believe that."

Peggy paid no more attention to this intervention than she had to his previous admonitory glance. She chewed and gulped down another sardine and then pronounced: "This is the last country in which to look for the truth. You have the choice between a number of lies. From time to time, I catch out one of the servants in a lie—about what something has cost, about why they failed to serve up a meal on time or to clean out a room, about what the children have been up to—but all that happens is that they substitute one lie for another. They rarely tell the truth, even if they know it—which I often doubt."

"That sounds terribly discouraging," Ruth said. "Except that so many of the people from whom I want to learn the truth are not Saloumese but foreigners."

"Yes, but anyone who lives any time in Saloum catches the infection. I've caught it. Yes, I have! One lies to excuse oneself, as one does back home. But one also lies for the sake of lying. Which few people do back home."

"More than you think," Rawson interjected. Face averted from them as though to disassociate himself from the whole conversation, he had been staring morosely out to sea.

Peggy ignored him. "I never used to be a good liar. But here I got the hang of it at once." She raised her glass and sipped meditatively. In the last rays of the sunset, the Muscadet glinted pink. "Tell me, Ruth—I may call you Ruth?—what do you think happened to your son, if he didn't hit his head on a rock and drown, as everyone said?"

"I don't know. How can I know? That's what I'm here to find out. I only know that he didn't drown, he couldn't have drowned. Not by accident, not in that way." She pushed her plate away, her sardines only half eaten. All at once she had no more appetite.

Rawson leaned across to the ice bucket beside him, took out the bottle, and spattering the tablecloth with drops of water, began to refill her glass.

"Thank you." She gave him a clouded smile. Then she looked down over the balustrade to the shore far below. A boat had come in, and a number of muscular men, their bodies naked but for loincloths and gleaming in the late, pearly light, were shouting, now at one another and now, it seemed, merely for the pleasure of shouting, as they lifted coarse round woven baskets full of still-wriggling fish from the boat to the shore.

Peggy said: "You'll meet Eugene Diamont in Bissance, I imagine." Head turned sideways and upward, Denzil was now staring at a group of children flying a kite made of newspaper from a bare, dusty mound behind the restaurant. Even more than before, he seemed deliberately to be distancing himself from all that was passing between the two women. Ruth had noticed that Peggy had pronounced "Diamont" as though the name were English. It was confusing, some people did, some people didn't. She would somehow have to discover which was correct before she met him. "He's an odd bird," Peggy added. "Or an odd fish. That might be a better description. There's something very fishlike about him."

"Do you know this woman in—in Ellampore? The one they all call Mother."

"All?" Peggy laughed, her mouth full of the piece of roll that she had just stuffed into it. "I've never called her Mother, and neither has Denzil—at least not in my presence. No, I've never come across her, since I've never been to Ellampore and she never comes here. But one hears about her, of course. One couldn't help hearing about her."

"What does one hear about her?"

As Pierre deftly removed the plates, stacking them one on top of another before passing them to a black waiter behind him, Peggy smiled up at him, her head on one side. Then, when he had left, she answered: "Clearly she's a woman of tremendous strength of character. Capricious. Willful. Charming. A cross, I should guess, between Mary Baker Eddy and Gurdjieff." Ruth was not sure who Gurdjieff was. "People as dominant as that always attract poor wretches who want to be dominated."

"Perhaps that's why so many people worship God."

Peggy stared at Ruth. Then, "Come again," she said.

Ruth merely shrugged.

"There was this English boy," Peggy said. "Last year. Or was it the year before? Anyway, he arrived not all that long after we had got here. He had an introduction to us, to me, because he'd been a ballet student and I was once a dancer. He'd given up ballet school—the school at which I trained—because, as he put it, he wanted to find himself. He had heard, read, about Ellampore and Mother, and he had obviously persuaded himself that to find himself he had to find her. So he set off on the boat. I rather liked him, I went down to the harbor to see him off. Well, he returned on the same boat some five, six months later. He was like a skeleton, he recognized no one, he seemed to remember nothing about his past life. He was, well, stark, staring mad. Denzil had to arrange his repatriation. Didn't you, darling?"

Rawson nodded, twirling his empty wineglass in his hand.

"How did it happen?" Peggy went on. "Well, people do go mad, we all know that. And someone who gives up a promising career in ballet—friends of mine, teachers at the school, all said he had promise—in order to travel to Saloum in search of a female guru, well, that sort of person may well be unhinged already. So it could be that even if he had stayed on in England he would eventually have lost his marbles. Who knows? But one does wonder."

"What became of him?"

Peggy shrugged, shocking Ruth with her indifference. "God knows! Dead perhaps?"

Pierre had returned, not with the waiter of before but with a diminutive child in attendance. The child, draped in a white apron that reached almost to his bare ankles, was carrying two plates aloft, one on either upraised palm. Pierre was carrying the third.

"Our lobsters!" At the sight of the three lobster halves, Rawson had jerked out of the reverie into which he had been sinking deeper and deeper. "Now this really is something, Ruth. You won't forget this treat. The Saloum lobsters are generally agreed to be the best in the world. You'll have to admit that you've never eaten any so good."

Pierre set down the plate he had been carrying before Ruth. Then he took the other two plates from the child waiter, hissing at him: *"La mayonnaise!"*

The child scurried off, his apron flapping about him to reveal that under it he was wearing only the scantiest of cotton shorts.

When she had helped herself from the sauceboat, Peggy asked: "Have you ever seen lobsters of such a size?"

Ruth shook her head. There was something monstrous about them, as though they represented some weird genetic mutation of lobsters as she had always known them.

The light was now so dim that, matchbox in hand, Pierre had returned to light the two candles stuck in what looked like champagne goblets. The flames flickered, strengthened, mounted higher.

"Aren't they pretty?" Ruth exclaimed, suddenly overcome by the beauty of the soft light flickering across the table, with the gray-blue sky beyond it.

"Bon appétit!" Pierre sang out gaily, as he left them to greet some other customers, three white middle-aged men and an Indian woman in a sari.

Peggy forked out some lobster from its shell, placed it in her mouth, and then sucked on it as though it were a boiled sweet. "Marvelous!" she cried out. "Try yours."

Ruth lowered her three-pronged silver fork and dug into her lobster. There was something gray there, something soft, something amorphous, which stirred lazily as she touched it. "Oh!" She recoiled in dismay.

"What's the matter?" Rawson asked.

"*That!*" She pointed with her fork.

He peered. Then, unable to see anything in the light from the candles, he drew the plate toward him. He lowered his head, like somebody extremely shortsighted trying to decipher the small print in a book.

"Oh, Christ!" He wrinkled up his handsome nose.

"What is it?" Peggy asked.

"I'd hate to say. Something not very nice. Something that has no business being there." Angrily he looked over his shoulder. "Where's Pierre?"

When, summoned by the child waiter from the table of the three men and the woman in the sari, Pierre did at last appear, Rawson was apologetic rather than indignant. The two men whispered together in French, their heads close. Then Pierre whisked away Ruth's plate, saying to her in excellent English, such as he had so far not used: "I must ask your pardon, madame. I will speak to the cook."

Totally unfazed by Ruth's discovery—she might, after all, have been served the other half of the same lobster—Peggy had continued, through all this, to excavate with her fork, to tear at a claw, to suck, to masticate, to swallow.

Ruth had to ask the question. "Do you suppose that was something that got into the lobster before it was caught—in the sea? Or did it get into it on the beach or in the kitchen?"

"Who can say?" Rawson gave a dry, mirthless chuckle. "You heard what Peggy said. In Saloum the truth is something one seldom discovers."

Ruth had to ask the next question. "What exactly was it?"

"Your guess is as good as mine." He picked up his fork and began to dig into the lobster half before him.

"A sea slug?"

Chewing, neither he nor Peggy answered.

"*Voilà, madame!*" Pierre spoke with the triumph of a Brillat-Savarin setting down a masterpiece before a customer. He was holding the plate high above his head. Then, with a flourish, he

73

swept it down before Ruth. *"Je vous demande pardon, madame,"* he leaned over to whisper, so close to her that she could feel his breath on her cheek. *"Bon appétit!"*

But Ruth's appetite had gone. She stared unhappily at the lobster while, oblivious to her, the other two gorged themselves. She had better make some pretense of eating. Reluctantly she picked up her fork and raked the firm, white flesh now in one direction and now in the other. She wondered if this was the same half of lobster, that gray, soft, amorphous intruder now ejected from it, or another half. She almost asked her host and hostess what they thought, then decided that it would be better manners not to do so.

Suddenly, miraculously, she became aware of a long, emaciated orange cat, with a broken tail and ears so large they would have been more appropriate on a donkey, pressing itself insistently up and down against her leg, with a repeated miaow like the hoarse squawk of a crow. She forked up as much of the lobster as possible and then, making sure that the others were too absorbed in eating to notice, raised the fork and dropped the contents on the floor. But the cat went on with its rubbing and squawking, ominously indifferent to the gobbet of lobster.

Again Ruth raked her fork back and forth across the firm, white meat.

At last the other two had finished. "A pudding?" Rawson asked.

Ruth shook her head.

"You've hardly eaten anything," Peggy said. "Wasn't it all right?"

"Jet lag," Ruth said. "I seem to have no appetite. Sorry. A waste, I'm afraid."

"Coffee, then?" Rawson suggested.

"Yes, coffee. Please."

"Oh, go away!" Rawson kicked out at the cat, which had now deserted Ruth's leg for his. "Pest!"

"Denzil, don't!" Peggy reproved him.

"Might have rabies."

"Nonsense."

Ruth was only half listening to them. Try though she might, she could not put out of her mind that gray, soft, amorphous thing lazily stirring at the heart of the lobster.

III

WITH ITS CLASSICAL portico, as of some Roman temple, beneath which cars would halt for one of the two uniformed guards to leap forward to release the passengers imprisoned in their air-conditioned comfort, its verandahs with their huge terra-cotta urns of red and purple flowers ranged symmetrically along them, and its oasis of a garden in which near-naked men staggered between scrupulously weeded beds, with yokes supporting buckets of water across their muscular shoulders, the Embassy struck Ruth as belonging to the Siné not of television, elevators, and air-conditioning, but of French colonials sweltering sleeplessly under mosquito nets, dying of sudden, mysterious fevers, and having servants flogged for minor derelictions of duty.

When she told this to Rawson, who had brought her there from her hotel in his car, he was delighted. "Ah, I see now that you're what I never suspected! You're a romantic like myself! But I'm sorry to have to tell you that, so far from being a relic of a murky colonial past, the Embassy was built only nine or ten years ago—after a fire had destroyed most of the original building."

Within the Embassy, he introduced her to a number of his colleagues in turn, sometimes knocking on a door before he ushered her in and sometimes merely opening it. She wondered on what principle a knock was deemed to be necessary or superfluous. In each case he would say, "This is Mrs. St. Just," without any further explanation, so that Ruth could only infer that everyone must know already who she was. Then, again without any further explanation, he would say the name of the man or, in one case, the woman who put out a hand to shake hers.

"You're on your way to Bissance?"

"Well, really to—Ellampore."

"Yes, of course. The death of your son."

"The death of my son. I want to know what really happened."

Each time the brief conversation seemed to traverse the same predestined route, to end in embarrassed silence when she made that avowal: *I want to know what really happened.*

Only the head of chancery—Rawson made an exception of him in not merely giving his name, Pinder, but also stating his function—continued with the conversation after the avowal had been uttered. He was a brisk man, with a pink, puckered, hairless face like that of one of the tiny monkeys that had chattered at Ruth from a tree as she had eaten her breakfast by the then deserted pool. He took her up at once: "There I fear that I must differ from you, Mrs. St. Just. We already know what happened. More or less. I do a lot of skin diving, the coastline here is perfect for it. There are innumerable rock pools, like the one in which your son had his accident. One thinks that they are deep, for the most part they *are* deep. But they often do have these treacherous shelves, and on a moonlit night . . ."

With a weary attempt at patience, she repeated what she had so often repeated before. Not only did Jim not dive, he did not even swim; and not only did he not swim, he had a terror of water.

Pinder smiled indulgently, his hands crossed, stubby fingers laced over his small paunch, as he tipped his chair backward. "It's one thing to have a terror of water back home—frankly, I have one, it's always so cold—and another thing to have a terror of water in a country like this. One of my little girls refused to learn to swim in our local pool in Hampstead. The mere suggestion would start her screaming. But as soon as we got her out here, there was no stopping her."

Ruth could not be bothered to argue with him. She stared out over his head to where, in the garden beyond the sealed window, an ancient-looking man—probably, she reminded herself, he was in fact younger than she—was teasing a flower bed with long, slow, meditative strokes of a wooden rake; his eyes, now returning her gaze, were misty with cataracts. Another, younger man squatted on the grass beside him, the fingers of a hand picking at the toes of a foot. It was as though the two of them took turns to labor.

Pinder had put a question to her. She gave an involuntary jerk of her body, as though some insect had suddenly stung her, as she switched her attention from the two black gardeners outside in the heat to the two white men with her in the air-conditioned coolness. "Sorry?"

"I was asking when you were planning to set off for Bissance." Impatience gave a jagged edge to his voice. That evening he was to say of Ruth to his wife: "Such a vague, disorganized, dreary woman."

"As soon as I possibly can. But I gather there's a strike of the local airline. I thought of taking a train, but Denzil—Mr. Rawson—says that's the worst way of all. Then I thought of a bus or a share in a taxi. But he's promised to try to get me on the boat."

Pinder nodded emphatically. "Yes, yes, that's what you must do, get on the boat. Much the pleasantest journey—if you're not in too much of a hurry. The only thing is, it's not always that easy to get a cabin, and you must have a cabin. But Denzil may be able to help you there." He looked across at Rawson, who was sitting, a faintly bored expression on his face, with one long leg resting unusually high over the other and a cigarette in his hand. "Old Angelopoulos owes us, doesn't he, Denzil?"

Rawson blew smoke out through his nostrils. "Certainly does."

The men exchanged knowing smiles. Ruth wondered what it was that had caused this old Angelopoulos to "owe" them.

Pinder heaved himself up off his chair. It was a clear indication that he had more important things to do than talk about the best means of travel from Siné to Bissance. "It would have been nice if you could have come to us for dinner tonight. But we have the F.O. inspector here until the end of the week—always rather a nerve-racking experience—and by that time I imagine you'll already have departed."

FRANCIS KING

"Oh, long before that—I hope."
"Perhaps on your return . . ."
"That would be nice, yes."
"Well, it only remains for me to wish you *bonne chance* on your—
er—mission of discovery." There was irony in the last phrase.
Ruth smiled. "You're very kind," she said, attempting to match
the irony.

In the back of the air-conditioned car on the way to the office
of the shipping company, Rawson told her: "I'd like to have
introduced you to H.E. But with the inspector here . . ." Ruth
knew that he was lying. Inspector or no inspector, the ambassador would never have wished to see her.

The car drew up before a long two-story building, set askew
on the docks; shacks of corrugated iron, their entrances filled
with lengths of sacking instead of doors, were scattered haphazardly around it. The building looked isolated, even abandoned,
with an emaciated goat tethered under a clump of bushes by its
entrance—it bleated desolately when it saw them—and no
human in sight. Across its front there was a faded sign, "CHÉNIER
ET MOGDAD, COMPAGNIE DE NAVIGATION," with a steamship with
three funnels painted below the lettering. A large, rusty-looking
bird with a cruelly hooked beak was perched on the sign.

As Ruth passed through the swinging door ahead of Rawson, a
giant of a man, slumped on an upright chair, his head lolling back,
eyes closed, and one bare foot resting on top of the other, awoke
and staggered upward, as though from a drunken stupor. A
swollen hand went up to the braided cap tilted over one of his
eyes, in a sketch of a salute.

Rawson asked for "Monsieur Angelopoulos" in a tone far
crisper than Ruth had ever heard him use before. The orderly,
bare feet splayed outward, then pattered off down the corridor.
Rawson pointed to the chair in which the orderly had been
sleeping. Ruth shook her head.

Eventually, after several minutes of being left on their own, the
orderly returned to show them into an air-conditioned office,

78

with three windows reaching from ceiling to marbled floor, over-looking the docks. An extraordinarily tall, extraordinarily thin man was looking out of these windows, his back to them as they came in. Deliberately, it seemed, he did not at once turn around to greet them.

"Taki!"

"Denzil!" Coarse black hair sprouted at the soiled opening of his shirt, on the backs of his bony hands, and on his high cheekbones. His complexion was an unhealthy yellow, two of his front teeth were chipped. Yet despite all these unprepossessing features, Ruth soon decided that he had a jolly, easy, jaunty charm.

When Rawson introduced them, the Greek gripped Ruth's hand in his and then, still holding it, subjected her to a careful, appreciative scrutiny, his eyes traveling down, up, down. "Please, madame." He pointed to a rattan easy chair.

Once all of them were seated, the Greek put out a hand and tinkled a bell on his desk. "You will drink some Greek coffee, *chère madame*? You will notice that I say *Greek* coffee and not Turkish coffee, as our friend Denzil likes to tease me by doing." He pronounced "Denzil" to rhyme with "pencil." "I have taught the boy how to make it." He leaned forward to her. "It is *good*." It was as though he thought her a finicky child who needed persuading.

"Coffee's just what I need. But, please, may I have a glass of water as well?"

"Of course!" He laughed, with a curious tearing sound from deep within him, as though she had said something peculiarly droll. "No Greek serves coffee without water. But this water will be out of a bottle. Much safer. In Greece it would be from a well or a spring."

Once again a "boy" in Saloum turned out to be an elderly man.

Having given the order for the coffees, Angelopoulos picked up a fan from the desk before him, pulled his shirt aside and out, and began to fan his narrow, hairy chest. He smiled over at Ruth. "Hot. This air-conditioning is no good. Needs replacement." Again he fanned himself. Then he asked: "You like it here?"

"It's—strange," Ruth said truthfully, holding his gaze.

Angelopoulos threw back his head and guffawed. "Strange! Very strange!" He leaned toward her again, his hands gripped between his bony knees. "My wife hates Saloum. My son and daughter hate Saloum. All live in Kavalla. But I—I like Saloum. Yes!" He spoke as people do when unjustifiably proud of some eccentricity. "I *love* Saloum! Yes!"

When Ruth raised her cup and sipped at the bittersweet, gritty coffee, he watched her from under bushy eyebrows. "Good? Good?"

"Good." They smiled at each other.

Rawson, clearly feeling excluded, as Angelopoulos had no less clearly intended, began: "You know, Taki, I've tried to get Peggy to prepare me Turkish coffee—"

"Not Turkish, Greek, Greek, *Greek!*" Angelopoulos shouted in interruption. It was clear that the two men were playing a game long since familiar to them.

"Well, *Greek* coffee, then—though everyone knows that the whole so-called Greek cuisine is Turkish in origin. But somehow she just doesn't seem able to do it."

"Send her to me one evening. I will teach her." The tone was suggestively jokey. He looked across at Ruth and gave her a wink.

At last the time came for Rawson to broach the object of their visit. "Mrs. St. Just wants to get to Bissance as quickly as possible. I've persuaded her that much the pleasantest way is to travel on the *Reine d'Afrique.* She sails tomorrow, doesn't she?"

"She sails tomorrow. But"—the Greek extended the palms of his hands to them, the sweat glistening—"there are no cabins." He shrugged. *"Je regrette."*

"No cabins?" Rawson spoke ironically, clearly not believing him.

The Greek shook his narrow head.

"But you wouldn't want poor Mrs. St. Just to have to go through all the horrors of a journey by train or bus—or in one of those overcrowded taxis? Where's your chivalry, Taki?"

"What can I do?" Again the Greek showed them those glistening palms. "I want to oblige such a charming English lady, a friend of yours . . . but . . ." He picked up the glass of mineral water before him and, head thrown back, drained it. Then, as he set it down, he asked: "What can I do, my dear Denzil?"

"There's always something you can do, you old rogue. Come on! Think of all the times I've come to your assistance when you've been out on a limb. Only last month . . ."

Angelopoulos thought or pretended to think, his head on one side and a hand to his unshaven chin. He sighed and grunted. Then at last he said: "There is one possibility. But I must send a telex to Monsieur Chénier for his permission."

"What is this possibility?" Rawson asked, in what was clearly pretended innocence.

"Monsieur Chénier's personal cabin. *La cabine du propriétaire.* Sometimes—as you know, Denzil—for an important traveler, for a special traveler . . ." He sucked in his breath. "Yes. *C'est possible.*"

When at last they had left, with Angelopoulos promising to telephone Rawson at the Embassy just as soon as he had heard from Monsieur Chénier in Lyons, Ruth turned to Rawson to ask: "What are my chances, do you think?"

"Your chances?" As they walked past the goat, it leaped away from them wildly, its udders swinging. "Oh, you've got that cabin."

"Got it?"

"Of course! He took to you, took to you at once. And you won't mind paying a little more than you'd pay for any other cabin, will you? He won't telex Chénier, because he knows that Chénier— being the snob that he is and therefore prepared to have his cabin used only by cabinet ministers, visiting bigwigs, or ambassadors—would certainly say no. But Taki will let you have it. Even if he hadn't taken to you and even if he didn't owe me a favor, he needs the money. After all, it costs him quite a bit to keep his wife in Kavalla and his mistress here both satisfied."

"A black mistress?"

"Of course. What else? White mistresses, like white chauffeurs, are enjoyed only by top people in Saloum. Taki's not one of those."

They clambered into the car.

"Where to?" the driver asked, his cheerful, pockmarked face turned to them over his shoulder.

"Where to?" Rawson asked Ruth.

Ruth looked at her watch. It was almost noon. "I think I've taken up enough of your time. I'll go back to the hotel."

"I'm sure Peggy'd be happy to take you shopping in the bazaar this afternoon, if you'd like that."

"Yes, she sweetly offered yesterday. But I think I'll take things easy. I'm still not over my jet lag."

"Well, just as soon as I hear from that old rogue, I'll give you a ring with all the details. If I'm not needed for something urgent at the Embassy tomorrow, I'll come to see you off."

"Oh, don't bother to do that! Please!"

"No bother. No bother at all." All at once he sounded grumpy, even offended.

IV

IN THE LATE AFTERNOON, Ruth went out to the swimming pool in her bathing suit, even though she had no intention of entering the water. She selected a deck chair under a red-and-green-striped umbrella and, having lain back in it, began to read a copy of *Vogue* bought at Heathrow. It would have been cooler and more comfortable to have gone on lying on her bed in her air-conditioned room, but suddenly she had felt a desire for people, even if those people were strangers. But here, in the trough between one party of tourists who had been carried off in a bus and another who would arrive in one later in the evening, there were now no people other than the tall, silent, courteous white-uniformed servants, so many of them with so little to do, who either stood in corners, their hands clasped behind their backs as they stared impassively ahead of them, or else strode, in the pretense of some urgent errand, from reception desk to bar, from bar to elevator, from elevator to baggage room.

A beautiful black boy, in a pair of shorts that had all too clearly once been a pair of trousers, now truncated above the knees, was making sweeping movements over the pool with what looked like an outsize shrimping net. When Ruth was not eyeing him, she knew that he was eyeing her; but as soon as she looked over in his direction, he put on a show of being totally absorbed in his task. Eventually, eyes lowered, he circled the pool to reach the side where she was sitting, and stooped and raked the net over the surface of the water. Ruth noticed the rivulet of sweat that trickled, molten gold in the sunlight, down the indentation of his backbone. She also noticed the small ulcer on his right ankle, and how widely his bare toes were spaced, as though he had never worn shoes.

His desultory task finished, he wandered off and placed the net against a tree. He then went over to talk to the solitary sentry who sat, a rifle slung across him, on the earth rampart, surmounted by rusty barbed wire that separated the grounds of the hotel from the highway and the public beach beyond it. From time to time, as they talked, the two looked in her direction. She wondered what they were saying about her. Was it complimentary or derogatory?

Eventually the boy pattered off down the concrete walkway that led around the side of the hotel to what Ruth assumed to be the servants' quarters. The sentry surreptitiously shook a cigarette out of a crumpled paper packet removed from a pocket of his tunic. He lit the cigarette and took rapid little puffs, when not hiding it behind his back. Ruth put down the *Vogue*, closed her eyes behind their dark glasses, and began to drift in and out on slow tides of sleep.

She was aroused by an incoherent screeching. Like some huge, white bird, its plumage blown now in one direction and now in another by the capricious wind off the sea, a man was standing, as though impaled on the rusty strands of barbed wire, at the farthest end of the high rampart separating the grounds of the hotel from the highway. Something waved in the air, right, left, right. A crutch, she realized, made amateurishly from two lengths of wood spliced together with rope. Again she heard that incoherent screeching.

She screwed up her eyes to see him better. Her heart began to thud. Yes, yes, of course. It was that beggar who, disheveled and demented and in danger of being knocked down by the speeding traffic, had hopped out over the highway toward the becalmed car in which she had been imprisoned at the traffic lights on her journey into the city from the airport. She could make out the emaciated arm, like the dried root of a tree, the fuzz of white hair on the chest where every bone was distinct, the similar fuzz of white hair, a little tuft of it, on the pointed chin. A gust of wind all at once twitched at the luxuriant, matted locks and whirled them upward.

It was at her that he was staring with that demented fixity of gaze. It was to her that he was calling with that demented incoherence of utterance. She was certain of both these things, even if, the sun now low in her eyes, she could not be sure of the direction of his gaze, and even if, as the torrent of sounds cascaded over her, she could not have told if they would have any meaning for a native of the country or not. Terrified now, she turned her head to seek out the sentry at the other, far end of the rampart. But mysteriously he had vanished.

She rose from the chair, feeling a momentary giddiness. She stooped and picked up her bag from the ground. She opened the bag. The white-robed figure, seemingly impaled on the rusty barbed wire, was now so still and silent that he might have expired from sunstroke or thirst. She began to walk around the pool, the chessboard of black and white tiles scorching her bare soles, and then, steeling herself, she ventured onto the grass.

With huge, fanatical, red-rimmed eyes, the man watched her as she drew closer and closer to him. His body leaned against the

barbed wire, and he held the crutch aloft as though in preparation to strike her as soon as she came into range. Words no longer
spouted from his mouth as though from some moss-fringed
faucet. Instead, he was dribbling a tacky saliva.

Like a child, half fascinated and half terrified, approaching
some wild beast through its bars in a zoo, Ruth held out the note
that she had taken from her bag. She stretched a plump, white
arm through a coil of barbed wire. He stretched an emaciated,
black one to meet it. Wolfishly he snatched at the note, with a
wild cry that could have been expressive equally of rage or
delight, of despair or triumph.

Suddenly the sentry was behind Ruth. He shouted gutturally,
stepped forward, and began to jab with his rifle through the
barbed wire. In terror, the beggar flung himself away, fell to his
knees, tipped over, and lay sprawling, the makeshift crutch just
out of his reach. With a retching groan that seemed to come from
somewhere deep within his bowels, he pivoted around first on his
elbows and then his knees. On all fours he lurched toward the
crutch and grabbed it. Then he rolled over and over down the
rampart, struggled upright at the bottom, again with that hideous
retching groan, and began to move, in gigantic hops, using the
crutch as a fulcrum, across the road and down the steep bank to
the sea on the other side.

The sentry beckoned her away from the wire. "*Venez, madame!
Venez!*" He made a gesture with the rifle, as though, if she dis-
obeyed the command, he would be obliged to shoot her. Then, as
she stumbled down the rampart, the coarse, dry grass lacerating
her bare soles, he extended the hand that was not holding the
rifle in an effort to steady her. "*Ces gens-ci—mauvais, mauvais!*" he
said in imperfect, sibilant French. "*Méchants! Il faut prendre garde!*"

"*Il est pauvre,*" Ruth said, remembering nothing of her former
terror.

"*Non, non!*" He was indignant, shaking his head vigorously.
"*Non, non! Pas pauvre! Riche, riche!*" The claim would have been
laughable if it had not been so sad. "*Il demande. Les touristes donnent.
Riche, riche, riche.*"

The words *"Riche, riche, riche"* pursued Ruth like some all-pervading stench as she made her way first to the deck chair, to snatch up her bag and the copy of *Vogue*, and then back into the air-conditioned room, at once prison and haven, up, up, up on the seventh floor of the hotel, far above the beach.

JOURNEY

I

THERE WAS AN AIR of tranquil resignation about the people penned together between metal barriers at the far end of a shed so cavernous that it might have been an aircraft hangar. Most of them were black, with mountainous bundles or rattan cases piled up around them; the larger of the cases looked like laundry hampers and the smaller like cat baskets. Those who were white were mostly young. Eerily quiet in a country so noisy, the queue did not move. Vendors marched up and down hawking wares transported on their backs or on carts with wheels that had a malevolent tendency to skitter, squeaking, swaying to one side or the other. Under the corrugated iron roof the air was hot and thick, with a metallic taste to it.

A policeman leaned against the wall beside the queue, his tunic unbuttoned to reveal a grubby undershirt and a gold chain from which dangled what appeared to be an eyetooth set in silver. He coughed, the phlegm rattling, and then spat out a gob of greenish mucus which all but landed on Rawson's highly polished left moccasin. All at once there was the sound of a harmonica, quaveringly lachrymose, playing "The Last Rose of Summer." A tall, handsome, blond youth in a floppy straw hat, his nose and forehead red and peeling from sunburn, held the harmonica to his lips, a long-fingered hand cupped around it, as he slouched, rucksack on back, against the barrier. There was a weary-looking

89

girl in a loose blouse and a full skirt reaching almost to the
ground—both garments looked Indian in origin—squatting on
the concrete floor at his feet, with a baby slung papoose-fashion
across her strong shoulders.

"Do I join this queue?" Ruth asked.

"Good God, no! This is for the deck passengers. You come
through here." Rawson led Ruth over to a door beyond the line of
people. As he showed her ticket to the policeman slouching there,
he said to her: "Aren't you glad you're not a deck passenger?"

"Yes, I suppose I am."

"You ought to be."

They entered a small, airless room, with wooden benches, many
of them with slats broken or missing, lining three of its four walls.
The benches were crowded with people showing the same tranquil resignation as those in the queue. But here everyone was
dressed as though for the Champs-Élysées in a heat wave. There
were black children in spotless white dresses or spotless white
shorts and shirts, their shoes polished and their hands and faces
clean. There was a beautiful black girl, in a full yellow skirt and
what was little more than a brassiere, also yellow, attached by a
halter to her long neck. There was an elderly white man, with liver
blotches on his face, who was fanning himself with the panama hat
that had left a red crease like a scar across his lined forehead. There
were two young whites, a boy and a girl, sitting close to each other,
hands clasped, with the smiling boy from time to time leaning
even closer to the smiling girl to whisper something in her ear.

"What's happened to the boy with my luggage?" Already Ruth
too had unconsciously assimilated the practice of referring to
grown Saloumese as boys.

"Don't worry. He'll have taken it out onto the quay. We'll find
him in the cabin with it when we get on board." Rawson inspected the people around them, swiveling his body with no
attempt to conceal his curiosity. "No one here I know. I was
hoping to see someone into whose charge I could put you."

Ruth smiled. "I don't need to be put into anyone's charge."

"Why don't you sit?"

"Where?" She could see no room.

"Over there. Those kids can move over."

He crossed to the bench at which he had previously pointed, and said something politely in French to the large, placid black woman who seemed to be in charge of the children, the boy unhealthily bloated and the girl with fingernails inexpertly painted crimson. The mother put one arm around the boy and the other around the girl and drew them both toward her ample hips. She smiled up radiantly at Ruth, who smiled back before squeezing herself into the space vacated. "What about you?" she asked Rawson.

"Oh, I'm quite happy standing."

From far away, through the half-open door, Ruth could still hear the tremulous sound of the harmonica. What was the lanky, handsome youth playing now? She could not be certain. The melody evoked the image of a cowboy sitting astride his horse, in total solitude on some bleached plain, while the sun sank behind distant cactuses. It made her feel uneasy and depressed, as the crowds and the prospect of boarding a strange ship to a strange place had not done.

The woman with the two children took an orange out of the string bag at her feet and began to tear at its peel as though she were plucking a chicken. The pungent odor pricked Ruth's nostrils. Having stripped it, the woman broke the orange into two and handed a half to each of the children. With anxious concentration, they tugged off segments, placed them in their mouths, and sucked on them. From time to time they spat out the pith on the floor. Again the woman smiled radiantly at Ruth. Then she took another orange out of the string bag and offered it. Ruth shook her head. The woman offered a banana. For fear of offending her, Ruth took that, peeled it, and began to eat it. She looked around for somewhere to put the skin and then dropped it to the floor, to join the gobbets of chewed and saliva-soggy orange pith.

She realized that the old man constantly fanning himself with his panama hat was staring at her. But he was doing so without any disapproval, merely with curiosity.

Eventually a door opposite the one by which they had entered creaked open, and a black man, in a once white uniform, shouted out in a high-pitched, nasal voice: *"Messieurs! Mesdames! Venez, s'il vous plaît!"*

At that, all the people previously so apathetic on the crowded benches leaped to their feet, shouting, jostling each other, and grabbing their cases and bundles.

"No need to hurry," Rawson said. "No need for anyone to hurry. The cabins have been allocated. It's not a case of first come, first served." He laughed, gazing around at all the frenzy. "But they always do this. There's always this rush."

Apart from the old man, who stood aside courteously in the doorway, gesturing with his panama hat for them to precede him, Ruth and Rawson were the last to leave the stifling room.

Looking back over her shoulder from the gangway, Ruth could see the deck passengers still penned, docile and silent, in their straggling line, even though the doors through which they too would eventually pass out onto the quay appeared to be open. "They won't be allowed aboard until all the cabin passengers have been settled," Rawson told her, also looking back. "There's something to be said for privilege."

"If one is one of the privileged."

An officer, a clipboard under one arm, fussily insisted on guiding them to the owner's cabin, even though Rawson kept insisting that he already knew the way, from previous journeys to Bissance.

There was a semicircle of windows, encrusted with salt, one of which gave access to a small private deck.

"One couldn't ask for better," Ruth said, looking out through the windows at a broken deck chair, lying on its side, and the sort of stool, white-painted and cork-seated, that one would normally expect to find in a bathroom.

"Well, one could anywhere else. But not in Africa."

The porter, now patiently waiting for his tip, had been joined by an Indian steward, hair shiny with macassar oil above a mischievous, eager face.

"Very nice cabin," the steward said. "A-1. Owner's cabin. Madame will be happy here." His attention distracted, he peered beadily to see how much Rawson was tipping the porter.

With the ruefulness that Ruth had now come to know so well, the porter was turning the three coins over and over in his palm. Then, beseechingly, he gazed up at Rawson.

"*Assez!*" Rawson turned to Ruth, even though the porter still stood beside him, palm outstretched, with the three coins resting on it. "The food's not all that bad in the first-class saloon. You'd better reserve a place."

"Lunch, *monsieur*? Yes, *monsieur*! Lunch for madame!"

Rawson handed some coins to the steward, who, unlike the porter, pocketed them without argument and then hurried off. Muttering under his breath, the porter trailed after him.

Rawson looked at his watch. "Well, I'd better go ashore. Though I wouldn't mind a little break in Bissance. Just what I need after an F.O. inspection. They're late—as usual. You should have sailed twenty minutes ago."

"You've been so kind to me." Ruth meant it. All at once she felt despondent at passing out of his care.

He smiled. Although she was almost old enough to be his mother, it was the smile of an indulgent, fond father at an errant daughter. "Delighted to have been of help—if I have been of help."

"There was something I meant to ask you." It was only now that she realized how odd it was that she had not put the question already. "You never met Jim—my son—did you?"

He shook his head, pulling down the corners of his mouth. All at once his face darkened, lost its previous friendliness. "Nope. Sorry. Can't help you there."

The ring of his heels gradually diminished on the metal of the passageway as Ruth, standing in the doorway, looked after him; she was disappointed that he never once glanced around to wave or say a last good-bye. When he had gone, she once again inspected the cabin. It was ample enough to contain not two bunks, as she had expected, but two beds, each with a festoon of yellowing mosquito netting suspended above it. She touched the pillow, lumpy and hard, on the bed nearest to her, and then pulled back a cotton bedspread to reveal sheets that looked suspiciously creased. She lowered her head. Pillow and sheets both had a sweetish scent clinging to them.

She crossed over to the bathroom, and stared at the toilet, bare porcelain without any seat, at its farthest end. Its bowl was clogged with a detritus of coarse, beige paper. Beside it there was an ancient shower, its rusty hose hanging askew from a metal pipe that had come loose from its bracket. Some long strands of black hair lay by the drain. Par for the course, she told herself. At least she had cabin, bathroom, and that private deck all to herself. From beyond the bathroom window, its wire mesh eroded here and there by rust, she could hear a scamper of feet and high-pitched children's voices screeching to each other in French. She decided to unpack. Then, after taking out her cotton nightgown and throwing it across one of the beds, she instead decided to go out onto the main deck.

The other passengers, toting their bulging cases, baskets, bundles, and rucksacks, were now thrusting their way up the narrow gangway. A mother gripped a small, simian child by the arm as though she were a doll, and jerked her up after herself. Some kind of altercation was taking place between two men, one old and one young, who stood aggressively facing each other at the top of the gangway, blocking the other passengers, until the officer with the clipboard under his arm stepped forward to intervene. A suitcase in one hand and a shopping bag in the other, the rangy, handsome youth who had played the harmonica now passed beneath; the baby, previously carried by the girl, was astraddle his back. The girl herself followed wanly, the straps of her rucksack biting deep into shoulders that looked no longer muscular but fragile and vulnerable. Drawn to the couple, she did not know why, Ruth leaned far over the rail to watch them for as long as it was possible.

Last there was a middle-aged white man, who, unlike all the others, pushing and jostling each other and even shouting abuse, seemed not to care about his ignominious place in the queue. An unlit pipe pulling down one corner of his mouth, a paperback in one hand, and an expensive-looking reflex camera slung across his white linen jacket, he alone of all the deck passengers had a porter, straining under two heavy suitcases, in attendance. Ruth stared, fascinated, as though she knew, even then, that their lives would improbably touch and mingle. He was tall, knobbly, and bald on top, with orange freckles on his bare arms and legs—he was wearing khaki shorts—and a ginger moustache under a large, beaked nose.

Passing beneath her, he all at once looked up, raised the hand holding the paperback in a roguish salute, and gave her a wink. French? English? American? She could not be sure. But the paperback had looked like a Penguin.

When he too had disappeared, she returned to her cabin.

As she was once again bending over one of her suitcases, searching for her toilet kit, there was a rap at the door. Then, before she could answer, it swung open to reveal a well-dressed middle-aged black couple. Totally unembarrassed, the man explained in French that he and his wife would like to look over the owner's cabin. On a previous trip the occupancy of the Foreign Minister had prevented them from doing so. Would madame mind?

Without waiting to hear if madame minded or not, the two of them crossed over to the windows and peered out at the small private deck. "Bon, très bon," the man said. "Joli," his wife agreed. The man then said "Permettez, madame?" and, again without waiting for an answer, opened the door to the bathroom. His wife, on tiptoe, peeped over his shoulder. They turned, smiling. Clearly they approved of everything—clogged and stained toilet bowl, broken shower, strands of hair—that they had found there. "Très agréable," the man said, nodding vigorously. No less vigorously his wife now joined in the nodding. "Très agréable," she seconded.

Eventually, with effusive thanks and a lot of bowing, they left. Fearing that there might be other, similar visits of inspection, Ruth locked the door.

For a while after that she stood out on the private deck, watching the shore, with its white or ocher office blocks and apartment blocks, its gantries and its factory chimneys, its occasional patches of green where trees and flowers, laboriously watered for some government official, diplomat, or businessman, shone out of a surrounding dryness and dinginess, all slowly wheel around, recede, dissolve, vanish. The ship was now gliding down an estuary as down a green tunnel, with mangrove swamps trailing on either side. Large, dark brown birds, harshly cawing, from time to time creaked up from them on ungainly wings that looked and sounded as if they had been constructed from cardboard.

Depressed by the monotony of the scenery and scorched by the sun reflected off the waves, Ruth picked up the rickety, white-painted stool and carried it into a corner where she saw a wedge of shade. She sat on it, she leaned back against the wall, she stretched out her legs, and closed her eyes. Soon, despite her discomfort, she drifted into a sleep troubled by dreams, terrible but impossible to recall in any detail on waking, of Jim, her darling Jim, as a small child somehow ravished from her.

"Lady! Lady!" Her eyes fluttered open. She gave a snort, then a gasp. It was the Indian steward, now changed into a grubby, creased mess jacket, with a napkin over one arm.

"Yes?" She squinted up at him, head throbbing as she tried to recollect the dream. The throbbing seemed to be a reverberation of the throbbing of the ancient engine of the ship.

He bunched his fingers together and raised them to his mouth, in simulation of the act of eating in his native India. He gave a sunny smile. "Chow is ready, lady," he said.

She wondered if, having previously called her "madame," he had now decided that she must be American. "Oh, thank you." She rose unsteadily to her feet, ignoring the hand that he extended to help her. "Where do I go?"

"If you wish, I will bring you food here. Monsieur and Madame Chénier always eat in cabin. No problem."

"No, no. I'll come along to the saloon."

Having opened the door for her to pass through, he then daintily eased around it ahead of her, so that he could precede her as her guide. He looked over his shoulder: "This way, please!" He looked over his shoulder again: "Not far now!"

The saloon looked surprisingly attractive, with its glistening mahogany paneling, its white tablecloths and napkins, and its vases of flowers. Ruth peered about her. Every table appeared to be occupied. But the steward marched across to the far end, turned, and beckoned. "Lady! Please! Please!" Tucked away in a corner, a single table, laid for two, was vacant. "I keep this for you," he said triumphantly, drawing back a chair. There was something extraordinarily touching about his eagerness to please, just as there had been about Rawson's.

"Thank you." She smiled up at him as she took the chair.

"One moment, please."

He wove his way sinuously through the tables, passed out of sight, and then eventually hurried back carrying a menu. He held it out to her, its edges dented and frayed and its surface spotted with grease. "May I recommend?"

"Yes, please recommend."

"Madame would like the *potage du jour*?"

"What is the *potage du jour*?"

"Good, good," he replied, without being more specific.

"Very well. I'll start with the *potage du jour*."

"And then madame would like lobster? Special lobster, king-size."

Ruth thought of that gray, soft, amorphous thing stirring lethargically at the heart of the lobster brought to her by Pierre. "No, no lobster."

"No lobster?" He sounded vaguely affronted. "In Saloum best lobsters in world, lady."

"No lobster." The recollection had made her feel vaguely sick. "An omelette. That's what I'd like. An omelette."

"Ham omelette? Cheese omelette?"

While they were discussing first the omelette and then the wine that she should drink with it, Ruth became aware that the ginger-haired passenger with the pipe and the paperback had entered the saloon. Under his shorts, his bare knees were as bony as his nose. One of the other waiters was saying something to him, shaking his head and pointing at the tables. But the man remained immovable, legs wide apart and one hand clutching the bowl of his pipe, as he peered crossly around him. Then he spotted Ruth's table in the corner, smiled at her, and, followed by the anxious waiter, stalked over. "You're English?" he said.

Ruth nodded, while the two waiters took up positions on either side of her chair, as though to guard her from this invader.

"You won't mind my sitting with you, will you?" Before Ruth could answer, he turned to the waiter who had trailed him, and told him in voluble but atrociously pronounced French that he would be eating with "cette dame-ci."

In silent disdain, Ruth's Indian waiter handed the newcomer the menu for which he had now asked. "I come back," he said.

"Are you sure you don't mind?" the man asked Ruth, leaning over the table, crossed arms resting on it.

"It would be a bit late if I did."

"They don't want to accommodate me here because I'm a deck passenger. If you haven't got a cabin, then you're a deck passenger. Crazy! If you could see the food on offer to the deck passengers—and if you could see the flies on it—then you'd understand why I had to throw myself on your mercy." He examined the menu, affectionately stroking his moustache as he did so. His pipe lay on the table. "H'm. I think I'll have the lobster."

"Oh, please don't!"

He looked up at her, surprised. But when she told him of the lobster at the restaurant in Siné, he said: "Well, perhaps after all I'd better opt for something else. Some chicken perhaps. Chicken's always safe—even if it's nearly always stringy in this country." He picked his pipe up off the table and put it into his mouth, unlit. "Don't worry. I'm not going to smoke this. But I find it comforting just to suck it. I daresay I was weaned too soon—something like that."

Later, after she had offered him some of the rough, astringent Burgundy that the waiter had proposed, he asked: "And what, if I may be so bold, are you doing in this godforsaken country?"

"Godforsaken?" She thought of the long, deserted beaches; of the fishing boats bobbing far out to sea as the sunset spread, a darkening stain, across it; of the bougainvillaea frothing down from the high walls of rich people's houses; of the handsome men, women, children, with their proudly erect bodies and shiny skins. "But Saloum can be so beautiful."

"God forsakes beautiful places and people, just as He forsakes ugly ones. Anyway, you haven't answered my question, have you?"

Should she tell him, a total stranger? Suddenly, on a crazy impulse, she decided to do so.

At the end of her narrative, he nodded, pipe still in mouth. "Yep. I read something about it. There was a piece in my paper." When he said "my paper," she assumed he meant the paper he usually read. It was only later, when she in turn asked him what he was doing in Saloum, that he revealed he was a journalist.

"I've come to do a feature on old Mamadan—the president. He's paying a state visit to England next month, as you probably know." Ruth had not known. The news made the vacillation and inertia that she had encountered at the Foreign Office all the more explicable. "I had an interview with him in Siné—not a very satisfactory interview, since the old boy has become as deaf as a post—and now I'm going to Bissance because that's where he hails from. A poor family. Father a schoolmaster. It's amazing, with a background like that, that he should have acquired a real education, won a scholarship to France, made a name as a philosopher, and then survived all these years as president of this, yes, this godforsaken country." Taking the pipe out of his mouth—he had been talking through it—he gave her a wicked smile from under the straggly ginger moustache.

"You've been in Africa before?"

"Oh God, yes. I've been in most parts of the world. But this is my first visit to Saloum. Africa is full of places far worse, I'll grant you that. There are no atrocities here—I mean, no government atrocities, though private citizens from time to time get up to horrendous things, just as they do back home—and there's probably no more corruption than on many of our local councils. People always hold Saloum up as a model. In Africa there aren't that many of them."

The bean soup, crisp croutons floating in it, was delicious when at long last it arrived. Between greedy gulps, head lowered to his spoon, he said: "Better introduce myself. Dave, Dave Millett. And you're—I've read your name in the paper but of course I've gone and forgotten it. Memory like a sieve."

She had always had an irrational reluctance to reveal her name to strangers. Perhaps savages were right in thinking that to reveal one's name was to put oneself in the power of the person to whom one revealed it. "Ruth St. Just."

"Shall I call you Ruth?" He was dabbing soup off his moustache with a corner of his napkin.

Ruth was surprised. But she said, "Why not?"

"It would be a bit forward of me at a first meeting in England. But since we're two English people thrown together on a Saloumese tub where almost everyone else speaks French, if not languages even less welcome, I have an excuse. And you must call me Dave—unless you want to be more formal and call me David."

Ruth nodded.

"I suppose you booked your cabin from England?"

She told him of the meeting with Mr. Angelopoulos and of the owner's cabin.

"Lucky you. I don't imagine he'd have been so helpful to a bloke."

"It was simply a matter of paying twice as much as for any other cabin. Of course he'll pocket the difference—or most of it."

"How cynical you are! Or is it only in Saloum that you take such a low view of human motives and behavior?"

"I don't have many illusions. Not at my age."

Another man might have protested: "Not at your age! What are you talking about? You're still young!" She felt at once riled and respectful of him for not having done so.

Without asking her permission, he kept reaching out for the bottle of wine, to pour from it into both their glasses. "Drink up," he chided her at one moment, when he found yet again that, whereas his glass was empty, hers was still full. "It's not all that bad, and it kills off the bugs. Yes, truly! I always find that in any country, however dirty and disease-ridden, if one can get a bottle of wine, then there's far less likelihood of succumbing to parasites or food poisoning. Once I was in Zaire with this young German who wouldn't touch a drop of alcohol, not a drop. Well, he caught *everything*—in the end he all but died of amoebiasis. Whereas I . . ." He laughed at the recollection, twirling his half-full glass round and round in both his hands, while he squinted down into it.

At the end of their prolonged meal, it was Ruth who eventually called across the now empty saloon to ask for their bills. Although she had deliberately used the plural, the Indian steward, who had already embarked on his own lunch at a corner table as far away from theirs as possible, leaned forward to inquire sotto voce: "One bill or two bill, lady?"

When Millett said nothing, Ruth replied firmly: "Two bills. Separate bills." She was sure that Millett had been expecting her to treat him.

Counting out coins on the tablecloth before him—he moved them about as though they were pieces in a game of chess, in which he could not decide what next to do—Millett did not offer to pay for a share of the wine, even though he must have drunk three-quarters of it. "A tip?" he queried. He hesitated, searched in his trouser pockets, and eventually added two small coins to one of the three piles before him. He examined Ruth's bill, his head on one side to see it better. "Aren't you rather overdoing things?" He sounded shocked.

"How do you mean?"

"That tip. It's probably as much as the poor bugger earns in a day."

"Never mind. A rich bugger in England would regard it as an insult to be left something so tiny. Besides, he's been good to me."

"Women are lucky. People *are* good to them." He sounded aggrieved.

Ruth got to her feet. Although she had drunk so little, her face felt flushed and taut, as though she had been out in a drying wind. Perhaps it was the air-conditioning, she decided, pumped out from a grid just above the table, where a blue ribbon fluttered outward to show that it was working.

"Are you going to show me your cabin?"

She stared at him, nonplussed. He grinned back at her.

Then he threw back his head, the fringe of overlong ginger hair at its back touching the collar of his bush jacket and the bald expanse in front glistening. "Don't misunderstand me. Please. I merely want to see what it's like to travel as a privileged guest of Chénier, Mogdad et Compagnie, instead of as one of the hoi polloi on that stinking lower deck."

She nodded. "Come and see. No objection."

He peered around the cabin, and then, so suddenly that it startled her, he lunged out to stamp on something on the floor beside the bed onto which she had thrown her nightdress. "Got him!" He examined first the crushed shape on the floor and then the sole of his sneaker.

Ruth peered. "What is it?"

"What *was* it, you mean. A cockroach. Rats and cockroaches—they have so much intelligence, so much fecundity, so much sense of self-preservation that one day they'll take over the world. But that poor bloke"—he indicated the black and yellow mess with the toe of his trainer—"he was an exception. No intelligence, no sense of self-preservation at all—though no doubt he was fecund." Again he began to peer around the cabin, even tilting his head up to examine the grimy ceiling. "Not bad, not at all bad. Lucky you." He went to the windows and then walked out to the small deck. Ruth followed him.

"*Bolong*, that's what they call these." He pointed.

They were juddering up a murky channel, with mangroves,

their roots chocolate-brown below the fleshy green of branches, forming an endlessly receding tunnel before and behind.

"*Bolong?*"

"These tunnels in the mangrove swamps. Perhaps, if we're patient, we'll see a hippopotamus. Or an eland. Or a hyena." He turned away from the rail and began to reenter the cabin. "My trouble is that I'm so bloody impatient. That's why I'm not all that hot as a journalist. I can't be bothered to hang around and wait. If there isn't a story, I make a story." He was staring reflectively down first at one of the beds and then at the other. "Two beds," he pronounced.

"Two beds." She knew what was coming.

He raised a hand, as though he were about to take an oath in court. "Now please don't misunderstand me. *Please!* I'm not about to proposition you. I am merely throwing myself on your mercy. D'you think you'd allow me, out of the goodness of your heart, would you be terribly decent and kind—to a fellow countryman in distress?"

Ruth laughed, then nodded. "Oh, all right."

"Really? You mean it?" Clearly he had had little hope of her agreement. Had she refused, he would have merely shrugged and said something like, "Well, there's no harm in trying, no feelings hurt, and no bones broken." He lowered himself onto one of the beds, which it was obvious he already regarded as his own. "If you could see the conditions down there. If you could *smell* them. And I'm bushed. I need a really good sleep."

"You must take me down below."

"Oh, I don't know. One should resist the temptation to see how the other half lives. It only makes one feel guilty and depressed."

"If you're allowed to trespass up here, I don't see why I shouldn't trespass down there."

He shrugged. "Well, that's logical." Reluctantly he got up from the bed. "Do you want to go down now?"

"Why not?"

Having eaten heavily, from the fly-ridden canteen or from the food that they had brought with them—some of them had even set up portable stoves, around which they had chatted in convivial groups—the deck passengers had now sunk into either torpor or sleep. Stretched out on rugs, newspapers, or the bare boards, they gazed up with dull, bleary eyes at the red-faced, ginger-moustached white man and the tall, handsome white woman with him. Two children—were they the same, Ruth wondered, as the two who had sat next to her in the waiting room?—squatted cross-legged opposite each other and played some game with open and shut fists that seemed to be a Saloumese version of "Scissors, Stone, Paper." They were so absorbed that they did not look around when Millett and Ruth halted behind them for a moment to watch.

"Hi!" The rangy blond youth who had played that quaveringly melancholic music on the harmonica called out to them. He was resting with his back against the rail of the ship, his legs stretched so far out across the deck that Millett and Ruth had had to step over them. The youth had removed his T-shirt to reveal a narrow torso, a damp line of hair running up between the breasts and then expanding above them. The girl lay, eyes shut, on her side on the removed T-shirt, with the baby on her coat beside her.

"Hi!" Millett answered, giving a jaunty salute with forefinger and middle finger raised to where a military cap might have been.

"I guess you haven't got a cigarette, have you?" the youth asked in a lazy voice with an American accent. His air, half defiant and half hangdog, reminded Ruth of that young scavenger, so long ago it now seemed, in the Kensington High Street restaurant.

"Sorry, old boy. I smoke this filthy thing." Millett took his pipe out of the breast pocket of his bush jacket and held it out for inspection.

"I've got a cigarette." Ruth drew a packet out of her handbag, opened it, and offered it. The long fingers, their nails far from clean, twitched slightly as they went out. "Mind if I take two? One for—her." With his head he indicated the woman sleeping beside him.

"Help yourself."

He drew out the two cigarettes, placed one in his mouth with a little sigh, and then placed the other in the palm, open on the deck, of the sleeping woman.

"Take care that doesn't roll away—or get crushed," Ruth said.

He laughed, as though she had said something deliberately funny. "No light."

As she stooped and held out the lighter to him, he grasped at her wrist. Perhaps he merely wanted to steady her, as she swayed before him with the gentle movement of the ship. Perhaps he wanted to make physical contact. She could not be sure.

Millett said: "Going to Bissance?"

The boy sucked deeply on the cigarette, filling his lungs. Then he replied: "Yeah. Well, really to Ellampore. You know Ellampore? It's this island, not far from Bissance."

Ruth did not reveal that her ultimate destination was also Ellampore, and she was glad that Millett, whether out of tact or lack of interest, also did not reveal it. She wondered if the couple were prospective disciples of Mother. It seemed unlikely that they would otherwise be visiting the island.

Millett moved on, raising a hand in what appeared to be more a silent benediction than a farewell. Ruth followed him.

"Wasted lives," Millett said, when they were out of earshot.

"Who can tell when a life is wasted?"

Millett halted, and for a while they leaned over the rail, watching the sluggish water beneath them. Then Ruth said: "I think I'll return to the cabin and my book."

She was relieved when he made no attempt to accompany her there. "Fine." He took his pipe from his mouth and raised it in the air. "Do we meet for dinner?"

She wanted to say: "I suppose that's inevitable." But she nodded: "Why not?"

"About eight?"

"All right."

"The same table?"

"If that steward gives it to us."

"He damned well ought to, after that tip of yours. If he doesn't, I'll kick up one hell of a shindy—if I don't kick his arse."

II

RUTH ALTERNATELY DOZED and listened to the voices, some in French but many more in languages incomprehensible to her, ricocheting, dangerously sharp, about the creaking ship. Repeatedly she looked at her watch, each time to wonder that so little time had passed, when so much had taken place in her dreams.

An insect looking like a dwarf cockroach, with disproportionately large wavering antennae, flicked through a crack in the mahogany headboard of the bed and then froze. She stared at it, trying to convince herself that it was staring back at her. She supposed that if it had been Millett and not she lying below, he would have at once leaped off the bed, grabbed a shoe, and battered it to fragments. She spoke to it. "How ugly you are. But I suppose you're one of God's creations, like all the other ugly things in this world." The antennae moved back and forth. Was it trying to signal some answer to her? Then with a whisk it scuttled back into the headboard.

Soon after that, she heard a gong, advancing, retreating, advancing, and finally reverberating right outside her door. She imagined the Indian steward standing there, mouth straining open as he thumped it again and again with all the force of which his thin arm was capable. Once more she peered at her watch. Quarter to seven. So, whatever Millet's plan for meeting her at eight, she would have to get up if she hoped to be served. Unsteady, she stood by the windows, massaging her arm, which was tingling with pins and needles. The ship was now out in the open sea, and cirrus clouds, faintly stained with pink, curled above a pale gray, lifeless, limitless expanse of water.

Later, seated on the toilet, the bare porcelain cold on her flesh, she realized that this was the first time that she had urinated since getting on the ship. Hadn't Rawson said something about an English tourist dying of dehydration?

As she sat down opposite Millett at the same table that they had occupied at lunch—he too had been summoned by the unexpected gong, while reading his Penguin novel on the first-class deck—she said, "I must have some mineral water. Do you think they have mineral water?"

"Of course."

The water, brought by the assiduous Indian waiter, was not merely suspiciously murky but also lukewarm. "Perhaps he could fetch me some ice," Ruth said, having sipped at it.

"No!" Millett was vehement. "No ice. The most dangerous thing of all in a country like this."

"Even more dangerous than snakes and mad dogs?"

"You never know where it's been." He threw back his head and laughed, although Ruth could see nothing particularly funny in the remark.

As they waited for their food, he began to ask her about herself—whether she still had a husband, whether she had other children, whether she worked or was, as he put it, "a lady of leisure." Take care, give nothing away, stall, she told herself. Journalists were never to be trusted, as they grubbed for their filth. Yet against her will, she felt the answers being slowly drawn out from her, as though effortlessly he were winding them onto an invisible spool held in the knobbly hands clasped before him on the table.

Eventually she said: "Your turn. Now you tell me about yourself."

"Oh, Christ!"

"Why should I be the only one to be interrogated?"

"Because you have an interesting story, I haven't. But"—he shrugged—"ask anything you want."

She hesitated, not knowing how to begin.

Without waiting further for her, he then volunteered: "I'm

married. My wife's a country-lover, daughter of a farmer, and so she lives in the country, in Dorset, for most of the time, and I live in London." Ruth thought: People are so vain, it's never difficult to get them to tell one everything about themselves, however uninteresting and banal. He was going on: "I have two grown-up children, a boy and a girl, whom I now rarely see. We never really hit it off from the start, and in any case I was so often away from home that their mother got in ahead of me." He lowered his head to the soup the Indian steward had just set down before him, as though he were about to lap it up instead of taking a spoon to it. He sniffed. "Smells all right." Then he looked up at her with a grin. "What else do you want to know?"

"Is this the work you've always wanted to do?"

Rightly she had guessed at an unassuaged desire, an unfulfilled ambition. He shook his head ruefully, as he stirred the soup. "Nope. I wanted to be a novelist. Yes, that, believe it or not, was what I wanted to be. I had a novel published soon after I left Cambridge. It was easier in those days to get a novel published. Not much good. I wrote two more, but nothing came of them." He raised a spoonful of the soup and slowly slurped at it. "I still think . . . I still have this crazy idea . . ." He broke off.

"Yes? What crazy idea?"

"That somehow—bugger me if I know how or why—I'll cough up one good novel before I've had it. Just one. But I'll have to get a move on. Time's running out." His last words made her try to guess his age. Fifty? Fifty-five? She could not be sure. At all events, it seemed early to begin to think of imminent extinction.

Dinner over, they sat out in rickety deck chairs set up for them by the Indian steward. An extraordinary sunset, of throbbing greens, oranges, reds, and yellows, spread wider and wider across the sea and the huge sky beyond it, then darkened, then faded. "Beautiful, beautiful," Millett said at one moment, hands clasped behind his bald head as he gazed first ahead of him into the distance and then, craning his neck, upward. "It means nothing to them," he said at another moment, indicating the black passengers crowding the deck. They were shouting across to each other, laughing, sipping drinks. One group, well dressed and elderly, were playing rummy at a table brought out for them by the steward. None of them ever glanced even for a moment at the sky or the sea.

Ruth felt obliged to defend them from his contempt. "I suppose they're as accustomed to sunsets like this as we are to rain clouds. Nothing to make a fuss about."

Still staring out to sea, he repeated sarcastically, "Nothing to make a fuss about."

Soon after that she said, "I think I'll turn in. It's been a long day. And this heat makes me tired."

He nodded. "Better if you go to the cabin alone. I'll slip in later. Don't worry about me. I'm good at being quiet. I won't disturb you."

"Then I'll leave the door unlocked." As soon as she had said that, she wished that she had not done so. Rawson had warned her about thieves in Saloum, and about their violence if their victims tried to thwart them.

"Yes, leave it unlocked."

Ruth took a shower, moving under the trickle of water so that it coursed now down one area of her body and now down another. She had forgotten about the hair by the drain. She gave a little shudder as accidentally she stepped on it.

In her nightdress, dressing gown, and slippers, she went out onto the private deck, her hairbrush in her hand. Leaning against the rail, she began rhythmically to brush the hair that the wind was blowing away from her face. There was something pacifying in the regular motion of her arm and the regular tingling of her scalp.

. . . Then suddenly, with a piercing sorrow, she thought of her darling Jim, a gawky, pale-faced boy standing to attention beside her as she sat before her three-sided dressing-table mirror. "Mummy! Mummy! Mummy!" he pleaded. "Let me, oh, let me!" Eventually she would hand him the silver-backed brush. First he would take a bunch of her hair in his hand and hold it to his cheek. Then he would begin to brush, mouth pursed and eyes half closed in concentrated effort. Best of all he liked to brush the hair at night, with the light off, so that sparks showered from it. "You're full of electricity, Mummy. You could make a thunderstorm. You could electrocute someone." Pressing her body against the rail, the brush now motionless in her hand, she could hear him saying that to her and her laughing reply: "Oh, I don't think I'd ever want to electrocute anyone." But now? If she could ever find the person or persons who had caused him to die . . . Implacably, feeling as though electricity were indeed now crackling through her, she raised the brush again and swept it back and forth, back and forth over her scalp, until it began to feel raw, and the throbbing of before dinner once again started up in her head.

She returned to the cabin, took a sleeping pill out of its bottle, and then, without thinking, ran some water from the washbasin into the chipped glass from the shelf above it. She threw back her head, placed the pill on her tongue, gulped at the water. Oh, Christ! What had she done? Well, at least she had been inoculated against typhoid, cholera, and hepatitis.

She first knew Millett was in the bed next to hers when, sweat-sodden, her heart beating wildly, she was startled into consciousness by a deafening grinding and clanking, as though a chunk of metal were being gouged out of the ship. As she sat up, she heard a stertorous breathing, broken by the mumbling of something so unintelligible that she thought it might be a foreign language. The grinding and clanking continued, to be followed by the din of voices shouting to each other.

Millett now also awoke, jerking up in the bed, a hand to his forehead. "Christ! What the hell's all that? We can't have arrived. We're not supposed to reach Bissance until eight."

"I think this must be a call en route."

Millett crawled across the bed, revealing that under the tangled sheet he had been totally naked but for a pair of undershorts. He put out a hand and grabbed an undershirt off the chair over which he had carelessly thrown all his clothes. As he struggled into it, he said: "Let's take a look." He jumped off the bed.

"You're not going out like that, are you?"

He looked down at the undershorts. "Indecent? But most of the Saloumese wear far less."

"You're not Saloumese."

"Yes, I suppose I've something to be thankful for."

Stationary, the ship was rocking gently on the swell. There was a gunmetal-gray cloud over the moon, so that but for the searchlight that held in glaring focus a motorboat and some half-dozen narrow pirogues, the light was diffuse and dim. Another pirogue approached. Caught in the searchlight's beam, the figure wielding its single paddle from a stand-up position looked gigantic. On the deck below—Ruth and Millett now peered over the rail—half-naked, muscular figures were manhandling crates and bales, while a few passengers, most of them also half-naked, looked on.

"Let's go below," Millett suggested.

"All right." Ruth drew her dressing gown closer about her.

The straining, sweating bodies of the stevedores gave off a pungent, gamey odor, in no way unpleasant. The two siblings who had been playing their version of "Scissors, Stone, Paper" on the deck in the afternoon now leaned close together, the boy's hand on the girl's naked shoulder—neither was wearing anything other than cotton pants reaching almost to the knees—as they stared, rapt, at the men heaving and toting with no sound other than a sudden grunt, snort, or inexplicable hoarse, staccato cry.

All at once, from the last of the pirogues to arrive, a party of people, all black, began to ascend the companionway. There were two young men in cheap cotton trousers and shirts and no less cheap Western-style shoes, with white daubs of paint on their foreheads and cheekbones and with their long hair, reaching to their shoulders, elaborately interwoven into plaits, to make for each what was in effect a casque. Behind these two was an old man, in a long white robe embroidered in a key pattern on its

111

square neck and hem. His forehead and cheeks were similarly daubed, his gray hair similarly plaited. His long, narrow feet were bare. His lips glistened scarlet in the glare of the searchlight, as though they were made-up. Once on the deck he looked majestically about him and stroked a small, sharply pointed gray beard with a hand whose nails, like those of the child standing close by him with her brother, were painted red at the tips to make them look as if they had been dipped in blood. An officer who had been supervising the loading and unloading, his uniform jacket abandoned, now stepped forward to address the old man with what struck Ruth as reverence, even awe. In response, the old man raised his left hand in what was simultaneously acknowledgment and benediction, the fingers extended to reveal a rosy palm.

"Who's he, do you imagine?" Ruth asked.

Millett shrugged. "Some local bigwig, I'd guess. Perhaps the local witch doctor?"

Two other men, similar in age and appearance to the first two, had now emerged on the deck behind the old man. The old man said something imperious to the quartet and jerked back his head, and they all then moved down to the farthest end of the deck, where a group of people, blankets shrouding them despite the heat, had been huddled in silence on two benches. The occupants immediately shuffled off, so that the newcomers could take their places.

"Yes, you're right," Ruth said. "Some bigwig. How I hate bigwigs, whether here or in England!"

Soon after that, Ruth and Millett returned to the cabin. Surprised that she should feel no embarrassment at the presence of this stranger sharing it with her, Ruth peeled away her dressing gown, kicked off her slippers, and climbed onto the hard, uneven bed. She propped her head on an elbow, not fully lying down. Equally unembarrassed, Millett pulled off shirt and trousers and threw them across the chair nearest to him. Then, letting out a groan, as though from a twinge of rheumatism, he stretched out on the bed in nothing but his undershorts; he stared up at the ceiling for a few moments and then turned over, away from her.

On his back there was a puckered crescent-shaped scar. She wondered if it were the result of an accident or an operation. Perhaps a war wound? He might just be old enough to have been in the war. One day she would ask him, she thought. Then she told herself that it was unlikely, the journey over, that they would ever meet again.

The ship gave a shudder, like an animal rousing itself from a deep sleep. There were more clankings and creakings, more hoarse staccato cries. She stretched herself out, then turned herself away from him. She stared at the door to the bathroom, glimmering palely before her.

He spoke in an already drowsy voice: "Do you think you'll manage to get to sleep?"

"Oh, I expect so."

She fell asleep almost immediately, to be again awakened by all the din of another halt. This time, when she looked across to the other bed, it was empty. Millett must have heard the din earlier and slipped out to watch the same mysterious procedure of loading and unloading, of pirogues bringing travelers to the gangway, of the searchlight swiveling around to cut glaring swaths through the surrounding darkness. Should she go to join him? She hesitated, her feet to the floor. Then she drew them up again, replaced her head on the sweetly scented pillow, and lapsed once more into a sleep so profound that she never heard Millett tiptoe back.

By the morning, he was again gone. But he must have returned in the interval, for the only one of his three bags he had brought into the cabin with him—the other two, he explained, he had put in charge of one of the stewards on the lower deck—had vanished.

Millett was not in the saloon for breakfast, served by an unfamiliar steward, tousled and constantly yawning. Nor was he there when Ruth wandered the lower deck—"Hi!" called out the young American, while the girl with him lifted something on a spoon to the mouth of the whimpering baby. But when, soon after eight, the boat had docked and she was descending the gangway, the Indian steward following with her luggage, she all at once saw him already on the quay below her. She wondered how he had managed to precede everyone else, since the deck passengers were not supposed to disembark until the cabin passengers had.

His luggage stacked around him, with a porter in attendance, he waited for her. "I forgot to ask where you were staying in Bissance."

"At the Hôtel L'Escale—I think that's what it's called."

"Now how the hell did you manage that? You really are a one! When I phoned for a reservation from Siné, they told me that every room was taken. Some French tour."

"The Embassy got me in."

"Ah, the Embassy! Now why couldn't the Embassy do something like that for me? That prissy information officer of theirs told me that L'Escale was the only place to stay—modern, clean, out of the town, by the sea. But did he offer to get me a booking? Not on your life!"

Ruth had at first thought that he was pretending to be disgruntled, as a joke. Now she realized that he was being serious. "So where are you staying?"

"At the only place that could come up with a room. Hôtel de la Poste. The guidebook says five rooms, Saloumese food, hair dryers soon to be added, no air-conditioning, very economical. I have a feeling I'm going to enjoy myself there."

She laughed. "Well, don't come along to L'Escale in the hope of sharing my room again." Then, fearing that he might take that amiss, she added: "But I hope we haven't seen the last of each other."

"Perhaps we could share a taxi, at least part of the way?"

It was the Indian steward who answered before Ruth could do so. "No good, sir. L'Escale—there!" He extended a skinny arm to point. "Town and Hôtel de la Poste—over there!" He pointed in the opposite direction.

Millett shrugged. "Well, that seems to be it. But—as dear old

Vera Lynn used to tell us—'We'll meet again, don't know where, don't know when.' " Passengers looked round in amazement as he sang out the two lines of the song in a shrill falsetto. Then he turned to the porter beside him: *"Allons-y!"*

At that, without saying anything further to Ruth or even looking at her, he marched off.

BISSANCE

I

ALONG WITH A large key to her hut and a small one to her minibar, the reception clerk at L'Escale had handed Ruth a brochure. In English, French, and German, with a number of photographs of glamorous, half-dressed white people being looked after by jolly, overdressed black ones, it weighed in her hand like some glossy flight magazine. From it, she learned that the "complex" contained ninety-four huts, with one hundred sixty-seven beds; that each hut had electric light, air-conditioning, a warm-water shower, and a telephone; that she could choose among three restaurants and a discotheque; that she could receive instruction in waterskiing, windsurfing, and sailing; and that if she applied to the reception desk she could ride horseback or even, if she so wished, on a camel.

The hut, set in a carefully watered garden and surrounded by hedges thick with small flowers smelling unaccountably of over-ripe cheese, was a Marie Antoinette version of the kind of huts, circular in shape, constructed of bamboo with a disheveled thatch on top, that were inhabited by whole families in the villages.

Ruth wondered whether it was too early, at just after nine, to telephone Diamont. She had better wait, she decided, and while she waited she might as well have a cup of coffee in her little garden, before the sun rose too high and it became intolerable to sit there. She picked up the sleek modern telephone and pushed its buttons repeatedly. Although lights flashed off and on, she could establish no connection. Eventually she went out of doors, in the hope of finding the "boy" who had brought her and her luggage to the hut.

The "boy" was nowhere in sight. But from the hut next door, a real boy of not more than sixteen or seventeen emerged in bathing trunks, with a jazzily patterned towel slung over a muscular, sunburnt shoulder. He smiled vaguely at her before taking the path leading down to the beach.

She called after him. "Excuse me!"

He turned, screwing up his eyes against the sunlight. "*Oui, madame?*"

She went on, still in English: "Is your telephone working?"

"Sure. I think so. Isn't yours?"

"Seems not. And I wanted to order something from room service."

"You are an optimist. But try my telephone if you wish."

"I suppose you're French," she said, as he walked back to his hut with her.

"Belgian."

"You speak marvelous English." She almost added: "My son used to speak marvelous French."

A small smile was the only acknowledgment of the compliment.

He ushered her into the hut, standing aside to allow her to pass in before him. A facsimile of hers, it was in a state of total disarray, with clothes, maps, shoes, and empty bottles scattered everywhere. "The boy has not yet made the room," he said. "He is always late. Sometimes he comes at one, two o'clock. Last night we had a little party here."

"It looks as if it must have been fun."

The telephone worked, and she was able to give the order.

"Now you will wait for your coffee to arrive," the youth forecast, as they came out of the hut. "You will wait. And wait. The service is terrible!"

"Oh, well, never mind. I'm not in all that much of a hurry." But in reality she was nervously eager to see Diamont as soon as possible.

The boy hastened off down the path again, calling out *"Ciao!"* over a shoulder. Then a girl appeared, also in a bathing suit, far ahead of him; he quickened his pace to a run, shouting after her: "Marguerite, Marguerite!"

The coffee arrived sooner than the boy's pessimism had led her to expect. Having placed the tray on the rickety garden table and handed her the bill for her signature, the waiter (how appropriate, she thought, was the word) remained at her elbow, silent and patient. She had left her bag on her bed. She looked up at him, the coffee cup in her hand. "I'll see you later." Either he did not understand or, not prepared to be seen later, he pretended not to do so. Handsome and tall, his face gleaming in the early-morning light like some luscious fruit, he continued to wait, completely motionless beside her. With a sigh she got up, went into the shadowy hut, and brought back the tip. Still saying nothing, he took the coins from her, slipped them into a pocket of his starched white mess jacket, and began to walk away. She watched him. So leisurely were his movements that he might have been some guest strolling up from his hut to the main building.

She savored the coffee, which was excellent. From time to time, other guests passed. Some called out *"Bonjour, madame!"* Others smiled or merely glanced at her. They all appeared to be French. Then an elderly English couple, arms linked, walked past so slowly and so carefully that they looked like convalescing patients. "It's a nuisance to be so far from the town," Ruth heard the woman say in a cross, fretful voice, and the man then answered: "Who'd want to be near a town like that?" Unlike the French, they did not greet Ruth or look at her.

All at once, on one of the red bluffs that rose one above the other to the left of the hotel—tiny streams trickled down them, glinting threads in the sunlight—Ruth saw the silhouette of a woman on a horse. Woman and horse were motionless for a moment; then the woman jerked the horse's head to one side, and they disappeared downward, toward the beach. Ruth wondered if she would next see a woman on a camel.

When, eventually, she went back into her hut and telephoned

the Consulate—this time, there was no difficulty—a woman's voice answered, sounding both distracted and bossy. "Mr. Diamont? You wish to speak to Mr. Diamont? Who is it, please?"

"Mrs. St. Just."

"Oh, Mrs. St. Just." Clearly the woman, who spoke with a South London accent, knew who she was and had been told to expect the call. "I'll try to find him. Please hold on a moment."

As she listened to Diamont's voice, Ruth again found herself wondering: English, French, African? There was something unnatural about the accent, as though it were a composite of many other ones.

At first Diamont suggested that she should come to see him in the late afternoon—"As you probably know, it's siesta time from one-thirty to four-thirty." But when Ruth, obdurate, replied that she would like to see him now, at once, just as soon as she could get a taxi into town, he gave in: "Oh, all right. Fine. Why not?" She guessed that in reality his morning was free of appointments.

The taxi, a seemingly brand-new Citroën CX, with a smartly uniformed driver—she knew, even as the hotel porter held open the door for her to enter, that it would be far more expensive than any taxi she had so far taken in Saloum—at first sped down a highway between the kind of stumpy red bluffs that she had seen from the little garden of her hut. Then they were bumping and sliding down a narrow dirt road, with ramshackle market stalls on wheels on either side of it. The driver blew his horn constantly, but none of the people strolling negligently down the center paid the smallest attention.

Having hurtled through a crowded, dusty square, with more stalls piled high with fruits, vegetables, and brilliantly colored sweets, they emerged onto a broad, paved avenue, shady with cedars, margosas, and mango trees. Drives, their gravel pink under the dark green of foliage, swept upward at intervals, leading to houses that looked as if they were replicas of Edwardian villas in Menton or Hyères. Down one of these drives, grander than any of the others, a young woman with a cheerful black face and immensely wide hips waddled with what Ruth took to be a bundle of washing on her head. She smiled at the passing car. She was the only person Ruth saw on foot in the area.

The Consulate was clearly a building older than the villas, with broad verandahs and, above them, on the first floor, an open gallery from which bougainvillaea tumbled in gaudy profusion. As at the Embassy in Siné, a uniformed orderly rushed forward to open the taxi door for her. "*Combien?*" she asked the driver, and as she had expected, he then calmly named a daunting sum, as though certain that she would not argue. She did not do so.

There was another Saloumese, neat in gray linen trousers and a white open-necked shirt. He sat at a desk in the cool, cavernous hall, from which a mahogany staircase arose grandly.

"Your name, please, madame?'" he asked, courteously correct.

As so often, Ruth felt a reluctance before giving it.

He ran a forefinger down one side of the appointment book open before him, each hour demarcated. But Ruth could see that there was no name in it but hers.

He came out from behind his desk. "I will tell Mr. Diamont of your arrival. Please wait in here for a moment."

He showed her into a small, mahogany-paneled room, with a worn sofa and two no less worn armchairs, all covered in the same faded cretonne, and an elaborately carved Victorian table, clearly in need of a dusting and a polish, on which she was astonished to find, as in the waiting room of some impoverished or stingy dentist or doctor, ancient issues of *Punch, Country Life,* and *Vogue.* She placed herself in one of the armchairs. But having done so, she at once jumped up to inspect a reproduction, its mat blotched with damp orange stains, of a Turner watercolor of Venice.

As she was gazing at it, she heard from behind her: "Ah, Mrs. St. Just."

She swung around. "Mr. Diamont."

His hands clasped behind his back and his short legs straight together, he gave her a little bow from the hips. "I'm so sorry to have kept you waiting so long." But she could not have been waiting for more than five minutes.

Although he was clearly middle-aged, Ruth found something disconcertingly boyish about him. His thick, graying hair, parted low on one side as though by an incision, had been cut not merely extremely short but also extremely badly, as though by some school or army barber. His gray trousers appeared to have shrunk, revealing at least an inch of sock. His shoes, with their rounded toes and worn-down heels, were dull and scuffed. The knot of what looked like a club or old school tie was tight, hard, and shiny. The round face had no lines on it and was therefore devoid of any reassuring indications of experience.

As she was taking all this in, she heard him say: "Shall we go upstairs?"

His hands still clasped behind his back, he again gave a strange, formal little bow as she passed through the door ahead of him. She began to mount the stairs. "It's wonderfully cool in here."

"We had the air-conditioning put in last year. Ridiculous they wouldn't agree to put it in earlier."

"One wonders how, in the past, all those colonial officials managed without air-conditioning."

"I managed. For years and years."

"So you've been a long time in Africa?" Although the stairs were shallow, she felt breathless as she reached the top.

"Yes. I'm what's called an old Africa hand. Colonial Service. But now there are no colonies, so I was shifted over to the F.O." He indicated the way with a tilt of the head. "The room over there, on your right."

Ruth stepped through the already open door. "What a beautiful room!" It was not politeness that prompted the exclamation. She had not expected this long, shadowy room, with its high, vaulted ceiling and its French windows giving out onto the gallery she had seen from the car.

"Yes, I always say it's the most beautiful room in Bissance. Which is not saying much. This is one of the oldest houses, of course. The French official who was the equivalent of what we used to call a collector used to live here. This was his ballroom."

The round face broke into a grin. "We don't have any balls here now. Please. Do sit down."

She sat down in the chair opposite his desk, with its litter of files, books, letters, pens, pencils, and two chunky glass ashtrays piled with cigarette ends and crumpled pieces of paper. He stared at her for a disconcerting moment, face suddenly blank. Then he too sat down.

All at once he removed his right hand from where he had constantly kept it behind his back, and placed it on the wood of the desk before them. It was as though he were presenting a credential or perhaps even a threat.

Ruth knew that she must not look at the hand for more than a fleeting second, and yet she could not stop herself from doing so. She had seen such hands on the otherwise beautiful daughter, a thalidomide victim, of a friend of hers. It was as though each finger had only a single joint. But Diamont was too old for his mother ever to have taken thalidomide before he was born. The hand remained there between them, with an almost malevolent insistence that she must continue to be aware of it.

He was speaking to her: "I gather you saw Mr. Rawson in Siné."

She nodded, turning her head aside to look out of the French window closest to her. "He was very kind."

"He's probably told you as much as I can tell you."

"I'm sure you can tell me more."

As though it were some inanimate object, he now picked up the hand with his other and placed it in his lap. "I can?" He sounded both surprised and amused.

"You knew my son. He mentioned you in his letters. Often, often."

"Mentioned me?" She was aware of an uneasy tightening not merely of his mouth and his jaw but of something deep within him. "In what context would that have been?"

"He was a good correspondent. Until, that is, he went to the island, to—to Ellampore." She stared across at him, he stared back. "He wrote of you as a"—she paused and again stared across at him, to gauge his reaction—"as a friend."

He nodded, his tongue slithering over his lower lip. She felt as if she had given another cruel twist to the screw that had brought about that uneasy, even panicky, tightening within him. "I like to believe that I was a friend of his. As you can imagine, in a place like this, there aren't that many congenial people around. Jim was congenial, very congenial. I was happy to have him here. For the short time that he was here, that is."

Still watching him closely, she pushed on: "He used to write of his visits to your house. He said his happiest hours were spent there."

"He said that?" His voice trembled slightly.

"He said that. Yes." She paused. "I gather he used to spend most of his weekends with you?"

"Many of them. He had a wretched little flat, provided by the school. Noisy, no air-conditioning, in the native quarter. So I told him to use my house as though it were his own. In fact, I put aside a bedroom for his sole use. Not difficult. The house is large and I'm not a family man."

"Did you ever know him to swim?"

"It's not something I'd have known or not known. You see"—the confession was painful to him—"I suffer from a disease, a skin disease, called psoriasis. It's common enough in Nordic countries, it's disfiguring but not particularly dangerous, rarely fatal. But here, when the natives see it, they're apt to think that one must be suffering from leprosy or something equally dire. So I make it a policy not to expose my skin to them, unless I have to. A nuisance when the climate is as hot as this—and when the sea looks so inviting."

Although his embarrassment had affected her, she felt obliged to go on: "Did my son ever tell you that he had been swimming or was going swimming?"

He shrugged. "I honestly don't remember. I don't think so. He may have."

"You see, Mr. Diamont, for all the time that I knew him, lived with him before he came out here, my son had this irrational terror of the water. Not only did he not swim, he would not even paddle in the sea."

He gazed at her as though to say: "So what?"

"I find it impossible to believe that he drowned as the result of hitting his head on a rock when diving at nighttime."

"Yes, you told me that in your letter and also on the telephone." He sounded patiently weary. "Nonetheless, as I told you in answer on each of those occasions, death in precisely those circumstances was the finding of the coroner—or, as he is rather more grandly called in this country, *l'officier civil chargé d'instruire en cas de mort suspect.*"

"I want to see him while I'm here."

"Do you mean the coroner—or the body of your son?" There was a brutality in the way he put the alternatives.

"The coroner."

"Yes, I'm sure that could be managed. Until a few months ago a Frenchman held the post. His successor is his former deputy—a Saloumese. Perfectly competent," he added. "If you wished, you could, of course, also see the body. I'm sure Monsieur Thumy would make no objection. He's a very obliging young man."

Ruth shook her head. She knew that she ought to do so, but she could not bear the thought of gazing down at some swollen, stiff simulacrum of her own beloved Jim, preserved from dissolution in a mortuary locker. She started on another tack.

"You know this woman everyone calls Mother?"

"Yes, I know Madame Vilmorin—as I think I've already told you. I am not part of her sect, I do not share any of her rather nebulous beliefs. But yes, I know her. And like her. As I also think I've already told you, I often visit her on her island. It was I who first took your son over to see her."

"So, in a sense, you were responsible for what happened later?"

"By that, do you mean that I was responsible for his death? No. I don't accept that. Not at all. The chain that led from my introduction to the accident several weeks later had far too many intervening links." He smiled. "You mustn't be unjust."

"Why did Jim leave the school?"

"Didn't he tell you in his letters?"

"Not really. No."

"I think there were a number of reasons. He and the director, a Swiss, did not get on all that well. Jim became restless, bored. He began to hate the routine. He also felt that he was being exploited, the salary was so poor. There was not, you see, just one reason for his departure but many—a nexus of them."

"Did you encourage him to leave the school?"

"I?" He raised the deformed hand from his lap and rested it on his chest. "I neither encouraged nor discouraged him. Why should I do either? He was a free agent, he was not in the employ of the Foreign Office or even of the British Council. So I had absolutely no right to push him in one direction or the other."

"Why did he become a part of that—community?" She hesitated for what would be the right word. "It was after he'd settled there that his letters became so few. Also—so odd."

"Odd?"

"As though someone else had written them for him. Impersonal, uncommunicative. As if our whole life together, all those shared memories, had never been." She gazed across the desk at him and, now totally composed, he gazed back at her, with a kind of quizzical pity. "You saw him after he'd settled there?" she asked.

"Yes, of course. As I said, I often used to go over there at weekends. Sometimes I'd go just for the day, sometimes I'd stay overnight. I still go. I went the weekend before last. Madame Vilmorin is always most hospitable."

"And while he was there, you noticed no change in him?"

"None. Except that he seemed more composed, more in control of himself. Calmer, *clearer*. And yes—I think I can say that—happier."

"His letters didn't sound happier."

He shrugged.

"Some change came over him."

He said nothing.

"I'm going over to the island. Tomorrow. Madame Vilmorin

said I could stay with her. It struck me that I'd find out more that way than if I put up in a hotel. But I've not yet let her know that I'm here. Can one telephone to—to Ellampore?"

"Of course. It's not *that* primitive, you know. Would you like me to call her and tell her you're coming? I imagine that she or someone else from the community will be there to meet you. She's good about that sort of thing."

Ruth nodded: "Thank you."

Diamont picked up the telephone on his desk. "Oh, Madame Hoa, I wonder if you could come up for a moment?" He replaced the receiver. "My secretary. English, but married to a Saloumese lawyer. Her mother was his landlady when he was eating his dinners at the Middle Temple. Like all lawyers in this country, he has ambitions to be a cabinet minister, if not the big boss when old Mamadan finally quits."

Madame Hoa, who was clearly the person to whom Ruth had spoken on the telephone from the hotel, looked pallid and listless. She gave Ruth a fatigued smile and a faint "Pleased to meet you, Mrs. St. Just." Then she stood, head bowed and hands clasped before her, as Diamont instructed her to telephone Madame Vilmorin and tell her of Ruth's arrival. "Do that at once," he concluded curtly, as though Madame Hoa were someone who habitually procrastinated.

She nodded. "Amir wants to know if you'll be wanting the car. Otherwise he'll take those parcels to the post office."

"I thought I'd take Mrs. St. Just back home for lunch. That is"— he looked across at Ruth—"if you have nothing better to do, Mrs. St. Just."

"I have nothing to do. Nothing at all. Lunch would be nice."

Diamont turned to Madame Hoa: "Then tell Amir that we shall need the car about twelve-thirty. And be an angel and ring home to say we'll be two."

After Madame Hoa had left, Diamont said in a low voice, as though he feared that she might be listening outside the door, "That woman always looks so glum. It makes me feel glum too. I'm sure she spends every day regretting that she ever married

Hoa. He's such a dull dog, even ambition hasn't had the usual effect of giving him an edge. And they have this vast brood of children, oh, don't ask me how many. Fortunately she takes a minimum of maternity leave whenever one is due. She has all the facility of my cat, Bonnie. Whom you'll be meeting, of course." He looked at his watch. "Now . . . I ought to do something about some of these letters here." He indicated the letters strewn across the desk. "Would you like to go for a stroll, or would you like to sit downstairs and read something until I'm ready? I shan't keep you more than, say, fifty minutes."

"Perhaps I could stroll in the garden. It looked so pretty as we drove up."

"Yes. But take care of the sun. You've got some dark glasses?" She nodded, put her hand in her bag, and drew them out.

"Good. Wear them. For years and years in Africa every white man and woman went out in a pith helmet. Now no one does. But dark glasses are essential."

Out in the garden, Ruth pushed her way through the heat as though through a heavy curtain that had all at once fallen invisibly about her. The direction of her "stroll" was determined entirely by the incidence of shade and water. For a long time she lingered under a margosa, staring down into a cistern at the bottom of which she could see her face dimly reflected in greenish slime. A lizard, as green as the slime, flickered across the parapet of the cistern and was gone in a moment. Again she stared down at the reflection of her face, as though somehow, there far below her, she would find the key to the locked door that she was trying to open in—Millett's words came back to her—"this godforsaken country." Surely there was a god, some god of some kind, even in Saloum? And surely he would eventually give her her answer? She had never before believed in any kind of god, but now she found herself offering up a prayer to that god, whoever he might be: "Oh, show me, show me! Tell me, tell me, tell me!"

Eventually she walked on, down the hill that tilted away from one side of the house toward a dell of huge cotton trees, wound round and round with yellowing vines and lianas. But soon she realized that there was no way of reaching the dell, since a brick wall intervened, with murderous spikes of glass embedded along its top. Near at hand, however, there was a round pool, with fish, their gold peeling from them as though they had been lacquered with it; they moved sluggishly in the water's murky depths. Beside the pool stood a stone bench, shaded by a cedrat. She sat on the bench and leaned forward with her hands clasped between her knees.

. . . "But why do you want to go away? Aren't you happy here?" She heard her own voice, as in a dream.

"Of course I've been happy." There was a subtly cruel difference in the tense used.

"Then why, why?"

"Because it's necessary."

"Necessary? What do you mean?"

"Necessary for me. If I'm to become the person I ought to become."

"I don't understand you."

. . . *I don't understand you.* She repeated the words now, her lips moving as she exhaled them on a single breath. It was possible to love someone and yet be unable to understand him. That was the terrible truth.

Beyond the dell, where the ground once again tilted upward, there were some tall, slender coconut trees. Something moved at the crest of one of them. A bird, she thought, a huge, ungainly bird. Then she realized that it was a man, in nothing but ragged shorts, who was cutting the coconuts with a knife—from time to time it flashed in the sunlight—and then dropping them to the hard red earth below. She watched him, and soon, aware of her scrutiny, he began to watch her, in between his frenzied slashings at the fruit. There was a loud plop in the pool. Then she felt some insect alighting on her forearm. Impatiently she brushed it away, without once taking her eyes off the man in the tree.

All at once the man folded the knife and stuck it into the top of his shorts, where it still flashed in the sunlight when he made a movement. A hand went down, he began to undo the buttons of his shorts. Then, grinning at her—she could see the white teeth gleaming from the dark face—he brought out a swollen, purple penis. Still she stared as, now otherwise motionless, he massaged it back and forth, back and forth, in one hand. She felt no shock, no annoyance, no excitement, but only a devouring curiosity, until the climax was reached and the white semen spurted down through the branches of the tree.

After that she rose, with no hurry, and began to walk back to the house. Perhaps Diamont would say to her, "Did you see anything interesting on your stroll?" and she would reply, "Well, yes, I did see a man masturbating in a coconut tree." She smiled to herself.

Then suddenly, with the atrocious pang she always experienced whenever, unbidden, some memory of her darling, lost Jim flooded back to her, she saw his untidy attic bedroom, revealed to her as she pushed open the door, his unmade bed, and him sprawled across it, knees drawn up in a convulsion caused by her unexpected entrance. "What are you doing? What *are* you doing?" He did not reply. He did not reply now, as she heard herself saying the same words. She had walked out of the room and down the stairs. Later she had said to Mark: "You must have a word with the boy," and he had cried out angrily, "Oh, for God's sake!" By then Mark rarely spoke to Jim, other than to give him commands. He did not speak to him on that occasion.

Diamont looked up and smiled. "Yes, I'm ready now." He did not ask where she had walked or what she had seen. He screwed the top on his old-fashioned fountain pen and placed it in the breast pocket of his jacket, so that both the top and the huge clip attached to it were visible. Then he patted his side pockets, as though to assure himself they contained everything they ought to contain. He touched a file and said, "That can wait, I think."

In the car, he pointed with his deformed hand to a giant, wholly leafless tree. "A baobab," he said. "Of all the trees in Africa, it's the one I love the most."

Ruth peered out. "That one's dead, isn't it?"

He laughed, delighted that her response was precisely what he had expected. "No. It only *looks* dead. 'The tree of heaven' is what the baobab is often called. The myth is that the devil came and turned it upside down, so that the roots stick in the air and all the foliage is underground. The baobab is strong, it has an amazing ability to survive in any conditions. It grows where no other tree can grow."

"From time to time one meets human baobabs."

"Oh yes, indeed!"

The house in which he lived, isolated among bamboo on the outskirts of the town, was a long, low, white modern building. It had a small swimming pool, a badminton court, and at the far end of a stretch of high, yellow grass, a target for archery.

"Not a thing of beauty," he said, as she gazed at the façade. "Not like the Consulate building. It was put up by a Saloumese businessman, a crook really, who then went bankrupt and eventually landed up in jail. We—H.M.'s Government, that is—got it at a bargain price, with all his furniture in it."

This furniture consisted of clumsy Louis XVI reproductions in a soft, blond wood, clearly heavier than balsa but with the same porous smoothness to the touch. The chairs stood ranged around the walls of the rectangular room in which, without an intervening hall, they had stepped from the glare and heat. What appeared to be a dining table, in a similar parody of Louis XVI style, stood in the center, covered, as in the waiting room of a children's hospital, with innumerable puzzles and games. Ruth picked up one of the puzzles and gave it a shake. "Difficult," he said. "You have to get all six of those birds into nests of their own color. I've never managed it—though it has been done." He shouted: "René!" Then he shouted even more loudly: "*René!*" He turned away from Ruth, muttering, "Blast it! Where is he?"

An open-necked shirt hanging outside his cotton trousers, his feet bare, a slender, limping boy with a badly pockmarked face— he looked no more than fifteen or sixteen—appeared through a door at the far end of the room. "Sir! You are back!"

"Yes, I'm back." Diamont was curt. "Didn't you hear the car? Didn't you hear me calling?"

"Sorry, sir. Listening to radio. Football."

"Well, turn the bloody thing off. Have you got something for us to eat?"

"Yes, sir, plenty to eat. Ready in a jiffy."

"I know what your jiffy means."

While listening to this exchange, Ruth had also been glancing around the room. Everywhere on the walls there were photographs of black footballers, black hockey players, black tennis players, black athletes of every sort. Sport was the only subject.

"As you can see, I'm mad about sport. No good at it, never have been, but I'm a terrific spectator."

"Jim was no good at sport."

He nodded. "One of the many things we had in common." She wondered what the other things might have been. "Here, let me give you a drink." He removed the lid from a pineapple ice bucket. "For once that moron has remembered to put in the ice."

"He also seems to have remembered to bring you your slippers," Ruth said, seeing the boy standing in the doorway to the kitchen, a pair of light Japanese-style slippers in one hand.

"I don't want those when I have a visitor," Diamont told the boy fretfully. "Oh, go away! Go away!"

As they sat facing each other, on imitation Louis XVI chairs, Diamont said: "The F.O. wrote that you were putting round libelous things about me. They thought I could sue—not that they ever care for their employees to do so." His tone was good-natured, faintly mocking.

"I told a journalist what I thought. A dangerous thing to do. He printed it."

"Don't worry. If I did sue anyone, it would be his paper. There'd be little point in suing you, from what Jim told me about your circumstances."

She felt an inner rage that Jim should have discussed her finances with this man. But she smiled at him and said: "Yes, it would have been pointless to sue a pauper. Quite pointless."

The boy returned, carrying a tray. He swept the puzzles and games to one end of the dining table, and then put down some raffia mats, stepping back from time to time and appraising them, head cocked on one side, to make sure that their positions were exactly symmetrical.

"What have you got for us?" Diamont looked across at him to ask.

"Stew, sir. Lamb stew."

"Oh, my God!"

Ruth understood the reason for the exclamation when a plate of the stew was set down before her. Glutinous, fat-fringed gobbets of lamb swam in a floury gravy.

"He's a good boy," Diamont explained. "But I'm afraid I can't say he's also a good cook." He reached out for the bottle of iced beer between them and poured some into her glass. "Not bad beer. Local. Brewery run by a German."

At one point, attempting to swallow a lump of lamb, she asked: "Are there many English people here?"

"In Bissance? Too many. By which I mean that the few that there are, are all jolly boring. There are two lots of missionaries, who hate each other far more than they hate any of the heathen. There are some businessmen who spend all their spare time—of which they seem to have an abundance—drinking gin and playing bridge. There are some people working at the oil refinery down the coast—they're considered definitely non-U by the others. And, of course, there is our Mrs. Hoa. I try to see as little of them all as possible," he concluded.

As the meal progressed and her efforts to keep up some kind of conversation with him became more and more strained, it seemed as if her own increasing weariness were merely an echo of his. She guessed that he was saying to himself, "If only this woman would go!" just as she was saying to herself, "If only I could leave!"

The boy brought in an old-fashioned Cona coffeemaker, consisting of two glass globes, one resting above the other, and of another, smaller glass globe, full of purple methylated spirit. "The

Saloumese coffee isn't at all bad," Diamont said, pouring some out for her. "Not if it's made with care."

He was right. "This is even better coffee than they gave me at the hotel this morning. And that's saying a lot."

"I never mind what I eat. But the coffee and tea that I drink have to be first-class."

As she was finishing her second cup of coffee, the boy returned. He stood, seemingly embarrassed, by the door to the kitchen, saying merely, "Sir, sir, sir," and gazing toward the window.

"Yes, what is it?"

The boy was silent, head now lowered. Then he looked up. "Visitors are here."

"Visitors? Oh, those people about the garden. Tell them to wait."

"I'd better be going." Ruth put down her coffee cup and got to her feet.

"So soon?" But clearly he had no wish for her to stay longer. "The driver'll take you back. The office doesn't open again until four-thirty. So he can take you and then come back for me." Diamont swiveled round in his chair to address the boy. "Tell Amir we need the car."

"Amir still eating."

"Then tell him to stop eating."

"I can wait."

"Nonsense. He's had plenty of time to eat to his heart's content."

Unlike Rawson in Siné, Diamont made no offer to see Ruth onto the ship the following morning. As they shook hands beside the car—the driver, picking at his teeth with what appeared to be a splinter of wood, looked on sulkily—he said, "Perhaps I'll see you on the island at the weekend. If you're still there."

"I expect I will be. Are you planning a trip?"

"Thought I might come over. Probably just for the day."

As the car began to creak down the gravel of the drive, the driver, still sulky, asked, "Where to?" Diamont had already told him.

"The hotel."

"Long way."

She did not answer.

When the drive began to curve upward, making what was in effect a circle of the house, now below it in a shallow dip, Ruth, on a sudden impulse, looked back. The long, flat house lay exposed to the glare of the early-afternoon sun, with a white cat—presumably the cat, Bonnie, which he had promised she would see but which had never appeared—walking slowly toward it. Then, behind the cat, she saw three boys of nine or ten, who looked as if they had appeared not from the town but from out of the bush. Diamont stepped out of the house, to greet first the cat, which he stroked under the chin, and then the boys, throwing his arms around the shoulders of the two leading the way. In those trousers ending far above his ankles, and with that close, botched haircut, he looked like a boy himself.

Then the car swayed around another corner and the man, the cat, and the boys were lost to sight.

The driver repeated: "Long way."

"Yes. Long way."

She eased her body back into the seat.

II

FROM THE WINDOW of her hut, Ruth could see a mysterious reddish glare, as though beyond that strange-smelling hedge to her garden and beyond the pepper and eucalyptus trees there sprawled some vast industrial city. She went onto the little porch, the discreet hum of the air-conditioning now replaced by the crepitation, like the sound of a dripping tap fiercely amplified, of the frogs in the ornamental ponds dotted about the gardens. She could also hear, from far off, the reverberation of voices clamorous in a variety of languages, as though some cosmopolitan mob were in the process of sacking the city that had suddenly reared up, by magic, where the quiet, hazy sea had previously drifted in and out of the bay.

For a long time, puzzled, she listened alone on the porch, her arms clasped over her breasts and her head on one side. Then, drawn by curiosity, as by the tug of an invisible thread, she made her way down the narrow, sloping path, through the oppressive scents of the night, to the beach. At one point she passed one of the sentries who guarded the compound of the hotel from any intruders. A rifle slung across him, he was leaning against a tree smoking what, from an experience with Ned the waiter, the smell told her must be some kind of pot. He gave a vague smile, white teeth gleaming in black face, and then, still without ceasing to lean against the tree, muttered, in a deep, slurred voice: *"Bon soir, madame."* *"Bon soir,"* she replied, a recollection suddenly coming to her of the man up in the coconut tree in the heat and glare of the morning.

Walking on, she became aware of a dog, an emaciated mongrel, trailing behind her. She stopped for it more than once and even called to it, but each time she did so the dog also stopped, crouching low on the ground as though in a show of submission. When on one occasion she began to walk toward it, it bared its fangs, growled, and rustled off into the undergrowth. As soon as she walked on, she knew that once again, at a distance of some twenty feet, it was pattering behind her.

She arrived at a clearing, where two benches were placed side by side so that anyone who sat on one of them would have a panorama of the bay. Then, all at once, she saw the towering bonfire, its flames fountaining, yellow, orange, and red, into a sky grayish-pink where the flames seemed to touch it, and then gradually deepening to black. Naked or near-naked bodies kept approaching this bonfire, to feed it with driftwood. Similar bodies splashed in the shallows or could be seen, heads bobbing above the silver-crested waves, far out to sea, where a humped island, like a sleeping whale, all but blocked the entrance to the bay. Yet others sprawled out on the sand or walked, arms around each other's shoulders or waists, along the open beach or under the stunted, twisted trees.

As she ventured nearer, she heard someone shouting to her. *"Madame anglaise! Madame anglaise!"* It was the boy from the next-door hut, holding the hand of the girl whom, that morning, Ruth had heard him calling Marguerite.

"Hello," Ruth said, realizing at the same moment that the girl's breasts, gleaming in the moonlight, were bare.

"You would like something to eat?"

The girl shook herself, scattering drops of water from her body. She must have just emerged from the sea. "We are having a barbe-cue," she explained, in English. "We have many good things. Please!" She made an invitatory gesture toward the bonfire.

"I've only just had my dinner."

"Never mind!" the boy protested. "You eat something. Very good. I will fetch for you."

He ran down the slope to the bonfire, his bare feet scattering sand. Totally unself-conscious about her near-nudity, the girl tilted her head to one side and began to wring out her long, tawny hair. She laughed. She did not seem to be laughing for any reason other than her delight in the sea, the moonlight, the barbecue, and the company of her young man. "You are American, madame?"

"English."

The boy returned with a paper plate on which he had set out a charred leg of chicken, a sausage, and three jumbo prawns.

Ruth picked up the leg of chicken in her fingers and bit into it. Juice trickled down her chin.

The boy and girl watched her, smiling. Then the boy asked: "Good?"

"Marvelous." Despite the stringiness of the meat, she meant it.

The boy raised a hand to his forehead in a quasimilitary salute. Then, in silence, hands once again joined, he and the girl scampered off toward the sea. Ruth went on chewing at the chicken leg. When, having finished, she threw the bone away from her in a wide arc, there was a stirring in the undergrowth beside her and the dog then emerged to race after it. As he crunched and chewed in the shadow of a tamarind bush, he kept up a constant growling. Ruth, not feeling like eating the sausage and the prawns, tipped them off the paper plate onto the sand at her feet. No doubt, having devoured the chicken bone, the dog would find them. She walked on.

As she strode with spine straight and head erect past group after group of people, many of them naked or, like the girl Marguerite, wearing nothing but an exiguous *cache-sexe*, little more than a rag, she thought how beautiful they all were, with their well-fed, strenuous bodies, their blithe cosmopolitan racket in a variety of languages, and, above all, in their unassertive self-confidence and ease. Yes, beautiful. But, in this godforsaken country, as irrelevant as herself or her Jim.

She quickened her pace, now wanting to set as much distance as possible between herself and them. She tried to imagine Jim as one of such a party, emerging from the sea, the water dripping phosphorescent from his body, snatching at food from the leaping flames, wrestling with another of the boys, taking a girl by the hand and strolling with her down the beach until lost to sight. . . . No, it was impossible. The realization of that impossibility filled her with sadness. *He was not like that.*

A bamboo hut, clearly abandoned, stood at the point where the path around the bay gradually petered out in stones and rubble. There was a hole in its thatch and another hole in its side, as though some animal had charged it, shattering the fragile wood. She peered in through the hole in the side, half fearful and half excited. She could see nothing, but after a moment she heard a sharp intake of breath and then a high-pitched giggle. Beyond the hut, there was a refuse dump. As she breathed in its rancid odor, she imagined the rats and cockroaches—eventual conquerors of the world, according to Millett—voraciously swarming over it.

Hurriedly she turned back. Then, all at once, as she again looked down on the bonfire, now beginning to expire—there was a taste of ashes on the breeze coming up off the beach—she

thought of the white cat picking its way daintily toward Diamont's house, and of those three black boys tentatively following
it. She thought of Diamont stepping forward, a smile of greeting
on his strangely immature face, and then placing his arms one
around each of the first two of the boys. At the recollection, she
stood perfectly still, one hand to her lips, as though awaiting
someone or something. Then she felt knowledge glide into her,
as slithery and venomous as a snake.

. . . "Aren't you happy?"

"Not really."

"Not really?"

"I don't seem to fit in."

"What about all those eager, attractive students?"

The boy shakes his head.

"Why on earth did you come out here?" the man with the
deformed hand asks.

"Because I wanted to discover something."

"Discover something? This is not a land for discoveries. Nothing has been discovered here since God or the devil first created it."

"I want to discover who I am."

"Dangerous to discover that."

"I want to discover what I want."

"Even more dangerous."

There will be student excursions to a ruined Portuguese fort,
the boy will plead illness. There will be a dance at the French
Institute, the boy pretends to forget. There will be a letter, the
boy does not answer it. He lies on his bed in the narrow, suffocat-
ing room and stares up at the ceiling, asking himself: Who am I?
What do I want? Then, one day, he asks himself: Who is he?
What does he want?

The deformed hand holds a puzzle and shakes it. The boy
holds a puzzle and shakes it, tantalized by it and furious that he
cannot solve its mystery. Effortlessly, a black hand, as adroit as a
monkey's, shakes and nudges the six colored birds into their
appropriate nests. The man says: How about some archery? The

FRANCIS KING

man says: Bet I can beat you at miniature golf! The man says: Try
flying this kite. The three children scamper, one behind the
other, the first of them grasping the kite string. The kite catches
in the scarred, twisted, bare branches of a baobab tree.

The first of the children, the one who held the kite string, wails
his loss to the man, who stands smiling and shaking his head. In
the language of the children, with its sibilants and guttural click-
ings, he says: Lost, lost forever. The child begins to sob. The boy
watches from the shadow of the porch, as much afraid of the
glare and heat of the midday sun as he has always been afraid of
the infinite, restless sea. The man beckons to him. Reluctantly, a
hand shielding his eyes, the boy ventures out. Can you climb up
there and get it down? The boy shakes his head. The man gives a
contemptuous laugh and, watched by the trio of children, climbs
up and up and up into the tree of heaven. He disentangles the
kite, he shouts down to the child still holding the string, the child
jerks at it. Now, high over the baobab tree, the kite, streaming its
scarlet tail like a comet exhaling fire, swoops and soars. All the
children screech in delight.

The man tells the sullen boy-servant that he may have the
evening off. He peels some banknotes from a bundle taken from
the back pocket of those trousers that are too short for him and
hands them to the servant, who recoils slightly, as he always does
in superstition, when that mutilated hand comes close to him. We
are alone, the man tells the boy. But they are not alone. In the
dusk, the three children sit side by side on the imitation Louis
XVI sofa, each sucking up Coca-Cola through a straw.

The man, cruelly playful, tells the boy: When one is alone, one
discovers who one is and what one wants. The boy stares at him.
The man eases himself onto the end of the sofa. He tells one of
the children, in his own language, to sit on the other sofa. Then
again he takes the bundle of banknotes from his back pocket and
again he peels some off. He laughs. I wonder how long it would
take the father of one of these little bastards to earn this lot? He
waves the notes above his head in the deformed hand.

The boy timorously edges his way to the sofa on which the

child now sits alone. Nostrils flared, he places himself on it. The child glances sideways at him, sucks at the straw, although the can is now empty, looks sideways at him again. Smiles . . .

She has imagined it as a novelist might have imagined it. Imagination becomes knowledge for her, and knowledge becomes power. Never in her life has she felt so much power vibrating within her, like some gigantic engine.

Purposefully, the dog trailing behind her, she strides out for the hut.

III

BEFORE LEAVING for the docks and the boat that would take her to Ellampore, Ruth made a number of attempts to telephone Millett at the Hôtel de la Poste. The first time a woman's voice shrilled *"Comprends pas! Comprends pas!"* before the telephone went dead with a click. On the second occasion a man answered and told her to wait. She waited for a long time, imagining him going in turn to the five rooms of which Millett had told her that the hotel consisted. Then, in desperation, she replaced the receiver and dialed again. At her third attempt, the same man answered. *"Dehors!"* he shouted. She began to ask in French if he knew when Millett would be back, but the man interrupted her with a *"Merci, madame! Merci!"* and brusquely cut her off.

Eventually she sat down at the desk placed under the air-conditioning vent, and searched for a sheet of writing paper in the elaborate folder provided by the hotel. It contained only one, a yellow, greasy stain in its center, as though some sweaty hand had rested there. She began to write:

Dear Dave,

Before leaving for Ellampore, I tried, with no luck, to call you. Perhaps, sickened either by the Saloumese food of your

143

hotel or by the delay in the installation of those hair dryers, you have moved off somewhere else. I just wanted to tell you that I think I've already discovered something. What it is you will have to wait to learn. . . .

She wondered why she was writing like this to him, not merely a near-stranger but also a journalist and therefore someone who might indeed be useful to her but who might also obstruct her in her mission. Perhaps, by simultaneously telling him that she had made a discovery and yet withholding its nature, she mischievously wished to tease him? When she finished the letter, her writing getting smaller and smaller as she approached nearer and nearer the bottom of the second side of the sheet, she looked down at it, her head on one side and her eyes screwed up, as though in examination of something too bright for them. Reckless? Foolish? Pointless? She deliberated. Then she pulled out from the folder the only envelope remaining in it. She scratched out the *Madame* already scrawled on it by another, obviously Continental hand, and in her own firm, immature one, as of some unintellectual schoolgirl, wrote in his name and the name of the hotel.

As she waited in the main building for her bill and her taxi—both seemed to take an inordinate amount of time to arrive—she said to one of the clerks: "Would you please stamp this and post it for me?"

He looked momentarily surprised as he peered down at the address. "Hôtel de la Poste," he muttered, with obvious disapproval. Then he drew a ledger toward him, opened it, and began to tear off some stamps. Delicately he pressed the back of each into a small pot containing a dampened sponge.

"You won't forget to post it, will you?" she said. Rawson had told her that in Saloum it was unwise to entrust the posting of a letter to any of the natives.

The clerk did not deign to answer. Carefully he placed the envelope in a drawer and then asked her: *"Nôtre hôtel vous a plaît, madame?"*

"Merci, c'était bien agréable."
Knowing why he had asked the question, she opened her bag.
He took the banknote that she handed him and dangled it between thumb and forefinger as he stared at her.
She again put her hand into her bag.

JOURNEY

FLAT-BOTTOMED AND WIDE, with much of its deck space taken up by trucks, private cars, and taxis yellow with dust, the boat was classless. Rusty metal racks, doing service for benches, were packed with people jammed up close and even perching, like hens in an overcrowded coop, on top of each other. Ruth looked around with a sensation of despair.

The Citroën CX, driven by the same smart, supercilious driver who had taken her to the Consulate, had been held up first by a herd of lanky bullocks, totally out of control of their diminutive herdsman, who brandished a pole twice his own height, and then by some army tanks, parked in such a way that the first of them made it impossible for any vehicle other than a bicycle or a motorcycle to edge past. When, after two lengthy detours, they had at last arrived at the docks, the barrier had already been lifted and the passengers, good-humored but determined, were thrusting their way aboard. The driver, clearly not prepared to help with her luggage, had told her she must hurry. Ruth looked around for a porter, insulting a policeman by assuming him to be one. Finally an old man with bowed shoulders and sticklike legs had wandered over to her from where he had been squatting on the quay—whether he was an official porter or not, she was never to know—and, bending double, had heaved first one suitcase and then the other onto his back, so slowly that she might have had all the time in the world to get aboard and find herself a seat.

Later he surprised her by accepting her tip not merely without argument but with an obvious show of gratitude, bowing his shaven head and putting a cupped hand to his forehead before limping away.

One would have thought that one of these muscular, grinning men would have surrendered his seat. One would have thought that one of these vivid, jabbering children would have done so. One would have thought . . . But she was too hot, tired, and discouraged to think anymore. She saw a companionway and began to make her way down it just as two youths began to make their way up. They smiled at her but were clearly not disposed to retreat, and so eventually it was she who had to do so.

The saloon below was even more crowded than the deck, with people seated not only beside the long tables but also on top of them, their legs dangling, and others squatting or even lying full-length on the floor among a jumble of boxes, bundles, baskets, and even livestock. Again, as on the deck, Ruth looked around her with a sensation of despair.

Feeling an overpowering thirst, despite all the cups of coffee she had drunk for breakfast that morning, she pushed her way over to the murky hole through which a jolly, toothless man, a purple rag knotted around his head, was dispensing food and drink. She pointed to something colored bright pink and labeled "Cerise d'Été"—she could see no mineral water, Coca-Cola, or juice. The man opened the bottle for her and then, having plucked an unwrapped straw from a bundle in a glass beside him, thrust it into the bottle. "Combien?" she asked. "Deux cents." It was far too much, but she lacked the will to argue.

As she sucked on the straw, she remembered Rawson telling her: "Never suck from a straw that hasn't been sealed in paper. They recycle them here—take the used ones and hand them out again. Without even a wash in most cases." Oh, to hell with it!

As she was still sucking, she became aware of a stir at the entrance to the saloon and looked over to see what was the cause. Descending the companionway were the old man and, behind him, the four young men, clearly his attendants, who had boarded the boat from Siné to Bissance in the middle of the night. The sight of them filled her with a clammy unease, she could not have said why.

At their appearance, a man at once rose and dragged his child off a bench, and a group of women in garish loose gowns also lurched to their feet. Without a word of thanks or even of acknowledgment, as though the bench were theirs by right, first the old man and then the four young ones seated themselves. Once they had done so, they froze into impassivity, talking neither to each other nor to anyone else, and holding their bodies strangely rigid.

After what seemed a long time of leaning against a wall—a hen, tied by its legs, rested on the floor beside her—Ruth felt a touch on her shoulder. It was a member of the crew, his hair glistening with oil and his eyes and smile friendly. "*Venez avec moi, madame,*" he said. Then, when she hesitated: "*N'ayez pas peur!*"

He opened a metal door and signaled to her to enter.

There was a toilet, its seat lowered, with a washbasin beside it. "*Asseyez-vous, madame!*" He pointed, fingers bending backward to reveal a pink palm, to the toilet.

There was an overmastering smell of ammonia. But reminding herself that Diamont had warned her that the journey could take anything up to two hours, Ruth went and sat.

The man came close to her and looked down, absolutely still and smiling.

Ruth opened her bag.

ELLAMPORE

I

INEVITABLY, Ruth was almost the last to leave the boat. The stout, cheery member of the crew who had accommodated her in the bathroom now helped her with her luggage. He put on a comic performance of being unable to lift even the smaller of her cases, groaning and saying, *"Lourd! Lourd! Très lourd!"* before effortlessly hoisting one up onto a shoulder and hefting the other in a vast, purple hand. Turning his head as he preceded Ruth down the gangway, he laughed boisterously before again groaning out: *"Lourd! Lourd!"*

Still on the deck, the truck drivers, eager to start on their way, were blowing their horns and shouting from their cabs at the passengers streaming off with their bundles and cases. One of these passengers, a woman in a long, full, crimson skirt and white blouse, her callused feet bare, had collapsed in what appeared to be a fit between two trucks. Another, younger woman was bending over her, mopping at the saliva at one corner of her mouth with the hem of her own long, full skirt. No one else paid any attention, the man with Ruth's suitcases even stepping indifferently over the outstretched, rigid legs. Ruth felt a compunction about doing likewise and, after a moment of hesitation, during which she looked down into the rolling whites of the victim's eyes, she instead edged around one of the two trucks.

There was no way of not instantly recognizing Madame Vilmorin in the mass of people, some there to meet relatives or

155

friends and others merely for what they regarded as a social occasion. Tiny, the ivory-colored skin of her face puckered around her small mouth and her mica-bright, almond-shaped eyes, she was wearing a beige Chinese pajama suit with flat-heeled Chinese-style slippers. She looked ageless; her black hair, streaked with a few threads of gray, was drawn back tightly from a center parting to make a compact bun low on an unnaturally long, thin neck. She was not looking around for her visitor but was absorbed in talking to the quintet of people, the old man and his four obsequious acolytes who had been Ruth's fellow passengers—so eerily, it had seemed to her—on both of the boats.

"*Là! Là!*" As Ruth pointed, directing the man with her luggage, she all at once felt a constriction of the throat, as though an invisible hand had first gently closed around it and had then begun to tighten its grip. There was a throbbing behind her eyes. With that sense of near strangulation came the realization that, yes, she was afraid of this tiny, ivory-colored woman, with—only now did Ruth notice him—a white-haired military-looking man beside her. His freckled hands, one with a heavy signet ring on it, rested on the rail of what looked like an airport cart.

"Madame Vilmorin?"

"Mrs. St. Just!" Ruth had not expected the American accent. Still less, from someone so fragile-looking, had she expected a voice so vibrant and deep. "I saw you a little while ago up on the deck and decided it must be you. Not difficult, since there was no other white woman aboard! Excuse me one moment." She turned back to the imposing, gray-bearded old man with those strange splashes of white paint on forehead and cheeks, while his attendants, their luggage spread around them, stared now into her face and now into their master's, in the manner of people trying to understand what is being said in a tongue unknown to them. Madame Vilmorin was speaking in a sibilant rush, so low and so quick that, so far from making out a word, Ruth could not be sure if she were speaking in French or the vernacular.

The military-looking man said: "Mother hasn't introduced us." There was something absurd in his referring to a woman younger than himself as "Mother." "I'm Tom Guthrie." Later Ruth was to learn that he had been a colonel in a Guards regiment.

"And I'm Ruth St. Just."

"Yes, that was clear." The smiling mouth under the white, nicotine-stained moustache was full and moist, the teeth tiny and crooked.

"You're English?"

"And that must be clear too." Again he smiled. "You had a good journey?"

When she told him that she had spent it perched above a toilet bowl—"I suppose there must have been another lavatory somewhere else, since no one tried to unseat me"—he shook with silent mirth, the wattles of his neck wobbling from side to side and his shoulders heaving. "I've never thought of doing that," he said.

"I didn't think of doing it. It was this man here"—she pointed to the crew member—"who thought of it for me."

"I'm sorry, my dear." Mother—as Ruth was from that moment reluctantly to come to think of her—had turned away from the old man with a final *"Bien entendu."* She rested her fingers, strangely dry and cold in the afternoon heat, on Ruth's bare forearm. Again Ruth experienced that constriction of the throat, accompanied by a feeling of dread, as though, by that mere fugitive contact, this tiny, self-confident woman might steal something invisible and yet vital from her. "You must be tired."

Ruth had not thought it before, but now she nodded. "Yes, very tired. It was a tiring journey."

"All journeys are tiring in a heat like this. Do you mind walking?"

Ruth did mind. But she nodded. "No, that's fine."

Under Guthrie's direction, the man from the boat was loading Ruth's cases onto the cart. Having finished, he executed a military-style salute, legs straight together, clearly in jest. "I'd better give him something," Ruth said, opening her purse. But when she held out the coins in the palm of her hand, she was amazed to be refused. Eyes fixed on Mother, the man vehemently shook his head. Ruth tried to insist, once again extending her hand, until Mother told her in a quiet but authoritative voice: "He doesn't want it. He's happy to have helped you for nothing. You must allow people that happiness."

"He's the first person I've met in Saloum who's wanted that," Ruth retorted.

"Then you've been unlucky, I'd say." Guthrie had already set off with the cart, and now the two women followed. Mother looked over to Ruth. "We have no car. We could have taken a taxi." Why they had not taken a taxi, she did not go on to explain.

Ruth had often imagined the island. Except for that long, low, dilapidated building, half palace and half penitentiary, looking like the skeleton of some prehistoric animal, bleached by sun and spray, and a few of the round, thatched huts where the natives lived, the island would be all but uninhabited in its uncontrollable lushness. If one took any of the vestigial paths away from the house, bursting one's way through the jungle fetters, one would come on wild pigs, bustards, lynxes, iguanas, gazelles. In clearings, shepherds would squat, conical straw hats shading their faces, as they watched their lean flocks. On the silvery beaches, gaily painted pirogues would be hauled up and splay-footed fishermen would mend their nets.

That was how she had imagined it. But now she was walking up a macadamized, potholed road, past corrugated iron sheds and lean-tos, with Mother beside her and Guthrie pushing the cart ahead of them. Cars rattled past. A bus, crammed with people—some were even stuck to its exterior, like flies to flypaper—belched blue, noisome fumes. A bicycle bell rang out and then the bicycle, ridden by a laughing youth with another laughing youth astride the bar, all but lurched into her. There were tangled creepers, often thick with flowers, cascading from high, crumbling walls, behind which stood eighteenth- and nineteenth-century houses, many of them deserted in their overgrown gardens. There were stalls, shops, modern houses with brass plates announcing lawyers, doctors, dentists. There were beggars, tugging at her dress or hobbling behind her, as they jabbered incomprehensibly; stalwart women with silent, dull-eyed children strapped to their backs; loitering men who whistled at these two white female foreigners walking past them; scavenging dogs and goats.

"Do you know the story of the island?" Mother asked, clearly used to all this turmoil and paying no attention to it.

"No." Ruth had never imagined that there had been any story.

"Ellampore was a slave island. Men, women, and children—often sold by their own chiefs—would be brought here, to be transported to the New World that, for them, was to be even more terrible than the Old World from which they came. If they tried to escape and were caught, they were thrown to the sharks." Mother spoke with quiet vehemence, her head turned toward Ruth as she strode up the hill to which they had now come. That Ruth had difficulty in keeping up with her and Guthrie, she either did not realize or ignored.

"That was rather uneconomical, wasn't it?"

Mother ignored the flippant remark. "Our community is housed in one of the buildings—the chief building, the only surviving one—in which the slaves used to be held. We hope we've succeeded in exorcising their troubled spirits."

A majestic woman, her skin the ivory color of Mother's, swayed past them, a bundle on her head. "Do you see that woman? She's one of the Lignares, as they're called. They're the result of unions between the Portuguese masters and the natives."

Turning her head, Ruth stared after the woman.

Through all of this, sweating and silent, Guthrie pushed the cart on up the hill. It struck Ruth as odd that, in a country in which labor was so plentiful and so cheap, he should be performing this menial task. Eventually she quickened her pace to overtake him and said, "I hate to see you pushing my luggage, but I really don't feel like offering to push it myself. Couldn't we find someone else to push it?"

Mother had now joined them where they had halted, her arms rigid at her sides and her eyes, naked of the dark glasses usually worn by foreigners, wide open to the glare. It was at her and not at Ruth that Guthrie looked as he said: "No, no. I want to push it. There's no need to get anyone else, no need at all."

"I'd willingly pay someone," Ruth persisted, feeling that she and Mother, silent beside her, were engaged in a contest of wills.

"No, no!" Guthrie was vehement as, with a lunge, he pushed on.

In that quiet but authoritative voice, with its American accent, Mother said to Ruth: "You've forgotten what I told you."

"What was that?"

"You must allow people the happiness of helping you for nothing."

Ruth felt first chastened and then angry. In silence, the two women continued their ascent of the hill.

Then Ruth said, in a manner that she knew to be ungracious: "It's really very kind of you to have me to stay. If I'd known that Ellampore would be like this, I'd have arranged to go to a hotel, so as not to put you to any trouble."

Mother smiled. "You've again forgotten what I told you." Then she added: "But perhaps you'd have been happier in a hotel?"

"No, no, not at all. Hotels can be so lonely."

Mother turned her head, gazed at her, and then gave a small smile. "You suffer from loneliness." It was a statement, not a question.

They had walked through some high, elaborate wrought-iron gates, one of them hanging askew from the side of a gatehouse built of a friable red-brown sandstone. On the inside walls of the gatehouse, but not on the outside ones, innumerable names had been scratched. Within the compound names had similarly been scratched on walls and carved on the trunks of the giant baobab and eucalyptus trees. Later Mother was to explain that these were the names of both slaves and tourists. Sometimes, she added enigmatically, a signatory had been both of these things simultaneously.

The main house was built of the same stone as the gatehouse. Three stories high, with four towers at each corner of its rectangle and a bigger circular tower above its center, it was forbidding in both its bareness and its isolation on a slope covered with nothing but yellow-brown scrub. Around it there were a number of smaller buildings, clearly more recent in date.

Halting, Ruth looked about her, until her eye was caught by what was no more than a glittering thread far away at the bottom of the slope on whose summit the main building stood. The beach! Again she felt that constriction of the throat, that throbbing behind the eyeballs, as she thought of her Jim. It must be down there that he was supposed to have had his fatal accident.

Suddenly she was filled with a hatred of the woman waiting beside her.

As though she had sensed that hatred, Mother now spoke with a steely hardness. "I'm afraid our community may turn out to be not quite what you expected. For one thing, we don't care much about creature comforts. There's no air-conditioning and most people do most things for themselves."

By now they had arrived at the house. A huge, elaborately carved door stood open to reveal a marble-paved hall on some of whose octagons names had also been incised.

"Oh, I'm used to doing everything for myself," Ruth said, wondering at the total absence of people. Perhaps all the other members of the community were resting in the heat of the afternoon.

Instead of entering the house, Mother now turned aside, as though she had changed her mind on a capricious impulse. Guthrie was standing near her, patiently awaiting her instructions. "I've put you in one of the annexes." Again she seemed to read Ruth's thoughts, as she went on: "No, it's not the annex where Jim lived. He lived in another one, you can't see it from here. This is our guest annex. It's where Mr. Diamont sometimes stays." She had pronounced the name as though it were French. "It's marginally more comfortable than any of the others. Which is not saying much." She turned to Guthrie, who had drawn a crumpled handkerchief out of a pocket of his khaki trousers and was mopping his forehead and the raw-looking back of his neck. "Let's go to the annex first. We can leave the luggage there and

Mrs. St. Just can have a wash and a rest." She turned to Ruth and, her tone suddenly becoming curt, added: "Then we can talk."

"I don't need a rest. But I'd like to have a wash."

"Only cold water," Mother said, as though pleased to be able to say it.

"Oh, in this heat . . ." Ruth murmured between parched lips.

The annex, to which they descended by a gravel path sprouting dry blades of grass, was a gimcrack modern building, with a faint smell of disinfectant clinging to it. There was a narrow corridor, its white walls bare but for a calendar, two years old, showing a color photograph of bookstalls by the Seine. On either side there were three shut doors. Mother walked first down this corridor, followed by Ruth and then by Guthrie, who was now carrying the luggage. "No," he had said obdurately to Ruth when, as he was taking the cases off the cart, she had tried to seize the smaller. Mother, arms crossed in wide, fluttery silk sleeves, had pursed her lips.

The trundle bed, laid with coarse sheets and a single pillow, might have come from a hospital. There was an enamel washbasin, chipped in many places, with an enamel jug in it, and a row of hooks along one wall, from two of which wire coat hangers dangled. Beside the bed there was a frayed rag-mat, such as Ruth had seen hanging for sale outside stalls in both Siné and Bissance. Under the bed was an enamel chamberpot. The window looked out on a clothesline, tied between two stunted trees, with some sheets, as coarse as those on the bed, flapping from it in the dry wind.

"Do you think you'll be happy here?"

Happy? Ruth had never expected to be happy on this strange mission. "It's fine," she said, looking around her.

Mother laughed briefly. "Don't exaggerate!"

Guthrie stood at the head of the bed, one hand resting on top of bars that might be those of a cage. He held his body stiff and erect, as though on parade.

"Next door there's a shower—cold water only, as I told you. Washbasin. The other thing. You can wash here, of course. As you can see." Mother pointed to the enamel basin and jug. "But in that case you have to lay in a store of water for yourself." Yet again seeming to read Ruth's thoughts, she added: "There are no paid servants here."

Ruth thought: Presumably the colonel is an unpaid one.

"Well, we'll leave you now. For how long?" Mother consulted her watch, set in gold encrusted with what Ruth took to be small diamonds. She wore it pinned to her blouse, just above her small left breast. "Shall we say an hour? Then we'll have our talk. Things may have cooled off by then."

Ruth wondered if the last sentence were intentionally ambiguous.

"Where shall I come to? The main house?"

"Oh, I'll come to fetch you. Or I'll send someone to fetch you. Perhaps Tom here. He's good at fetching—and also, as you've seen with your cases, at carrying."

II

RUTH WAITED FOR more than two hours. Had she misunderstood what Mother had told her? Was she expected to make her own way up to the house? She read a novel, by turns acrid and sugary, about life among the intelligentsia of Camden Town. She wondered why, when it had seemed so entertaining to her on the plane and in Siné and Bissance, it should now seem so trivial and tedious. She threw it to one side, got off the bed—there was only one uncomfortable wooden chair as an alternative—and crossed to the window. Half open, it had none of the usual wire netting across it. In consequence, the room was full of flies. Would there be mosquitoes at night? There was no mosquito net above the bed. She stared out at the washing flapping on the line. One sheet, coarse and gray, had jerked free of its peg at one corner, so that the wind alternately tossed it up into the air and swept it across the ground.

Then, behind the sheet, she saw the shadow of a woman.

Again the sheet whirled upward, this time to reveal not some stranger, as she had expected, but the American girl who had been traveling with her baby and her lanky husband or lover on the boat from Siné to Bissance. The girl had a basket on the ground beside her, into which she placed the laundry after having clumsily folded it. A clothespin in her mouth, she was attempting to fold the sheet—in its wild movements, it might have been some living creature, terrified of being captured or constrained. As she folded the sheet she became aware of Ruth gazing at her. She stared, not with the pleasure of achieved recognition or even with the bewilderment of recognition attempted, but with what struck Ruth as something not far from dread. Her mouth open, she now clasped the sheet, at last roughly folded, against her breast, as though for inadequate protection against a possible assault.

Ruth smiled and leaned out of the window. "Hello! Do you remember me? From the boat to Bissance? I gave you a cigarette."

Still the girl stared, making no response. At last she muttered "Oh, hello." Then hurriedly, with small, panicky movements, she placed the sheet on top of the rest of the washing, picked up the basket under an arm, and hastened off around the side of the house. Were she, her baby, and the man also living in this annex? Or was she making her way to some other annex?

Bewildered and uneasy, Ruth retreated from the window, once again to stretch out on the bed. All at once she thought of Jim carefully washing out his clothes in the bathroom of the upstairs flat. "Let me do those for you," she would offer. But obstinately he would answer: "No, I prefer to do them myself. Really." She would persist: "You can put them in the washing machine. Why go to all this trouble?" "Because the machine would ruin them." Dreamily, for minutes on end, he would knead the pants, undershirts, and socks in the soapy water, taking obvious pleasure in feeling the suds squelch upward over his hands and then, as he loosened his grip, once more sink back into the fabric. He had always been so finicky. How had he managed in this country where nothing was ever wholly clean? She could not imagine him using a choked-up toilet like the one over which she had perched on the boat, drinking from a straw already used by someone else, or putting his head on a pillow stinking of an alien perfume or hair oil.

"You were thinking of your son."

Without knocking, Mother had appeared silently at the door. She put her back to it, so that it clicked shut. Her small, ringless hands, the nails shaped into sharp diamonds, in a manner long since gone out of fashion, were clasped before her. She was wearing not the beige pajama suit of the walk up from the docks but a mauve one, identical in cut. She had colored the slanting lids of her eyes with the same mauve, somehow muting the previous energy with which they had glittered.

Ruth was taken aback. "Yes," she admitted reluctantly, "I was thinking of my son. How did you guess that?"

Mother gave her small smile. "I didn't guess it. I knew it. What else would be in that sad, distracted mind of yours on arriving at the place where he died?"

Ruth got off the bed. Mother was trying to impress her—as she had already tried to impress her—with a show of apparent clairvoyance. But she was not going to be impressed.

Mother stepped forward to pick up one of the medicine bottles that Ruth, with her usual sense of order, had set out on the rickety bamboo dressing table, thinking: This bamboo table is like the bamboo tables in seaside boardinghouses in England. She peered at the label on it, screwing up those mauve-lidded eyes. Perhaps she was too vain to wear glasses, Ruth thought. "Mepacrine?"

Ruth nodded.

"Not necessary."

"You mean there are no mosquitoes? People don't get malaria here?"

"There are mosquitoes. Some people get malaria. But it's not necessary to get malaria, and it's not necessary to take mepacrine in order not to get it."

"You've never had malaria?"

"Never." Mother was still holding the bottle in her hand. Ruth felt an impulse to snatch it from her. "Never," she repeated.

"Perhaps you're going to tell me you've never been ill."

"Oh, I've been ill, very ill. They thought I was dying," Mother said in a voice so low that it was almost a whisper. "But I've not been ill for a long, long time." She put down the bottle and then, moving a hand behind her back, while her gaze was still on Ruth, she opened the door. "Are you ready?"

Ready for what? Ruth wanted to ask. But she merely nodded.

"Good." Mother turned and walked out of the room. Then, without once looking around to see if Ruth were following, she made her purposeful way, her slippers soundless on the bare concrete, down the long, narrow corridor.

From behind her, Ruth said: "I saw someone I know. From the window. Well, actually, not someone I know but someone I've met before. On the boat from Siné to Bissance."

Mother made no reply until they were outside the annex in the dimming light of evening. "Perhaps it was only someone you thought you had seen before."

"No, no. I'm sure. I gave her a cigarette on the boat—her and her husband or boyfriend." She laughed. "I didn't imagine it. I promise you."

"Well, it's not of great importance, one way or the other. You'll probably see her again. Then you can check."

"Are they also living in my annex?"

Mother ignored the question. Ruth still following behind, she went through the door, open as in the afternoon, of the main house. She turned, after Ruth had also entered. "You can shut that door now." As Ruth was about to do so, she repeated, as to a dim-witted child: "Shut it, please." Ruth shut it behind her.

The high-ceilinged hall, with a wide stone staircase at its far end, was dim and cool. For the first time, Ruth realized that there was not only no air-conditioning but also no electric light. Presumably there was none in her annex either. But she could not remember having seen any candle or oil lamp.

Having led Ruth up the staircase and down a corridor, its whitewashed walls bare, Mother stopped before a door, drew a key out of a pocket of her pajamas, and inserted it in the lock. She smiled at Ruth—who almost expected her to exclaim "Hey, presto!"—before giving it a quick turn. She pushed open the door to reveal a wide, airy room, in the Japanese style. Ruth gazed around her, at what was clearly part of a separate flat. There was a disturbing incongruity in the paper screens, tatami matting, and contrasting unvarnished woods, in this house that had once been a seventeenth-century Portuguese staging post for slaves.

"You're partly Japanese, aren't you?" Ruth said.

"Partly, yes. My mother was Japanese, but she spent all her life in America, she was even born there. A *nisei*—that's what they call such people. My Japanese grandfather was an orange farmer in Florida. During the war they took away his orange farm and interned him and my grandmother. By then my mother had married a *real* American—even though his family were first-generation German—so she was left at liberty. People were foolish then," she added without rancor. She gestured to the cushions scattered about the floor. "Do please sit. If you don't mind sitting on the floor. I could get you a chair."

Ruth sat, feeling ungainly and uncomfortable. Perhaps Mother had intended this? "You've been a long time in Saloum?" she said, shifting her buttocks on the cushion, which seemed to her extremely hard.

"No. Not all that long." Mother shook her head, a hand to the bun coiled low on her neck. She did not elaborate.

As they gazed at each other, Ruth felt that they had embarked on some kind of dangerous game. But it was a game that she, unlike her opponent, had never played before. Nor did she know the rules.

"You've made a long and expensive journey, Ruth."

Ruth was surprised and annoyed by the use of her Christian name without permission asked. "Yes. Long and expensive. But I had to make it. Even though it meant selling my restaurant," she added.

"Had to?"

Looking at Mother, her legs tucked neatly beneath her and her small body upright, Ruth felt even more bulky and gauche. "As I wrote to you—I had to discover how my son died."

"But we told you! All of us told you. He went out alone to swim. Late at night. He dived. He hit a rock, was concussed, drowned." She recounted each event in the sequence as though it were something mundane and trivial.

"I don't believe that. I can't. And you know why I can't."

Mother leaned forward, her hands in her lap. "Then what do you believe?" It was getting dark in the room, the paper shutters gleaming faintly pink as the sun sank behind them. Her eyes glittered under the mauve lids as she repeated: "Then what do you believe, Ruth?"

Ruth wanted to say: "I believe that someone—or a number of people—murdered my son." But restraining herself, she merely turned her head aside.

Mother rose from the floor, in a single movement graceful in its effortless fluidity. She crossed the room to a bell-sash of the same beige satin as the pajama-suit that she had worn that afternoon, and gave it a tug. Ruth could hear a distant jangle.

"Would you like a lime-juice soda? Or some mango juice? Or there's alcohol, if you prefer that."

"Whatever you're going to have."

"You must have not what I have but what you yourself want. In this community everyone has what she or he wants." She smiled. "That is, of course, sometimes different from what he or she *thinks* that he or she wants."

"Then I'd like a lime-juice soda. That'll be refreshing."

An extraordinarily emaciated boy, the skin taut over the sharp arch of his nose, over his naked ribcage, and over his long, bare legs below ragged shorts, entered the room without knocking. Silent, expressionless, he looked at Mother out of huge, pale-blue eyes. His blond hair was cropped, and he wore an earring in one of his oddly pointed ears.

"Two lime-juice sodas."

The boy nodded, but made no move.

"That's all," Mother said.

On naked feet, the boy padded out.

"What nationality is he?"

Mother ignored the question, as though Ruth had had no right to put it. Again she seated herself, legs folded neatly under her. "You're uncomfortable. Do let me get you a chair."

"No, no, I'm fine, thank you."

"Lean your back against the wall, then."

"Thank you, I'm fine." But she was far from fine. Her shoulders and haunches were aching, and she had pins and needles in one of her legs. She shifted, then resolved not to shift again. She must endure this discomfort, as she must endure everything else, in this dangerous game, which she had never played before and of which she did not know the rules. "Are there many people in your community?"

"It's not *my* community, my dear. It's no one's community. It is just *the* community."

"That man, that Indian—whatever he was called—founded it, surely?"

Mother shook her head, with a kind of weary indulgence. "No, he did not found it. He gave us, all of us, both those who knew him before his death and those who never knew him, the knowledge to found it. There's a difference."

"But surely you're now its director?"

Again Mother shook her head, with the same weary indulgence. This time she also smiled, like a schoolmistress with a not too bright child. "No, I'm not the director of the community. What directs us is the knowledge that he left with me. There's a difference there too."

"Why did my son come out here?"

At that moment the emaciated boy shuffled back into the room, carrying a tray that seemed, with its two tall glasses and its ice bucket, too heavy for arms that struck Ruth as having all the brittleness of dry twigs. He stooped, one leg going down to the floor, so that the tray tilted dangerously. Mother put out a hand. He gave a sharp sniff, almost a sob, as Mother placed the tray on the ground between herself and Ruth. Then he stood there, silent and still, his hands clasped before him, looking down at the tray. Mother said no word of thanks, she merely gave a curt nod of dismissal. The boy hurried off. How could Mother maintain that she was not the director of the community? She was its dictator.

"Why did my son come here?" Ruth repeated.

"I've no idea." Mother picked up the tongs beside the ice bucket, dropped two cubes of ice into one of the glasses, and then held out the glass. Ruth took it, remembering all that she had been told about the risk of ice in Saloum. Well, she would have to accept that risk. Mother would see it as another sign of weakness if she were to ask for the glass to which no ice had yet been added. "Did he never write to tell you?"

"No. No, he didn't. That was one of the things that struck me as odd—still strikes me as odd. After he came here, he wrote so seldom. And when he wrote, the letters were so *impersonal.* Anyone could have written them."

"If you lose yourself, then inevitably you seem impersonal. He wanted to lose himself. Perhaps he succeeded."

"Perhaps? Don't you know?"

"No, I don't know. How could I know? Not for sure." Slowly she dropped a cube of ice into the tall glass before her. She raised the glass to her lips and sipped delicately at it.

"What brings people here?"

"You've already asked me that question."

"No. I asked you what brought my son here."

Mother gave that weary, indulgent smile, as though to a dim child. "Isn't that the same question?"

"Not to me."

"How dark it's getting!" Mother again rose gracefully and crossed over to the bell-pull. "Have you noticed the abruptness of the division between light and dark in the tropics? There's the same abruptness in the division between life and death. One moment the sun is blazing down on one, the next moment it has sunk beneath the horizon. One moment someone is talking, laughing, eating, the next moment . . ." She shrugged.

The emaciated boy returned.

170

"The lamp," Mother told him.

"Is there no electricity in Ellampore?"

"Of course there is!" Mother laughed. "Didn't you know that the French brought all the advantages of civilization to Saloum a long, long time ago? But somehow some of the advantages of that civilization failed to reach this old prison."

Boldly Ruth persisted: "You've still not told me what brings people here."

"You imagine—as many outsiders imagine—that people come here because they want something. But the truth is that they come here because they want nothing. Then, having wanted nothing, they discover what it is that they really want."

Absurd mumbo-jumbo! Yet even though she wished to despise and laugh at this diminutive, domineering woman, Ruth found that she could not do so. She felt baffled, uneasy.

The boy came back with the lamp cupped in both his hands. As he knelt to set it down between them, the huge eyes seemed even huger, the beaky nose even beakier. Once again he gave that little sniff that was almost a sob, as he straightened up.

After he had gone, Mother said: "Tell me about your life."

Ruth stiffened. "I don't want to talk about myself."

"Your son never spoke about you."

Ruth did not know whether to be glad or sad at that. "He seems to have become singularly uncommunicative," she said drily.

"Oh, he communicated," Mother said. "Oh, yes." All at once she became brisk and practical, looking at the watch on her bosom and then jumping to her feet. "Goodness, I've been so absorbed in our conversation that I've quite forgotten that you must be hungry."

Strangely, although she had not eaten for several hours, Ruth felt no hunger.

"Come!" Mother put out a hand to help Ruth off the floor. But deliberately Ruth ignored it. "Let's see what they've prepared for us."

Ruth followed Mother out of the flat—Mother turned the key in the lock and then tried it, to make sure that it was secure—and down the stone stairs in a light so dim that at one moment she tripped and all but fell. In the distance she could hear an excited babel of voices. Somehow, after the sense of a place deserted and, but for Mother's electric presence, sunk in torpor, Ruth felt cheered by the din. Mother put a hand to the latch of the high door at the far end of the tunnel-like vaulted passage along which they had walked, and pushed it down. She entered.

At once there was total silence. Eleven people were seated at the long oak refectory table, its inelegantly bulbous legs pitted with wormholes. Everyone had frozen at the sight of Mother, eyes fixed on her, not the newcomer. A hand held a half-raised fork to a mouth; a napkin rested against a lower lip. Behind the table, there was a dais—Ruth was reminded irresistibly of a college hall—and on this, at a smaller oak refectory table, the old man and his entourage from the two boats were placed.

Mother raised her small hands, as though to call to everyone for the silence that already existed. "Good evening, everyone."

"Good evening, Mother." The chorus was ragged but loud.

"This"—one of the small hands indicated Ruth, in the manner of a chairwoman on a public platform—"is Mrs. St. Just. Mrs. St. Just is on a visit—a brief visit—to us from England." She touched Ruth's arm with those strangely cold and dry fingers of hers. "Over there." At the far end of the larger of the two refectory tables, distanced from anyone else, two places had been laid. As the two women made their way toward these, the old man on the dais rose to his feet, to be followed by his attendants. Hands lifted together as though in prayer, they bowed to Mother. Then they resumed their places.

Mother sat down, her back straight and her eyes glinting as they darted hither and thither. "You may talk," she said in her low, vibrant voice. But the diners, so noisy before, all remained silent as they once more began to eat.

Ruth glanced at them in turn. Over there were the two Americans from the boat, but without their baby. Next to them was the emaciated youth who had brought first the drinks and then the lamp to Mother's quarters. Close to him, so close that she might be either protecting him or seeking his protection, there sat a humped, elderly woman, with her white hair piled up like a cottage loaf on her head. Ruth next took in two nondescript girls, their pale, plain faces untouched by makeup, and then, beyond them, a woman, her face bizarrely made-up like some pantomime dame, whose orange hair, teased into the semblance of a giant chrysanthemum, towered above everyone else's, male or female. Next, Ruth saw a black man, with graying moustache and beard; another, older white man, with many large rings on his long, narrow fingers, who would raise only the tiniest of morsels to his mouth and then spend what appeared to be minutes on end patiently chewing; and a muscular youth, no more than fourteen or fifteen years old, who, somehow distanced from the others, ate with scowling concentration, round head low over his plate. Of Guthrie, the colonel, there was no sign.

"You can eat fish?"

"Thank you, yes."

"Patrice!" Mother called down the table to the muscular youth. The youth went on eating, either too absorbed to have heard or pretending not to have done so. "Patrice!" The voice now had an edge to it. "Please go and tell Tom that Mrs. St. Just and I are ready."

The youth now got up, revealing that he was wearing a pair of swimming shorts under his short-sleeved, almost transparent voile shirt, and went through a swinging door that clearly led to the kitchen. Ruth heard him shouting: "Tom! *La mère désire manger!*"

Mother raised the wooden pepper mill before her and banged it on the table. "Why this silence?" she demanded. The question seemed to be put half in earnest and half in jest. At once the diners turned their heads to each other and began to converse. But it was not with the uninhibited excitement with which they had been conversing when Ruth and Mother had walked down the tunnel-like passage to the hall. Ruth wondered what the black men behind her on the dais were doing. She could hear no sound from them.

"Don't imagine this hall to be as old as the rest of the building,"

Mother said, when Ruth had tilted up her head to examine the barrel vaulting. "Built in the thirties. For a time there was a Catholic school here. This was where they held assembly."

His face flushed and glistening with sweat, a blue and white butcher's apron around him, Guthrie pushed his way through the baize-covered service door with a plate in either hand. Each plate had on it a half of one of the giant avocadoes so common and therefore so cheap in Saloum, with vinaigrette dressing already poured into its hollow. He did not look into the face of either of the women as, head turned sideways, he leaned across Ruth to put Mother's plate down before her. Ruth raised both hands to take hers from him. "Thank you," she said to him. Still he did not look at her. "Bread," Mother said. At once he hurried down the table to fetch the basket in which the coarse, gray bread lay in thick slices.

After he had gone, Ruth asked: "Does he always do the waiting?"

"No, not always." Mother crumbled her piece of bread between delicate fingers.

"And does he also cook?"

"Sometimes." Mother gouged into her avocado with the spoon she had taken up. Ruth followed.

"What nationality are these people?"

"All kinds." Mother smiled, once again digging her spoon into the avocado. "Does it matter? People are people. Except those who are merely spirits or merely animals." Suddenly, half rising, she called down the hall: "Lucy!"

"Yes, Mother." It was the grotesquely tall woman with the towering hairdo who answered, the deep voice unmistakably North Country.

"Take over from Tom."

Lucy got up from her seat, docilely accepting the command, even though her plate of what looked like some sort of pilaf was only half-eaten. As she swayed toward the service door on extremely high stiletto heels, her black miniskirt was pulled taut across her bony buttocks.

174

"Well, she's English," Ruth said. "That's obvious."

"Is it?" Mother gave that irritating small smile, almost a smirk. "Well, you may be right."

Clutching a plate piled high with the same unappetizing-looking pilaf that the others were consuming, Guthrie now emerged through the service door. As he looked around for somewhere to sit, Mother called out: "Over here!" He hesitated momentarily, then crossed to them, to seat himself next to Ruth.

"Why the hesitation? Didn't you want to sit with us?"

"Of course, Mother." He raised an edge of the butcher's apron and began to mop at his flushed forehead with it. "I'm delighted to sit with you and Mrs.—er—St. Just. If you want me, that is."

"If we hadn't wanted you, would I have called you over?"

"Of course not."

"Now you can talk to Mrs. St. Just. My voice is tired. I've talked long enough."

Nervously Guthrie looked at Ruth. "Everything all right?"

"Oh, yes, thank you."

"Good." He inserted his fork into the pilaf before him, and raised some of it, gray and glutinous, to his mouth.

Mother turned round in her place. "What's happened to Lucy and that fish?" She pushed her plate away, the avocado half now scraped clean, and leaned down the table. "Patrice! Do see what Lucy's doing."

Again the muscular boy got up and strode out through the service door, and again his rough, immature voice—it sounded as if it had only just broken—could be heard shouting out, this time in English: "Lucy! Mother waits her fish!"

"All right, all right! I don't imagine she wants her fish half-raw!"

Mother burst into laughter. "Lucy has spirit," she told Ruth. "It may be the equivalent of wood alcohol, which can leave one with a terrible hangover, destroy one's sight, or finish one off forever. But spirit she has."

Soon Lucy flounced through the service door with the two plates. "There you are, Mother. I broke one of the buggers while turning him over in the pan. Do you want me to give that one to Mrs. St. Just or to you?"

Again Mother laughed with sheer good humor. "To me, of course, you silly girl! Mrs. St. Just is our guest."

The mullet, served with snow peas and crisp little balls of millet, was excellent. "You'd like some wine," Mother said with that inflection that implied a statement, not a question.

"No, no."

"Yes, I'm sure you'd like some wine. We have a local wine here in Ellampore. Tom"—she touched him on an arm—"fetch us a bottle of the white. And make sure it's cold."

Guthrie got up.

Suddenly Mother was calling down the table once again: "Frau Wertheim! Frau Wertheim!" Ruth wondered why, when she had so far addressed everyone else by a Christian name, Mother should in this case have used the surname.

The humped, elderly woman with the white hair piled on top of her head looked up nervously, mouth ajar.

"Come and sit with us."

"Now?"

"When else?"

The old woman got up stiffly. She had a pair of glasses hanging around her neck on a gold chain. These she now put on, so that all at once her previously vague, easygoing face seemed to sharpen. "Excuse me," she said, sitting down where Guthrie had been sitting. She placed her hands, fingers extended, on the table before her. The fingers of the right hand trembled in what Ruth thought was probably the first symptom of parkinsonism.

At that moment Guthrie returned. He set down two glasses and a misty bottle. As Ruth was wondering how it had been chilled, Mother put out a hand and touched it. "We have a refrigerator that runs on oil," she explained. "It was a present from Frau Wertheim."

The old woman bowed her head, as though in acknowledgment of applause.

"Frau Wertheim has been very generous to us. She has made us many gifts. Haven't you, Frau Wertheim?"

Frau Wertheim now raised her head again. In a tremulous voice, she said: "To be rich can often be more of a deprivation than to be poor." Ruth guessed that this impoverished-looking but clearly rich woman was quoting one of Mother's sayings.

"You remember Mrs. St. Just's son," Mother prompted. "You remember Jim."

Frau Wertheim's small blue eyes moved slowly sideways, as though to squint at something that she had been forbidden to look at. She said nothing.

"Did you know my son?"

"Yes, I knew Jim. Yes, of course. He and I read Goethe together. We walked together. He liked walking." Suddenly the old woman looked carefree and radiant. "I know much about trees, plants, birds. He knew nothing, nothing! So I tell him. I say, 'Jim, look at the pelicans.' I say, 'Jim, look at the cedrat.' I say, 'Jim, look at the neem flower.' Jim learned from me."

Ruth felt a sudden gratitude to her. "And his death? What do you know about his death?"

Frau Wertheim lowered her head. Suddenly she looked furtive and frightened.

"Frau Wertheim knows no more and no less about his death than the rest of us. Do you, Frau Wertheim?"

Frau Wertheim hesitated, her eyes still lowered. Then she muttered: "Sad, sad."

"Yes, sad," Mother agreed. "What did Silesius say? 'Die before thou die, that so thou shalt not die.' Perhaps Jim died for himself before he died for us. We must hope for that." She stared down into her glass, her lower lip trembling. To Ruth's astonishment, she seemed genuinely moved.

The old woman drew in her breath and then exhaled it on a deep sigh. "He was a good boy," she said. "Good, but troubled."

Guthrie, who had been standing behind Frau Wertheim without making any attempt to reclaim his seat, now wandered off

177

and sat down next to the black man with the beard and moustache at the far end of the table.

Suddenly, Mother picked up the pepper mill and again banged with it on the table. "Have we any entertainment for tonight?" She looked down the table. "How are we going to amuse our guest?" Once more, it was difficult to know to what extent she was joking. "Tom?" Guthrie jerked up his head, half delighted and half appalled. "You'll dance for us." She beckoned to him with both her hands. "Lucy will dance with you. Patrice— call Lucy."

At the summons, Lucy came out unself-consciously through the service door, wiping her large, bony hands on the apron that she had tied over her miniskirt. She went up to Guthrie, who was standing awkwardly beside the table, one knee on the bench and a hand on his hip. She took the other hand, then drew him away from the table. They smiled in complicity at each other, as though they had suddenly become oblivious of everyone else in the room.

Mother leaned across the table and gripped Frau Wertheim's arm. "Play for them."

"Play?"

"Play."

Frau Wertheim rose and shuffled over to the piano, which Ruth only now noticed stood in one corner. She placed herself on the stool and played a series of arpeggios, her shoulders hunched and her elbows lifted high. The piano was hideously out of tune. Then, head on one side, she began to play the waltz that Ruth recognized as "Destiny."

Lucy drew close to Guthrie, putting a bony arm up around his neck. He put an arm around her narrow waist. They began to waltz together, at first with a grave decorum, and then whirling faster and faster, bodies soon close and cheek pressed to cheek. Round and round they spun, like huge mechanical toys. Ruth looked across at Mother. Cheek resting on hand, she was smiling with pensive indulgence. Then Ruth looked once again at the dancers. They were out of time with the music, constantly anticipating the beat. They were ungainly, Guthrie's feet stomping down on the cracked, pockmarked marble of the floor, and Lucy's body jutting out now in one direction and now in another. Yet there was something strangely moving about their fanatical absorption.

At last the dance ended, to be applauded by the five black men on the dais. No one else clapped. "Thank you, Tom. Thank you, Lucy," Mother said. Both of them were breathless and sweating, their faces blank, as though they had performed under hypnosis and still did not know what they had been doing.

Mother peered again down the table. "Now Arlen will play for us."

It was the young American of the boat, his blond hair falling around a long, lean face that now looked not merely open but also defenseless. With those spidery fingers of his he drew the harmonica out of the breast pocket of his crumpled seersucker jacket and then, perching on a corner of the table, a leg raised with his foot on the bench, he began to quaver out "The Last Rose of Summer." There was something absurd to Ruth in hearing the reedy, melancholic notes in a country in which it was always summer and she had yet to see a rose. The American girl watched him intently as he played, in rapt adoration. Frau Wertheim, having swung round on the piano stool, looked more critical.

Before he had finished, Ruth felt Mother's cold fingers on her arm. She whispered, as though she were imparting some secret for Ruth alone: "If we do not die, then we cannot be resurrected. Remember that."

The American played other ballads, while the rest of them listened, silently passive. Then, in the middle of one of them—it was "Blow the Wind Southerly"—Mother surprised Ruth by suddenly rising, with a scraping back of the bench. At once the American lowered the harmonica from his lips. Without any apology for the interruption, Mother said: "Who'd like a game of Ping-Pong?"

The boy Patrice raised his hand.

"No, not you, Patrice. Not tonight." She pointed to the elderly white man who had been eating so fastidiously. "You," she said.

"Me, Mother?"

"Yes, you."

"But I haven't played Ping-Pong for, oh, donkey's years." The voice was soft, the faint accent middle-European.

"Never mind."

Reluctantly, fingering his bow tie, the man followed Mother toward the door. Before going through it, Mother turned and said over a shoulder: "Ruth."

Ruth wanted to say: "Thank you. Ping-Pong doesn't interest me in the least. I'd rather stay here." But politeness restrained her.

Some four or five of the others came too, along the vaulted corridor, down another, narrower one, and then on to a verandah, where there were a rickety Ping-Pong table and a single pressure lamp, its globe thick with insects burning white above it.

Mother was an expert. She took a mischievous delight in making her increasingly breathless and sweating opponent race from one corner of his side of the table to the other. She always left it to him to retrieve any ball that went astray. When she made a smash, it was with venom, as though she would really have preferred to slam the paddle across his face. "Out!" she would cry exultantly. "My point! Thirteen three!"

Then suddenly, in the middle of their second game, she flung down her paddle. "Enough! I've had enough." She laughed, throwing back her head. "Well, you must agree, I'm not a bad player," she said to Ruth. "Do you play?"

"Not for years. And I've no intention of starting again," Ruth said firmly.

Mother, no longer paying attention to her, was looking over Ruth's shoulder. Ruth turned. The five black men, almost invisible in the darkness but for the weird splashes of white on their foreheads and cheeks, were making their way across the moonlit expanse of ground between the verandah and a building that Ruth assumed to be another annex. *"Bonne nuit, messieurs!"* Mother called out, and there came echoing in ragged chorus: *"Bonne nuit, Madame Mère!"*

Breathing so effortfully that he might have been in the throes of a heart attack, Mother's opponent was wiping his forehead and the palms of his hands with a handkerchief. Mother went over to him and touched him lightly on a shoulder. "Every stick has two ends, the good end and the bad end. All that matters is to be beaten by the good end," she told him. He gazed at her with a yearning gratitude.

Mother then turned to Ruth. "You'll want to go to bed now."

Ruth felt rebellious. "But there's so much that I still want to ask you, talk to you about."

"Sufficient to the day is the good thereof. Let's leave the evil—if there is any evil—till tomorrow." Her tone was as crisp and dry as newly fallen snow. "Lucy, you will take Mrs. St. Just back to the annex. See that she has everything she wants. Within reason," she added, smiling.

III

WITH A BONY HAND shielding the flame of the lamp, Lucy walked ahead of Ruth down the path. In the wind that had arisen, her beehive of hair swayed from side to side like a giant puffball. She set her stiletto heels down smartly on the unevennesses between the paving stones. Her long, muscular legs were set wide apart and her broad shoulders were thrown back. "Mind that wide hole!" she warned at one moment, and at another, "Oh, some bloody dog's been and pooped here. Take care, take care!" On the last of these two occasions, she also made a fastidious grimace, so that her face, plastered in makeup, with its strong, jutting jaw, looked like a grotesque mask.

"Do you also live in this annex?" Lucy was setting down the

lamp on the plain table, where Ruth, always so tidy, had carefully arranged her things.

"I? Oh, no. I live on the other side of the main house. I lived here once, for a few days, but then I moved over there."

"Weren't you happy here?"

"It was okay. But Mother said I should move, so I moved."

"Do you always do what Mother says?"

"Usually. Not because one has to. But because she has a way of being right."

"Like God."

Lucy had picked up the opened packet of cigarettes that Ruth had left on top of the novel she had impatiently thrown aside. "May I have one of these?"

"Of course."

"I don't usually smoke, but from time to time I like to have one."

Ruth drew her cigarette lighter out of her bag and flicked at it. Lucy lowered her head, the puffball of hair bouncing up and down. "I didn't smoke all evening," Ruth said. "I wasn't sure if Mother would approve." She realized, with a shock, that it was the first time that she had referred to her hostess not as Madame Vilmorin but as Mother. Afterward that was how she would always refer to her.

"Mother doesn't approve or disapprove of anything. She sometimes quotes from that man—what was he called? I don't remember. Anyway, he said, 'Do what you will is the whole of the law.' "

"Crowley, Aleister Crowley. 'Love is the law, love under will,' " Ruth completed. "Jim used to be interested in him when he was a teenager."

"Really?" Lucy was surprised. She drew deep on her cigarette and then expelled the smoke through flared nostrils. Seating herself on the bed, she let her body slip backward, emitting a sigh as she did so. She ended up sprawled across the bed, her legs dangling and her head against the wall. She had a curiously disjointed look, as though she were a puppet. Clearly, unlike Ruth, she did not feel like sleeping.

"You came here about your son?" she said in her deep voice, with its North Country accent.

"Yes."

Lucy gave a brief, explosive laugh. "That's crazy!"

"Why is it crazy? Any mother would want to know how and why her son died."

"What does it matter? *Now?*"

"One has to keep faith with the dead. Not only with the living."

"It must have cost you a bomb to get here."

"It must have cost *you* a bomb to get here."

Lucy straightened herself on the bed and then inspected the glowing tip of her cigarette. "I was *paid* to come here. In a sense."

"*Paid?*"

"Sure." She drew on the cigarette, the nostrils once again flaring in the strong-jawed face. "I was on a cruise ship. It called at Bissance. There was an expedition to Ellampore."

"Well, that cruise must have cost you something."

"I wasn't one of the cruisers, I was one of the crew."

Ruth wondered what Lucy's job on the ship had been. She could easily see her as a stewardess, looking like a guardsman, with a beehive of hair for bearskin. Less easily she could see her as an entertainer, microphone in hand, jollying along rich, elderly, somnolent "cruisers." She wanted to say, "And what were you doing on the ship?" but something restrained her. Instead she said: "So you jumped ship?"

"If you put it like that. There was this guy, this guy I'd met in Cape Town on another cruise, and he told me about the community and Mother. He'd been here for a time. He said his life had been changed and *he* had been changed. So I thought: Why not? Try it! I left my mates and came up here and I never went back. It was easy. Far easier than I'd imagined. That's what Mother always says. If you really want something, then it's always far easier than you imagined. It's only when you don't really want something but think that you do that it's difficult."

"I really want to discover what happened to my son."

"He was drowned, yes? It was before I came here, but I heard about it. Everyone said he'd drowned. The sea is beautiful here, but it's easier to die in it than back home. A week—no, I lie, a fortnight ago—there was this French tourist, he looked quite a dish in the photograph in the local rag, and he was killed by a shark, swimming only two or three hundred yards out, at a camp in Bissance. A girl, a little Dutch girl, was drowned not so long before that. She was paddling and this wave swept in, and whoops! she had vanished. Oh, and there was an old man— American, I think—who was finished off by a heart attack just as soon as he had stepped into the water." She took obvious pleasure in relating each of these macabre happenings in turn.

Ruth yawned, not bothering to put a hand to her mouth. "I must get some sleep. I'm done in."

Slowly, as though she were reassembling legs, arms, feet, and hands, Lucy clambered off the bed. "Got all you want? Mother told me to be sure to see that you had all you wanted."

"Thank you, yes." Ruth pointed to the lamp. "Look at all those insects. I wonder if they're planning to make a meal of me."

"Should have closed the window before bringing in the lamp. My fault."

"Take a cigarette with you." Lucy had thrown the butt of the one that she had just consumed, until it was no more than a scorched shred of paper, in a wide arc out of the window. Ruth had been fascinated by the way she had held it, her large fist cupped around it, the long fingernails painted so deep a red that they looked black in the lamplight.

"Thanks. In fact, I'll take two." Lucy gave an impudent grin, as she pulled out a couple and tucked them into the vee of her blouse.

"Are you alone in your annex?"

"People come, people go. Mother says one must learn to expect only one thing, and that's the unexpected." She went to the door. "Well, good night. Sleep tight."

"Mind the mosquitoes don't bite?"

Lucy gave a hoarse laugh and closed the door behind her. Ruth

184

stood motionless, listening to the receding click of the stiletto heels on the concrete floor. Far off, a dog was howling. Perhaps it was the same dog that had "pooped" on the pathway.

She shut the window and picked up the mosquito spray, bought in Siné, which she had set out with her row of medicines and cosmetics. She began to spray savagely, as though to kill a mortal foe.

IV

IN THE NIGHT Ruth awoke. She had forgotten to reopen the window after her spraying, and now the room was so airless and hot that the sweat was pouring off her body under the single coarse sheet. She crawled off the bed, opened the window, and then stood beside it, looking out on the bare expanse of earth, yellow in the moonlight, which sloped upward to the main building. High up in the main building, on the third floor, a single lamp still burned. Perhaps in a hallway? Or in a bathroom? Or was someone reading or writing or merely sitting, so near to the dawn? She looked at her watch. Almost four o'clock. How dreary everything seemed at this hour!

Back in bed, the sweat still running off her despite the now open window, she could not again fall asleep, however much she willed it. Instead, she began to go over in her mind that extraordinary talk with Mother, the meal, and everything that had followed it. Oh, she hated that woman, despised, and yes—she had to admit it to herself—feared her.

All at once she began to compose in her fevered mind a speech that she might deliver or a letter that she might write to her. But she knew that the speech would probably never be delivered, the letter would probably never be written.

. . . *You are a charlatan. You love power, and you know how to gain it, use it and abuse it. But with the sort of feeble, broken, vaguely questing people that you have gathered around you, the acquisition of power and its use and abuse are not all that difficult. It is no more difficult than imposing your will on a troupe of performing dogs.*

You think that you are God. And with apparent omniscience and omnipotence, capriciously bestowing and withdrawing your favours, performing some act now of kindness and now of cruelty, you have managed to persuade these poor deluded creatures that it is God they have found in you.

What you have to offer them is pitiably little. "Do what you will is the whole of the law. Love is the law, love under will." The love is their love for Mother. The will is yours, not theirs.

Unwise, they hunger for wisdom. Uncertain, they hunger for certainty. The wisdom that you give them consists merely of paradoxes and utterances so gnomic that they simultaneously mean nothing and everything. The certainty that you offer them is merely the certainty that everything is uncertain.

You tell them that they cannot live unless they die. But what you have not understood is that they cannot die unless they live. . . .

She closed her eyes, lying on her back, arms straight to her sides, a patient awaiting some terrible ordeal. But now she would sleep. She would not dream. Whatever the ordeal, she was ready for it.

V

MOTHER HAD TOLD Ruth that the muscular boy, Patrice, would bring her breakfast at seven. "We eat dinner together. The other meals we eat apart," she had explained. Then she had added: "I hope seven isn't too early for you. We go to bed early, we get up early."

It was not Patrice who bought the breakfast, but the emaciated youth who had waited on Ruth and Mother the evening before, and he arrived not at seven but an hour later. *One must learn to expect only one thing and that is the unexpected.* Perhaps Mother had decided to rub in that lesson.

The boy, with his ragged hair bleached almost white and his painfully thin body burned almost black by the sun, was silent while he effortfully transported the tray over to the table, balanced it perilously on one corner to enable him to move aside the novel and a toilet kit, and then set it down. Even when Ruth had greeted him with a cheerful "Good morning," he had merely responded with what was more a nervous tic than a smile.

"What's your name?" she now asked.

He cleared his throat, shifting from one bare foot to the other. At the sides of his mouth there were raw grooves, and the whites of his eyes were inflamed. "Vilho," he muttered at last, edging toward the door.

Ruth could smell the sourness of his breath. "Vilho." As she repeated it, she realized in a terrible moment of clairvoyance: *This boy is going to die.* Probably even younger than Jim, he was going to die as Jim had died, even though the manner of his dying might be wholly different. She wondered what was the source of this knowledge mysteriously bubbling up within her like some acrid spring. She repeated the name again obsessively, as though, by thus insisting on his identity to him, she might somehow avert his fate. "Vilho."

Then she asked: "Where are you from, Vilho?"

"I am from Finland."

"Oh, where in Finland?" She spoke as if she had been there.

"Tampere." His voice was hoarse and strained.

"And are you ever going back there?"

He stared at her out of his huge, pale eyes. Then he shook his head mutely. He edged once again toward the door.

"Do you know when Mother is coming for me? Or does she want me to go to her?"

Again he shook his head, before he disappeared.

Overcome by a terrible sadness, Ruth went over to the tray, with its dented metal pots of coffee and milk, its two rolls, its wrapped rectangle of butter, and its honey in a minute plastic container. "Like a hotel," she thought, as the patter of the boy's feet faded into nothing. "Like a second-rate hotel." She poured

187

out some coffee and then added milk. The coffee was weak and tepid, the milk had clearly been boiled. She put down the cup and stared into it.

Once again she experienced that terrifying moment of clair-voyance: *That boy is going to die.*

VI

WHEN BY NINE O'CLOCK Mother had still neither come herself nor sent anyone to fetch her, Ruth left the annex and walked, slowly because she felt unaccountably tired even at this early hour, up the uneven path to the main building.

All at once, the American girl, her hair now dangling in braids on either side of a face that, before so lackluster, now looked red-cheeked and wholesome, appeared walking down toward her, a heavy shopping bag in each hand.

Uncertainly Ruth smiled at her. As though Ruth were a stranger, the girl then smiled back.

"Where's your baby?"

"My baby?" The girl, the sweat glistening along her beautifully formed upper lip and her wide forehead, looked taken aback by what was, after all, the most ordinary of questions. "Someone—someone is looking after her for me."

"Have you been shopping?"

"Yeah. I went down to the market. Not the main market, that's far, but the little one at the bottom of the road. There's not the same variety there, Mother says, but I guess the prices are cheaper." She began to walk on.

The door of the main house was open, so Ruth, having wondered whether to pull at the rusty bell-pull, eventually walked in. Looking around the lofty hall, she called out in a voice she wished did not sound so nervous and shrill: "Anyone there? Anyone there?"

Eventually one of the two pallid girls who had been seated

together at dinner the previous evening looked over the staircase from the floor above. There was a cloth bound round her head and she was holding a dust rag. Ruth assumed that she must have been cleaning Mother's quarters. "*Oui?*"

"I was looking for Mother," Ruth said in English.

"*Pas ici.*" Then the girl went on in English. "She go to market with Tom for shop. She say tell you back eleven, maybe eleven half."

"Thank you." *One must learn to expect only one thing and that is the unexpected.*

Ruth walked around the main house, past what had once been flower beds and were now no more than areas of baked mud demarcated with broken bricks. Somewhere over there—she raised a hand to her eyes—she had, on her arrival, seen that glinting thread she had assumed to be the sea. She began to walk in that direction, first across some sharp scree and then, finding another path, along it.

The cicadas were so noisy, clattering away invisibly all around her, and the path was so rough that there were times when she wished that, instead of setting out on this walk, she had returned to the coolness of the annex to read. She was ruining her shoes, her dress was already moist under her arms and between her shoulders, and her head was aching.

Eventually she realized that what she had imagined to be a glint of the distant sea must have been the sun flashing on the new sheet of corrugated iron used to patch the tile roof of the square two-storied house that she could now see in the distance, at the bottom of an incline. Trees, like huge, dusty mops, stuck up around it, and bougainvillaea trailed from a porch that was little more than a half-hoop of far older corrugated iron, tawny with rust. Clearly this was another of the annexes, even less attractive and welcoming than the one in which she had been housed. She wondered who lived in it, if anyone did. Everything was totally still and silent.

She walked around the building, at one moment stepping over the frame of a bicycle rusting, without wheels, in the long, yellow grass, and at another moment starting when a huge bird threshed out of a bush and took off, like an overloaded plane, toward the horizon.

There was an empty swimming pool on the other side, reminding her that Mother had told her that for a while the estate had housed a school. Many of the tiles either had fallen off or were cracked. At the bottom, a jumble of objects lay piled together: melon rinds, scraps of paper and clothing, a rusty roll of barbed wire, a saucepan with a charred hole in its base, a short length of raveled rope, a single gym shoe, its sole half torn away, a book, lying open and face down, the title on its spine now no more than an indecipherable blur. Fascinated and repelled, Ruth stared down at this detritus. Then, in one corner, lying with its head propped, as though deliberately, on the jagged edge of an empty Heinz baked beans can, she saw a dead rat, its belly swollen and its teeth, tiny and yellow like grape pips, revealed in a rictus of death. It could not have been there for long. Had it been so, its flesh would have long since been stripped off.

She stared at the rat, wondering how it had met its death. Caught in a trap, hunted by a dog or cat, from old age, from disease? She would never know. But still she stared down at it, her eyes screwed up behind her dark glasses and an insatiably curious look about her tilted head and the mouth that she had compressed into a single line.

With a sigh, she eventually turned away. She would go back, without having found the sea, let alone the place where Jim was said to have died.

Wearily she retraced her steps and then began to ascend the stony path.

VII

FROM HER ROOM, where, seated uncomfortably on an edge of the bed, she had been brooding, the unread novel in her hands, on a son lost and a marriage spoiled, Ruth was eventually summoned by Frau Wertheim. "Mother asked me to see to your lunch," the old woman said, as though she did not welcome this duty. "I eat very little in this heat at midday. But of course I am happy to share with you."

Frau Wertheim led her out of the room and down the corridor to a small kitchen, its walls white-tiled, with a stove, fed from a cylinder of butane gas, in one corner and a cold-water sink in the other. She reached up into a cupboard and brought down two cans. With a trembling hand she raised the glasses dangling round her neck and eased them over the bridge of her nose. She peered. "You can eat spaghetti?"

"I can eat anything," Ruth said untruthfully.

Frau Wertheim peered at another can. "Here are tinned sausages. You can eat tinned sausages?"

"Oh, yes, yes."

"Let us eat both. Better." Frau Wertheim dithered, as she looked in a drawer for a can opener while holding the can of sausages to her chest.

"Shall I open that?"

"Please." All at once Frau Wertheim's previous mood had changed. Now, clearly, she was childishly happy to have Ruth's company and help. She passed over first the can and then the opener. She stooped and opened the door of a cupboard below the sink. As she reached for a frying pan, a cockroach scrambled out of it, dithered on the rim, and then plopped down to the concrete floor and scuttled off to safety.

Frau Wertheim made a clucking noise. "Everywhere. Everywhere. Yesterday I take a blouse, a clean blouse, out of my drawer and one of these—these creatures is sitting on it."

Ruth had opened both the cans. She put the spaghetti into a saucepan, which Frau Wertheim had just passed to her. Then she held the frying pan under the antiquated brass tap of the sink, letting the cold water, the pressure even lower than when she had washed that morning, trickle over it. If her former staff could see her now! Obsessive about cleanliness, she had constantly demanded that their hands be washed, thrown away food kept for more than two or three days in the refrigerator, and scoured the filter of the dishwasher after each use. As she now picked up a sour-smelling cloth, held it under the tap, and then rubbed it over the bottom of the frying pan, she heard herself upbraiding Jim, then only a boy, as he helped her with the dishes: "No, not that cloth, not that one! That's filthy! And use some hot water!"

Eventually, facing each other across the bare kitchen table, the two women sat down to their unappetizing meal. While Ruth had been preparing it, Frau Wertheim had wandered off without explanation, to return with two lukewarm cans of the local beer. "You like beer?" She had held up the cans triumphantly.

"Lovely," Ruth had said.

"Have you been here long?" Ruth now asked.

"Yes, I am one of the first. I meet Mother in Nice. I am staying in Nice in hotel, Mother is staying in same hotel. She speaks to me of her dream. I help a little to make the dream real." Frau Wertheim sucked noisily on a strand of spaghetti that was in danger of slithering off her fork.

"And now you'll make your permanent home here?"

"*Natürlich.*" Frau Wertheim was surprised, even shocked, by the question. "Where else do I go? Here is now my place."

"You're a widow?"

"Yes, a widow. You also?"

Ruth shook her head. "Divorced. Jim was my only child. You have children?"

"Yes, I have children." Frau Wertheim drank from her glass of beer. Then she raised her trembling hand to wipe away the froth glistening along her long upper lip. "And my children have children. Now they have no interest in me."

"Oh, surely!"

Frau Wertheim shook her head. There was no sorrow or indignation, merely a wish to get the record straight. "They write to me, *ja*, they write to me. Sometimes I write to them. But they expect nothing from me, I expect nothing from them."

"You're happy here, then?"

Head on one side and mouth bunched, Frau Wertheim considered that as though for the first time. "Yes, I am happy. Or I am not unhappy. For many years I was unhappy. For many years I was afraid." She lowered her head and stabbed at a section of sausage with her fork and then piled spaghetti on top of it. "Now I am not unhappy and I am not afraid, not at all."

"What made you afraid?"

"You know the fear of falling? Many people have it. They cannot go up to a high place because they fear to fall. So with me. I was on a high place, my father had been a famous musician, known all over the world, my husband had been a famous doctor, I had this position, I had these children, I had this money. And I am afraid, afraid, afraid, because maybe I lose all these things. But now they are all lost, I am nothing, I live here and I am nothing, and so—no more fear! I cannot fall. I am so low, I cannot fall." She looked up and across at Ruth, to give her a glowing smile.

"You helped Mother to buy the estate?"

Frau Wertheim nodded. "*Ja.* But that is not important. I give half of my money to my children, half I give for the estate. Now I have no money, none, none, none! That is fine!" Suddenly she burst out laughing, and Ruth found herself joining in. Frau Wertheim raised her half-drunk glass of beer. "*Prosit!*"

"*Prosit!*"

While their glasses were still raised, Ruth became aware that some people had appeared in the open doorway behind her. As Frau Wertheim looked up and smiled at them, so Ruth now swiveled around.

It was the old man and his four followers. The followers were carrying the bundles and bags that they had had with them on the boats. The old man was now wearing a skullcap, embroidered white on white. None of them even glanced at Ruth, all of their attention was directed at Frau Wertheim. The old man put his hands together, and the others then did likewise. They all gave a ragged bow to the old woman, who, fork still in hand, had now scrambled to her feet. "*Au revoir, madame,*" the old man said. "*Nous allons partir. Au revoir.*"

Frau Wertheim made a tentative movement with her right hand, then withdrew it when it was clear that the old man was not going to shake it. *"Auf Wiedersehen,"* she said in a reverential tone.

Again the quintet bowed, then silently they were gone.

Frau Wertheim reseated herself, pulling her plate toward her. "Who are they?"

Frau Wertheim swallowed, then answered. "They are friends of Mother. You know that there are two religions in Saloum?" Frau Wertheim leaned back in her chair, her food forgotten, as though about to deliver a lecture. "There is the old religion, which is animism, and there is the new religion, which is Muslim. There are also, of course, Catholic, but few, few, they are unimportant. *Ja?* This old man comes from a tribe far east. He is leader. Also priest. When Mother was very ill, soon after we come here, the French doctor cannot cure her but this man cures her. Magic, maybe!" She laughed delightedly. "You believe in magic?"

"Not in Europe. But in Africa . . . Who can say?"

"Ja, ja!" Frau Wertheim nodded her head vigorously. "In Africa there is much magic, everywhere magic!"

A voice from the doorway behind Ruth put in: "Yes, Africa is full of magic." It was Mother. "In Europe magic is created by machines. Here it is created by people." She came forward and put a hand on the back of Ruth's chair. "Have you had a good morning?"

"Thank you, yes." But the morning, most of it spent either in trudging about in the heat or in introspection, had hardly been a good one.

"I'm sorry if I've seemed to neglect you. But I had to go down to the market, and then I had to consult with our black visitors from Haute Bassari. They've just gone."

"Yes, they came to say good-bye. To Frau Wertheim."

Momentarily Mother looked disconcerted. "They came *here?*" Ruth nodded.

Frau Wertheim interposed: "They have a long, long journey. I wonder if they will stop off anywhere."

Mother ignored her. "I expect you'll want a siesta now," she said to Ruth. "This is the hottest time of the day."

"Oh, I don't feel like sleeping."

"Well, lie down at least. You'll find it'll do you good." She smiled and turned away. Then she turned back. "Later, if you want to see the place where Jim had his accident, I can take you there. Do you want to see it?"

"Yes, of course I want to see it. I said that yesterday."

"Good." Mother became brisk, even curt. "Then I'll come for you at about four. All right?"

Ruth thought: If form is anything to go by, that means that you'll come for me at three o'clock or five o'clock, or else you won't come at all. But she nodded. "Fine."

Saying no further word, Mother left them.

"Let me wash those things," Ruth told Frau Wertheim, who was carrying their dirty plates over to the sink.

Frau Wertheim, clearly delighted, made no objection. "Very well. Thank you." She made for the door. Then she turned: "If you wish for hot water, you can use the kettle. There is also Nescafé if you wish for it—up there, there." She raised an arm and pointed. "Now I think I go to siesta. Thank you." She gave a little bow. "I enjoyed greatly."

Ruth wondered whether to put on the kettle for hot water for the washing up, and then decided that it would be too much bother. She thought: I'm going to pieces here. Like everyone else. I was always shouting at Jim, "Oh, why can't you realize that, if you have to do something, it's better to do it properly?" and now here I am washing up greasy dishes in cold water, without any detergent and using a filthy cloth. And I no longer care, I no longer care.

VIII

MOTHER WAS WEARING a coolie hat of rough straw, tied under her small, pointed chin with a pale mauve ribbon. In the silk pajama suit of the previous afternoon and the same silk slippers—they struck Ruth as wholly impractical for a walk over rough country—she looked remarkably elegant and youthful.

Ruth herself felt neither of these things. She had made the mistake of falling asleep fully clothed while reading on her bed, with the result that her dress was crumpled and she felt lethargic, bad-tempered, and headachy.

"It was good of you to let me stay here," she said in an attempt at graciousness. In fact, it seemed to her not so much good as puzzling.

Mother clambered nimbly over a low wall and then waited on the other side, hand extended, for Ruth to negotiate it. Ruth, feeling clumsy, did not take the hand. "I'm sorry to bring you this way, but it does make the walk so much shorter than if one goes by road," Mother said. She stooped to pick a tiny wildflower, its yellow trumpet spotted with brown, growing out of a crevice in the wall. She held it up to her nostrils. "No smell. It looks so pretty and it smells of nothing." She tossed it away. Then, as she walked on ahead of Ruth, she turned her head to say over her fragile shoulder: "There's nothing *good* about letting you stay here. You're welcome, as anyone is welcome who's interested in our little community. During the tourist season—it's too hot now—we have lots of visitors, you know. They're always torn between wondering how we can bear to live here in so much isolation and discomfort, and wondering why they're not living here themselves. Is that your reaction too?"

"Not really. I think I've begun to understand what everyone finds here. But I don't think I'd want to find it myself."

"You might find it without wanting to find it. That's how some of them began."

They walked on in silence. Ruth was thinking of the denunciation of Mother that, lying sleepless the night before, she had begun to compose in her fevered mind. Eventually she said: "I thought you'd react to me differently."

"How do you mean?"

"Well, here I was, convinced—as I'm still convinced—that Jim could not have died as everyone tells me he died. It would have been perfectly natural if you'd sent me packing."

Mother laughed cheerfully, with no derision. "You mean it would have been perfectly human."

"Do I? Anyway . . . You've been magnanimous. I admire magnanimity."

Ruth had frequently imagined the beach. There would be golden or—why not?—silver sand, stretching on and on, and there would be the blue, blue sea, with small islands, uninhabited and rarely visited, dotted across it. There would be palm trees, swaying in a breeze that, as evening approached, cooled all the fevers of the day. There would be a goat tethered in some scrub. There would be a half-naked child building a sand castle. There would be two old women gathering driftwood in straw panniers. There would be no one else.

Now, as they walked beside the choppy, misty-looking sea, they repeatedly had to avoid treading on the scurf of fruit and vegetable skins, fishheads, condoms, rags, tins, and bottles that had been tossed up to make a high, malodorous rampart. There were white bodies being toasted by the sun and black bodies being cooled by the water. An elderly bearded man cycled past with an ice cream cart, ringing his bell persistently as he did so. His trousers were rolled up to knobbly knees, a panama hat was tilted rakishly over an eyebrow. Inevitably, there were importunate children, jostling around the two women and demanding over and over again: "Donnes! Donnes! Donnes!" There was a handsome youth in a suit, his hair glistening with oil, who strolled past them with a mockingly provocative stare out of brilliant eyes under thick, arching brows.

Then suddenly, as though he had materialized out of one of the sand dunes, there was a beggar with a crutch, who hopped along beside them, his toothless mouth twisted to one side, while strange, guttural sounds erupted from it. Ruth, her face drained of blood, as her body seemed all at once to be drained of it, stared at him in fascination and fear. Could it—could it—could it possibly be the same beggar who had pursued her in Siné? He looked exactly the same, the makeshift crutch looked exactly the same, and those unintelligible grunts and wails were the same grunts and wails that she had heard—yes, now, now she remembered, she remembered!—in those kaleidoscopic dreams in which England and Africa, past and present, Jim and Mother were all mixed up together, like murderously sharp slivers of glass. But it was impossible that he could have traveled the hundreds of miles from Siné to this island. She must be imagining it.

Mother drew a banknote from her purse and handed it to the man, who at once snatched at it with a crow of glee. But then, having examined it, he began to wave it in the air before her, shouting hoarsely.

"Nothing is ever enough for the very poor or the very rich. That's how they differ from us." Mother walked on, indifferent to the beggar's renewed protestations. Ruth, heart beating violently at the encounter, followed her.

Eventually, realizing that the man had abandoned them, Ruth looked back over her shoulder. He was now half leaning and half sprawling against a beached boat, waving no longer the note but now his crutch in the air, as he continued to scream out imprecations.

"Pay no attention," Mother said. "Poor man—he's not cursing us, he's cursing the world."

Ruth was not so sure.

The beach petered out in a blunt escarpment of rocks, elephant-gray strangely fissured with dark red. Mother touched one of the rocks with her hand. "These rocks are famous for their color. A geological freak—so Tom is always telling me. Strange." She gave the rock a pat, as though it were a sleeping animal. "Beautiful."

A path had been gouged into the escarpment, and up this Mother now began to climb, turning back at one moment to ask Ruth: "Can you manage this?"

Without answer, Ruth merely quickened her pace.

Someone had excreted where two rocks made a hollow. Ruth wondered if eventually the sea, which had failed to wash away that scurf of rubbish along the beach, would wash away the turd, coiled and glistening like a snake. There was no paper beside it.

As Mother continued to ascend, agile and energetic ahead of her, Ruth felt suddenly breathless and giddy.

Mother turned to repeat her previous question: "Are you sure you can manage this?" It was as though she had intuited the breathlessness and giddiness.

"Oh, yes, thank you."

From up here, Ruth could see another beach, the mirror image of the one they had just traversed. No doubt beyond that there was another, and another, and another. . . . Ruth imagined an infinity of bathers and sunbathers, of children, boats, rubbish. Perhaps even an infinity of beggars, all like the beggar who had screamed his incoherent abuse? She felt suddenly exhausted and dispirited.

Mother halted. "Isn't the sea beautiful from here?"

Yes, it was beautiful. Ruth had been so intent in gazing at the beaches on either side of her that she had not noticed the extraordinary gradations of blue and purple, broken by sudden flashes of refracted sunlight so brilliant they burned themselves on the retina. "Not much farther," Mother said.

They trudged on. Then Mother once more halted. Small hands on narrow hips, she looked down. Then she pointed. "Here," she said. "It's called Le Chaudron du Diable. God knows how long it's been called that. I suppose some romantic Frenchman gave it that name. One would have supposed that the devil would have made himself a deeper caldron than that."

Far below, jagged rocks formed a semicircle around a seething press of water. There were trails of yellow and green seaweed over the rocks, looking as though they were geological stria, similar to the red ones running through the elephant-gray rocks farther back.

199

"He dived in here?"

"Yes."

"Unless he fell."

"That wouldn't have been consistent with his injuries. If he'd slipped in the darkness, he wouldn't have landed with that force on his head."

Ruth had to say it: "Someone might have pushed him."

Mother answered calmly: "The pathologist came to the conclusion that that was also inconsistent with the injuries."

"I don't see why," Ruth retorted stubbornly.

"Well, you can have a word with him and he'll explain it to you. As I understand it, if there'd been a struggle, there would, firstly, have been abrasions on his bare feet from these rocks here, and perhaps also abrasions or at least bruises on his bare body, where the assailant grappled with him. Secondly, it's most unlikely that he would have struck the rock under the water with the top of his head."

"I still don't see—"

"Well, you must talk to the pathologist." At last Mother was losing her patience.

Ruth stared down into the frothing water below her. She imagined it as a novelist might imagine it, and doing so, she felt a piercing intensity of grief. But he could not have died here, he had not died here. There was imagination, there was reality. On her bare arms she could feel the chill spume of the water threshing below her, she could taste its salt, stinging on her sun-cracked lips. But nothing else came up out of the caldron to her. If he had truly died here, she would truly have known.

She turned to Mother. She shook her head. "No," she said, with absolute conviction.

For a moment Mother seemed to be totally thrown off balance by the one word. Then she shrugged. "People can rarely be persuaded to believe what they don't want to believe."

"But I *want* to believe that he died in an accident!"

"Do you?" Now Mother was implacable.

"Of course I do! But the trouble is—I can't, I can't."
"It would be better for you if you could believe it," Mother said.
To Ruth it sounded like a threat.

IX

THAT EVENING, feeling herself unable to endure dinner
again in the refectory, Ruth pleaded a headache—which, in fact,
she had—and sent a message up to Mother, through Patrice,
whom she had seen returning from the beach, to ask if she could
have something to eat in her room.

Patrice had been shocked, explaining that every member of
the community and every guest was expected to dine with the
others. That was the rule, the rule could not be broken.

Ruth, a hand pressed histrionically to her forehead, had then
repeated in bad French, *"Je suis malade, j'ai mal à la tête,"* until
Patrice, only half convinced, had trudged off, shrugging his
broad shoulders. Eventually he had returned, still in his damp
bathing trunks, with a tray on which rested a slice of watermelon,
a cold chicken leg, two wrinkled tomatoes, some scraps of wilted
lettuce, and a hard, dry whole-meal roll. With an ill grace he set it
down on the table, muttering, *"Bon appétit, madame!"* though clearly
he did not mean it. Then he hurried off.

Ruth ate a few mouthfuls and then took up her book. When
the sun had set with its usual precipitate splendor, she got up and
lit the lamp. But that meant shutting the window because of the
mosquitoes and shutting the window meant that, even at this
hour, she began to stifle. Eventually she decided to go to bed. She
undressed, pulled on her cotton nightdress—tomorrow, she
decided, she must wash it—and taking up her toilet kit and the
small, coarse square of toweling provided for her, walked down
the deserted corridor to the bathroom. Thank goodness the

soiled underclothes—man's or woman's, she had not been able to decide—had vanished from the towel hooks, where she had found them hanging when she returned from her disturbing expedition to the beach and the escarpment of rocks beyond it. The underclothes could not have belonged to Frau Wertheim; it was inconceivable that she would wear underclothes so grubby or, if she did, that she would leave them in a bathroom shared with others.

Slipping out of her dressing gown, Ruth stepped under the shower. What had been a lukewarm trickle of water in the morning had now both strengthened and chilled. As she experienced the fierce rain on shoulders and breasts, she revived and was invigorated. She began to regret her decision to dine alone. Had she gone up to the main house and joined the others, she might have discovered something. But what did she mean by "something"? All at once it came to her that she now wanted to discover not merely the truth of Jim's death but also the truth of the relationship of all these various people to Mother. Why? To that, uneasily, she could not find the answer. After all, she was not naturally inquisitive, as Jim had been—often provoking her to protest, "But what's that got to do with you? Let people get on with their lives, while you get on with yours."

As she lowered her head to dry her hair, something glinted up at her from beside the porcelain toilet bowl. Had she dropped the wedding ring which, despite her divorce, she still wore? No, it was on her finger. Had someone else dropped a ring? She stooped, put out a hand, then stiffened and recoiled.

What she had touched was a used hypodermic syringe.

Later, sleeplessly tossing on the hard, lumpy mattress, the top sheet tangled about her, she began to tell herself a feverishly jumbled story.

. . . He is the beautiful, brilliant, spoiled son of a rich industrialist (politician, newspaper proprietor, banker) and a successful actress (dress designer, businesswoman, singer). The father is so busy growing richer and richer and the mother is so busy growing more and more successful that they have little time for their beautiful, brilliant, spoiled son.

The boy gets in with the wrong set at university (school, parties, place of work). Or he has a disappointment in his examinations (love affair, job, ambitions). At first, it is easy. He snorts the happiness powder through a silver funnel or he injects the happiness ichor through a plastic-and-glass syringe. He seems more beautiful and brilliant than before, to both himself and others. Like some monstrous, invisible tumor, the hunger grows within him. He spends what money he has. Then he steals from his business (friends, parents, shops). There is an appearance in court, and a period of confinement in a clinic in Switzerland. There is another period in court, and a period of confinement in a prison in Finland. The rich father and the successful mother have even less time for their beautiful, brilliant, spoiled son. They give him more money than ever before and suggest that he should make a journey, somewhere, anywhere, in order to cure himself (find himself, make a new start in life, start out afresh). But he leaves his homeland with that monstrous, invisible tumor still ravenous within him. He goes to Paris (London, Rome, Athens). He buys the happiness powder and the happiness ichor, and then, when he has no more money left, he steals yet again and is imprisoned yet again. Eventually, like one of those objects that has formed that malodorous rampart of detritus on the beach, he is washed up in Saloum (Siné, Bissance, Ellampore). He meets Mother.

Do what you will is the whole of the law. Love is the law, love under will. That is Mother's rule and he is prepared to immolate himself in obeying it. As he begins slowly to die, like a plant blighted beyond cure, he fetches drinks or food and carries trays or messages. Mother's love holds out to him the promise of the oblivion that, secretly, he has always craved. Mother's law is only that he must crave that oblivion enough. . . .

Is this it? She thinks that this is it. Lying awake on the hard, lumpy mattress, the top sheet entangled about her, she is certain that, yes, this must be it.

* * *

203

Later that night, not long before dawn, Ruth had a strange and terrible dream. Unlike most of her dreams, it was not one that she forgot on waking or, indeed, ever forgot.

The light was soupy, so that she seemed to be viewing everything through cataracts of the kind that she had so often seen in this country, even over the eyes of the young. She was standing motionless by the empty swimming pool, staring down into it as though in search of an answer to a question that she had not yet wholly formulated to herself. Yellow threads of famished grass now trailed from the cracks in the tiles, and grass pushed up among the piles of scattered rubbish in the bottom. She could see the rusty Heinz baked beans can, but she could no longer see the rat, with its pointed head resting along the murderous serration of its lid. She blinked against the film that expanded, like some giant cobweb, between her and everything at which she looked. Then she raised her eyes and, all at once, miraculously, the film had dissipated.

On the other side of the pool, oblivious to her watching presence, the emaciated Finnish boy, Vilho, sat with his legs, two sticks charred black by the flames of the sun, suspended stiffly over its rim. He picked up the same soiled underwear that she had seen draped in the communal bathroom and tore off a thin strip. Across the pool, she could hear the sound. Then he extended a skeletal arm, and round and round it he wrapped the strip of soiled material. His teeth were clenched as he drew it tighter.

At the increasing constriction, the thin, fragile arm began to swell monstrously, a bruiselike lump appearing and then expanding, a larger and larger balloon. He reached beside himself. The needle flashed piercing diamonds of light in his hand. He raised the bruiselike bulge and, with a cry of mingled anguish and terror, his lips drawn back from his teeth in what was almost a snarl, he plunged the needle home.

For a time, eyes closed, he rocked back and forth, the syringe still in his hand. Then he set it down and, with the strip of cloth still bound tightly around his arm, he tore savagely at that bruiselike lump of flesh until at last, after much desperate effort, it came away in his grip. He stood up and with a scream flung it outward and downward into the cracked, empty pool.

Ruth looked down. What she had supposed to be a lump of bleeding flesh was the rat, dead now, its small yellow teeth revealed, like grape pips, in a rictus of death.

X

AS THEY HAD MADE the precipitous descent from the escarpment of rock, Ruth had asked Mother: "Who found him?"

"Who found him? Some children found him. Early in the morning. They were looking for crabs, shrimps, mussels—I don't know. They recognized him at once, they had seen him before, they knew he was one of us." She went on to describe how the three children had arrived, breathless with triumph rather than horror, to report their discovery. A number of the members of the community had then rushed over to see what could be done, while she, already knowing that nothing could be done, had telephoned to Dr. Leroi, the Paris-trained doctor who looked after the community on the rare occasions when one of them needed him.

"Could I talk to the children?"

"Yes, I imagine that you could. Though whether they would understand you is another matter. Children of that class don't speak French, much less English. In any case I don't think they'd have anything to tell you that they didn't tell us. They saw the body floating face downward in the Chaudron du Diable. They couldn't possibly have touched the body even if they had wanted to. You've just seen the drop for yourself."

"This doctor—could I speak to him?"

"Why not? He's an agreeable man. Civilized. Friendly. A great lover of France and French culture. Like the president."

So it was that on the following morning Ruth and Mother set

off to visit Dr. Leroi. Mother, as always energetic and impervious to the heat, had suggested they should walk—"There's a footpath, really rather pretty, for most of the way across open country, not more than two or three miles"—but Ruth, suffering from an upset stomach, lethargic after her night of alternating sleeplessness and vivid, terrifying dreams, and exasperated by the mosquito bites now causing her constantly to scratch at her bare arms and legs, had for once been successful in opposing that inflexible will.

"We have no car," Mother had said. "Or were you thinking of asking Tom to push you on the trolley?" she added sarcastically.

"I was in fact thinking of a taxi. . . . I'll pay for it, of course."

The taxi was a battered Renault 5, without air-conditioning and with a jagged dent in one side that made it impossible to open one of the two rear doors. The driver was cheerful and loquacious, holding forth in sibilant, unidiomatic French, most of it unintelligible to Ruth, about some Russian cruise ship due the next day. *"Personne russe n'achete rien! Rien! Rien du tout!"* Mother tried in vain to explain that though the ship might be Russian the passengers certainly would not be so.

"This is where the French officials used to live," Mother said, as they began to lurch and grind up a hill, with a dizzying view of the sea at each hairpin bend. "Now it's where the Saloumese officials live. *Plus ça change, plus c'est la même chose."*

Carefully kept drives, shaded by cedrats and neem trees, swept up to low, white bungalows, many with cars, far larger and smarter than the Renault 5, parked outside them.

"Il me faut vous attendre, madame?"

"Oui."

"Pendant combien de temps?"

"Une demi-heure, une heure," Mother said indifferently over her shoulder as, followed by Ruth, she crunched across the gravel in her delicate slippers.

"It seems so much cooler up here," Ruth said, as they waited for someone to answer the bell.

"And cleaner. Another world. The Greeks used to imagine that the gods lived on Mount Olympus. The people of Ellampore might be forgiven for imagining that they lived up here."

A black girl in a nurse's uniform opened the door to them, greeted them in French, and showed them into an air-conditioned waiting room with bright green wire netting over windows beyond which Ruth could glimpse a formal garden of ponds and fountains, stone urns and stone seats, neatly clipped bushes, and a lawn far lusher than any she had yet seen in Saloum. The furniture, in metal, plastic, and unstained woods, was modern and had clearly been imported with considerable expenditure of the hard currency of which the country was said to be in such desperate need.

Mother sank into a settee and then crossed her legs, in their rustling Chinese pajamas, high over each other. She put out a hand for a copy of French *Vogue*. "It's only here that I now ever see *Vogue*."

"Dr. Leroi must have an affluent practice. I'd never have imagined that in a place like Ellampore . . ."

"By no means all his money comes from his work. He owns estates, both on the island and, more important, on the mainland. He has an uncle who's minister of tourism, and another uncle who's one of the president's oldest and closest buddies. All these things help in a country like this. In fact, they help in any country, don't they?"

At that moment Dr. Leroi stepped quietly into the room and stood silent before Mother, smiling gently down at her. Despite his thinning hair, streaked with gray, Ruth guessed that he could be only in his early thirties. She also guessed, so straight was his hair and so pale his complexion, that he must be of mixed blood.

Mother jumped up. "Michel!" Her small, pointed face was illuminated with pleasure. She held out a hand, which he took and kissed.

"This is Mrs. St. Just. You know about Mrs. St. Just. I explained on the telephone."

He nodded at Ruth and then, as though on a second thought,

extended a hand. "Mrs. St. Just," he repeated, as Ruth took it. "Do we speak English or French?" His accent was American.

"English, if you don't mind," Ruth said. "My French is appalling."

"My English is appalling. Even though I studied for two years in Boston after Paris. But if it's English you want . . ." He shrugged his narrow shoulders. "Why not?" He turned to Mother. "Shall we go into the consulting room?"

Mother and then Ruth preceded him. From behind them he said: "Eleanor, why haven't I seen you for such a long time?" It took Ruth a moment to realize that he was putting the question to Mother. It was the first time that she had heard anyone call her anything other than Mother or Madame Vilmorin.

"Because you've never bothered to ask me over."

"But you hate my parties."

"You don't have to invite me to a party."

Like the waiting room, the consulting room was cool, clean, and expensively modern in its decor. Dr. Leroi stooped to pick up a crumpled paper tissue and dropped it, distaste flickering across his face, into a gleaming metal pedal-bin. "Please." He pointed to the chairs opposite the one he was himself about to take, a huge desk between him and his visitors.

Mother looked about her. "This is such an elegant room. But you know—I have to say it—it gives me the creeps. When I'm in it, I always think of all the disagreeable things you must have had to tell people while you've been sitting over there and they've been sitting over here."

"Think of all the things that I've told them that have brought them relief."

He placed his elbows on the desk, so that the sleeves of his shimmering gray silk suit, riding upward, revealed heavy cuff links, set with what Ruth took to be rubies. The material of his voile shirt was almost transparent.

"Well, Mrs. St. Just." He smiled at her with his white, even teeth. "Your consultation with me is not of the usual kind, I gather."

"No, I haven't come here to tell you what is wrong with me."

"Or even that nothing is wrong with you?"

"No, not even that." She looked into his eyes, which had a kind of misty, vague kindness about them. "I want you to tell me about my son's death."

"What can I tell you that our good friend here hasn't already told you? I was called to the community that morning, early; Madame Vilmorin called me. She was agitated, explained how the body of your son had been found. There seemed to be no doubt, no doubt at all, that with that kind of injury to the skull, he must have hit some hard object after a fall."

"There's no possibility that—he might have been pushed?"

"Not in my view."

"Or died in some other way?"

Dr. Leroi reiterated what Ruth had already been told so often. There had been an autopsy, conducted not by him but by a pathologist in Bissance—Dr. M'Tami. The body had been transported there, refrigerated, of course. It was—he looked at her with what seemed to her at once sympathy and reproach—still being kept in Bissance, awaiting word from her and her husband for its burial or cremation. He understood her concern, he felt deeply for her. But . . . He shrugged his narrow shoulders. There seemed to him no doubt that her son had died precisely as it had been decided at the inquest. Sadly, accidents often occurred.

He fell silent, elbows still on the desk between them and chin propped on hands; his head tilted to one side, he looked across at Ruth with that same mixture of sympathy and reproach.

"Thank you," she said, in a suddenly weary voice, even though there had been nothing in his narrative, other than its grave, measured tone, for which she had reason to be grateful. "It's difficult to explain this to you. You see, Jim—Jim was my only son. We were very close. And when—when people are very close, they somehow *know* things about each other. It's a kind of ESP, I suppose."

He nodded encouragingly. *"Bien entendu."*

"Well, that ESP tells me that he didn't die as the result of an accident. Whatever anyone else may say. I know, I *know* that it didn't happen like that."

He looked across at Mother. Mother looked back at him. He raised his eyebrows and gave a small smile. Mother shrugged her shoulders and stared down at the toe of the slipper on the left foot crossed at the ankle over her right. It was as though he were saying to her, "Poor, deluded woman—what are we to do with her?" and she were replying, "What indeed?"

"Did you ever treat my son?" Ruth now asked.

"Treat him?"

"I mean, was he ever your patient?"

He seemed to hesitate for a second before he replied. Then he said: "No . . . Oh, of course I have patients from time to time from the community—even though I think that our good friend here does not really believe in my kind of orthodox Western medicine. But your son was never my patient. Never. He seemed to be a strong, healthy boy. I cannot say that I ever got to know him well, but on my visits I'd often run into him, even chat with him for a few moments." He frowned, as though trying to recall something. Then he went on: "Once we had a longer conversation at dinner in the refectory. Yes, yes, I remember that. He struck me then as—intelligent. Well-read, too."

They looked at each other in silence. Then Mother touched Ruth lightly on the arm. "Is there anything else you wish to ask Dr. Leroi?" she prompted.

Frustrated, baffled, and obstinate, Ruth felt an illogical anger against both Mother and this quiet, courteous doctor, whom she could see only as Mother's ally. She shook her head. "I don't think so."

"Unless, of course, you want to ask him for something for your upset stomach?"

Ruth, who had told Mother of the upset stomach in the car, did not know if the question were kindly or malicious in intention. "Oh, that seems all right now," she said. "I took some Lomotil I brought with me."

Dr. Leroi got up from his chair. "Then may I offer you a drink?" He consulted the watch on his thin, hairy wrist. "I have twenty minutes before my next patient is expected."

Mother looked at Ruth inquiringly. Then, when Ruth made no response, she too got up: "All right! Thank you! A drink!"

They returned to the waiting room—Ruth wondered what scruple had prevented them from remaining in the consulting room—where a servant in white, baggy trousers and white mess jacket brought them gin slings. Mother and the doctor, seated side by side on the low sofa, began an animated conversation in French about social events and mutual friends on the island and in Bissance. Ruth was convinced that they were deliberately excluding her.

"Please forgive us. We're being very rude," Dr. Leroi interjected at one moment. But even after that he and Mother made no attempt to draw Ruth in.

As she heard but did not listen to their brisk French, letting it spray over her as the bitter spume from the Chaudron du Diable had sprayed over her while she had stared down into its turmoil, all at once a realization came to her. On the doctor's huge desk, there had been a photograph—she had had to tilt her head in order to see it—of a beautiful white girl, presumably his wife or his fiancée. But despite that, there was something deeply erotic between these two people, sitting so close to each other and talking to each other with such animation and, yes, joy. There was a light on both their faces, and the light was reflected back and forth, back and forth, constantly gaining in intensity. Mother, usually so direct, even abrupt in her conversation and general behavior, had now acquired an insinuating languor, as her tongue kept flickering to the corners of her small mouth, her hands kept stroking her knees under their silk pajamas, and her eyebrows kept arching in surprise, amusement, or mock alarm.

Eventually the nurse came in. The patient had arrived.

"Damn these patients!" Dr. Leroi at last reverted to English.

"Why are there always patients to see when I'm enjoying myself? I'm sorry." He got up. "What can I do?"

"Give up your practice," Mother said mischievously.

"Give up my practice! I might as well tell you to give up the community."

"You don't need it."

"But of course I need it. Just as you need the community. What else would I do with my life?"

"I can think of many things." Mother, followed by Ruth, went out into the hall. Then she turned back: "Oh, I forgot to ask—what news of Annette?"

"Still in Paris. Her mother gets better, her mother gets worse. She always gets worse when Annette announces her departure. What can I do?"

Ruth presumed that Annette was the beautiful white girl whose photograph stood in the elaborate Art Nouveau silver frame on the consulting room desk.

Dr. Leroi bowed so low over Ruth's hand that she thought he was about to kiss it, as he had again kissed Mother's. "I'm afraid I've disappointed you. But isn't it better that your son died of an accident than"—he paused—"in some more sinister way?"

"I must know the truth." Ruth almost added: "I must know the people who killed him."

In the ramshackle taxi—where, waiting for them, the driver had gone to sleep in the back—Mother said: "He's charming, isn't he? The best sort of Saloumese."

Ruth nodded, staring, as the taxi lurched and grunted around yet another hairpin bend, at the sea far below them.

"In a place like this, it's nice to have someone like him."

"Why doesn't he work in Siné or Bissance? Or abroad, if it comes to that?"

"His career's not that important to him. His work is. Yes, of course, if he set about it, he could be successful in Paris, New York, or London. But this is his kingdom. Far better to be a king in Ellampore than some junior court official in one of those other places."

212

Ruth gathered her courage. "I can see that you and he get on well."

"Yes, we get on well. We're rather alike, really."

How they were rather alike, she did not specify.

XI

OUTSIDE THE MAIN building, Ruth paid off the repeatedly yawning taxi driver. Presumably because Mother, a resident of Ellampore, was present, the charge was about a third of what other Saloumese taxi drivers had demanded of her for comparable journeys.

As the taxi lurched off in a crunch of gravel and a cloud of dust, Mother said: "Well, that's taken care of that. Is there anyone else you want to see?"

Ruth sensed that behind this question there was another one: How much longer must we expect you to stay here? To that second, unspoken question, Ruth herself did not know the answer. No road that she had taken since her arrival had turned out to be straight; eventually every road had ended in a cul-de-sac. She felt an overwhelming weariness of the spirit. Yet beneath that weariness she was buoyed up by that same obsessive determination that had brought her all the way from the restaurant in the Cotswolds to this weird little community on this island in the south Atlantic.

She now answered Mother's question: "For the moment I can't think of anyone else, no. I wish I could. Back in Bissance I've still to see Dr. M'Tami and the coroner, Dr. Thumy. Both were away when I tried to call them." Had they really been away? Increasingly she wondered.

Mother put out a hand and gave Ruth's arm an affectionate squeeze. "Sooner or later, my dear, you're going to have to face up to the fact that that accident really took place."

Ruth shook her head. "Never."

"It would be so much better for you if you could accept it." The fingers squeezed the arm stiffening in revulsion and fear. "Really. Try."

Back in her room, with no appetite for the luncheon that Mother had told her one of the two plain, pallid girls would be bringing, Ruth made a deliberate effort to follow Mother's council. *Accept it. Try.* But however much she tried, however much she exerted her will, acceptance eluded her. She sat on the bed, plump body erect and strong hands clasped in her lap, and stared out of the smeared window at the washing on the line beyond it. This time there was a cotton dress that she recognized as having seen on Frau Wertheim the day before, and a shirt, striped a faded blue and white, that she persuaded herself was the property of the Finnish boy.

All at once surmise became a process of anguished creation. . . . In that Japanese-style suite of rooms, Mother is speaking, while the body lies out on some sacking, a sheet over it.

"I thought I could always rely on you."

"You can always rely on me."

"Well then?"

"It'll cost money. If I were to do the autopsy . . . Thumy's all right but unfortunately M'Tami's less corruptible than most. Perhaps the result of his years abroad!"

"Less corruptible? You mean more expensive?"

"Precisely."

"But you must have influence with him."

"Some. Not enough."

"You know I'd do anything in return."

"Anything?"

"Anything."

"Well, clearly, it has to have been an accident. Now what sort of accident should it be?"

"There was that Canadian—do you remember? Two or three years ago. He was diving, hit his head on a submerged rock. Why not? That could easily have happened."

She goes to him, stepping delicately over the body on its bed of coarse sacking. She puts her arms around his neck, slowly, first the one and then the other. "You're clever," she says. "You can solve anything, can't you?"

"Not as clever as you." . . .

The plain, pallid girl came in with the tray. Her sharp knock startled Ruth. Today there was a *gratin* of aubergine in a tomato-and-cheese sauce, fresh bread with scrolls of butter beaded with moisture, equally fresh lettuce, vinaigrette dressing in a small pottery jug, grapes, mangoes.

"What is this?" Ruth pointed.

"Mother said to bring it for you," the girl replied brusquely. Along with everything else, there was a half-bottle of chilled Louis Roederer champagne.

Ruth was astonished. "But I'm not celebrating anything."

The girl shrugged and turned away.

The thought came to Ruth that perhaps Mother was celebrating something.

XII

THAT AFTERNOON, having eaten the unusually delicious food—who could have prepared it?—and drunk the champagne, Ruth decided that after her insomnia of the past night she had better try to sleep. But she found it impossible to do so. She even found it impossible to concentrate on the Siné French-language newspaper, three days old, passed on to her by Mother. She felt herself to be like that ravenous fire on the shore of her hotel in Bissance. There was a still, white-hot core, and from it the incandescent particles of ideas constantly whirled around, upward, and away. Terrible things had gone on here on the estate, from the days when prisoners, failing in their attempts to escape, had been thrown to the sharks, to Jim's death, to the present.

Now in her mind all these highly combustible things fed the flame at the heart of her being.

She threw aside the newspaper, put on her dark glasses, and reached for her sunhat. Having slipped her feet into sandals, she then suffered a momentary giddiness as she stooped to fasten the straps. Outside the annex, the heat struck her a poleaxing blow. There was no one about, there was no sound but the clatter of cicadas from the arid scrub. Mad dogs and Englishmen, a mad Englishwoman and dogs, she thought. But there was no sign of any of the dogs that from time to time she would see wandering about, emaciated, limping, covered with sores, on their furtive scavengings.

Where should she go? To the Chaudron du Diable? As she thought of it, she could again taste the spume bitter on her lips, could again feel it cold and sticky on her bare arms and legs. But there was no point in trekking out there. The message that the threshing waters had held for her—which was merely that they held no message—was one already transmitted.

At random she took a path she had never taken before, winding down erratically from the annex, past another annex, silent and still in the afternoon heat, and then under the grateful shade of some trees. She had a curious sensation of weightlessness, as though, after the diarrhea that had afflicted her in the early morning, she was now no more than an empty husk. Even her head, previously heavy with so many dark suspicions, now seemed puffball light.

A goat lay tethered under a tree, its sides heaving and its eyes glinting like two topazes at her. The rope of its tether had become entangled, so that the plastic bucket of water set out for it was far beyond its reach. Ruth approached, picked up the bucket, and set it down beside the creature. It lumbered up, raising first its rump and then its narrow head. It gulped greedily as Ruth watched.

Soon after that, she came on a trio of completely naked children, no more than three or four years old, who were playing with some pieces of wood in the dust by the path. At the sound of her approach, they looked up, clearly terrified, as though they thought she might snatch their playthings from them. She smiled, but that only precipitated a wail from the smallest. She walked on. She decided that she must be near some houses or huts.

In a clearing in the jungle into which the path had now wound, there were three huts made of *banco*, a mixture of earth and straw, supporting a tousled thatch of mangrove leaves. An ancient woman was squatting in the shade, with a dog asleep beside her and, on a coconut mat, what Ruth, peering with the sun low in her eyes, at first took to be a puppy. Then she all at once realized with amazement that it was not a puppy but a white baby.

Seeing her, the woman leaped to her feet, the dog barking frenetically. She stooped to yank the baby up into her arms and then scuttled—like some shiny dung beetle, thought Ruth—into the nearest of the huts, from which she could be heard gabbling in a high-pitched voice, almost a wail, to someone invisible within. A white baby? How was it possible? Ruth remained transfixed there, staring at the dark hole that provided the hut with its entry, and wondering if she ought to force her way in. Suddenly there came to her a memory of meeting the young American girl and asking about her baby. "Someone is looking after her." Wasn't that what she had said, with furtive, embarrassed guilt? Was it possible that here, in this little circle of untidily thatched huts, the girl had found that someone?

Ruth put a hand to her brow, pressed downward, and left it there. Words were hammering, blow on blow, in her head.

. . . "She gets in the way," the girl says. "How can one think about what's within one, as Mother tells us to do, if one must constantly think of someone outside one?"

The American boy nods, with sage resignation. "Yeah, I guess it's hard."

"Hard! It's impossible."

"Then what's the solution? Mother says that every problem has a solution. Right?"

"No. She says that every solution has a problem. Not the same thing." The girl is brighter than the boy.

"Of course it is! Anyways, we'll have a word with Mother."

The American girl stares down not with love but with baffled curiosity at the child staring up at her. The child looks very old, the girl looks very young. She says: "It's odd. Since I came here, I feel nothing for her."

"That's because you feel for other things."

"More important things?"

"Guess so. Yeah, they've got to be more important." . . .

The children playing in the dust stared up at Ruth, mouths open and eyes wide, as she hurried up the path toward them. Then the oldest emitted a scream, to be followed by a hysterical burst of sobbing, face screwed up and knuckles pressed to eyes. The others also screamed. At that, like animals before some jungle predator of a kind never before encountered, they jumped up and scattered in different directions, plunging into the bush.

XIII

PANTING, her face blotched and glistening with sweat, Ruth raised a hand and rapped repeatedly on the door to Mother's quarters. There was no answer. She leaned her head against the door and, hand still raised, listened intently. At this hour of siesta, she was certain that Mother was within. She was lying on the couch in those pajamas of hers, the beige or mauve or pale blue silk fluttering in the breeze from the open window. Or she was reading on the floor, squatting before a copy of *Vogue* given to her by Dr. Leroi—"No point in keeping it for Annette. By the time she returns, it'll be months out of date, and in any case she's certain to have seen it in Paris." Or she would be sitting motionless and silent with someone, both of them conspiratorially watching the door, behind which they knew that she, Ruth, was knocking with so much vehemence.

Eventually Ruth grasped the handle of the door and shook it, first gently and then violently up and down, up and down. It was locked, as she had known that it would be locked. "Madame Vilmorin!" She no longer called her Mother. She hammered again with a fist. Silence. Or did she hear a rustle, a whisper, a titter? The two people in there were having difficulty restraining their laughter. She could see them. There was Mother and there was —well, it could be any of them.

Furious and frustrated, Ruth at last left the door and walked jerkily, as though her movements were not properly coordinated, down the corridor to the window at the end of it. She looked out into the glare of the late afternoon, as it impartially bathed in its fiery radiance a stretch of brown grass, a cracked and empty fountain—the spout, protruding from the mouth of a stone dolphin, was emerald with verdigris—and a sheet of newspaper which, blown against a tree, twitched there from time to time as though it were some spread-eagled creature in the final throes of dying. No one. Nothing.

She walked back down the corridor, hesitated for a moment outside the locked door, wondering whether to hammer on it yet again, and then hurried down the stairs, at one point all but slithering downward on the marble. She did not even know if any members of the community lived in this building with Mother. There were doors to the right and left. Would they also be locked? Tentatively, she opened one. There was nothing behind it but a broken deck chair, some brooms, a bucket, and a great deal of dust. Perhaps there would be someone in the refectory? But although the long table and the smaller one on the dais had both been set out, it was empty but for the flies noisily buzzing around it, and a small lizard, emerald flecked with rust, which rested, motionless but for its wildly palpitating throat, on the cracked stone of one of the window ledges.

From beyond the baize door that led to the kitchen, she heard a metallic sound, as of two pots colliding. She pushed the door open. "Is anyone there?" She did not know why her voice should sound so faint and tremulous. She edged down a dark corridor toward the wedge of brilliant light slanting into it from another door.

Around that door, Guthrie's head now appeared. He was wearing nothing but a pair of khaki shorts, reaching almost to his knees, and an apron suspended from his neck and tied about his waist. Even his feet were bare, revealing hornlike toenails.

He was jovially surprised to see her. "Hello, hello!" She could smell onions cooking in the kitchen behind him. "Just preparing the vegetables for dinner. Got some aubergines in the market."

"Where's Mother? Do you know?"

"Mother?" He put his head on one side, as though trying to remember. But Ruth knew that it was all a pretense.

"I knocked and knocked on her door. No answer. And yet I knew . . ." No, that was foolish. Better not to reveal to him that she had known that, all along, Mother had been within. "I've something important to ask her."

"Well, it'll have to wait." He slapped his forehead with the back of his hand. "Yes, I've just remembered. She's had to go across to Bissance. With Arlen and Harriet—the American couple."

He was lying. Ruth was convinced of it. "With the American couple?"

"That's what she said."

"Why?"

He jerked his head back, like a horse jibbing at a fence too high for it. "No idea, I'm afraid. She said they might get back this evening or they might not. Nuisance because it's difficult to know how much to cook. Mother hates waste—for aesthetic and not economic or moral reasons, she says."

"Did the Americans take their baby?"

"Not *their* baby. *Her* baby," he corrected with a smile. "A lot of people make that mistake. Brother and sister."

"Brother and sister!"

He nodded.

"But one would never have imagined . . ." She broke off. An

220

even more sinister suspicion had crept into her already turbulent mind. "Where do they live?"

"Where do they live? Somewhere in the Midwest. No idea of the precise location. Why?"

He was looking at her as if she had taken leave of her senses.

Fool! "I mean here." She made an effort to control her irritation. "Where have they been put up?"

"Oh, some way away. There's an annex with an empty swimming pool in front of it. When this place was a school, the kids used to use it because the sea was thought too dangerous for them."

"I know that annex," Ruth said, turning away from him. "My son used to live there."

"So he did." As she began to walk away, he called out after her: "No use to go down there. I told you—they're away in Bissance."

There was anxiety in his voice; he was trying to put her off course.

"Never mind," she replied, hurrying on. "That's all right."

XIV

BY THE EMPTY POOL, Ruth remembered her dream of the emaciated Finnish boy, first wrapping the strip of cloth round and round his arm and then plunging the needle into it. She stared down, half expecting to see, down there below, the lump of flesh that in the dream he had torn from himself and then hurled into the dryness of cracked tiles, rubbish, and dust. But even the rat was now gone, although the can, with its cruelly serrated edge, still remained.

Hands clasped and head bowed, as though in silent, agonizing prayer, she continued to stare downward.

. . . That dung beetle of a woman has somehow scuttled out of

221

the back of the hut and made her way, faster than Ruth, up to Mother's quarters. The two of them then hurry down to the American couple.

"That's the last thing one wants her to see," Mother says. She is annoyed that the woman has not brought the baby with her. "That creature spells trouble, constant trouble. The sooner we can get rid of her the better."

"Rid of her?" Has the American, echoing the words, misunderstood Mother, or has he understood her only too well?

"Anyway," Mother says, "let's stall for the moment. We'll tell Tom to tell her that we've all three—no, four, the baby too— gone to Bissance. Then we'll work out something.". . .

She has imagined it as a novelist might imagine it, but somehow the imaginings do not quite fit. Something terrible is going on with the American brother and sister, who are—yes, Ruth is sure of it—also lovers, abandoning the child of their incestuous relationship—yes, Ruth is sure of that too—to an old black woman who looks like a dung beetle.

Ruth's head began to ache all of a sudden. "One of my migraines," she used to say to her staff, and they all knew then that they would be on their own, since she would have to go lie down in her darkened bedroom for a few hours or even for a whole day. But she could not go lie down now. She must see whether the Americans were skulking in their quarters; and if they were not skulking in them, she must at least see what those quarters were like.

She passed through a swinging door, which grated shut behind her, into a large hall. There was an air of dereliction about it, the cement floor crisscrossed with cracks and the once white walls scribbled on, presumably by pupils of the past, with childish pictures and characters. She walked up to one door and tried it. Then, when it proved to be locked, she walked up to another.

A voice at the top of the staircase suddenly called down: "Mrs. St. Just! What on earth are you doing here?"

Ruth looked up, startled. Then she saw Lucy. Foolish of her not to have recognized that deep North Country voice. "Lucy!" But this was a different Lucy, without the grotesquely smeared makeup and without the huge chrysanthemum of orange hair. The face looked vulnerable in its paleness. The eyes, with their short, sandy lashes—the thick, long, black false ones had been peeled off—looked extraordinarily small. Around the head there was wound a towel.

Ruth began: "I was looking . . ." Then she broke off. "What are *you* doing here?"

"Me? I live here, sweetie."

"Here?"

"Yes. Why not? I told you. I used to live where you are living. Then I moved down here."

Ruth stared at her. Was this another lie? "I thought—Tom told me—no one lived here but those two Americans. The brother and sister."

"Tom knows nothing. Takes nothing in. Talks awful balls." Lucy came down the steps toward Ruth, placing her large feet, in their feathered mules, firmly on the concrete steps; she stared into Ruth's face with growing concern. When she reached the last step, she asked: "Are you all right?"

"Of course I'm all right!" Ruth detected something false in the inquiry. "I was just looking for the Americans."

"You seem somehow . . . Oh well, never mind. If you say you're all right."

"I do say it." Ruth stared at the heavy mannish jaw, and at the wide mouth, which looked brutal now that it was not glistening with lipstick.

"I was just about to have a shower. This heat! One sweats and sweats. And stinks."

"Where is the Americans' room?"

"Rooms," Lucy corrected. "The first two on the right, at the top of these stairs. But they're not there."

"Not there?"

"Nope. They and Mother went into Bissance. They took the afternoon boat. Some trouble over residence permits, I can't think why. I got mine just like that. People in the community usually do." She put out a large hand, the nails long and painted crimson, and rested it on Ruth's arm. Ruth felt her flesh crawling where that other flesh was touching it. But she must not pull away, that would only arouse suspicion. "Are you sure you're okay? You could sit in my room for a moment, if you wanted. I might even have a drop of something stashed away."

"Yes, of course I'm all right. Perfectly all right. Thank you."

Why did first Tom and then this freakish woman, with her wide, bony shoulders and splayed feet, keep asking her if she were all right? Unless, of course, the question concealed the hope that she was not.

"Did the Americans take the baby with them?"

"I've no idea. Why?" Lucy was now staring at her, towel over arm and toilet kit dangling from wrist, with what Ruth could interpret only as a mixture of alarm and hostility.

"I just wondered. I've not seen them with the baby since we first ran across each other on the ship."

"Well, it's around. Sometimes, in fact, it's a bloody nuisance. Kept me awake last night and then woke me early in the morning."

Ruth forced herself to smile. On no account must she give this woman any excuse for reporting back to Mother. That could, she now decided with a chill tremor within her, be dangerous. "I mustn't keep you from your shower," she said. "In fact, you've given me the same idea. One gets so sticky here. If only there were electricity, so that one could have a fan."

"It's just a question of having a new generator installed. It's not even necessary to be connected to the mains. Or I shouldn't wonder if the old generator—in that shed beside the swimming pool—couldn't be mended."

"Then why isn't something done about it?"

Lucy rubbed thumb and fingers together. "Cash, darling."

"But surely there's no lack. . . . I thought . . ."

"Somehow we keep going. But there's never enough cash. Mother, with her love of turning everything on its head, says that one of the principles of the community is: 'To each according to his ability, from each according to his needs.' But it doesn't always work out."

Was Lucy mocking Mother? Ruth could not be certain. As they began to walk together back down the corridor, toward the front door and away from the staircase that would have taken her to the Americans' room or rooms, Ruth said: "Do you have a high opinion of Mother?"

Lucy halted and turned. She replied vehemently, even angrily. "Have a high opinion of her! I adore her! I don't know where I'd be—where any of us would be—without her."

"Somehow I can't myself accept her as God." As soon as she had said that, Ruth realized that it would have been wiser not to have done so. It too would no doubt be reported back to Mother in due course.

"I don't think any of us accepts her as God. But she's a wonderful person." Lucy turned away from Ruth, putting out a hand to the handle of a door beside her. "Well, I'll have my shower," she said. She peered back at Ruth, the small eyes, set wide apart, with their short, sandy lashes, scrutinizing her with what to Ruth seemed curiously like pity. "You should have a shower too," she said. "And a lie-down. It's no good rushing around too much in this heat."

As Lucy opened the door, Ruth had a glimpse of a toilet without a seat, and of a shower across which hung a plastic curtain printed with a design of small sailing ships rocking on a pale blue sea; it was torn diagonally at one corner, askew from its rail. There was a lisping sound as water dripped from its rusty spout.

"Bye then!" Lucy called.

"Good-bye."

Ruth pretended to walk on to the front door; she then turned and, with unusual nimbleness, glided back to the staircase and up it. She guessed that Lucy, deafened by the shower, would not hear her. The first two rooms on the right—wasn't that what Lucy had said? She opened the first of the doors, not knowing what she expected to find. Two mattresses lay side by side, with sheets and pillows in disarray; a rucksack, open and half empty, a shopping bag, and a gaping suitcase, seemingly full of dirty clothes, lay scattered around. A brush, trailing long black hairs similar to the girl's, rested on the windowsill, with a paperback lying facedown beside it—hurriedly Ruth picked it up and looked at the title: *Psychic Archaeology* by someone named Jeffrey Goodman. Passages had been marked with a red pen. Below the window were a pair of sneakers, one on its side. They were the sneakers usually worn by the boy.

She must hurry if Lucy were not to catch her.

The other room had a sour odor, as though milk had been spilled and then inadequately mopped up. There was no bed, not even a mattress, merely a basket in the center. The basket was empty, the bedding in it soiled. There was a closed suitcase and, hanging from the hook behind the door, a cotton kimono and, over that, a pair of tights.

Ruth hurried down the stairs and toward the front door. As she reached it, she heard that deep North Country voice behind her. "Mrs. St. Just! Are you still here?"

"I've dropped a handkerchief somewhere. I thought it might have been here—while we were talking. But there's no sign of it."

"I see." Clearly Lucy did not believe her. Fronds of wet hair, not the orange hair of the chrysanthemum wig but short black ones, curled from under the towel bound turbanwise around her head. The other towel, now sopping wet, was over her muscular arm.

"Perhaps I dropped it somewhere on the way over here. It doesn't much matter. But it was rather a pretty one. Embroidered."

Ruth walked to the front door, opened it, and emerged into the heat and glare. She walked quickly, halfway around the pool to the path that would take her back to the annex.

. . . So they didn't have separate rooms, those two, brother and sister. They could not be sleeping apart, when the one room contained those two mattresses, set side by side, and the other contained neither bed nor mattress but only that basket, with soiled linen in it. She felt an excitement that seemed to seize her by the throat in its viselike grip; as she walked up the uneven path, the cicadas noisy all about her, she had to pause at one moment, hand pressed to chest, in order to suck in breath.

Strange, terrible things were happening here. The death of Jim was only one of them.

XV

THE BLACK MAN with the closely clipped, graying moustache and small, pointed beard—Ruth had never learned his name—stood in the doorway. Ruth, awakened out of a shallow, restless sleep by his knocking, had jerked up, face creased, damp, and flushed. Hurriedly she drew up one side of her nightgown where it had slipped off a shoulder, and croaked: "Yes? Who is it?"

"It is I," the man said, with odd formality, his lips parting in a smile. His voice was deep and beautifully modulated, his accent American. "I'm truly sorry. I always hate to awaken people. I always hated to awaken my younger brother, when my parents sent me up to do so. It's"—again he smiled—"too much like jerking a fish up out of water."

Ruth stretched a hand out to the dressing table for her watch. Having noticed that constant sweating was rotting its leather, she had gotten into the habit of taking it off whenever she could.

The man drew an old-fashioned watch from the breast pocket of his fawn bush jacket. "Four minutes past eight. We were worried about you. Don't you wish for some dinner?"

"Dinner." Ruth repeated the word as though she had never heard it before. Then she swung her feet off the bed, aware that the man was staring down at them with a fastidious expression. "Yes, dinner. I'll slip into something and come up."

"We've never really been introduced. I'm Warren Grant."

Ruth rose unsteadily, putting out a hand to the bedpost. "And I'm Ruth St. Just."

He nodded. "Yes, I know that." He turned away. "Well, we'll expect you in a moment. You know how to get there?"

How could he imagine that after two days she still did not know the way to the main building? Picking up her dress from the chair across which she had thrown it, she called out, just as he was about to close the door behind him: "Oh, Mr.—er—Grant!"

He halted. "Yes, Mrs. St. Just?"

"Is Mother back?"

"No, Mother is not back. That's why no one came to fetch you earlier. Mother sees to all such things. Without her, we are rather, well, rather like motherless children!" He gave a brief chuckle at what he had clearly intended to be a little joke.

As she toiled up the path to the main building—was this sensation of physical weakness, contrasting with feverish mental activity, an aftermath of her recent stomach upset?—Ruth all at once remembered, with an access of nausea, her dream. Eddying round in it, now asleep and now half asleep, she had been drawn up from it by Warren Grant like some threshing fish from a millrace.

. . . Yet again she had been standing by the waterless swimming pool, but this time it was night, so that all the abandoned objects in it—the bottles, cans, newspapers, rags of clothing, rusty kitchen utensils, broken crockery—might have been floating on a yellow tide of moonlight. From across the pool, from within the house, she could hear the tremulous whine of a harmonica, floating down from the first-floor window of the room in which the two Americans, brother and sister, slept closely, side by side, on the two mattresses. The music was—was . . . What *was* it? Yes, "The Last Rose of Summer." But notes smudged each other, like tints in an amateurish watercolor; they were constantly flattened. It hurt her, hurt her physically, to listen. She stopped gazing up and across at the window, as though by doing so she would somehow cease to hear the sounds coming from it. Instead, she now stared down into the pool.

Then she saw it. It lay with its head resting on the serrated edge of the Heinz baked beans can. It was white. It was vulnerable. It was human. It was—she knew it, from its rictus of agony, so similar to the rat's—dead. Dead. She struggled to move away, she struggled to awaken. She woke briefly. But then, as though she had been pulled out of a tumultuous sea only to be irresistibly sucked back in again, she was once more whirled away in the frothing eddies of that terrible dream.

What did it mean? she asked herself as she walked toward the babble of voices on the other side of the dining room door. The dream was telling her something, as her dreams often did. If she relived it enough and thought about it enough, then she would discover. But now she had no time. Now she must face all these strange, hostile, perhaps even dangerous people, each of them bonded so closely to Mother, grown-up children who could survive only under the awesome shadow of her presence and authority.

"Ah, there you are!" It was Tom, clearly in command in Mother's absence, who rose to greet her. A strip of raw, sunburned skin dangled from the tip of his nose. "My fault. I ought to have sent someone sooner."

"No, it was my fault. I fell asleep."

As Ruth began to gaze about her—the emaciated Finnish boy, Vilho, caught her glance and gave her what struck her as a surprisingly grateful smile—Tom said: "An old friend of yours has come to visit us. Just for one night."

An old friend? Then Ruth saw Diamont, who had pushed back the bench on which he was sitting, with a grating sound of its legs on the cracked, dusty marble floor, and had begun to move toward her, right hand extended. As she took the hand, she felt its deformity, the truncated fingers pressing against her palm. Had he deliberately inflicted that shock? It was the first time he had ever shaken hands with her. "Mrs. St. Just!" he was saying. "I was hoping you'd still be here. Today's Saturday, so I thought I'd make the trip."

His ill-cut hair stuck up in damp tufts. He must have been swimming, she decided. Unless, of course, he had just had a shower. "You came here for the swimming," she said.

"No," he said. "No, I don't swim." Of course! She had forgotten what he had told her about the skin disease that the natives mistook for leprosy. "I came for the company—especially yours. Here!" He pulled the bench back even farther. "Come and sit beside me."

Tom, still standing, called out, presumably to one of the plain, pale French girls, neither of them visible: "Marianne! Marianne!"

The girl appeared. "*Oui?*" she asked sulkily.

Tom merely pointed at Ruth with a forefinger. The girl gave her a baleful look and then went out, the baize door creaking back and forth behind her.

Diamont, reseated beside Ruth, picked up his knife and fork and sliced into the fried fillet of fish before him. He pulled at the small bones revealed, with thumb and deformed forefinger. "This fish is known as *baloumi*. It has a wonderful flavor, but these bones are the devil." He put a chunk of the fish into his mouth, and then began to pull out more bones, his tongue protruding from between his teeth.

Ruth scrutinized him, chin supported on palms and head tilted sideways. His white shirt was too tight, emphasizing those breasts that might belong to a pubescent girl. His thighs were almost hairless, and his shorts cut into them each time he leaned forward for a mouthful.

"So," he said. He smiled at her. "What sort of time have you been having?"

He talked as though she had been on holiday here. She shrugged, turning down the corners of her mouth.

"Find out anything?"

She nodded. "Yes." She was not going to be specific to this man whom she saw as certainly one of Mother's allies and probably one of those involved in the death of her son.

He shook his head, as though in disbelief. "But there's nothing *to* find out! I wish I could persuade you of that."

Ruth thought of the three near-naked boys approaching his house as the car had driven her away from it. "You'd be surprised."

Marianne banged down a plate before her. The portion on it

230

seemed to consist chiefly of the tail of the fish, with some greasy fried potatoes and some kidney beans in a tomato and onion sauce.

"Thank you," Ruth said. But Marianne had gone. Once again the baize door creaked back and forth, as though possessed of the same anger as the girl.

"It's unfortunate I've missed Mother. Things here are never the same without her. My boat passed hers, but I'd no idea she was on board."

"Why did she have to go to Bissance? Have you any idea?"

Did he realize that she was counterchecking? At all events, it was casually that he answered: "Those Americans. Something wrong with their residence permits. Or they failed to get them issued at all. Something like that. The bureaucracy in this country is appalling. They took it over from the French, of course, but unfortunately there are no longer any French to run it. You get a similar situation in the former British colonies."

"When will they come back?"

"No idea. There's a late boat tonight, gets in after midnight. But I'd imagine they'll put up in my house."

Ruth could not conceal her astonishment. "In your house?"

"Yup. I gave Mother a key a long time ago. That way she can use the house whenever she wants, even in the absence of myself and the boy. That's our arrangement. She stays there when she wants, ditto for me here."

Frau Wertheim, who had been slowly masticating her food, with her head lowered, on Diamont's right, now looked up, her pale blue eyes vaguely seeking out Ruth's face. "I have stayed in Mr. Diamont's house." She pronounced his name "Dee-oh-mont." "With Mother," she added. She put a forefinger to her front teeth and then pushed up her upper lip. "I break these teeth. Mother says dentist here is no good. So we go to Frenchman in Bissance."

There was a burst of laughter from Patrice and the old man, usually silent, who wore many rings on his long, slender fingers. The old man shook his head rapidly, leaned sideways, and whispered something into the boy's ear. As Ruth looked at the two, they both looked at her. Then they laughed again, Patrice on a shrill, almost hysterical note. Ruth knew that it was about her that they had been talking and at her that they were laughing. But she resolved not to show that she knew. She pushed her plate aside. She could not eat any more of the greasy fish and fried potatoes. She wondered if Marianne, clearly annoyed by her lateness, had deliberately given her so unappetizing a helping.

The other French girl now flounced in, to remove first Diamont's plate and then Frau Wertheim's. As she leaned across the table, her body interposed between Englishman and German woman, her dress, loose at the neck, fell away to reveal that under it she was wearing nothing else. Her nipples were large and plum-colored. *"Vous avez terminé?"*

"Thank you, yes." Ruth lifted up the plate and handed it to her. The three plates, now piled one on top of the other, all but toppled. The girl made an angry moue, and cried, *"Merde!"* She then lowered the plates again onto the table, placed knives and forks all together on one, and re-formed the stack.

"She will never be a *Hausfrau*," Frau Wertheim said, with a shake of her head and a gentle little smile. "But Mother says that one way to learn to love life is to learn to do the things we hate."

Diamont glanced sideways at Ruth, and then almost imperceptibly raised his eyebrows. He seemed to be saying: "God, these sayings of Mother's!" The momentary disloyalty took Ruth by surprise.

Again Patrice and the old man laughed, even louder than before.

Lips trembling, Ruth stared down the table. Then she asked Diamont: "Why are they laughing?"

Marianne had just set down a bowl of fruit salad, most of it canned, before him. He gave it an unenthusiastic glance, as he replied: "I've no idea. Patrice is always full of silly jokes—a rather childish sense of humor. But the jokes are less harmful now than when he was a delinquent in Cherbourg."

Ruth shook her head, frowning. "It's me they're laughing at.

They first look at me and then they burst out laughing. Why? What is it? What's the reason?"

"Oh, I don't think it's anything to do with you. You're just imagining it." He plunged his spoon into the fruit salad and raised it to his mouth. Mouth full, he went on: "You know, Mrs. St. Just, I'd say you've got a pretty powerful imagination. A novelist's imagination."

He too, in his more subtle way, was laughing at her.

Angrily Ruth turned away from him and gazed down the long table to where, at its farthest end, Lucy—in a bright green dress that fell off her bony shoulders, and long earrings, each a green glass globe the size of a pigeon's egg—was talking animatedly to Vilho. Vilho nodded lethargically, gave his slow, sweet smile, nodded again, said nothing. Soon he would have another fix. Soon after that, another. Soon, soon, soon. Soon he would die. *Do what you will is the whole of the law.* Do what you will to kill yourself. All at once she was again consumed with pity for the sad, tormented, emaciated boy. Somehow she must save him.

Diamont had caught the direction of her glance. He leaned toward her and whispered: "Lucy looks even more outrageous than ever tonight. All that green eye shadow and all those green baubles. She wants me to take her to Les Pirates."

"What's that?"

"The Pirates."

"No, I wasn't asking for a translation. What is it? A nightclub?"

"I suppose you could call it that. The only one on the island. Care to come?"

Ruth calculated. She still felt the lethargy of her walk up from the annex but not, now that she had eaten some of the greasy food and drunk a lot of the thin, chill wine, as acutely as before. If she did not go with them, she would probably pass the evening alone. She did not want to lie out on that hard, lumpy bed, trying to read by the inadequate light of the lamp, while the mosquitoes whined around her. Much less did she want again to dream, sucked down into that vertiginous whirlpool full of images which all seemed to hold some arcane message, as though in a code to which she still lacked the key. "All right," she at last said. Then, realizing how ungracious that must sound, she added: "Why not? Sounds fun. I never thought I'd go to a nightclub in Saloum. It's years since I went to one in England."

Pushing back the bench so violently that he all but dislodged Ruth, Diamont half stood up to shout down the table: "Lucy! Lucy! Mrs. St. Just would like to come with us to Les Pirates."

"Oh, lovely," Lucy called back in a bored, nasal voice between clenched teeth, clearly not thinking the prospect of Ruth's company anything of the kind.

"Ought I to smarten up?" Ruth asked Diamont, conscious that her dress needed ironing and her shoes needed polishing.

"If you want to." It was obvious that he thought she ought to.

XVI

RUTH WAS WEARING a black silk dress, black pumps, which she had had difficulty in getting into, since the heat had caused her feet to swell, and a large, circular brooch, an eighteenth-century cameo in a Victorian setting, pinned on one breast.

Holding open the door of the car for her, Diamont said: "I hope that brooch isn't valuable."

Ruth touched it. "It's about the only family heirloom I have left."

"In that case, I'm not sure it's all that wise to wear it."

"Oh, do you think someone might steal it? Would it be better to leave it in my room?"

He pulled a face and shrugged.

"It's just as likely to get stolen there," Lucy said. "Anyway, no thief in Ellampore would know its value. I'm far more likely to have these earrings ripped off me. And they're just glass."

The two women sat side by side in the back, with Diamont alone in the front. That was how he had seemed to want it.

Lucy turned to Ruth, again looking her up and down. "You look smashing," she said. "Very much the lady, of course." She grinned impudently. "But smashing." She put a hand over Ruth's knee and gave it a squeeze.

"Thank you."

"And so do you, Eugene," she told Diamont, who was still wearing the open-necked shirt and shorts.

He realized she was teasing him, and clearly did not care for it. "Ought to have changed. But in this heat . . ."

"I'm surprised you've brought your car just for a weekend," Ruth said.

"Oh, it gives me a certain freedom. From the community. Even from Mother. If either gets too much for me."

"Didn't you bring your driver?" Lucy asked.

"Nope. Gave him the weekend off. His family lives somewhere out in the bush."

"He's a real dish," Lucy said. "And I'm ravenous. Pity."

"No doubt you'll find lots of dishes at Les Pirates."

"One can only live in hope." Again Lucy's hand squeezed Ruth's knee. "Nice scent. Sometime you must let me borrow some of it."

"Of course."

A pall of dust had settled over the town, so that the widely spaced street lamps seemed even dimmer than usual, and the sea, from time to time glimpsed in the distance between trees or houses, was faint and blurred. Diamont had lapsed into a sulky torpor, as—low in his seat, shoulders hunched, and face set in a constant scowl—he stared out at the winding road ahead. When some cart drawn by a donkey, some group of obviously tipsy youths, or some mischievous children, grimacing, waving, and eventually running along beside the car, obliged him to slow down, he would press irritably on the horn for seconds on end.

At one moment, when they were stationary behind a dust-coated bus—the passengers in the rear were all staring out at them, grinning—a child carrying a long wand of sugarcane lashed out with it at the rear mudguard. Clearly the action was a joke. But Diamont at once jumped out of the car, leaving the engine running, and set off in pursuit. The boy, thinking that this was also a joke, scampered zigzag among the crowds of people alighting from the bus, turned to put out an extremely long tongue, made a gesture of shaking his balls with a hand, laughed uproariously, and vanished from sight.

Puffing, Diamont returned. "Little pest," he muttered.

Lucy gave a raucous neigh.

"It's all right for you to laugh. You won't have to pay for the damage. This isn't the Consulate car. This is my car."

Again Lucy gave the same raucous neigh, looking sideways at Ruth for approval. "No damage has been done, Eugene."

"How the hell do you know that? You can't see from where you're sitting."

Having left the town, they began to bump over an unmade road through countryside that seemed strangely deserted and forlorn. Beyond stretches of marshland, the sea was a milky streak. Each time the car hit some particularly bad bump, Lucy would let out a little scream and clutch hold of Ruth.

"Oh, for God's sake!" Diamont eventually exclaimed in exasperation. "Do you have to carry on like that?"

"I don't *have* to. But I like to." Lucy seemed to be set on annoying him.

Les Pirates was a circular, thatched building, close to the sea, with some huts roofed with corrugated iron clustering around it. Parked haphazardly like toy cars thrown down by a child were a number of small Citroëns, Renaults, Volkswagens, and three long American limousines, one with a driver asleep at its wheel. Diamont did not bother to park his car any more tidily than the others.

Tumbling rather than clambering out, Lucy ran a hand through her chrysanthemum of hair. She turned to Ruth: "Do I look a perfect fright?"

The truthful answer would have been yes. But Ruth said: "No, of course not. You look fine."

"No one's going to care a damn how you look," Diamont told her rudely. "Stop being so self-conscious."

An urchin, with scabs on his chin and bare arms, came over with the usual offer to mind the car. Diamont sighed, then agreed irritably: *"Bien, bien!"*

At the door, a man dressed as a pirate, his chest bare but for an embroidered waistcoat and his belly bulging mountainously under cotton pantaloons, waddled forward. A cloth painted with a skull and crossbones had been tied so low over his forehead that it was impossible to see his eyebrows. Clearly he knew Diamont; he linked his own arm in his and drew him close as they entered the crowded, smoky room. By a fortunate chance he had a table just for them, he explained. Another time they ought to book. He turned to Ruth and, showing his large, irregular teeth in purple gums, he said: *"Ami, ami, mon ami,"* as he hugged Diamont even closer.

"The owner," Lucy explained. "A terrible old crook. Has his finger in every kind of criminal activity from burglary to prostitution."

The owner turned to grin at Lucy, nodding his head vigorously. There was no way of telling whether he had understood what she had said and was flattered by it, or whether he had understood nothing and had imagined something much less libelous.

"Please, madame." He pulled back a rattan chair for Ruth. His half-naked body, so near to hers, had that gamey odor, by no means unpleasant, which she had by now come to know so well.

"Thank you."

"Champagne, monsieur?"

Crossly, Diamont shook his head.

"Scotch?"

Diamont turned to Ruth, ignoring Lucy. "Scotch?"

"Some wine, if that's possible, please."

"I'd like some Scotch," Lucy said. But again ignoring her, Diamont ordered wine.

"Et des fruits?"

"Bien, bien."

Ruth was gazing about her. For the most part, the customers were black. Everyone was well dressed, the woman usually in gauzy, lacy white, as though for a communal wedding. Like the owner, the waiters were all in pirate costume, many displaying the sort of physiques that in Europe would be seen in such numbers only at a bodybuilding contest.

Ruth could hear the sea behind her shushing inward, then crashing down on the sand, and then withdrawing with a strange rustle, as of dead leaves being blown across gravel. There was such a desolation to this sound of constant withdrawal and resurgence, eventually obliterating for her all the din inside the room, that Ruth was glad when five men, also dressed as pirates, clearly the band, shuffled in through the door to what she took to be the kitchen. One was wiping his mouth on the back of his hand, another belched with no attempt at concealment. They must have been eating.

The men mounted a dais, in no hurry, as they chatted now to each other and now to the customers nearest them, negligently took their seats, picked up their instruments, and mopped at their foreheads or the palms of their hands with clean white handkerchiefs.

Diamont leaned across to Ruth. "They play atrociously. But never mind."

"Are you going to dance with me?" Lucy asked, as a tall, thin man, an accordion strapped to him, struck up the first notes.

Diamont yet again ignored her. "Strange to come all this way to hear the sort of music you could hear in some dive in Toulon or Marseilles."

Couples were getting to their feet with a strange formality, the men putting out hands to lead their women. A waiter set down a bottle of wine, already opened, and three glasses, which he had been holding by their stems in a cluster in one fist. Diamont pointed at the bottle and said something not in French but in one of the three vernaculars that Ruth had been told were spoken in

Saloum. Visibly annoyed, the waiter picked up the bottle again and went off with it to the kitchen.

"He should open the bottle before me," Diamont said. "I'm certainly not going to drink the dregs from other people's bottles and even glasses."

Lucy had now swiveled her chair around in such a way that, her back to Ruth and Diamont, she was facing the dance floor and the band on its narrow dais.

Having returned, the waiter ostentatiously bent over to display the bottle to Diamont. Diamont nodded curtly. The waiter stepped back, inserted a corkscrew, and, breathing heavily through his nose, jerked the corkscrew out. The cork broke off, with at least a half of it still embedded. The waiter smiled, whether in pleasure or embarrassment, Ruth could not have said.

"Oh, bugger!" Diamont exclaimed.

Again the waiter inserted the corkscrew and, after repeated efforts, grunting and gasping, he eventually managed to dislodge the remaining piece of cork. *"Monsieur?"* He held the bottle over Diamont's glass and poured out half an inch of wine.

Impatiently, without tasting it, Diamont gestured at Ruth's glass, saying what she presumed to be the local equivalent of: "Oh, get on with it!"

Having filled all three glasses, the waiter went off, to return with a large cut-glass bowl of fruit. There were mangoes, smelling of turpentine, small red bananas, and a bunch of grapes with drops of water glistening on them.

Diamont pulled off a grape and popped it in his mouth. "Have something," he said to Ruth.

Ruth took one of the bananas and began to peel it. Diamont eyed her. Then he said approvingly: "A good choice. Safe. You won't get an upset stomach from a banana."

Lucy had started up a conversation with one of the male dancers, half in atrocious French and half in a rapid, slangy English, which he clearly did not understand. He was a large man, in a baggy white linen suit, white shirt, and white tie; a ring with a chunky red stone was on the middle finger of his left hand.

Despite the tribal scars on his forehead and cheeks, he was extremely handsome. The tiny woman dancing with him, clearly much older than he was, smiled nervously now at him and now at Lucy.

"Lucy has got off," Diamont said. "That doesn't surprise me. Have you ever known anyone so brazen?"

Ruth pulled off a grape from the bunch and sucked on it. The juice, cold and sour, seemed to fizz in her mouth.

The two dancers had moved on. Swiveling back in her chair, Lucy said to Ruth, not to Diamont: "Not bad, that one. Not at all bad. Wouldn't you agree, Ruth?"

Ruth merely smiled.

"God, Lucy, you're incorrigible. No wonder you were the toast of the lower deck. Isn't she incorrigible?" Suddenly his mood had improved. He raised his glass. "To your health, ladies."

Silently Ruth raised her glass and sipped from it. Meanwhile, leaning across the table, Lucy crashed her glass against Diamont's with so much force that it was a miracle both did not shatter.

The band had embarked on another number, with a noisy rock beat. Lucy began to sway from side to side in her chair, raising her large, clumsy hands in an imitation of playing the maracas. "This is all so wonderfully out of date. But, oh, how I love it, love it!"

Diamont was now looking neither at her nor at Ruth, nor even at the band and the dancers, but furtively sideways, at a table set in a corner. Ruth followed his gaze. There were two young black adults, he in a white cotton suit and she in a full-skirted white dress, her hair straightened and pulled taut from a center part into a bun. Beside them were two children, a boy in a sailor suit and a girl in a dress similar to her mother's, her fingernails painted crimson and her hair tied in bows of crimson ribbon. Eyes lowered, both children were greedily scooping ice cream out of high glasses.

Suddenly Diamont realized that Ruth was also watching the quartet. But instead of showing any embarrassment, as she had expected, he merely smiled at her: "Aren't the children here beautiful? It's a pity that most of them grow up to be so ugly."

A man had appeared, perspiring freely, on Diamont's right. He bent down, one hand on the back of Diamont's chair. It was the dancer with whom Lucy had carried on her badinage. It soon became clear that he was asking Diamont if he might dance with her.

Diamont threw back his head and laughed. Then he waved a hand in Lucy's direction. *"Volontiers, volontiers!"* he said, adding in English: "Take her, take her. I'm prepared to give her away to anyone with the proverbial pound of tea."

Lucy pulled a face at him. Then she rose, giving a reassuring pat to her bouffant wig, grabbed the astonished man by the hand, and dragged him, at a run, onto the floor of genteel dancers. At first, as she circled him, shaking her shoulders and bending at the knees, he was all too clearly embarrassed. Then, infected by her desperate high spirits, he too began to leap about the floor, in time to the accelerating beat of the music.

People at the surrounding tables began to clap and shout encouragement at the couple, while the other dancers, sheepish and in a few cases even shocked or affronted, began to drift back to their seats. Eventually Lucy and her partner were alone. With her mouth stretched wide and her tongue protruding between her teeth, she was grinning wickedly. The man, sweat glistening on his scarred forehead and cheeks, was grinning back at her. Their hands joined, separated, joined again. He swung Lucy up into the air, making her emit a shrill scream, as though on a switchback. Then he pulled her to him, as though she were some huge, ungainly doll on the end of an elastic string. Again she whirled away, again she bounced back. Ranged along the walls, the owner and the waiters were also watching. Then they were joined by a number of kitchen hands, clad in nothing but shorts, many of them barefooted. One of these had emerged through the service door holding a dripping ladle. Another had a mountainous chef's hat, stained from long use, balanced on top of his egg-shaped head.

Ruth heard laughter behind her. She turned. Beyond the windowless arches of the room was a circular verandah, and beyond that a palisade woven of palm branches. Above this palisade, she could make out faces in which only the teeth and the whites of the eyes were in focus, the rest blurred. She thought: Here, in this room, is civilization—or what we regard as civilization. Out there is the jungle, waiting to strangle and devour us. The palisade is so flimsy.

Lucy's partner was now whirling her round and round, his hands at her waist and her legs high off the floor. Lucy's eyelids, lurid with green eye shadow, were closed; her mouth gaped open, like that of a fish when it has been jerked from its element. The green balls of glass dangling from her ears caught the light and returned it in jagged splinters.

Again Ruth looked back over her shoulder. A shrouded figure had somehow clambered up onto the palisade and was now crouched there, head and shoulders above all the watching faces. Ruth stared, her eyes widening in terror.

Diamont followed her gaze. "Oh, they're always there," he said. "It's a kind of allegory of life. Those within and those looking in from without. Sometimes the two groups change places. But not all that often." It was eerie to hear him voice what had been approximately her own thoughts a few moments before. Somehow it made the presence of that figure on the palisade even weirder.

Diamont turned away from her. He put out a hand, plucked another grape, and popped it in his mouth.

"That man," Ruth said. Her voice wobbled, however much she tried to steady it.

"Yes?" He gave her a glance, looked away, and then looked back at her, in a delayed reaction of concern. "Which man?"

"That man on the fence. Over there." She pointed. "He's been following me. A beggar. First he was in Siné, then Bissance, then here."

"It can't possibly be the same one. How could it be? Where would he get the money to travel all those distances? This country's full of beggars. They all look much alike. Some have shriveled arms, some have shriveled legs, some are blind, some"—he hesitated—"have loathsome skin diseases. There's a terrible monotony about human suffering in any part of the world, but more here in Africa than anywhere else."

"But it *is* the same man. I know it's the same man." Her voice rose, broke. Diamont stared at her, eyes narrowed. "Why does he keep following me? What does he want? Who is he?" The words tumbled from her with sudden obstructions, often between one syllable and the next. She had gripped his forearm as it rested along the edge of the table.

He spoke firmly, as though to a child who had awakened screaming from a night terror. "Now don't be silly. No one's following you, certainly not that beggar. Or any beggar. If you were a Getty, I suppose a beggar might just follow you the length of Saloum. But why on earth do you suppose. . . ?" He broke off, his gaze returning to the dance floor. The music had stopped, and Lucy, face flushed and with dark stains of perspiration under the arms of her dress, was being led by her beaming partner to a table at the far end of the restaurant. The tiny woman with whom the man had originally been dancing and three other men, all in white suits and gaudily patterned ties, smiled up at Lucy as she approached. She put out a hand and roguishly raked it through the brilliantined coiffure of one of the men. He laughed in delight.

"So many odd things have happened to me here. Odd, frightening. At first they seemed to be just coincidences. . . . But one after the other . . ."

But Diamont, still gazing across at the far table, was not listening to her. "We shan't see Lucy back at this table, that's for sure. I doubt if she'll even come home with us." He gave a derisive laugh. "I'd say she's set herself up for the night. Wouldn't you?"

Ruth was looking back over her shoulder again. Everyone, as though at a prearranged signal, had suddenly vanished from the palisade. Perhaps some watchman had dislodged them? Through the chinks in the woven branches, Ruth could see the glitter of waves as they swept in on the beach.

"He's gone." She felt a great relief. But also, strangely, she felt a disappointment.

243

"Oh? Has he?" Although vague in his response, Diamont had heard her this time. He peered. "They've all gone. This is late for them, you know. They start work at first break of day."

The owner waddled over. Body tilted backward, legs wide apart, and huge belly thrust out before him, he looked like a woman in the last month of pregnancy. His small eyes glittered under the absurd skull-and-crossbones scarf. "*Tout va bien?*" he asked in a French that made it seem as if he were clearing his throat to spit as he uttered it. He put an arm round Diamont's shoulder, and then raised a hand to pinch his cheek. Diamont's immediate reaction was one of pleasure; then he began to blush in embarrassment. "*Joli garçon, très joli,*" the owner said. "*Mais méchant, très méchant.*" He picked up Lucy's half-finished glass of wine, tipped it up at his lips, and drained it. He winked at Ruth. "*Bon vin! Bon!*"

As he waddled off, Ruth put a hand to her forehead. The band had just struck up again. "All this noise is giving me a headache. Are we going to stay much longer?"

"No longer than you want. I've had enough myself. And as I was saying, Lucy seems to have fixed herself up for the night."

Even while he was speaking, there were screams from the far end of the room. Having jumped to her feet, Lucy had begun to belabor her partner about the head with her handbag, shrilling "*Bête, bête, bête!*" He raised his arms to shield himself. It was all a joke, and everyone at her table and the surrounding tables was laughing.

Diamont clicked his fingers at a passing waiter, who swept on, ignoring him. "*Garçon!*" he called to another. He too swept by. Finally Diamont attracted the owner's notice.

"It can't be this much," he said, scowling down at the bill, when at last it was before him. "Unless, of course, Lucy has been ordering drinks and telling them to . . . Oh, what the hell! I can't be bothered." He pulled a wad of notes, soggy with sweat, out of the back pocket of his shorts. He peeled off three. "That should be okay. No one could say that either the wine or the service was brilliant."

"Let me pay my share."

"I wouldn't dream of it. No, no!"

Diamont got heavily to his feet. As she got to hers, Ruth once again looked back over her shoulder, out toward the palisade. But apart from a wolfish dog, sitting on its haunches beside the fence, as though on guard, there was no one there now.

Diamont had noticed where she was looking. "No, he's not there." His tone combined mockery and exasperation. "Your beggar isn't there. Never was there, if you ask me." He crossed stiffly to the table at which Lucy was sprawled. Her head lay on the shoulder of another of the men and her long legs stretched out before her; her dress was rucked up to her thighs. "We're on our way," he said.

Lucy waved a dismissive hand. "Then on your way, Buster!"

Her former partner jumped up, put an arm around Diamont's shoulder, and gave him a vigorous hug. Seemingly as drunk as Lucy, he began to say something in slurred, hissing French, nodding his head up and down as he did so. Then he pointed at Lucy and got out: *"Elle est ma soeur. Ma très chère soeur."*

"Idiot!" Diamont exclaimed, as he and Ruth walked away. She did not know if he was referring to the man or to Lucy.

Outside, Diamont peered around him, as though he had forgotten where he had left his car. From the shadows a tiny figure pattered up, to grab him by the side of his shorts with what was more a prehensile claw than a hand. *"Msieur! Msieur!"* The boy clinging to him, Diamont let himself be guided. When he reached the car, he inspected it from all angles; only then, satisfied that it had suffered no damage, he put a hand into his pocket and pulled out some coins.

The boy took the coins greedily. Then, having looked at them in his cupped palm, he shrilled out: *"Non, non! Encore plus! Encore plus!"*

Diamont negligently tossed a few more coins into the dust, where the boy went down onto his haunches to scrabble for them.

Starting the car, Diamont muttered: "Poor little bugger! What a life! But he's luckier than most. That concession must be worth something."

"Do you think Lucy'll be all right?"

"Lucy? Of course. All those years before the mast must have taught her how to look after herself."

"I wonder if we shouldn't have waited for her."

"Oh, she'd finished with us. Lucy's pretty ruthless." He swerved to avoid a truck that had lurched out of a dark side street into the main road, its driver hooting frenziedly. "God, these drivers! Apes would be better at it."

Ruth had begun to feel an increasing tightness about the temples, an increasing throbbing behind her left eye. It was odd that she had not had the usual warning symptom of visual disturbance before the pain started. She opened her bag and searched in it for her pills. But she had forgotten to bring them.

Diamont's voice swept in and out, with a shushing sound, like the sea beyond the restaurant palisade: "One can't . . . help . . . admiring Lucy. . . . A mad . . . kind of . . . courage . . . To do . . . what she did . . . is something that . . . I just can't understand . . . but I suppose . . ."

Ruth leaned her head back against the upholstery. She gave a small, involuntary groan.

"Anything the matter?"

"Just a migraine. I'm used to them. Perhaps I've had too much sun. Perhaps all this noise . . ."

"You mustn't overstretch yourself."

Overstretch herself? What did he mean? And what was all that about Lucy and a mad kind of courage, and her having done something that he just couldn't understand? She knew that sometime, somehow, she must work both these things out. But for the moment the pain was too severe for her to do more than rest her head against the upholstery and feel the car bucking and rearing like some mettlesome horse over the potholed road. From time to time, she became aware of Diamont glancing across at her with pitying, fastidious distaste.

On their arrival, Ruth staggered out of the car. She looked up at the windows of the main building. A lamp burned in one of the top-floor rooms, as she had seen it mysteriously burn there late on her first night in the annex.

"I wonder if Mother and the Americans are back."

Diamont looked at his watch. "The late boat won't have got in yet. And I doubt if she'll have taken it. Rarely does."

Ruth began to walk toward the front door. "Perhaps I'll go up and see."

"No, no." Firmly he gripped her arm. "Much too late. She won't be there, and if she is there, she certainly won't want company or conversation now. I'll walk you back to your annex." He gripped her arm more tightly—the next morning, under the lukewarm shower, she would see his fingerprints, a greenish purple, on her soft flesh—and propelled her down the path. "Have you got something to take for your migraine?"

"Yes, yes, I have." Her voice was forlorn.

"Good."

"Where are you staying?"

"I? Oh, I'm in the main building. That's where Mother usually puts me."

Ruth imagines what will follow on his return to that building. The images and sounds sparkle and crackle like fireworks in her aching head.

. . . He knocks on the locked door.

"Who is it?"

"Eugene."

"Oh, Eugene!"

The key turns in the door, it opens. Mother is wearing a nightgown, so transparent that the dark aureoles of her nipples and her darker sex are visible through it.

"I just thought I'd look in before going to bed."

"I hoped you would. How did you get on?"

"Oh, Lucy took up with this man. So I jettisoned her. Or, rather, she jettisoned us. I only wish I could have jettisoned the other one. But no man would be interested in *her*, would he?" They both laugh. "She's a dreary one, that," he adds.

"And dangerous."

"Yes, dangerous." . . .

The annex was dark. Presumably Frau Wertheim had long since gone to bed.

"Is there a lamp in your room? I didn't think about one."

The moonlight was so bright that they could see each other's faces as they stood in the silent corridor, the front door open beside them.

"Yes. But I'm not sure I've got my lighter." She began to look in her bag. "I think I must have left it on the restaurant table when I smoked my last cigarette."

"Then you won't see it again." He patted a pocket of his shorts. "Never mind, I have a box of matches. I always remember to carry matches with me when I come here. Matches and a bottle of whiskey. Both essential."

He began to walk ahead of her down the corridor, the back of his head silhouetted by the moonlight. Ruth thought: He knows which is my room! How does he know that?

Unerringly he went to it and, not waiting for her, opened the door and entered. She followed. He scratched a match on the box. It spurted briefly into flame, then went out. He threw it away from him. "Christ! The matches they make here!" He lit another, shielded its flame, and stooped to the lamp. As he adjusted the wick, he said: "That seems all right." He turned to her, smiling: "How is your head?"

"Oh, better." In her growing unease, she had forgotten about it. But at his reminder, she once again felt that tightness around the temples and that jagged throbbing behind her left eye.

"You need a good night's sleep. I'll leave you to it." He backed toward the door.

"Thank you," she said. "Good night."

"Good night."

She stood listening to his footfalls slowly receding down the corridor. Then the front door clicked behind him. She seated herself on the edge of the bed and eased off first one shoe and then the other. There was a purple line, like an incision, where they had bitten into the flesh of her insteps. Slowly she began to draw down the zipper of her dress. What was it he had said about Lucy? She saw those wide mannish shoulders and those large mannish hands. She saw the long legs sticking out into the dance floor, with their knobbly knees and outsize feet. She saw that orange chrysanthemum wig. Lucy was dancing, the hands of her tall, burly partner at her waist. He hoisted her up into the air, then whirled her round and round in a circle. Lucy was belaboring him with her handbag. Lucy was speaking in that deep North Country voice of hers.

Of course! Suddenly it came to her, even as she once again felt the hand squeezing her knee in the car, and once again heard that deep North Country voice telling her of quitting a cruise ship, of coming here, of finding both freedom and herself. Finding herself. He had found herself. That was how he and she—Luke and Lucy?—might have put it.

Seated on the edge of the bed, her fingers pressed to her trembling lips, she sees and hears it unroll before her.

. . . "Do what you will is the whole of the law. But do you really will it, want it?"

"Yes, yes, I do. All my life I've willed it and wanted it. Otherwise I'll never be happy."

"You shall be happy. There's this surgeon here, this brilliant surgeon. He's a friend of mine. Dr. Leroi. If you really will it and want it, then he'll bring it to pass."

"I'll be reborn."

"Yes, you'll be reborn. With me as your mother." . . .

Again Ruth sees and hears it unroll before her.

. . . "She knows too much." It is Mother speaking.

Or is it Eugene Diamont speaking?

Or Dr. Leroi?

No, no, that's not it! (Never mind who is speaking.)

"He knows too much."

It is Jim, her darling Jim, not she, who knows too much. He

dived not into the rock pool but into something far more murky and dangerous. He died by an accident not of nature but of knowledge.

And she, too, has now dived into that same abyss.

XVII

MOTHER WAS SEATED, legs tucked under her, on a cushion on the floor, neatly darning a minute hole in the sleeve of one of the silk tunics that she wore hanging loose outside her Oriental-style trousers.

Ruth stood in the doorway, the door open behind her. "I didn't know you were back," she said accusingly.

Mother gave a small smile, then lowered her head and bit off the thread between her small, even teeth. "Then why did you come up to my room?"

"When did you get back?"

"About an hour ago. We took the same boat that you took when you came here last Tuesday. We missed the one last night, so we stayed in the house of a friend."

"In Mr. Diamont's house."

"Yes, that's right. In Mr. Diamont's house." She extended a hand and slowly beckoned. "Why don't you come and sit down? Why stand there?"

Ruth came in, but instead of sitting on one of the cushions arranged around Mother, she went over to the window and sat on the bare wood of the floor, her back against the wall and her legs stretched out before her. Her mouth felt dry, the skin of her face scaly and taut. "I had to see you."

"Yes." Mother looked up from scrupulously folding the blouse on the floor before her.

Ruth ran her tongue over her lower lip. "Yesterday—I saw

something so strange. I came here to tell you. But you'd already left."

"And what did you see?"

Before Ruth could answer, a door on her left, which she had always assumed to lead to Mother's bedroom, jerked open. Lucy, her head bound with a scarf and her face devoid of makeup, so that she looked much as she had looked on the previous day on her way to the shower, stood there, a mop in one hand and a bucket beside her. She made no acknowledgment of Ruth, as though, now reduced to the status of servant, it would be improper of her to do so. "I've done the bedroom. Is there anything else?"

"The bathroom." Then Mother added, as though as an after-thought: "Please."

Lucy disappeared.

Mother looked across at Ruth. "Yes?"

"Yesterday afternoon I went for a walk."

"Silly to walk in the afternoon sun. That way you'll make yourself ill. You're not used to it. You should have a siesta—or read quietly in your room."

Ruth braced her back against the wall and stretched her legs to their fullest extent. "I came to this settlement. This little settlement." Head tilted to one side, she eyed Mother askance in search of some betraying reaction.

But Mother merely nodded. "Yes, there are a number of native families squatting on the land. People tell me that either I should force them to pay some kind of rent or I should evict them." She shrugged. "But they do no harm. And anyway they haven't the money to pay rent." She picked up the folded blouse and stroked it as it rested over the crook of her arm. "They were here before we came. They'll be here long after we've gone."

"There was a baby." Again Ruth sought for some reaction from Mother.

"They breed like rabbits. But, of course, they also die like flies. The rate of infant mortality is appalling, as is the birthrate. Dr.

251

Leroi had started a number of immunization programs. But they just can't see the point of bringing their children to the hospital to have needles stuck into them. There was this child, it was obviously dying. Dr. Leroi prescribed something for it when I called him. It didn't have to die. But the parents just never gave it the antibiotic pills. I think they were more frightened of those pills than of the child's death."

"This baby was white."

"*White?*" Mother looked and sounded convincingly incredulous. She was cool, oh so cool, and oh so clever.

"Yes, white."

"I think you must have imagined that. You tend to imagine things, don't you, Ruth?" Her head to one side, she smiled at Ruth.

"I didn't imagine it. I saw a white baby, lying out there in the dirt, with flies crawling over it. And then, when this old woman saw that I'd seen it, she snatched it up and hurried away with it into a hut."

Mother frowned, drawing down the corners of her mouth. "Well, there *are* albinos, you know. It could have been an albino, I suppose. Not impossible."

"It looked like that baby belonging to those Americans."

Mother laughed outright. Then her face clouded over, as though at last, belatedly, Ruth had succeeded in touching on a nerve. "Americans?"

"That brother and sister—Arlen and Harriet."

"It could hardly have been *that* baby, since they and the baby came with me to Bissance. In any case, why would they leave her in charge of some natives? A number of people here would have been perfectly capable of looking after her, and perfectly willing." She raised her eyebrows in interrogation.

"That's what I wondered. Why?"

Mother said nothing, merely staring at her.

Ruth repeated: "Why?"

Still Mother stared at her, with a disquieting intentness.

"Did they give the baby away?" Ruth demanded.

"Of course they didn't!" Mother laughed. But her unease was obvious.

Ruth twisted her hands in her lap, suddenly losing all composure. "Things are going on here," she said. "Terrible things. Not just the death of my son, not just that. I've found so many terrible things here."

Mother rose to her feet, with the agility of a teenage girl. "Really, I can't listen to all this nonsense, I'm afraid. No, really, I can't. I've tried to do my best for you, to help you as best I could. But it's—it's beyond me. Quite beyond me."

Ruth now also rose. Staggering and all but falling, she put out a hand to the window ledge for support. "You've done nothing to help me. You've obstructed me at every turn. Tried to pull the wool over my eyes. Thought me an utter fool."

"Oh, for heaven's sake!" Then, the blouse over an arm, Mother crossed over to the door to the bedroom, opened it, and disappeared. Ruth could hear her talking to Lucy, but what they were saying she could not make out, strenuously though she tried.

Mother returned. "Lucy's going to make us a tisane. It may soothe your nerves."

"What is it?"

"One of the native remedies. Something I often take. The old man—the one who traveled on the boat with you—brought it to me. He always does, it's from his part of the country. Good for the nerves."

"My nerves don't need soothing."

"The death of your son, these long journeys in a totally strange environment, the heat, isolation . . . I think it's all been a little too much for you." She went up to Ruth and took her gently by the forearms. "Come on, Ruth. Sit down, relax."

Ruth jerked herself free. Then she lowered herself again to the floor, her back to the wall.

Mother looked down at her. "Poor Ruth. Jim told me you were—not strong."

"I'm sure Jim told you nothing of the kind. I'm extremely

strong, I always have been. How do you think I brought him up virtually singlehanded for all those years, when his father couldn't be bothered with him?"

Still Mother stared down at her. Then she turned away with a light sigh. "Yes, you've had a tough life."

Ruth loathed her for the pity in her voice. "Because I sacrificed so much for Jim, he became particularly dear to me. Sacrifice has that effect."

Lucy came in with two cups on a round lacquered tray. Her large, clumsy body dipped downward, until her head was on the same level as Ruth's. "This is wonderful stuff," she said, as though she were a hospital nurse offering a patient a pill. "You'll see. One of nature's cures. I often take it myself when I feel that things are getting too much for me. Much better than Librium!"

Ruth was about to take the cup nearer to her. Then some instinct made her reach for the other one. She watched closely as Lucy then dipped down in the same way beside Mother, and Mother put out a small, ivory-colored hand and took the remaining cup. She raised it to her lips, she sipped ruminatively.

Ruth sipped too. Involuntarily she swallowed. Then she banged the cup down on the floor beside her. "It's bitter!"

Lucy had gone. Mother said: "Oh, don't let that put you off. I find it rather pleasant, in fact—that bitterness. You can have some sugar, if you like."

"No. No, thank you." Ruth pushed the cup away from her, splashing some of the liquid into the saucer.

Mother sipped again, her eyes on Ruth. "I wish I knew what to do for you."

"Tell me the truth."

Mother sighed. She opened her mouth, as though about to say something, and then clearly decided not to.

"Tell me the truth," Ruth repeated.

Mother ignored her. "Drink that, my dear." Ruth shook her head. "It can't possibly do you any harm, and it may do you some good. Go on." Ruth remained obstinately silent, gazing up at

Mother with eyes heavy with suspicion. "Have you any pills of your own?"

"Pills? What kind of pills?"

Mother looked embarrassed, as she turned her head sideways to gaze out of the window. "Well—tranquilizers."

"Tranquilizers? But I don't need tranquilizers! Why should I need tranquilizers?" Suddenly Ruth felt her mouth filling with bitterness. She knew she should have spat out that first sip, not swallowed it. Like a cold, clammy snake—she had dreamed of such a snake, she remembered it now—fear glided through her entrails. "I'd like to see the baby."

Mother was disconcerted. "Well, I suppose that sometime . . ."

"Now."

"Now?" Mother was taken aback.

"Yes, now."

"But perhaps Arlen and Harriet may not want—"

"Why shouldn't they want me to see the baby? I want to make sure—make sure they still have her."

Mother heaved a sigh. "Very well," she said, rising once more to her feet. She crossed over to Ruth and put out a hand to pull her off the floor. But Ruth did not take the hand; she first went on all fours, then raised her torso, and then scrambled up. At the effort her face grew congested. "But nothing convinces you of anything," Mother went on. "Does it? So what's the point of showing you the baby? You'll only decide that they've reclaimed it, or substituted another baby for it, or—oh, God knows what else you'd imagine."

"I want to see it. I'd recognize it."

"Would you? One baby looks very like another, if it's not your own. Ah, well! Never mind!" Mother crossed gracefully, taking small, swift steps, to the door of the bedroom. "Lucy, if anyone wants me, I've just gone down to the Americans. I'm taking Ruth with me."

Again Ruth felt that bitterness welling up within her and flooding her mouth. But this time, instead of swallowing it, she drew a handkerchief from the pocket of her dress, held it to her lips, and spat twice. There was an icy sweat breaking out on her forehead, and it seemed as if at any moment her legs would buckle under her.

"Are you really all right?" Mother had drawn close to her and taken her arm.

Ruth jerked herself free. "Yes, of course I'm all right!"

The staircase, as the two of them descended it in silence, seemed interminable to Ruth; it was far narrower and steeper than she recollected from her previous journeys up and down. What had been in that cup from which she had sipped? Mother must have known that, suspecting something, she would reach for the cup farther from her. She was cool, oh so cool, and oh so clever.

"It's crazy to come out in this heat. This really is a fool's errand." Mother put up a hand to adjust her dark glasses. "Haven't you got your dark glasses?"

"Forgotten them."

"No wonder you're not well. No one from a temperate country should go out without dark glasses in a subtropical one."

But Ruth had often seen Mother out in the glare of midday without dark glasses. "I'm perfectly well." It was not true. She was experiencing a growing sense of nausea, her bowels were contracting in increasingly painful spasms. Ruth thought: Am I dying? Am I dying? Is this what they did to Jim?

They approached the dry swimming pool and began to walk around it. Ruth, stumbling along beside Mother, caught the toe of her shoe in a crack in the surrounding tiles and all but pitched forward.

Mother put out a hand. "For heaven's sake! Do be careful! We don't want you falling in. That would really be the last straw."

Ruth felt her gorge surging upward, her bowels once more contracting, this time with excruciating pain. She leaned over the pool. She seemed to void her whole self into it.

XVIII

DR. LEROI WAS LEANING over her. She could see, as his pale gray open-necked tussore shirt fell away, that around his neck he was wearing a thin gold chain with, on the end of it, dangling against the shiny, beige flesh—well, what, what, what? It was not a cross, not a locket. Some kind of talisman, she thought, yes, it would be some kind of primitive talisman.

"What happened?" she asked. But she knew what had happened. She had sipped that bitter liquid handed to her by Lucy. She had vomited. She had become unconscious. If she had drunk all of it, she might now be dead.

"You ate something that disagreed with you. Or it may have been an attack of sunstroke."

Behind Dr. Leroi a voice said: "I thought you were going to fall into the pool. Lucky I grabbed you in time! Lucky too that just then Dr. Leroi called in just by chance when he was passing by! I had quite a struggle getting you into this room, I can tell you!" That was Mother, even though her voice sounded subtly different—deeper, more nasal, what was the change? Yes, Mother had been with her. They had been going to see the Americans, Arlen and Harriet, and Harriet's baby. Or Arlen and Harriet's baby. Fortunately for them, and unfortunately for herself, she had never gotten there.

She tossed her head from side to side on the hard, lumpy pillow. "I can still taste it," she said.

"Taste what?" Dr. Leroi asked.

Again she peered at the object dangling at the end of his chain. "A bitterness."

"Bile," he said. "When you've vomited, that's common enough."

"It was that—that tisane. That's what made me ill. That was it."

257

She saw that, as Dr. Leroi straightened himself and stood back from the bed, he and Mother exchanged glances of complicity. She should not have said that, she should not have let them know that she knew. They were cool, oh so cool, and oh so clever. She must show a similar coolness and cleverness, if she were ever to get out of here alive.

Mother was saying: "But you hardly drank any of it. You took one sip and left it. I drank almost a whole cup. I've never known it to upset anyone. Totally harmless."

We are not talking of a totally harmless tisane, we are talking of something else. But she must not say that, she must not let them know that she knew. She closed her eyes. "Well, I don't know," she said. "Perhaps you're right. Perhaps it was the sun. I forgot my dark glasses," she added, suddenly recollecting that, as they had neared the cracked, empty swimming pool, Mother had told her of the danger of not wearing dark glasses when the sun was high.

Again she became aware of Mother and Dr. Leroi exchanging glances of complicity, Mother's eyes narrowing as they focused on his and his then responding with a sudden deepening.

"Perhaps it would be a good idea if I gave you an injection. How about that?"

She could feel, as before her collapse, a twisting of the bowels, and the sweat breaking out, icy, on her forehead. "Injection? Injection of what? I don't need any injection."

"Now come on! There's no need to get upset. If you don't want an injection, how about a tranquilizer? A mild tranquilizer. Just to make you sleep. You'll feel easier." His voice was soothing, gentle, sympathetic. But of course that was all a diabolical trick, to get her off her guard.

"No," she said. She controlled her mounting hysteria. "I don't think I want—need—an injection. Or a tranquilizer. I'll just rest here for a little. Then I think—I think I'd like to catch the late boat."

"You're planning to leave?" Why should there be that note of relief, even joy, in Mother's voice? What was she playing at now?

"Yes, I think so. I'll have time, won't I? I haven't much to pack."

"I think it would be extremely foolish of you to travel after such an attack," Dr. Leroi said. Mother looked at him and, not realizing that Ruth was watching her from the bed, gave a little shake of her head and a frown.

"But I feel much better now. Fine. Once one's vomited . . ."

"Why not wait till tomorrow?" Dr. Leroi continued.

No, no, at all costs she must get away now, before it was too late. "There's nothing more here for me, really. I've seen all I wanted to see, heard all I wanted to hear." She became conscious that on either side of the bed Dr. Leroi and Mother were now staring down at her with a strange mixture of pity and revulsion.

Mother turned away. "Well, if that's what you want."

"Yes, that's what I want. I don't want to be any more of a nuisance to any of you any longer."

"Then I'll send Lucy over to the annex to help you with your packing."

"No, no!" she protested vehemently, then wished she had not done so. She must not let them know that she knew Lucy was their accomplice. "But if Frau Wertheim . . ." She was sure that Frau Wertheim, with her sweet, absentminded innocence, could not also be involved. Perhaps she was the only one of them not involved.

"Frau Wertheim?" Mother was clearly taken aback. "You want her to help you with your packing?"

"Please."

"But she's an old woman. Not very strong."

"Please!"

Mother shrugged. "Very well." She made for the door. "Anyway, you'll be able to travel on the boat with Mr. Diamont. He can drive you down to the docks in his car and keep an eye on you."

"Mr. Diamont?"

"Yes. It's lucky he didn't take the earlier boat—the one he usually takes."

She must on no account show that the thought of Diamont as her traveling companion filled her with new terror. She must

259

accept his presence with an appearance of gratitude and relief. But she would have to be careful, terribly careful, she must never be alone with him on the deck.

"Yes," she said. "Yes. That's lucky."

JOURNEY

ON THE FERRY, teeming with people as before, Diamont sprawled across the backseat of his car, now working lethargically at a crossword puzzle in an airmail edition of *The Times* many days old, and now, his head back against the upholstery and his mouth open, dozing.

Ruth was uncomfortably perched among a covey of black women on a bench from which two slats were missing. Paying no attention to her, after a preliminary scrutiny and some giggling, the women screeched to each other over her head or across her, those on either side of her from time to time brushing her with their hair or bare arms. But she preferred to endure all this than to risk being alone with Diamont in the car.

"You could stretch out in the back," he had said.

She had shaken her head.

"Or in the front if you prefer. I can take the back."

"It'll be cooler on deck."

"Not in this sun."

"There'll be a breeze."

"As you wish . . . Anyway, what about a drink? I have a Thermos here." He had produced it from the back of the car. "Iced tea. Nothing like it to quench the thirst."

She had thought of that horrible bitterness welling up in her mouth, her uncontrollable vomiting into the swimming pool, and her collapse. "Thank you." Again she had shaken her head. "I'm not thirsty." In fact, her mouth and throat had been parched.

He had stared at her for a moment, with that same odd mixture of pity and revulsion with which Dr. Leroi and Mother had stared at her. Then he had shrugged. "Please yourself. At all events, I'm going to have a nap. The best way to make the time pass. I must say I've come to loathe this journey. I cannot imagine why they don't have at least one boat with first-class quarters and air-conditioning."

Ruth now leaned forward on the long bench, so that the two women on either side of her, one young and beautiful and the other ancient and wrinkled, could no longer talk across her and were obliged to talk behind her instead. She could see Diamont's face in profile, blurred, as though all its previously decisive lines had been smudged by the act of sleeping. Perhaps now it would be safe for her to go to the hole in the wall from which, on her journey out, that jolly, toothless man had dispensed synthetic fruit drinks, bottle-green, scarlet, and purple in color, to the people pressing around him.

It was the same man in charge, a rag knotted around his head and a brass bangle with strange markings on it dangling from a wrist. But this time, instead of welcoming her with a smile, he seemed deliberately to be ignoring her, as he served people on either side of her and even behind her. Finally she commanded in a harsh, husky voice: *"Attendez!"*

He took some coins from an outstretched hand, and then turned to her with what struck her as a smile of insolent irony. *"Oui, madame? Vous désirez?"*

She pointed to the bottle of bright pink liquid labeled "Cerise d'Été." Once again, having opened the bottle, he reached for an unwrapped straw from a bundle in a glass. But this time she jerked the straw out of the bottle and threw it to the ground, clearly to the man's annoyance and surprise. She would drink from the neck. Safer, though not all that safe. *"Combien?"* she asked.

He replied not *"Deux cents,"* as on the previous occasion, but

"*Cinq cents.*" It was plain to her that she was paying for having rejected the straw.

"*Cinq cents?*"

"*C'est ça, madame.*" As he said the words he looked at the man standing beside her, and she was convinced that between them there passed a fleeting smile at the absurdity of this rich white woman daring to question the sum. Well, she had better hand it over. It was, she had to admit, not all that much.

She tipped back her head and then placed the bottle to her lips. She knew that everyone was watching her with amusement. They had all seen her pluck out the straw and throw it away.

Having replaced the bottle on the counter, she wearily remounted the companionway up to the deck. Of course some-one—a pregnant woman with a completely naked boy on her lap—had now squeezed into the place that she had previously been occupying. It was no use to attempt to reclaim it or—with people squatting out on the deck, perched on the rails like brilliantly plumaged birds, or resting on the bumpers of cars—to look for somewhere else. Well, it hardly mattered. Soon they would arrive. Already the waters had narrowed to the estuary, and the mangrove swamps were now beginning to give way to bare, tawny slopes surmounted by factories and warehouses.

Diamont clambered out of the back of the car, one side of his face creased where it had rested against the window while he was sleeping. His shirt was stuck to his rounded back with sweat, and his socks, visible beneath his too-short jeans, rolled down to his sandals. He hitched at the jeans, then drew a handkerchief out of a pocket and rubbed it over his face. "Nearly there," he said. "Twenty minutes at most." He stretched back into the car and brought out the Thermos. "Sure you don't want some of this?"

"Sure."

He poured out some of the iced tea into the cup that also acted as top of the Thermos, and drained it at a single gulp. "What have you been doing?"

"Nothing."

"One does a lot of nothing in this godforsaken country."

This godforsaken country . . . The phrase, reheard, filled her with a sense of eerie disquiet.

As though seized with a sudden restlessness after his inactivity in the car, he now wandered off from her, pushing his way between the groups of people on the deck, with an occasional pause to scrutinize someone or other. Yes, of course he would look at that handsome boy, in the tattered trousers and the even more tattered shirt, a still-live turkey under an arm. And, yes, he would look at those two younger boys, crouched on their hunkers in a corner, as they played some game with frayed, grubby cards. It was all too obvious. And he did not care how obvious it was to her.

As the others rushed to leave the boat, pushing and treading on each other and banging each other with their baskets, suitcases, crates, and bags, Diamont told Ruth negligently: "No hurry. Wait. Wait here." He opened the door of the car for her. "We'll drive off when the time comes to drive off."

She hesitated, then got into the car. Surely nothing could happen to her when there were so many people all around them.

"Have you fixed up somewhere to stay?" he asked, when at last the truck before them had moved forward and their own turn had come.

"No. But I'll try L'Escale again. I liked it there."

"You're extremely unlikely to get in. It's the only good hotel in Bissance and all the tourist agencies use it."

"Then I'll have to find somewhere else. I'm not choosy," she added.

He laughed. "No one could be choosy after a stay *chez* Mother."

As they bumped up the track that led from the docks to the main road, he turned to her: "I can put you up, if you like."

He had said it casually, as though making an offer that he rather hoped would be refused. But at once she was on her guard. "That's very kind of you. But I'd hate to put you to any trouble."

"No trouble at all. As you saw, the house is large. The guest room has its own bathroom *en suite*, and you wouldn't have to see any more of me than you wanted."

"I'll try L'Escale first."

"Just as you like. In that case, I'll drive you there."

"I can easily take a taxi. It's such a long way out."

"No, I'll drive you there. No difficulty. I have a friend who works there. If there's no room, he might nonetheless be able to come up with one."

A friend? What friend? Again she was wary. "Oh, there's no need to worry him on my account. Please."

But Diamont did worry him. A young man with a *café-au-lait* complexion, he was behind the desk as Ruth and Diamont approached it. "Monsieur Diamont!" He ran around the desk and embraced Diamont, kissing him first on one cheek and then on the other. When Diamont spoke of the room, he sang out: "No problem, no problem!"

"I told you that if Jean were here he'd be able to fix you up." Diamont patted Jean on the back, as though he were some boisterous dog.

"Anything for you, Monsieur Diamont. Anything, anytime!"

"Jean will look after you," Diamont said, after Ruth had filled in the registration form and handed over her passport. "Won't you, Jean?"

"Of course, Monsieur Diamont."

Ruth gazed at Jean out of wary, apprehensive eyes.

BISSANCE

"THE UNHAPPIEST PEOPLE in the world are not those who have to sleep alone but those who have to eat alone."

An elderly widower who would each Tuesday eat an extravagant, solitary dinner in her restaurant had once said that to her, looking up at her with watery eyes under paper-thin, blue-veined lids, as she had set down a plate before him. During these days in Saloum, she had come to appreciate the truth of his dictum. Alone, one ate both too much and too fast. Time stretched like a frayed piece of elastic, and one imagined oneself neglected by the waiters. One looked at the other diners because there was nothing else to do, and then one resented it if the other diners looked back.

At a table on the corner of the terrace, as a fresh wind blew through her hair, which she had set herself that evening, Ruth now wished that she had had something sent to her hut.

"You did not like that, madame?" the waiter asked in English as he removed her half-eaten *crêpe aux fruits de mer.*

"It was fine. But in this heat I haven't much appetite, I'm afraid."

How would she manage to eat the duckling that he had persuaded her to have as her second course? Solicitously, he poured some more wine into one glass, some more mineral water into another. She raised the glass of mineral water to her mouth, sipped, and thought again of that bitter liquid in her mouth. She wished she could banish a memory so vivid that, each time it

271

returned to her, she would feel her gorge rise as though she were about to vomit.

The people around her were mostly French, mostly young, and mostly well dressed. She drew her packet of cigarettes and her lighter from her bag, lit a cigarette, and, chin cupped in palms, gazed at them. Fortunately they were far too absorbed in each other to be aware of her scrutiny. Youth, vigor, gaiety, wealth, good looks: they seemed to glisten with these things. Not one of them, she imagined, had been obliged, as she had been, to sell everything in order to come to this country on the edge of the Atlantic. All at once she was consumed by a sense of loss, loneliness, desolation. Under all the chatter, laughter, and clinking of crockery and cutlery, she could hear, from below the terrace, the sea thudding down on the beach, drawing back and then thudding down yet again. Were these the same tourists who had been here before? There was no way of knowing. Perhaps the young man over there, in the blue blazer, was the Belgian in the hut next to hers who had brought her those charred pieces of chicken and prawn from the barbecue. Perhaps he was not.

She drew deeply on her cigarette, then drew again. Once, when their relationship had been at its worst, Mark had said to her, "Those cigarettes will be the death of you," and she had then retorted, "They're the only things that keep me alive."

"Ruth!"

She turned uncertainly, not expecting her name and therefore wondering if she had really heard it.

Dave Millett was ambling toward her table.

"You! Hello!" Her pleasure at seeing him, which made her jump up from the table and rush toward him, with her hands held out in greeting, clearly took him aback. "How wonderful to see you!"

"Nice to see you, my dear." He took and then patted one of the hands that had been extended to him. "Didn't you go to Ellampore? I thought . . ."

"I went. I came back. Yesterday."

"Well, you certainly bring me luck. I shared your cabin when they told me I'd have to sleep on deck. And now, if you'll allow me, I'm going to share your table, because they've just told me there's not a single one vacant."

His trousers were soiled, his bush jacket creased. The hand with which he was holding a paperback against his chest had long, dirty fingernails and a jagged scratch on it, as though from a cat. But his presence, as he drew back the chair opposite her and then put the paperback down on the table beside him, continued to fill her with relief, even joy. It was as though, having survived a shipwreck, she had been swimming on and on over a dark sea toward a shore she had begun to decide was no more than an illusory smear on the horizon; now, all at once, a rower had borne down on her out of the murk.

He put out a hand to the bottle of wine resting in its ice bucket, took her half-full glass of mineral water, emptied it on the ground, and then filled it with wine. At no time did he ask her permission. But what had exasperated her on the ship she now accepted with total indifference. He sipped. "Hm. Not bad. You're clearly one of the few women capable of ordering a decent bottle of wine. But then you run a restaurant, don't you?"

"Ran. I just told the waiter to bring me a dry white wine. That's all. If the wine's all right, then that's my luck, not skill."

The waiter came over and asked if monsieur was going to eat. *"Naturellement!"* Millett told him. He leaned across the table, arms crossed. "I'm famished." He grinned at her.

Suddenly, for the first time in days, Ruth also felt hungry.

"How did you get on?" she asked, offering the question in trade for the similar one she hoped he would ask her.

"Well, it wasn't much of a story. The trouble with Mamadan is that he's far too decent and intelligent a man to make much of a story. When I interviewed him in Siné he gave me what was, in effect, a lecture on the nature of freedom. When I interviewed those close to him here, they had little more to say than how much they respected, admired, and liked him. Not quite what the readers of my paper want." Again he reached across for the bottle, this time emptying its whole contents into his glass.

"And what *do* your readers want?"

"They want the sort of crimes committed by an Amin or a Bokassa. They want mass murders, tortures, cannibalism. Or, at the least, a stable of women, black, yellow, white. Old Mamadan is as incorruptible as any politician is able to be."

"But what about the visit to the family?"

He was looking around for the waiter. "Let's have another bottle of this wine. *Garçon!*" As the waiter came over, Millett held out the empty bottle to him. *"Encore une!"* He turned back to Ruth. "The family was decent. That was their trouble. They were altogether too decent. They don't live in the capital, they prefer to go on living in the little village where generations and generations of them have lived. The father was a schoolmaster, now retired, very old. The sister is a primary-school teacher. Another sister is married to a local doctor. They've got nothing out of being related to the president. Even more surprisingly, they don't expect or want anything. Dull, good people. No use to a journalist."

"Has your piece appeared?"

"Not yet." He tilted his body sideways, so that the waiter, having set the second bottle of wine in the bucket, could lay a place before him. "Perhaps they'll spike it. I shouldn't be surprised."

"Spike it?" She had never heard the phrase.

"Chuck it into the wastepaper basket." He took the menu from the waiter and at once began to order.

"Are you staying here?"

"Yes, thank God. There were bugs in the other place, the Hôtel de la Poste. They wouldn't admit it, of course, not on your life. Said I must have been bitten by mosquitoes. But mosquitoes don't leave welts like this. Look!" He jerked up a trouser leg to reveal a leg knobbly with blue and purple veins.

"Goodness!" But her hurried downward glance had revealed nothing to her.

He scratched meditatively, his head concealed by the table, and then straightened up again. "They keep me awake, those bites," he said. "Yes, that was a hideous experience. It wasn't really a hotel but a *maison de passe.*" He squinted at the plate that the waiter had set down before him. "Hm, that looks not at all bad. Who would suppose that one would be eating a bouillabaisse in Saloum. Amazing!"

"So you'll be going back soon?"

"I should think so. Might go to the Ivory Coast. There are rumors of an imminent coup."

She fell deliberately silent, waiting for him to return her interest. But for a long time he merely spooned up the bouillabaisse, with his head lowered. Then, at last finished, he wiped his mouth on his crisp white linen napkin, stared ruminatively out at the darkening waves, and said: "And how did you get on?"

She gave a little shudder, as though the warm wind had all at once freshened. She hugged herself. She too now stared out at the darkening waves as they crashed down on the deserted beach with a roar and a hiss. "Horrible. It was far worse than I'd ever imagined."

"Tell me." He leaned forward, as one of his hands went out to take a cigarette from the packet she had left beside her on the table.

She told him: about the sagging electric wires no longer fed with current from the broken-down generator; about the swimming pool, dry and full of stinking refuse; about the main house and the annexes; about the quintet of natives, the old man and his followers, who had been her fellow passengers on both her trips by boat; about Dr. Leroi and the strange talisman that he wore around his neck; about Mother—"the Queen Bee of the whole show, its God really"—and all the other "weird" inhabitants.

He nodded, puffing on the cigarette and then, when it was burned almost to its filter, on another, also taken from her packet. Yes, he was interested, he was certainly interested. Ruth was in no doubt about that. Perhaps he would write about it all, and perhaps his writing about it all would force people, whether here or in England, to take action.

She described to him the various members of the community one by one. Disregarding the cassoulet that the waiter had now

275

set down before him, he leaned even farther across the table, his red-rimmed eyes, suddenly kindled out of their previous deadness, fixed on her face. "Yes, yes," he said from time to time. "I see. Gosh!"

"I had this terrible sense of evil. They all gave me this terrible sense of evil." She thought of Frau Wertheim. "Except that there was this German woman—the one I told you about, the one whose money . . . Even an old man to whom I never spoke— French he was, I think—seemed somehow . . . corrupt. And even that fifteen-year-old boy called Patrice and the two French girls . . . It's as though she'd hypnotized them all. It's as though they all believe her to be God, yes, really to be God. She quotes those words of—of Aleister Crowley, is it? 'Do what you will is the whole of the law.' But it isn't what they will, it's what she, Mother, wills. They are all this God-Mother's children, they must all do what this God-Mother says. Or else."

He began to ask her in greater detail about Lucy, with her gruff voice, mannish shoulders, and huge feet and hands; about Vilho, so emaciated, as if there was nothing left now but the sunburned skin, stretched taut, and the bones that it covered; about Diamont, with the three ragged boys turning up at his house, out of the bush, as it seemed; about the Americans, brother and sister, and the mystery of the baby; about Dr. Leroi, clearly so attracted to Mother, and about Mother, clearly so attracted to him. . . .

"And your son?" he at last asked. "What did you discover about the death of your son?"

She stared out to sea. As the light from the swaying lamp above them caught her face in profile, it suddenly looked not merely handsome but beautiful. It might have been carved from marble, Millett thought; like marble, it now had an extraordinary durability and strength, as well as that previously unsuspected beauty. "I think they killed him." Now she turned her head and gazed at him, her eyes implacable under her wide-arched brows. "I know they killed him."

"That's a terribly serious thing to say."

She gave a small, twisted smile. "It's a terribly serious thing to have happened. Isn't it?"

"But why should they have wanted to kill him?"

"He knew too much." Again she turned her head away from him, to stare out to the sea. Below them someone passed, a wild-looking man with a shriveled arm and leg, and a white fuzz of long, tangled hair, and a crutch. He raised an arm to the diners on the terrace above him and cried out to them in a high-pitched French: *"La charité! La charité!"* As a group at the next table began to laugh and shower small coins down onto the sand, where the man hopped hither and thither scrabbling for them, Ruth experienced a profound shock. In consternation, she whispered to Millett: "That man—he has something to do with them."

"What man?" He looked over her shoulder, imagining that she meant one of their fellow diners.

"That cripple, beggar. They've had him follow me, spy on me. I'd know him anywhere."

Millett looked bewildered. "I don't really think . . ."

The beggar, having retrieved all the coins, was now staggering off down the beach to where, in the distance, the lights of another restaurant were glittering through the dry evening air.

"Yes, yes!" She nodded emphatically. "I think there's some kind of link, secret and strong, between Mother and the people of this country. Between her religion and theirs. I mean, their primitive religion, not the Christianity or the Mohammedanism they've acquired in recent times. A primitive religion of devil worship and magic—and perhaps even human sacrifice."

He had at last begun to eat his cassoulet. "Oh, I don't know about that," he said. "But these cranky little sects—such as that one—can certainly be dangerous. Exploitative. And one knows of cases of, well, death. The sort of people drawn to them are, in most cases, psychological stretcher cases. So it's not really all that surprising. . . ."

"My son wasn't a psychological stretcher case." She was indignant. "He was sensitive, yes. High-strung. But he was totally normal, totally sane. That was why they decided to do away with him. At that place, there's no room for the totally normal, the totally sane."

"Why do you imagine he went there in the first place?"

"Well, he liked adventure. He liked what is new. And he had this idealism, the idealism of the young. At first he probably thought that the community—everyone sharing everything and taking a hand in everything—was something fine, noble. Then— as I see it—he must have started to question things. Notice things. As I started to question them, notice them. He must have realized that, whereas everyone else gave, Mother only took. Others lived in discomfort, others worked. Mother had her own private quarters and everyone else was expected to wait on her."

"Perhaps they like to wait on her. People of that kind have an innate masochism, a need to be punished. Anyway, it's all very fascinating." He took another mouthful, pondering all that he had heard. Then he said: "Interesting that she should quote Crowley. Because her community sounds not unlike his at Cefalù. That too ended in suspicions of murder."

She wondered whether to tell him about the bitter tisane, her vomiting and collapse into unconsciousness, and her terrified decision to flee the community as quickly as she could. She hesitated. Then she said: "If they thought that my son knew too much, then I think that in the end they came to think that I knew too much, guessed too much. Where Jim was concerned, I always had this kind of ESP."

. . . At a dinner party, she suddenly gets up from the table. She is clearly agitated. "I'm sorry. I've got to go home."

Home? Her host and hostess are amazed. Is she unwell? Has something upset her?

"No, I'm fine, nothing's upset me. It's Jim. I have a feeling. . . . I don't know why or what. But I must go back."

"You could telephone," the hostess suggests.

"No. I must go back."

Host, hostess, and guests look at each other in consternation. Ruth drives through the rain with her face set in anguish.

Perhaps she should have telephoned, but something kept telling her not to do so.

Mark is here. He has dared to come to the house from that woman of his, and he and the sixteen-year-old boy are talking together, side by side on the sofa in the sitting room. Mark's arm is along its back, so that he is almost touching his son's neck.

"What are you doing here?" she bursts in to demand.

He smiles up at her with unruffled insolence. "I wanted a chat with James."

"In that case, you should have asked me if you could come."

Jim gets up, excuses himself incoherently, and rushes up the stairs. Even now, at sixteen, he cannot bear to hear his parents squabble.

"See, you've upset him," she says.

Again he gives that smile of unruffled insolence. "*You've* upset him," he says. "This is still my house, as well as yours, let me remind you."

All at once she is screaming at him. Her screams sound like a knife being honed on glass. "Get out! Out! Out! You came here to try to win him over! Didn't you? Admit it! Your one object in life is to poison his mind against me—to make him hate and despise me!"

"Ruth, Ruth," he protests, raising his hands as though he were trying to halt an oncoming juggernaut.

But she rushes on: "You've got some little plot going. I can see it. Don't think I can't see it!"

"Ruth! Ruthie! Ruthie!" He backs toward the door. "This is bad for the boy. And so bad for you. You know what the doctor said."

"*You're* bad for me. You're bad for him too. And I don't care what the fucking doctor said. He was always on your side—two men together." . . .

Now she leaned forward. Yes, she must tell Millett about the drink. He must learn about that. Then, if anything happened to her in the future, he would be able to tell people the truth, he would be able to go to the police, he would be able to bring those devils to justice. "They tried to poison me."

"*Poison* you?"

"Yes."

She began to tell him what had happened.

At the end, he gazed down, frowning, at the tablecloth. His hand went out and took another cigarette from her packet. "Well, all that's something else," he said.

"What do you mean—something else?"

"I couldn't write about it. Could I? No proof." She opened her mouth, preparatory to making some outraged protest, but he hurried on: "I'm not saying it didn't happen. On the other hand, food poisoning—as I know from experience—and sunstroke are all too common out here. So . . . no, I couldn't write about it." He shook his head decisively. "But the rest . . . yes, that I can use. Yes, oh yes. A good story."

"But you'll remember, won't you?"

"Remember?"

"That they tried to kill me. If anything should happen to me— if, at some later date, they succeed in doing what they failed to do this time—you will remember, won't you? Won't you? You won't let them get away with it?"

"I'll remember."

His hand went across the table. She thought that he was about to take another of her cigarettes but, instead, he put it over her own.

He squeezed her hand in his, smiling across at her.

ELLAMPORE

THE DUTCH television director, wearing an undershirt and a pair of bathing trunks, black striped with dark red, which revealed plump, hairless thighs, told Mother: "That was very interesting, madame."

"I can't imagine what was interesting in it," Mother replied wearily and without insincerity. She had said the same thing or what approximated the same thing to countless other intruders who had arrived to pry into her life, the lives of the other members of the community, and even the lives of people who, except tangentially, had had nothing to do with the community whatever.

The Dutchman stroked his straggly, tawny beard, as his crew, one of them a wiry gray-haired woman in charge of sound, began to assemble their equipment in the hall. "We are sympathetic," he said defensively. Then, as though he were striving for greater accuracy: "We are trying to be sympathetic."

"I am sure you are." Mother's irony was lost on him. "Do you need any help with your things?"

"No, no. Please! You mustn't trouble yourself." Their olive-green van, hired in Siné, was parked under some trees.

"Then if you'll forgive me . . ."

"Of course, madame!" He put out his hand. "I am happy to have met you. I wish you all luck."

"That's something I need." Mother gave a small, bitter smile as

283

she took the hand. It was damp and yielding to the touch. Like a sponge, she thought. Well, he had been better than some of the others. Should she shake the hands of each of the crew members? Eventually she decided not to do so, merely smiling vaguely at them and sketching a farewell wave.

Tom Guthrie and Dr. Leroi awaited her in the sitting room; a bottle of English gin, brought by Leroi, and another of the local tonic water stood on the floor between them.

"Why, why, why?" Guthrie asked as she came through the door.

"Why what?" But she knew perfectly well what he meant. Graceful as always, she lowered herself on to a cushion, folding her legs beneath her.

"Why see those ghastly people? Why not send them packing?"

"Because then those ghastly people will imagine even more ghastly things." She reached for a glass and splashed gin into it. The two men exchanged glances. She had never drunk spirits in the past. "He was all right, that one. Stupid, clumsy, but all right." She raised the glass and gulped from it. " 'The truth will set you free.' One tries to tell the truth. But the more one tells it, the more inextricably one seems to be enmeshed."

After all the publicity first in Millett's "rag" (as he himself habitually referred to it), then in other, more respectable English newspapers, and then in newspapers all over the world, the community was breaking up. "I had always thought of myself as an ordinary woman," Mother had told the Dutchman, "and now I've learned that I am an extraordinary one, even a monster." The Dutchman, embarrassed, had demurred: "Not a monster, of course not a monster. But you *are* an extraordinary woman. Why not admit it?"

Leroi said: "So Vilho has gone?"

"Vilho has gone. He would have died happily here, and now he will die unhappily in Finland. People should be allowed to live as they want and to die as they want." Again she gulped the raw spirit. "But I'm sorry for you, Michel. Because you helped that poor boy and because you helped Lucy, now you have all this trouble and publicity."

Leroi shrugged. "It'll pass." But he was not sure of that. Like many countries that have recently achieved their freedom, Saloum was niggardly of the freedoms it allowed its subjects. "And Frau Wertheim—she's still with you?"

"Not for long. Her children are determined to get her away. It's odd. For years they were totally uninterested in anything she might be doing, they hardly wrote her. But now, with all this publicity . . . Her eldest son told the *Gazette* that he had come here to 'rescue' her. It was as though she had been my prisoner. The odd thing is that all the fight now seems to have left her. She just goes along with whatever those children of hers propose."

"At all events, you still have Lucy."

"Yes, poor Lucy. She'll stay on with me—as long as I myself stay on. But she's shattered that now her mother knows her secret. More shattered probably than her mother is in having learned it. Her mother wants nothing more to do with her—'My son's dead to me,' she told that awful journalist. Unless of course he invented that for her, I wouldn't put it past him." Mother was speaking with weary bitterness. If Lucy were shattered, then so was she.

"You'll build it all up again. Time will pass, people will forget about all this nonsense, and then you'll find that other people will come to you, there will always be other people to come to you, and with your unique gifts you'll make it all as it was before." Guthrie spoke with yearning tenderness, the fruit of long years of bondage to an inexorable will now broken.

Mother shook her head. "Never again. I haven't the heart, I haven't the spirit. I feel as I did when I was a child on a beach on Cape Cod—we were holidaying there—and I built a castle on the sand. The next day the castle had vanished, swept away by the tide. My father said he'd help me build another castle, it was the easiest thing in the world. But . . ." She shifted from one side to another on the legs neatly folded beneath her. "That was it. That's it now."

"You still have so much to give," Leroi coaxed her.

"Nothing more to give. And nothing more that I now want to take."

"You'll get it back," Guthrie said. "You'll get it all back."

She shrugged, as though indifferent whether she did so or not.

"What a terrible woman," Leroi said.

Mother nodded. "I thought she was only silly and sad. I never realized how dangerous she was. I should have guessed that—if only from what her son told me about her. But I thought he'd been blinded by his love—and by his hatred. Why did she want to do all this to us? It turned out that we were entertaining a devil unawares."

"No, not a devil," Leroi interposed gently. "Just someone—sick."

"If only you could have cured her!"

"I have a feeling she's beyond curing."

Soon after that, Mother said quietly: "I think I want you to go now. I'm tired, I want to think. Don't be angry." She rose, and then the men rose too.

Leroi always hated sitting on the cushions, but he never liked to ask for a chair. He put his hands on her fragile shoulders, leaned forward, and kissed her on the forehead. "I think that before I leave I'll go down and see the young Americans."

"Yes, see what you can do for them. They're in a bad way. She had a strange ability to see into people's hearts. One must give that to her."

"But all that nonsense about the baby!"

"Could it have been an albino? Or just a delusion?"

"We'll never know."

"We'll never know."

After the two had gone, Mother stood at the window, looking out into the light that was gradually softening and darkening as the evening came on. She felt enervated, despondent, useless. All her life she had never rested, and now she wished only for rest. All her life she had never hated, and now she was filled with hatred.

The two Americans would be in their room, with the baby in the basket between them. Perhaps Arlen, perched on the windowsill, was playing some melancholy air on his harmonica.

Perhaps Harriet was looking up at him, her eyes brimming with the love about which so many of the strangers who had come to the community had questioned Mother and had wanted to question them.

. . . "One feels dirty only because others tell one one is dirty," Arlen had said, resting his head on his outstretched forearms.

Like a beaten dog, Harriet had crept up to him and had hesitatingly put out a hand to touch the back of his neck.

"That woman thought us dirty," she had said.

"Oh, to her all things are dirty!" Mother had put in.

"What right had she to judge us?" Arlen had demanded.

Mother had given a dry laugh. "What right indeed? That right belongs only to God.". . .

Now Mother turned away from the window with a new resolution in her step and in her eyes. Energy all at once flowed through her. Her energy had been the energy of love. Now it had become the energy of hate.

She crossed to a Japanese *tanzu* bequeathed to her by one of the earliest members of the community, a Japanese potter now dead. The *tanzu* was made of cherry wood, polished to the color of an unripe nectarine. It had a secret drawer; opening it involved pulling out two other drawers and then pressing simultaneously on two small latches behind them.

Mother pressed on the latches and pulled out the small secret drawer. It was empty but for an envelope, its flap unstuck, with a name and address scrawled across it in an immaturely bold, sloping hand.

She picked up the envelope and rested it lightly against her lips. "Well, you've asked for it," she thought, knowing at long last in her life all the pleasures of hate, as she had for so long known all the pleasures of love. "You've asked for it."

HOME

"WELL, I'll certainly not leave the matter. No, I'll go on worrying away at it. In the end, that's the only way one gets anything done in this business."

His glasses had thick tortoiseshell frames, and behind them the blue eyes were cold, despite all the assumed warmth of his voice and his smile.

"I've been worrying away at it for an awfully long time. People are prepared to write about it, talk about it. But no one is prepared to *do* anything."

Something of her pathos at last communicated itself to him, and he felt momentarily ashamed that, while repeatedly glancing at the clock on the wall behind her, he had been wishing: "Oh, for God's sake, get on with it!" To get on with it was something that people sinking deeper and deeper into a bog of obsessional unhappiness could never do. He sighed: "Yes, I know, I know. But this is a difficult case. As I've already explained to you," he could not resist adding, "there's the whole question of jurisdiction."

"But that lawyer I saw . . ."

"Yes, you told me that." He quickly cut her off. If he were to get to the opening of that new shopping mall, he'd have to be nippy. She must once have been a beautiful woman, he thought, with a brief pang for the passing of that beauty. But people hanging onto a single obsession let everything else, including themselves, go. That she had let herself go, there could be no doubt. There was a greasy pallor to her face, suggesting something kept too long at the back of a larder. Her straight gray hair looked in need of a wash. From time to time a tremor passed through the hands clasped tightly in her lap, as through the limbs of a sleeping dog.

She licked her lips and raised one of the hands to brush a tendril of hair off her face. "So you think there's something you can do?"

"I hope so. Yes, I hope so. Another question in the House, that's the first thing. We all know what the Foreign Office is like. In cases like this, they don't want to know, they don't want to be bothered. Our relations with Saloum are—much to the annoyance of the French—getting better and better. There have been recent oil finds there—a British company's involved. The president is due to make a visit shortly. No one wants to rock that particular boat. It's understandable."

"Does no one care about justice?" She said it with a bleak, terrible anguish.

"In politics, I'm afraid that a lot of people care more about a lot of other things. But *I* care about justice and I think that in the House there are still some people who also care about justice—not only on my side of it. The first thing is to get the Saloumese to reopen the whole investigation. That, as I see it, is the first thing at which we must aim."

A weariness, penetrating deep into her entrails and her bones, overcame her like the first, inexorable symptom of a fatal illness. "Yes," she agreed. "Yes." She nodded her head. For so long so many people had told her that the first thing was to get the Saloumese to reopen the whole investigation. But many months ago a young man had suddenly and mysteriously died in a country in which innumerable people met with sudden and mysterious deaths. The Saloumese did not care. Did even this broad-shouldered, red-haired M.P. in the thick tortoiseshell-framed glasses care, except professionally?

He rose from his chair. "Well, Mrs. . . . . er" —he glanced down at the pad before him—"Mrs. St. Just. I have other people to see now, I'm afraid. But as soon as I have some news for you, I—or my secretary—will get in touch. I hope that won't be long. Meanwhile—keep cheerful, don't worry." He usually gave this last advice as a valediction to his constituents.

As she walked to the bus stop, Ruth thought: "He's right to call that his surgery. I feel as if I'd just come round from a major operation." Her whole body was aching, her breath came effortfully. But as soon as she had boarded the bus after a long wait in the murk and cold, she felt a miraculous revival, similar to many in the past. She was never going to give in, however much they wanted her to do so. Never, never, never. She would rather die than do that.

In the cramped suburban house in which she now rented two rooms, her landlady, Mrs. Sibson, was ferociously rattling a feather duster up and down the banisters. A widow, she seemed to use cleaning as her way of working off her aggression against a world in which her husband had died in his early thirties and she herself was childless.

"Hello, Mrs. St. Just. I didn't see you this morning, before you went out." How pale, thin, and bedraggled the poor soul looked! Like the M.P. before her, she felt a brief pang of compassion.

"I went out early. I had to go into town."

"There's a letter for you. Here." She picked it up from the table beside her. "That post is up the creek again. Didn't arrive till past twelve. Would you believe it?"

Ruth could believe it only too well.

Mrs. Sibson held out the airmail letter, with its many foreign stamps and its scrawled readdressings. Her hand once again shaken by a tremor, Ruth took it from her. "Thank you."

"I expect Mr. Samuel would like those stamps, wouldn't he?"

"Yes, I'll save them for him."

Staring down at the envelope, Ruth began to mount the stairs slowly. Mrs. Sibson, once again transfixed by a brief pang of compassion, called up: "If you'd like a bite of something with me in about half an hour, you'd be very welcome."

"That's very kind of you." Ruth halted and looked down over

the banisters. "But I had something to eat early in town," she said, lying.

"Well, that's all right, then." Mrs. Sibson was relieved.

Ruth went into the smaller of her two small rooms, took off her overcoat and hung it up, and then sat down on the bed, the envelope in her hands. She stretched her legs out before her. With a forefinger she then began to pick at the flap, as though undecided whether actually to open it or not. Finally she did open it, with a single tear, and drew out the sheet of paper inside.

With a mixture of terror and amazement, she stared down at the handwriting. It was the handwriting of her darling Jim.

For a second, an incredible joy burst upward like a fountain within her. Then, as she unfolded the flimsy airmail paper, her hands trembling so violently that they almost tore it and then almost dropped it, she knew that this letter was not from the living but from the dead.

The letter began not with the usual "Dearest Mother" but with no salutation of any kind whatever:

When you receive this, I shall be dead. I want to die because I have never been able to live. That I have never been able to live is because of you, and so, in a sense, it is you who are my killer. I tried to escape from you first to Bissance and then to this community, where I submitted to the will of another, kinder, wiser, more tolerant Mother, as I once submitted to yours. But wherever I went and whatever I did, I could not escape you. You have infected me, incurably, with yourself. You are the terminal illness from which all my life I have been dying.

I feel a terrible pity for you, not ill enough to be confined and not well enough to move about the world without harming others. You would have ruined Father's life with your obsessive suspicions, your certainty that he was always in the wrong and you in the right, your jealousy, contempt, hatred. But he managed to escape from you, as I, blood of your tainted blood, flesh of your corrupting flesh, could not do. Those phantom voices that used to speak to you out of a sulphurous cloud have now begun to speak to me. If I am not to inflict terrible harm on both myself and others, I must do what I have decided to do.

As I think of you now, it is of a mad, capricious God, recreating the world—which also consists of me—in Her own image. The world does not wish to be as this God would have it, and nor do I. But God does not care about the wishes of the world or of Her Only Begotten Son. She wishes Her world to suffer and Her Son to be crucified.

As I think of you, it is also of a no less mad, capricious novelist. The world does not wish to be as this novelist would have it be, and nor do I. But to the novelist what the world and I wish is of no importance whatever. The world must suffer and I must die so that the novelist can pursue her demented dream.

I have a terrible pity for you. I also have a terrible hate for you. And yes, I must admit it, I also have a terrible love. That love, more than the pity and the hate, has made me reach my decision.

Whatever I possess, I wish to go to the community. It has represented for me the only home that I have ever really known, just as Mother has represented for me the only mother I have ever really known.

The signature trailed downward from the page, an expiring comet: not Jim, not Jim, but, for the first time in all the years that he had written to her, James.

Below that "James," another hand had written something in small, neat characters contrasting dramatically with the large, untidy ones above it:

You said that you were determined to learn the truth, whatever it might cost. Well, here it is for you. At 5:30 A.M. on the morning of June 11, he jumped from the window ledge of his room, on the second floor, into the empty swimming pool below. He died of his injuries in my sitting room at 9:12 A.M. of the same day. Dr. Leroi was present. We decided that we must conceal from you both the manner of his death and this letter that he left for you. He had told us of your precarious mental condition. It seemed, in the circumstances—since we knew of your obsessional love for him—the kindest thing to do.

For a long time Ruth sat motionless on the bed, her face immobile, with the letter held in hands that, miraculously, had ceased to tremble. She was staring at her own reflection in the tarnished mirror above the old-fashioned washbasin.

Then she stirred herself. Holding it up to the light from the window beside her, she examined the thin sheet of paper once again, eyes screwed up and mouth bunched in concentration. She compared the handwriting of the letter itself with that of the postscript. She got off the bed and walked over to the window to see even better. Again she peered.

Suddenly an incredible joy once more burst up within her like a fountain.

It was obvious, obvious, of course it was obvious! That letter could not have been written by Jim, her son, her beloved. Those were not his feelings, that was not his handwriting.

Mother had forged it.

ABOUT THE AUTHOR

Francis King is the author of numerous novels, among them *The Dividing Stream* (winner of the Somerset Maugham Award), *Voices in an Empty Room*, and, most recently, *Frozen Music*. In addition, he has written five volumes of short stories and one of poetry. He is drama critic of the *Sunday Telegraph* and frequently reviews books for British press and radio.

Mr. King is president of International PEN. He lives in London.